SHAPERS
of WORLDS
Volume III

SHADOWPAW PRESS *Reprise*

New editions of notable, previously published books

The Legend of Sarah

Cat's Pawn

Cat's Gambit

Cat's Game

By Leslie Gadallah

Duatero

By Brad C. Anderson

Blue Fire

By E.C. Blake

Phases

By Belinda Betker

Stay

By Katherine Lawrence

The Crow Who Tampered With Time

Backwater Mystic Blues

By Lloyd Ratzlaff

The Shards of Excalibur Series

The Peregrine Rising Duology

Spirit Singer

From the Street to the Stars

By Edward Willett

SHAPERS
of WORLDS
Volume III

**Science fiction and fantasy by authors who were guests on the
Aurora Award-winning podcast The Worldshapers**

Edited by
EDWARD WILLETT

SHADOWPAW
PRESS *Premiere*

SHAPERS OF WORLDS VOLUME III
Science fiction and fantasy by authors featured on
the Aurora Award-winning podcast The Worldshapers

Published by
Shadowpaw Press Premiere
Regina, Saskatchewan, Canada
www.shadowpawpress.com

Trade Paperback ISBN: 978-1-989398-41-8
Hardcover ISBN: 978-1-989398-43-2
Ebook ISBN: 978-1-989398-42-5

Edited by Edward Willett
Cover art by Tithi Luadthong
Interior design by Shadowpaw Press
Created with Vellum

COPYRIGHTS

CONTENTS

INTRODUCTION

Until one begins a series of anthologies, one does not appreciate the challenges that such a project will entail.

I'm not speaking of the challenge of constructing each Kickstarter, or the challenge of collecting and editing the stories from the featured authors (which is more a pleasure than a challenge).

No, I'm speaking of the challenge of coming up with a fresh introduction for each volume.

The purpose of the introduction is to introduce (duh) you, the reader, to the anthology in a way that will hopefully entice you to read the whole thing. To do so, I like to use metaphor.

In the introduction to the first volume, where I laid out my own background as a long-time reader and writer of science fiction and fantasy and how I came to be hosting a podcast and then Kickstarting an anthology featuring authors who were guests on that podcast, I finished with a metaphor comparing authors to potters, shaping worlds out of the clay of their own experiences, thoughts, dreams, fears, and hopes.

Not a bad metaphor, albeit I stole it from myself—the leading character in my novel *Worldshaper*, which began a series for DAW Books entitled *Worldshapers* and whose release coincided with the beginning of my podcast, *The Worldshapers* (sensing a pattern here?) was, indeed, a potter, and the cover featured a potter literally shaping a world on the wheel.

Last year, I used what I think is the best metaphor of all, likening the anthology to a "cabinet of curiousities," those eclectic collections learned and curious individuals assembled in centuries past, precursors to natural history museums and other such delights. In a cabinet of curiousities, fossils, meteorites, artwork, cultural artifacts, and antiquities might all rest cheek by jowl to educated, entertain, enlighten, and intrigue viewers—just as, in these anthologies, tales of monsters, demons, and aliens, tales of magic and horror and humor, and tales of time travel, space travel, and post-apocalyptic wandering may all find a home under one cover.

But that brings me to this volume, and I find myself in need of a new metaphor. As it happens, the very day I'm writing this, I took a long walk in the prairie outside my home city of Regina, Saskatchewan. The prairie is deceptively simple in appearance. When you drive through it in a car, all you see is the flat land stretching to the horizon, brown or green or white, depending on the season, and it's easy to dismiss it as a monotonous place with little variety.

But when you walk on the prairie (or, indeed, in the forest or any other natural environment), you quickly discover that, in fact, variety is everywhere. On my walk this morning, I startled a bevy of quail from a wheatfield. Grasshoppers leaped out of my path; a yellow butterfly fluttered by; a hawk, circling overhead, called; a gopher skittered across the road; and once I was out of the wheatfield, there were more plants beneath my feet than I could identify (except for the nettles—they're hard to ignore when you're wearing shorts). And I know that in the soil, earthworms tunnel, microscopic fauna thrive, and microbes multiply.

All of these forms of life are different from each other: unique and fascinating. In a way, every species is a world unto itself, full of mystery. Scientists spend entire careers studying a single species without learning everything there is to know. Multiply that by the number of living things in every acre of prairie, and the complexity is mind-boggling.

Yet, when you view it from a distance, all you see is the prairie.

Similarly, when you look at the cover of this or any anthology, all you see is the cover. In this case, in addition to the (I hope) eye-catching image that draws you to the book, there is a list of names, the authors whose stories appear in this volume: Griffin Barber, Gerald Brandt, Miles Cameron, Sebastien de Castell, Kristi Charish, Cory Doctorow, K. Eason, David Ebenbach, Mark Everglade and Joseph Hurtgen, Frank J. Fleming, Violette Malan, Anna Mocikat, James Morrow, Jess E. Owen, Robert Penner, Cat Rambo, K.M. Rice, Walter Jon Williams, F. Paul Wilson, Jane Yolen, and me.

Some of these authors may be familiar to you. Some you may never have heard of. But all have crafted tales set in worlds of their creation. Each tale is a window into that world. Some of those worlds are much like ours. Others are very different. Some tales take place in a single corner of the world. Some span all of time and space.

And each author, like the multiple species I encountered on my walk in the prairie this morning, is a world unto him or herself, full of more stories for you to discover in novels and short stories and poetry.

The ecosystem of science fiction and fantasy, like the

ecosystem of the prairie or any other ecosystem on this whirling planet, is infinitely complex, infinitely diverse. This anthology is just one small corner of it: a few square feet of prairie, to continue (but hopefully not torture) my metaphor.

The variety contained within this book is immense, but only a fraction of the variety to be found in all the tales told by all the writers of wondrous tales in all the world.

Enjoy—and then continue your exploration in all the other stories written by these authors, and all the many others in the grand biosphere of fiction.

Edward Willett
Regina, Saskatchewan
September 1, 2022

THE WRITER SPEAKS TO THE NEW WORLD

By Jane Yolen

I am not a god, only an inventor
whose tools are words and imagination.
If I say, "Let There Be Light,"
it is not writ in thunder but in a description
of a cosmic light bulb,
or an apostrophe of many colours.
If I say, "Let There Be Creatures,"
They may be made of meat, iron,
Mold, sawdust, vegetation.
If I say, "Let There Be Wars!"
ignore me. I am only making a plot.
If I say, "Let There Be Rules,"
laugh at me, for I am writing a book
to tell other gods how to speak
to a New World.

AND THE WALLS CAME TUMBLING DOWN

By James Morrow

I. THE FALL OF JERICHO

When the callow but clever Yasha ben Ephod learned he'd been selected to fill the most important position in the Israelite Nation's military band, his initial confusion soon transmuted into exhilaration, which then became embarrassment, which quickly turned to terror.

"Joshua wants you as his new shofar master," declared Captain Abidan ben Ochran of the archery brigade.

"Why me?" asked Yasha.

"During the Battle of Jahaz, the sound of your ram's horn rose above every other instrument," Abidan explained, striding insouciantly around the little tent as if he owned the place, which in fact he did, Yasha having gambled it away the previous evening during a dice game (because Abidan had kept his own tent, he allowed Yasha to continue living in the latter's customary abode for a small montly fee). "Of all the horns on the field that day, yours was the one that most stirred the fighters' blood."

Although Yasha had never looked forward to the music lessons his mother had insisted he take as a child (while the Israelite nation wandered without purpose year after year through the wilderness of Kadesh), evidently all those tedious hours with Nahshon the trumpet teacher had finally borne fruit. Shofar master: a daunting yet thrilling responsibility—for not only would Yasha be commanding all the other shofarists during the imminent conquest of Canaan, he would also have authority over the tymbalists, flutists, and trigon players.

"I feel unworthy of so great an honour," he protested.

"A fleeting emotion, I'm sure," said Abidan. "When I report back to Joshua, I'll tell him you accepted the appointment without hesitation."

Confusion, exhilaration, embarrassment, terror—but it was the terror, Yasha knew, that would linger. An invading army's shofar master was always among the prime targets of the defenders' forces. Kill that particular musician, and you've killed the wellspring of the would-be conqueror's spirit. Moses's campaign against the Amorites had involved nine furious battles, and his shofar masters were always among the first casualties, variously felled by arrows, swords, spears, and stones.

"In homage to my late mother, I gratefully accept this position," Yasha told Abidan, making no effort to conceal his ambivalence.

———————

AS A DAZZLING morning sun burnished the alluvial plains of the Jordan basin, Yasha ben Ephod and the musicians under his command crossed the river in a hastily constructed but sturdy barge. Disembarking, they arrayed themselves along the west bank, then surveyed the flotilla of rafts, scows, and skiffs bringing the rest of the Israelite army—Captain Abidan's dauntless archers, Captain Uri's valiant swordsmen, Captain Zerah's implacable javelinists, Captain Machi's deadly sling-shooters—to the shores of the Promised Land. Shortly after noon, more such vessels crossed over, bearing priests, artisans, shepherds, tribal elders, women, children, flocks, and herds. *For four decades, we have been a nation on the move*, mused Yasha, *a ship forever in search of a harbour. At last, we shall anchor ourselves to the world.*

While the Twelve Tribes set about pitching their tents on the fringes of Canaan, Joshua dispatched spies to reconnoitre the nearest city, Jericho, bastion of King Jobab, and by nightfall, rumours were swarming through the camp like mosquitoes from the nearby marshes. The fight for Jericho, ran the hearsay, would begin in two days. Because the city's walls were high, its gates impregnable, and its granaries full, Joshua's campaign of attrition might last for weeks, even months, and yet he had no choice but to lay siege to Jobab's stronghold. Even with Yahweh's sponsorship, Joshua would not dare lead his people farther into the Promised Land with an enemy fortress at his back.

On the second night following the crossing, as the Israelites' cooking fires blazed in defiance of a moonless sky, the leaping embers mingling with the stars shining over Canaan, a courier came to Yasha bearing the news that Joshua wished to meet immediately with his new shofar master.

Yasha had no difficulty finding the general's quarters, for no tent in their itinerant community covered as much ground or flew so many standards. Sipping from a golden wine goblet, Joshua sat behind a table overspread with scrolls and papyrus sheets. An immense shofar, the largest Yasha had even seen, anchored a large map of Canaan. Further securing the map were a second golden goblet, empty, and a seven-socketed menorah, its candles blazing. Forty years in the wilderness had taken a toll on the late Moses's adjutant. Joshua's eyes and hairline had receded. His bald spot shone in the flickering candle flames. Tiny, worm-like threads of white and silver had infiltrated his black beard.

He instructed Yasha to sit down. The young musician accepted his offer of wine. A servant appeared and filled both goblets to the brim.

"Such a beautiful instrument." As he gestured toward the shofar, Yasha noticed that a skilled bone-carver had adorned the surface with scenes of Noah and his family navigating the Great Deluge. "May I hold it?"

"Yes, but you must not play it," said Joshua in his rattling sistrum of a voice. "Were you to blow on this horn now, our whole encampment would be swept away."

Taking hold of the shofar, heavy as a block of marble, Yasha admired its voluptuous curves and sensuous whorls. "Is it enchanted? Did you buy it from a sorcerer?"

"Israelites never traffic in talismans," Joshua insisted. "As we learn in Moses's chronicle of our flight from Egypt, the appendix to the Decalogue includes the directive, 'You shall not supply a sorceress with her means of livelihood.' "

"I was taught, 'You shall not allow a witch to live.' "

"As a fighting man, I rather prefer your version. Last night, while I was reviewing the day's dispatches, a radiance of surpassing intensity bloomed before me as if a shooting star had fallen into my tent. Gradually, the light coalesced into a tall female figure with bright wings and iridescent eyes. The vision gave her name as Hegeliel, the Angel of History, and she presented me with a strongbox containing that shofar."

"Obviously, you enjoy great favour in the eyes of our Creator," said Yasha.

"Hegeliel invited me to remember 'Abraham's primal act of compliance,' as she put it, 'that glorious inversion of Adam's primal act of disobedience.' You know the story. Not long after the fall of Sodom, Abraham, at Yahweh's direction, tied his son to a sacrificial altar. But then, as he was about to plunge the blade into Isaac's chest, Abraham noticed a solitary ram, feasting happily on the leaves of a thicket even though its horns were caught in the branches." Joshua indicated the shofar. "That instrument, the angel informed me, is from the very ram whose substitutionary death allowed Isaac to continue living—not only to continue living but to sire Jacob, progenitor of the Twelve Tribes. In a peculiar way, had this wondrous horn not bound the ram to the thicket, our nation would not exist."

"I shall guard it with my life," said Yasha.

"With your life and with the lives of the musicians under your command. Its powers are profound, or so Hegeliel assured me. 'Instruct your shofar master to summon seven mighty blasts from the Horn of Abraham,' she said, 'and the vibrations will shatter the enemy's ramparts, smash his gates, and turn his battlements to rubble.'"

"If I understand you correctly, there will be no siege of Jericho."

"Our army will be inside the city by noon," said Joshua, nodding. "Ah, but I see you have finished your wine." He gestured for his servant to refill Yasha's goblet. "Drink deep, my young trumpeter. The grapes of Hazoreth will reward you with a good night's sleep."

As AN EXUBERANT SUN rose over Jericho, glowing like a golden apple set upon a sapphire altar, Joshua ordered his chariots to parade seven times around King Jobab's city. Next, he instructed his infantry to march seven times along the very same route, and then he required the priests to do likewise while bearing the Ark of the Covenant. Even as he supervised these displays, Joshua made sure his shofar master stayed far from the ramparts—a wise tactic, Yasha decided: it would be madness to expose the most important soldier in the Israelite Army to enemy projectiles before Jericho had fallen.

At last, the time came for Yasha to perform. Positioning himself squarely before the eastern rampart, just beyond the range of Jobab's archers and sling-shooters, he sucked in a deep breath, raised the Horn of Abraham to his lips, and brought forth the loudest, longest note ever heard in the Jordan River floodplain. Reaching their target, the reverberations triggered the expected miracle, causing a thin but emphatic incision to appear in the nearest wall, like a single grapevine climbing toward the sun. Yasha released a second note, and two more fissures appeared, likewise dramatic and purposeful.

A third blast.

A fourth blast.

A complex mesh of fractures now crisscrossed Yasha's target as if the rampart were a vertical frozen lake sustaining the pounding footballs of a thousand Nephilim giants frantic to reach the shore while the ice still held.

A fifth blast.

A sixth blast.

As the walls came tumbling down, the other musicians added

superfluous though harmonious voices to the concert, the tymbalists banging on their drums, the trigonists twanging their angle
harps, the flutists chirping like metallic birds. By the time Yasha
released the seventh blast, not a single tower, gate, or battlement
protected the eastern wall of the city. The desert wind raised
silvery billows of dust and crimson clouds of sand from the debris.

Joshua lost no time giving his captains the orders by which
they would consummate the fall of Jericho. "*Cherem!*" he shouted.
"*Cherem!* Yahweh has given me to know the city is laid under ban!
No spoils, no prisoners, no mercy—*cherem!*"

"No spoils, no prisoners, no mercy—*cherem!*" echoed the
captains.

Cherem. Of all the words in the Hebrew language, *cherem* was
the one Yasha least wanted to hear at that moment. During his
long campaign against the Midianites, Moses had practised *cherem*
with a heavy hand, but Yasha had always run away after each
battle, thus sparing himself the sight of Israelite soldiers taking up
their swords and butchering every last surviving man, woman,
child, slave, and beast.

If called to account for this policy, Moses would have noted
he'd been following orders from On High. He might have added
that the kings whose forces his armies had crushed since the
twelve tribes escaped Egypt would have happily imposed their
local versions of *cherem* on the Israelites had the wars not gone in
the latter's favour. Yahweh's Chosen People were no more inclined
toward atrocity than Amalekites, Girgashites, Perizzites, Hivites, or
Jebusites.

Father, why is this cherem *different from all other* cherems?
Yasha shuddered head to toe.

*Because this time, the slaughter traces directly to a miracle
performed by Yasha ben Ephod.*

A convulsion of remorse coursed through Yasha's soul like an epileptic seizure. His internal organs spasmed in pain, as if he'd swallowed a ravenous demon from Sheol, and now it was consuming him from within, liver, lungs, belly, and bowels.

He pivoted on his heel and, still gripping the enchanted ram's horn, fled the scene of the imminent abomination, pointing himself in the general direction of Egypt. Because he could not swim, his decision to leap into the Jordan would surely have its intended result.

Soon his destination loomed up, and he waded into the marshes, straight away finding himself hip-deep in silt. He pressed on, tripping over a root, and fell facedown, whereupon the marshes, the river, the floodplain, and the universe turned black.

II. A PASSAGE TO BERLIN

Yasha, awakening, found himself afloat on some medium or other, air or water or perhaps preternatural braids of smoke from the inferno Jericho had doubtless become. He was lying on his back, staring at a clear cobalt sky. For a fleeting instant, he imagined he was indeed airborne, soaring across the heavens toward whatever shadowland, underworld, afterlife, or variety of oblivion lay on the other side of the grave. But then the scent of aquatic vegetation reached his nostrils, even as rhythmic splashes of water struck his cheeks and brow.

He lifted his head. The skiff was being poled down a narrow river by a tall woman with white, luminous, feathered wings sprouting from her shoulder blades. The Angel of History was a poor pilot. With every third stroke, she brought a measure of the river aboard, most of which landed on Yasha. He sat up. Flecks of mud from the Jordan marshes clung to his bare legs and woollen tunic. The air was cold. The birdsongs were strange. He was no longer in Canaan.

"I suspect you're hungry," said Hegeliel in a peculiarly accented Hebrew as she passed two dried figs to Yasha.

"I appreciate your interest, but I intend to finish drowning myself at my first opportunity."

"Then you will have a fight on your hands, young Yasha. You must wrestle with my determination to keep you alive."

"Are you helping me at Yahweh's behest?"

"I'm a freelance angel. Have wings, will travel. But you must not imagine my clients choose me. I pick them. The night before Jericho fell, I decided to bless Joshua, giving him the Horn of Abraham. This afternoon, I elected to intervene on your behalf, lifting you from the marshes before the mud could suffocate you. A day may come when I shall deign to assist the God of your fathers, though, in all honesty, I've never warmed up to that particular supreme being. From a theological standpoint, I prefer Ninhursag, Shakti, and even Zeus."

"I have no idea what you're talking about."

"Do you understand me when I insist that absolution is a condition far more desirable than oblivion?"

"Are you saying you can cure my remorse?"

"No, but I can create the conditions whereby you might cure yourself."

"Where are you taking me?"

"You should more properly ask, 'When are you taking me?' We are bound for the far future, over three thousand years after the fall of Jericho. Any century now, we'll reach the Spree River, which will take us north to our final spatio-temporal destination, the German metropolis of Berlin on the fourth of November, Anno Domini 1989. On that particular date, I am given to know, a massive political demonstration will occur in the Alexanderplatz, named for a Russian Tsar."

Yasha contemplated the passing landscape, a vertiginous blur of colours that had no name and shapes that lay outside his vocabulary.

"Is Berlin an Israelite city?" he asked. "Or do the people worship idols?"

"Primarily, it's a sad city, cleaved by a hideous barrier." The angel laid her pole athwart the skiff and pulled from her robe the shofar by which Yasha had razed Jericho. "On the eastern side of the Berlin Wall, millions of people are compelled to live under a morally and philosophically bankrupt system called communism. On the western side, by contrast, millions of people pursue their ambitions in thrall to an entirely different ideology, capitalism, notable for its moral and philosophical bankruptcy."

"I didn't know angels were so cynical."

"I didn't know mortals were so naïve." Hegeliel passed the shofar to Yasha. "I'm happy to report that we're already on the Spree. A major landmark lies dead ahead, the Oberbaumbrücke. Before the Communist Party tore down the dual gothic towers, it was among the most beautiful bridges in the world."

Yasha surveyed the city, a bleak concatenation of sterile buildings, stunted spires, crumbling tabernacles, sombre pedestrians, and self-propelled metallic vehicles.

"I don't think much of this Communist Party," said Yasha.

"Neither does anyone else, including the Communist Party."

"May I assume that when I bring down the Berlin Wall with my horn, the tide of humanity will flow from east to west?"

"Indeed," said the angel. "I'm convinced you will become a Moses figure to the people of East Berlin. They will hail you as the hero who delivered them from captivity by the cruel Erich

Honecker and the blinkered Egon Krenz, though neither leader is as bright or resourceful as Moses's nemesis, Ramses the Great. The Socialist Unity Party of East Germany has always been a breeding ground for people destined to leave the world a worse place than they found it."

"If I wrote down everything you're telling me, Hegeliel, I might make sense of it."

"At this juncture in history, words don't particularly matter, young Yasha. The moment belongs to your music."

WITHIN THE HOUR, the skiff reached Humboldthafen, a small harbour on the Spree. It was from this very spot, Hegeliel explained, that a brave young man called Günter Litfin departed on an ill-fated escape attempt in August of 1961. A tailor by trade, Litfin intended to swim from the docks to a small canal that branched off from the Spree and flowed across the east-west border.

"Alas, after entering the canal and swimming beneath a railway bridge, Litfin was noticed by East German police officers," Hegeliel continued. "As the hapless tailor tried to exit the canal on the western side, one of the officers killed him with a kind of mechanized slingshot called a pistol. In the years that followed, at least a hundred and forty more people were murdered in cold blood trying to get over the Berlin Wall."

Dressed in nonsensical clothing and displaying curiously pale skin, a crowd of demonstrators was gathering on the quay, having evidently decided to begin their march to the Alexanderplatz from a spot of great political and spiritual significance. While some of these East Germans seemed morose and even despondent, others joyfully flourished boldly printed banners declaring, among other sentiments, KEINE GEWALT.

"What does that say?" asked Yasha, pointing.

The angel translated the directive into Hebrew. " 'No violence.' This is the first time in East German history the authorities have permitted a demonstration organized by private individuals."

"*Keine Gewalt*," said Yasha. "In other words, the protestors fear some members of their movement might spoil everything by engaging in fisticuffs or throwing rocks."

"Actually, I'm afraid *Keine Gewalt* is the protestors' plea for the secret police, the Stasi, not to molest them."

Hegeliel secured the skiff by running a hempen rope through an iron ring embedded in the quay, then disembarked along with Yasha, who clutched the Horn of Abraham to his bosom as if it were a poultice treating a chest wound. The angel and the shofar master melded with the crowd. For the better part of an hour, the roiling sea of disgruntled multitudes rolled toward the heart of East Berlin, chanting their mottoes and waving their banners.

Once again, the angel became Yasha's interpreter, rendering German into Hebrew. PRIVILEGIEN FÜR ALLE, "Rights for all!" SOZIALISMUS JA, EGON NEIN, "Socialism yes, Egon no!" WENDE OHNE WENN ODER ABER, "Change without any ands or buts!" NAZI-METHODEN IM STRAFVOLLZUG BEENDEN, "End Nazi methods in the penal system!" UNABHÄNGIGE GEWERKSCHAFTEN, "Independent labour unions!" VIERZIG JAHRE SIND GENUG, "Forty years is enough!"

"They seem not to have noticed the angel in their midst," said Yasha as the multitudes at last reached the public square.

"I've reorganized the protestors' brains to preclude their ability to see me. I'm invisible to every mortal within a seven-thousand-cubit radius."

Abruptly a new voice, male and sonorous, joined the conversation, speaking in well-intentioned but awkward Hebrew.

"You are invisible to most people, quite so, but I see you clearly," said the protestor. "I am Kurt Schwabe." He exuded the sort of serenity Moses had displayed as he lay dying on Mount Hebo. "I learned Hebrew so I might read the Tanakh in the original. Languages come naturally to me—as does my ability to exempt myself from the sort of mass hypnosis being practised by this unhinged woman in the angel costume."

"It's not a costume," said Hegeliel. "Young Yasha ben Ephod and I have come from far away."

The protestors, Yasha calculated, now numbered many tens of thousands. As they surged toward the speaker's platform, Yasha, Hegeliel, and Schwabe lingered on the western side of the Alexanderplatz. Patrolling all four perimeters were scores of unsmiling men in black coats, most armed with projectile-firing weapons— "automatic rifles" Hegeliel called them—strapped to their shoulders.

"Half of them are doubtless Stasi agents," said Schwabe. "The other half report to the Komitet Gosudarstvennoi Bezopasnosti— the KGB—in Moscow."

"Pastor Schwabe is a famous and beloved figure in East Germany," Hegeliel explained to Yasha.

"Or *infamous*, if you ask the Stasi," said Schwabe.

"Pastor?" said Yasha. "Is he a shepherd?"

"More like a rabbi," said Hegeliel. "Back in Canaan, your Hebrew nation will in time forsake the priestly tradition and embrace its scholars and teachers instead."

"You're joking."

"Another day's discussion."

"For the past seven years, I've conducted peace-prayer services at the Nikolai Church in Leipzig," said Schwabe. "We regularly importune the Almighty with our dismay over the counterproductive and potentially cataclysmic nature of the Cold War."

"Cold War?" said Yasha.

"It's complicated," said Hegeliel.

FOR THE NEXT HOUR, Yasha listened to the impassioned, bizarrely amplified proclamations pouring from the rostrum. The speakers, Hegeliel explained, were expanding on the ideals expressed by the banners: freedom of speech, freedom of assembly, the end of consecrated torture, a vision of an East Germany where socialist egalitarianism had replaced the police state—but Hegeliel was so entranced by Pastor Schwabe's presence she neglected to provide a Hebrew translation (which frustrated Yasha, though he declined to complain).

"May I ask what brought you here today?" said Schwabe.

"Yasha is in need of absolution," said Hegeliel.

"Not my modus operandi," said Schwabe. "I suggest you take him to a Catholic priest."

"His ram's horn is imbued with supernatural powers." Hegeliel lifted the instrument from Yasha's grasp and showed it to Schwabe. "He's going to use it to topple the Berlin Wall."

"Who does he think he is, Joshua?"

"Joshua's former shofar master," said Yasha.

"Let's give Pastor Schwabe a demonstration," said Hegeliel, pointing to a derelict and gutted apartment building adjacent to the railway station.

The angel returned the shofar to Yasha. He faced the apartment building, placed the instrument to his lips, drew in a deep breath, and exhaled emphatically. At the sound of the blast, the protestors turned their heads toward Yasha. The violent whole note followed a true course to the ghostly edifice, whose façade instantly became a network of fissures hedging the windows, balconies, and zigzagging exterior stairways. Impressed but not overwhelmed, the protestors redirected their attention to the demonstrators holding forth on the rostrum.

"Perhaps I'm hallucinating," said Schwabe in a curiously level voice. "Perhaps I just saw a magic trick. It might even have been a tawdry sort of miracle. In any event, I can understand your impulse to bring down the Berlin Wall, young Yasha, but I insist that you forget the idea."

"Just as Yahweh softened Pharaoh's heart, so will this trumpeter shatter the barrier that divides this city," Hegeliel insisted.

"Thanks to Lech Walesa, a new day has dawned in Poland," declared Schwabe, his serenity dissolving into indignation, his voice rising toward well-earned righteousness. "Freedom is nigh for the people of Czechoslovakia. Even as we speak, Hungarians, Romanians, and Yugoslavians are casting off the yoke of totalitarian socialism. But know this, young Yasha. The bloodless battles of which I speak were hard-fought. The victories were hard-won. You must not trivialize these changes with a sonic rifle or a science-fiction raygun or whatever you call that thing."

Yasha endured a turning in his gut, as if he'd been stabbed with a sacrificial blade. The angel had promised him absolution in Berlin, and now this Pastor Schwabe, coming out of nowhere, was attacking Hegeliel's scheme with an argument he felt powerless to ignore and unable to refute.

"But wouldn't it be amazing to see the Berlin Wall come down in a matter of minutes?" Yasha pleaded. Again he aimed the Horn of Abraham at the vacant apartment building. "Wouldn't that send up a shout of joy such as the world has never heard?"

"The greatest peaceful revolution in European history is unfolding before us, and I won't allow you to take it away from its architects," said Schwabe. "Before the week is out, the border between East and West Berlin will be as porous as cheesecloth—this I sense with every particle of my being."

Yasha blew his ram's horn, and the cracks in the distant building grew wider. Stones fall away like teeth from a leper's mouth. The crowd glanced at Yasha, glowered collectively, and again focused on the rostrum.

Suddenly, one of the black-suited agents yanked the rifle from his shoulder and yelled at Yasha.

" 'Cease and desist!' " ran Pastor Schwabe's adequate Hebrew rendering. " 'Stop that immediately!' "

Holding his rifle like a cudgel, the agent strode up to the pastor, the trumpeter, and the invisible angel, then screamed at Yasha in the universal language of rage.

" 'You may not want to know who is tempted to break your skull, but I'll tell you anyway,' " said Hegeliel, translating. " 'I am Lieutenant Colonel Vladimir Putin of the KGB. Normally I perform my duties in Dresden, but today I was drawn inexorably to Berlin.' "

Hegeliel moved nimbly to thwart the Putin person, but the agent executed a cunning feint, then struck the shofar master with the butt of his rifle. Yasha felt warm fluid rushing down his face. He dropped to his knees and, before blacking out, watched his blood spill onto the Alexanderplatz and flow across the paving stones like a torrent of scarlet rain.

III. THE BOLLARDS OF YUMA

Once again, Yasha found himself afloat in Hegeliel's skiff. His head throbbed violently, as if his brain had grown too large for his skull. By the evidence of his wet cheeks and soggy tunic, the Angel of History was still an incompetent pilot. As Yasha levered himself upright, a smothering cloak of heat descended on the skiff and the waters beyond.

"I'm sorry I failed to deflect the lieutenant colonel's blow, but I drove him away before he could cosh you again," said Hegeliel. "He'd never been goosed by an invisible angel before."

"How long have I been unconscious?" Yasha brushed the linen bandage wound tightly around his scalp.

"Six days. The same interval, coincidentally, that Jewish forces needed to win the Third Arab–Israeli War and, no less coincidentally, that Yahweh claims to have expended in bringing the universe into being."

"So was Pastor Schwabe right? Did the Berlin Wall fall before the week was out?"

"Alas, young Yasha, you lay insensate through the momentous night of November the ninth, 1989. I shall never forget the spectacle—crowds surging unimpeded through all six checkpoints, adolescents dancing atop the wall, ecstatic anti-communists raising their voices in song, East and West Berliners spontaneously embracing each other despite being total strangers. As I look back from our current vantage in the early twenty-first century, I am reminded that unification was not without its ambiguities and complications, but it proved far superior to the status quo."

"And yet my remorse remains."

"Your second journey of expiation, I predict, will end much

better than the first. The redemption of Yasha ben Ephod begins on this waterway known as the Rio Grande, sometimes the Rio Bravo, which for many miles forms a natural barrier separating a heterogeneous people called Americans from the sovereign nation of Mexico. Just as vast numbers of East Berliners wished to become West Berliners, so do thousands of oppressed proletarians furtively appear along this border every day"—the angel pointed to the southern bank of the Rio Grande—"intending to cross over to America"—she indicated the opposite shore—"where they believe a better life awaits. The proletarians go by many names. Migrants, immigrants, refugees, aliens, illegals, wetbacks, job stealers, undesirables."

"I see no migrants at the moment."

"They move under cover of darkness. Sometimes they swim the river, sometimes they use inflatable boats, but in both cases, the risk is great. The American sub-nation of Texas maintains entire regiments of soldiers charged with imprisoning and mistreating migrants who lack the proper credentials."

"My horn can bring down walls. Can it also drain rivers?"

"After the Rio Grande turns northwest into the American sub-nations of New Mexico and Colorado," said Hegeliel, "the border becomes defined not by a waterway but by barbed-wire fences, concrete ramparts, and arrays of steel pales. But our next stop is not a wall segment but a zone that lies hundreds of miles from here"—she flourished a squat, cylindrical canteen—"deep in the southwestern desert of the sub-nation of Arizona."

"I've already spent too many days of my life crossing deserts."

"We shall reach our destination in less than an hour."

"How is that possible?"

"Do you think the appendages sprouting from my shoulder are

merely decorative? Climb onto my back, young Yasha, and together we shall outrace the wind."

LIKE AN IMMENSE KITE crafted from the finest linen, Hegeliel and Yasha soared at a mindboggling velocity across the parched reaches of southwest Arizona, the angel's wings beating up and down like the oars of a mighty ship. For Yasha, the flight entailed many discomforts—the hot wind scouring his throat, the sand grains pricking his face, the dips and swerves torquing his stomach—and yet he knew that henceforth he would pity anyone who'd never ridden on the back of an angel.

At last, Hegeliel touched down, though Yasha suspected she'd chosen the spot on a whim, for this particular patch of wasteland was surely indistinguishable from the surrounding tracts to the north, east, south, and west.

"Were you to walk due south," said the angel, pointing, "when you reached the Mexican sub-nation of Sonora, you would encounter no walls, fences, or spirals of concertina wire. You might not even realize you'd crossed over into another country. And yet, ironically, the Arizona desert is perhaps the most insurmountable barrier in all the sorry theatres of the American immigration tragedy." She stamped her feet. "This is the wall that blocks migrants from a better life—this rampart of sand and fire, forty miles of nothingness in all directions.' "

Hegeliel hung the cylindrical canteen around Yasha's neck as if presenting him with a military decoration. She pulled the shofar from her robe, pressed it into his grasp, and propelled him in an ever-widening helix through a world as hot, dry, and inhospitable as the Kadesh wilderness where, late in the twentieth year of the Israelites' epic wanderings, Yasha had been born.

Within an hour, they began finding testaments to the dark side of America's immigration policies, body after lifeless body, men, women, adolescents, and children, their clothes torn by the wind, their skin blistered by the sun, their tissues desiccated and already inclining toward bone. Every canteen was empty. Yasha suggested they accord the corpses rudimentary burials, but Hegeliel insisted there wasn't time: the musician's absolution hinged on his blowing the Horn of Abraham before nightfall.

———————————

AGAIN THE ANGEL and the shofar master took to the air, and after two hours of riding the thermals, they came upon a vivid artifact demarking the sub-nation of Sonora from the sub-nation of Arizona. To Yasha, the thing suggested an array of immense swords, at least thirty feet high, their handles and hilts buried in the sand, their points welded to ponderous blocks of metal.

"Behold your new target," said Hegeliel. "It's called a bollard wall."

As the angel led Yasha toward the barrier, he stumbled over the crumpled corpse of a man no more than twenty.

"Along this part of the border, you'll find a corpse every half-mile or so," said Hegeliel. "Two or three times a week, a band of migrants appears here bearing a ladder as long as the bollards. The nerviest among them scales the wall, climbs onto the steel block, and jumps into America, thinking the sand will break his fall. Instead, it breaks his back."

Peering through the interstices, Yasha observed mirages

dancing and swaying atop the hills of the Sonora wasteland on the other side.

"The brilliant design of this wall traces to ingenious engineers employed by a tyrannical American leader who, as it happens, greatly admired your assailant Vladimir Putin," said Hegeliel. "The four-inch gaps enable border patrols to monitor migrant activity on the other side—and to poke their rifle barrels into Mexico if necessary."

Even as Hegeliel spoke, twenty migrants of various ages—children, elderly people, adolescents, adults in their prime—mostly males, a few females (one pregnant)—appeared among the shimmering hills. They carried two very long ladders and a thick coil of rope.

"I am given to know they are an extended family from the nation of Honduras," said Hegeliel.

Elaborating, the angel explained that if the family could get across the border here, they stood a good chance of reaching the migrant detention centre near San Luis or, even better, the Sisters of Mercy Hospice outside of Yuma. But if the bollard wall proved insurmountable, they would probably trek southeast through Sonora until the human-made barrier disappeared and the desert took its place.

"And then they'll turn and head north," said Hegeliel, "into a world baked by a remorseless sun and seething with scorpions, venomous serpents, and Gila monsters."

"Seven blasts?" asked Yasha.

"As always," said Hegeliel.

Yasha marched north for twenty paces, pivoted 180 degrees, and placed the Horn of Abraham to his lips.

The first blast set fifty adjacent bollards to vibrating like strings on a gigantic lyre, each shaking at a slightly different pitch so that an otherworldly melody filled the air.

The second blast got another fifty bollards rippling inharmoniously.

The third blast turned the vibrations into a whirligig cacophony of metallic discordance.

The fourth blast caused the hundred bollards to sway back and forth like bulrushes in a gale.

The fifth blast fractured each bollard several inches above its base, the destabilized wall section remaining upright only by the grace of inertia.

The Honduran family, sensing what was about to happen, cheered wildly, laughed gleefully, applauded madly—and retreated to the safety of the nearest hill.

Yasha again placed the shofar to his lips, but before he could blow the sixth note, a peculiar vehicle came rumbling over the rugged terrain, a kind of four-wheeled chariot piloted by a florid-faced driver transporting two grim passengers, one gangly, the other obese.

"Alas, Arizona Border Recon is here," said Hegeliel. "Vigilantes with AR-15s and strong ideas about how to solve America's immigration crisis."

Flourishing their weapons, the passengers leaped from the vehicle. Their clothing was painted to suggest various shades of desert sand.

Yasha blew a sixth note. The hundred-bollard segment rocked back and forth like an overcrowded footbridge suspended above a gorge.

The gangly intruder barked a command that Hegeliel (who'd evidently made herself invisible to the vigilantes) translated for Yasha as, "Cease and desist!"

"Drop your fucking trumpet!" added the obese intruder.

Yasha blew a seventh note, and the hundred-bollard segment fell onto the Sonora side, sending up cascades of earth and leaving a breach that could easily admit the entire Honduran family even if they walked abreast.

Before Yasha knew it, the wiry vigilante had whacked the shofar from his grasp and placed it on a nearby slab. Like a physician grinding herbs using mortar and pestle, the stout vigilante pulverized the Horn of Abraham with the butt of his rifle.

The Hondurans continued cheering, as if the destruction of the ram's horn were somehow part of the miracle they'd just witnessed, but their merriment died when the vigilantes rushed into the breach (the rawboned one dashing pell-mell, his corpulent confrere huffing and puffing) and took aim with their rifles.

"Go back where you came from!" shouted the stringy vigilante.

Yasha unlooped the canteen from around his neck and, joining the Border Recon vigilantes in the breach, hurled it southward like a discus. The canteen landed at the bottom of the Hondurans' hill.

"Get out of here, you fucking wetbacks, or we'll blow your heads off!" screamed the obese vigilante.

"And who the hell are you?" the gangly vigilante asked Yasha.

"Just some wandering Jew."

An adolescent Honduran descended the hill and retrieved the canteen. His family formed a line behind him as he marched resolutely southeast. Doubtless, they intended to travel far into the Sonora wasteland—to the end of the wall—all the way to the southwest Arizona desert. To better lives, conceivably. To slow deaths, probably.

Satisfied that the migrants had no future, the Border Recon vigilantes returned to the vehicle. The driver engaged the propulsion system, and the vehicle sped away toward the western horizon.

"This is not the absolution you promised," said Yasha.

"The horn is shattered," said Hegeliel. "I cannot help you further."

"Then help the Hondurans!"

The angel clasped Yasha by the shoulders and rotated him until he faced due east. "Walk seven miles in that direction, and you will reach an unguarded well on the perimeter of the Tohono O'odham Indian Reservation. The shaft is deep. The water is fresh."

"In Yahweh's name, help the Hondurans! You're an angel! Help them!"

"True, young Yasha, I'm an angel, which means I shall never see the world as you do. Help these people? Alas, that's not how the supernatural works. It never was. It never will be."

Hegeliel transmuted, becoming a radiance of impossible intensity, then disappeared entirely, leaving behind only a single blazing feather and a lingering scent of myrrh.

―――――――――――

WITHOUT BENEFIT OF DIVINE INTERVENTION, Yasha reached the well, cured his thirst, and proceeded to the Tohono O'odham Reservation. Despite the language barrier, he managed to convince the inhabitants he was not from Washington and meant them no harm, so they agreed to let him stay on as a kind of guest worker. Owing to the government's policy of rationing all water supplies available to Arizona's Native Americans, agriculture had in recent generations become fearsomely difficult for the Tohono O'odham, and yet they remained determined to grow their traditional crops, and Yasha earned his daily bread and nightly bunk by helping them cultivate tepary beans, papago peas, and Spanish watermelons.

Although the Tohono O'odham were linguistically gifted, they had no interest in learning Yasha's language; but they were happy to share with him their native tongue, along with their considerable knowledge of English and Spanish. Thus it happened that Yasha became the only O'odham-speaking Jew in Arizona, regularly regaling his hosts with tales drawn from the Israelite nation's ordeal in the wilderness. They particularly enjoyed the legend of the prophet Moses fracturing a boulder with his staff and bringing forth water.

The path of Yasha's life took an unexpected turn when, three years after he stumbled into the reservation, a documentary-movie company from New York City, Gloaming Productions, arrived to shoot footage for their PBS-commissioned feature on the history of Arizona desert peoples. Yasha immediately hit it off with the director, a rabbi-turned-filmmaker named Mitzi Ginsberg. Throughout the shoot, the two of them had great mischievous fun speaking to each other in their secret language, Hebrew.

In time, Yasha and Mitzi fell in love, married, moved to New York, and bought a condominium in Chelsea with the sizable inheritance she'd received after her father passed away. When Mitzi offered to pay for his higher education, Yasha leaped at the opportunity, which is how he became a licensed clinical psychologist with a thriving practice in SoHo. Year in, year out, he treated Manhattan residents of various income levels (he used a sliding scale) and diverse religious, political, ethnic, and erotic allegiances. He also composed and performed trumpet solos for the soundtracks of his wife's documentaries.

Throughout his career, Yasha never ceased to marvel at the

unconscious but extraordinary measures people took to defend themselves from each other. Spouses shut out their mates. Parents built barriers against their children, children against their parents, siblings against their brothers and sisters, workers against their colleagues, addicts against their better selves, narcissists against everyone else. Occasionally, Yasha's therapeutic skills proved inadequate, and the client in question would resort to divorce, disownment, estrangement, bridge-burning, suicide, or politics. But on the whole, the shofar master knew what he was doing. The people in his care were paying him to knock down walls, and that's exactly what he did. Yasha ben Ephod was approaching absolution at last.

THRESHOLDS

By Kristi Charish

I've never much minded killing people.

I considered this as my boot heel clicked softly against the sterile, white tiles as I crossed the empty church. The locals had strung a makeshift morgue up at the altar and sealed the tarps around the corpse, one Peter Alder, age sixty-five. I pressed my face up against the translucent plastic that was a hair's breadth shy of opaque. I swore before switching on my gelskin's audio Feed.

"MAX, I can't see a goddamn thing. I thought we issued all these outlier settlements new containment systems." *Ones with a video hookup.*

The Feed snapped like an electric spark ahead of MAX's metallic voice. "Voluntary upgrade, Billie."

Fantastic. I'd have to wait for the nanobots to assemble a video link on the other side of containment before I could run any diagnostics on the cause of death.

I swear these frontier towns like making my job a bitch.

My audio feed snapped again. "The natives are getting restless,

Billie," MAX said. "I don't know how much longer I can hold them off."

For the love of . . . A year ago, a Mitigation Android X would have kept them at bay for hours. The only thing that scared them much nowadays was the hint of a mandatory tech upgrade and obligatory vaccine intervention.

I preferred the old days.

"Billie?" MAX said, prompting me for an order.

I peered through the out-of-date quarantine tarp and accessed the nanobots. Temperature, preliminary diagnostics . . . still no video link, not for another fifteen minutes.

I hate frontier towns. "All right, MAX, let them in." I took up position by an alcove with a bowl of water balanced on a stone pedestal and opened my jacket so the disrupters were in plain sight.

The heavy oak doors creaked open, and I counted fifteen people as they filtered in, scanning each one so their biocode appeared in my gelskin's visual Feed, superimposed over their faces as they shot decidedly unfriendly and surreptitious glances my way. Names, ages, serotypes, vaccinations. Immediate family only. Well, at least they hadn't broken that rule.

I pulled up their pathogen loads as they spread around the small church. A few active viral infections, pathogenic bacteria, and moulds. Not great, but about what I'd expect from the frontier. More importantly, none of them were positive for a Threshold Factor.

They squeezed into the benches, at least two rows back from the front.

Bluster over foolhardy bravery; that I could work with—

A woman with greying hair and skin damaged from decades of unfiltered UV exposure and age walked right past the rest until she was touching distance from the quarantine plastic, a child in tow, a girl, clutching at her long coat.

One in every crowd.

I accessed her personal file in my Feed. The one concession the CDC had won against the frontier and outpost settlements in the last year had been bio-registration. Caroline Alder, age sixty-eight, wife of the dead man, and the kid was Katrina Alder, age six, paternal granddaughter to the deceased.

Why the hell would anyone bring a six-year-old to a funeral? *Has to be frontier-specific,* I thought. *Not even the city Orthodox bring their kids to these things. Too risky once a population reaches threshold. Hell, even here in a frontier town, it ought to be too dangerous. Then again, it's at funerals and deathbeds I see people do the really stupid stuff—*

My gelskin audio Feed spiked ten decibels as the little girl started crying. It hurt like hell before I got the outer volume feed down.

"Billie, I'm receiving odd audio signatures," MAX said across our secure Feed line.

I muted my gelskin's outgoing audio so the locals wouldn't hear. "Screaming kid at a funeral, MAX. Put it in your frontier reference files—oh, hell." I sucked in a harsh breath I was glad the rest of the room couldn't hear as the kid reached out and brushed her fingers gingerly against the quarantine plastic. Out of reflex, my own fingers slid over my disrupters. You'd need a cauterizing blade to cut through even an old quarantine plastic like this one, but damn, the kid touching it had me jumping.

I caught a grieving sister glance over at me before I could cover my mishap, dark eyes accusing underneath her black lace veil. She tapped another sister on the shoulder, a thin-faced woman wearing a ridiculous, floppy black hat. Two sets of dark eyes sized me up, lingering on my disrupters. I stared right back.

MAX's clipped, metallic voice threaded through my audio feed once again. "Making friends, Billie?"

They had nothing to complain about. It was set on stun. If they thought a few old ladies were going to scare me into a polite demeanour...

One by one, the relatives walked up to the plastic and said goodbye to the deceased.

"What do you think?" I asked MAX. I checked the ETA to my quarantine video feed. I'd seen it before in the Orthodox city communities, but it still unnerved me. There was something perverse about talking to a corpse.

"I think you have company coming at three o'clock," came MAX's clipped, matter-of-fact voice.

I shoulder-checked the oak doors as they creaked open. Two large young men dressed in white smocks decorated with red crosses slipped in. Medics. They stopped just shy of the back bench. My Feed greenlit their credentials, but despite that, I zoomed in my optics. Both their shirts stretched tight around their chests, and the pant hem on one was an inch short.

Short uniforms?

"Fantastic," I said as if it were a curse.

"I ran their credential codes through the Feed twice. They say they're here to ensure no one breaks quarantine," MAX said.

My Feed chimed an alarm as it registered two T7 disrupters. A cantankerous, unreliable firearm model at least two decades older than the two medics concealing them, poorly.

"I'll just bet they did," I said, more to myself than MAX. Not only were the T7s prone to overheating, but they were notorious for their odd and unfortunate habit of slipping from stun setting to kill.

I watched as the men sized me up, backs straight, tense, as they wondered at first whether they could draw faster, then relaxing, settling in, as they decided they could.

I hate field medics. With few exceptions, every pandemic on the books could be traced back to a self-righteous medic without the guts to shoot the sick people . . .

I switched to a visual text feed. Never know who might read lips. *I do not like those T7s. What's it looking like out there?*

"Perimeter is secure, but I'm concerned about audio traffic. I intercepted a request for an in-town autopsy to determine pathogen infection and mutation risk. They're proposing a formaldehyde dip and local burial."

Yeah, that wasn't happening. I'd read the preliminary symptoms report: the pathogen matched a level-five emerging hemorrhagic fever, emerging meaning it was a few small mutations away from human-to-human transmission. Bacterial or viral, most likely, though I wouldn't rule out fungal just yet. Considering the forest terrain and heavy rainfall, the pathogen was most likely waterborne, introduced by rodents, waterfowl, or even the fish.

A pathogen jumping species was never a good sign, but more disconcerting was that there hadn't been another hemorrhagic-fever report in any other neighbouring outpost. Meaning the species jump was recent and fast. It was mutating. All the markings of a Threshold pathogen.

These idiots were going to start the next pandemic. *MAX, I don't care what channel you need to hack, shut down that request—*

Another chime in my Feed alerted me that the nanobots on the other side of the containment unit had finished building a video feed. I patched the video through to mine and MAX's local visual feeds. The nanocamera tracked my eye movement, and the Feed kicked in, recording our examination as we got our first clear look at the corpse of the late Peter Alder.

They'd covered his lower half with the same opaque plastic that screened the quarantine but left the torso exposed. Average size and build, unremarkable except for the genetic recessives he carried for blue eyes, light skin, and red hair turned grey and sparse by age. Typical of people who lived outside the city shields, the skin on his arms, hands, neck, and face were weathered a leathery red-brown from windburn and UV exposure. The rest of his torso, though, was yellowed, with a waxy sheen. Probably liver failure early on in the infection, but I wasn't about to rule out multiple organ failure.

"The primary infection was waterborne, Billie," MAX said as he analyzed the nanobots' test results. "Consumption of local water over CDC-approved water supplies. The preliminary reports omit any movements outside the outpost clean zone, but trace water microbes indicate he came into contact with the pathogen in an outflow stream three kilometres north."

Hunting or fishing. I grimaced. Not the first or last outpost to manoeuvre around buying CDC clean supplies, but stupid. Would have had clean water with him—no one was *that* stupid—so accidental exposure, falling or tripping in the stream.

Eyes, ears, nose, mouth; all his mucus membranes showed signs of hemorrhage. *This guy bled to death in under two hours.*

I had the nanocamera zoom in until I found what I was looking for: patches of pin-sized, dry, flaky scab-like sores that covered his face and body.

It's ready to go airborne, I messaged MAX. *I'm calling in a level-five Threshold pathogen.*

"Skin lesions are indicative of contact transmission, Billie, and

a pathogen carrying a Threshold vector in a population this size is
highly unlikely—"

Except for rare outliers. *Take another look at the symptom para-*
meters and those pinhole sores. I patched MAX back into the medical
records I'd received at two a.m., the ones that had had me out of
bed and on a CDC transport at two-fifteen.

There was a pause on MAX's end as he checked my notes and
the new visuals. "Revising my preliminary analysis on threat level
and concur with level five. Billie, these records have no digital
signature. Who sent them?"

I'm guessing the autoscan kicked in. The autoscans were a
mandatory piece of tech all the frontier towns and outposts had
been forced to adopt. Whenever there was a terminally ill individual, they kicked in and transmitted the symptoms to the CDC.

There was another pause. "Negative on autoscan. This town
isn't slotted for upgrades for another three months."

That surprised me. *Friendly medic?* I offered.

"Those would be them behind you, with their fingers hovering
over the T7 triggers."

Still watching me with cold eyes, they didn't strike me as the
sharing type. If not them, who had registered the symptoms with
the Center for Disease Control?

I scanned the family, who'd just about finished saying goodbye
to the deceased. None of them struck me as the type to share
anything with the CDC either. Not that it mattered. CDC enforcers
found the pandemic before it started and contained it. That was
my job. I could worry about where the report came from later, or
better yet, let someone at operations figure it out.

The last of the man's family took their seats, except for the
Widow Caroline, who disentangled herself from the little girl,
handing her off to the mother, before heading straight for me.

Out of the corner of my eye, I saw the two medics tense and straighten.

I've got one of my bad feelings, MAX. Trash whatever communication system they have that passes for a Feed and get these idiots offline. And watch the locals. Last thing I need is a lynched android.

"No, that is the last thing *I* need, Billie. And it will take me another minute to disassemble the medic's communication systems. Older suits. Shouldn't give me too much trouble."

I wanted some distance between myself and the T7s, so I met the Widow Caroline halfway. The rest of the family kept their eyes downcast, except for the kid. I wondered what a six-year-old made of all this.

"Ms . . .?" Caroline started. She gave me a terse smile that didn't hide the cold determination on her face.

"Holliday," I offered, keeping my hand on my disrupter.

Her smile fell, and she pursed her lips.

Here came the demands.

"We're well outside threshold population numbers and city infection limits, Ms. Holliday, so you understand we aren't used to dealing with . . ."

"CDC observers?" I said, offering the kinder euphemism for enforcer.

"Or your—*robot*," she added, her lips twitching in distaste at the word.

"Android," I corrected her.

Confusion flickered across her face. "Pardon me?"

"The correct term is android. Robots are machines that follow a set program. Androids learn and think for themselves. Robot is considered a slur in polite society nowadays, Ms. Caroline." I enjoyed watching her face go red and her lips tighten as she kept her temper in check.

"Billie, as much as I appreciate you defending the honour of androids everywhere, ever heard the term, 'picking a fight you can't win'?" MAX said into our private Feed.

Who said I can't win? I messaged back.

"Well, for starters, there are the two T7 disrupters."

Caroline didn't try to hide her hostility this time. "Regardless, Ms. Holliday, we aren't used to the CDC showing up for a run-of-the-mill flu. Not to be rude, but we'd prefer to bury our dead and grieve without an audience."

I kept my face blank as we stared at each other. I don't smile or offer platitudes. People convince themselves you empathize and start to think they have the moral high ground. It makes it easier to justify resisting, fighting. "I'm pretty sure you've already figured out I can't let you do either of those things, Caroline," I said.

Caroline regarded me for a moment, sizing me up with a pair of pale, crystal-blue eyes not common in the gene pool nowadays, then nodded. "I'm very sorry to hear that, Ms. Holliday," she said.

Without any other warning or signal, I heard the medics behind me unclip their firearms.

"T7s are such a finicky model," Caroline said.

"So I've heard," I replied, but she'd turned her back on me to rejoin her family. All of them had their backs to me, except the little girl, who craned against her mother, not old enough yet to know better than to watch.

I didn't bother shoulder-checking the medics and instead pulled up a 360 view on my visual Feed. The T7s were already drawn and aimed at me. I slid my fingers around my disrupter triggers, slowly.

"Billie," Max warned, "your gelskin indicates you just primed both disrupters."

"Good, then they're working." The medics were jumpy, lack of training, so when I scraped my heel against the wood floorboard, I knew they'd both retrain their eyes—which they did.

I spun on my heels and drew both disrupters, levelling them at the medics. The speed surprised them. One of the women in the funeral party behind me screamed—scratch that, it was the girl.

I clenched my teeth against the high pitch as it filtered through my gelskin audio. They should have known better than to bring a kid to a funeral.

"Might I remind you you're under special request to minimize antagonistic actions?" MAX said, his voice penetrating my Feed.

Oh, for— "Fantastic, MAX. Why don't you come in here and tell them that yourself? I'm sure they'd *love* to hear what you have to say about us not shooting them. Right after they riddle you with enough disrupter charges to scramble an air transport." I unmuted my outgoing audio. "Last chance, boys. Drop the T7s."

Surprising no one present, the T7s' laser sights locked on my head and chest.

MAX wasn't letting up either. "Someone in this town sent those files. They've made an effort to cooperate with the CDC. How will it look if you shoot everyone?"

First off, I couldn't shoot everyone—there were too many, and most would run. Second, MAX knew I didn't shoot kids. "Safe?" I replied as the people behind me scrambled out of range.

"Billie, we are trying to avoid an incident like last time, not rewrite standard operating procedure."

The hand of the medic on the left twitched, and a bead of sweat trickled down his face.

"In my opinion, standard operating procedure could use some rewriting," I said.

I could have sworn MAX sighed—or made a metallic facsimile

of one. "Heads up, Billie, you have one more incoming. The Feed and bioscan say he's the town preacher."

As if I didn't have enough people in here to worry about. A bench behind me crashed to the floor as the people in the church tried to get out of the way, but there was no way to leave without getting caught in the potential crossfire. Didn't stop them from trying, all except the girl, who was the only one smart enough to hide—or aware, as most children are, that there's no point doing anything else when the adults lose their heads. The mounting panic in the church infected the medics, making them jumpier.

I retrained a disrupter on the oak doors as they swung open and a man wearing a beaten and greyed canvas duster and telltale white collar stepped through. Mid-thirties, six o'clock shadow, brown hair in bad need of a haircut. Rougher and more worn around the edges than the religious-preacher type I was used to. Average height, build, and no weapons as far as my scan could see.

He raised his hands and took in the scene slowly, gaze lingering on my disrupters and the T7s before he let out a low, drawn-out whistle. His eyes caught mine. No panic, no anger. No fear. I eased my finger down on the trigger.

He held my eyes a moment more, then turned his attention to the crowd. "I see we're off to a good start with the CDC today, everyone." His voice was low, rougher than I'd expect for a religious type. He didn't speak with contempt but certainly with impatience. "But how about we try something different today and not kill each other in a gunfight on the floor of a church, hmm? Caroline? Ted? Marshal?"

And then he did something unexpected. He strode into my line of fire.

Out of the medics put his T7 down, but the second only tightened his jaw.

The preacher regarded him, the corner of his mouth curling. "You know, Marshall, unless you know how to service the plasma chamber in that old T7, it's more likely to backfire and take off your hands than kill her. If you can even fire it straight." The preacher then turned his eyes on Caroline. "Or did Caroline not mention that?"

The second medic, Marshal, lowered his gun. Caroline—well, if looks could kill . . .

The preacher turned to me last, his eyes drifting toward my two primed disrupters. He raised his hands and held them out to the sides. "I think I can speak for most of us when I say I'd rather not disintegrate today . . ." He nodded again at my disrupters as he trailed off.

Reading people isn't one of my strong suits. I used the Feed instead. No increase in heart rate or blood pressure. Not lying.

His eyes didn't waver as he waited, watching me. In the end, that's what convinced me. I holstered my guns.

Besides, if I couldn't draw faster than the two medics . . .

The preacher cleared his throat before tension ratcheted back through the air. He looked straight at me as he made his way to the small pulpit, which had been pushed off to the side of the quarantine. I caught the limp in his gait, subtle but there.

"Billie, your disrupters are offline. What's going on in there?" MAX said.

"Beats the hell out of me, MAX. Preacher threw a curveball," I said into our private audio. I figured we were past the point of caring about lipreaders. "It could all still go sideways, so stay ready." It usually did, though optimism never hurts.

"All right," the preacher said, raising his voice so it echoed in the small hall. "It's been a horrible twenty-four hours. There's nothing I can say here that's going to bring Peter back or lessen the grieving of you loved ones." His eyes turned from sympathetic to cold as he them at his parishioners. "What I can say is that the last thing he'd want is for his entire family to risk getting what killed him. Everyone go home, finish your mourning in safety, and let Ms. Holliday from the CDC do her job."

The words were even and measured, but even I didn't miss the subtle threat. *Strange preacher.*

The Widow Caroline was the only one who stepped forward, a hard set to her face. "I'll be damned if I'll let those butchers cut him up and send him back in pieces, Carmichael. There's no reason for it—"

"Caroline, you know as well as I do Peter didn't die from the flu," the preacher said, not unkindly but still firmly.

But the widow was having none of it. "None of us are sick. It's just their way of stepping on us as if we were savages and couldn't tell the flu from—"

"Caroline, *that's enough.*" His words rang out, sending the low murmurs of agreement with the widow quiet once more. "You're all so worked up that you're blind to the facts staring at us. If you wanted to pick a fight with the cities and CDC, you showed up at the wrong church. Now all of you *go home.*"

There were a few mumbles from the small crowd, but one by one, they filtered out, Carmichael corralling them until the last straggler, who happened to be the widow, was manoeuvred outside into the morning sun. She shot me the evil eye as the church doors swung shut behind her.

"They always this friendly?" I asked.

"The polite thing would be to say yes," the preacher said, then sighed. "You've got quite the reputation, Ms. Holliday," he said, evaluating me again before offering me his hand. "Word gets around, even out here."

By chance, stray sunlight from a cracked overhead stained glass window hit the right spot at the right time, and I caught the metallic flicker on Carmichael's neck, a metal disk under his ear surrounded by three angry red scars.

I was surprised my scan had missed it. The old gelskins from a decade back had used thread wires instead of a retinal scan for the CDC Feed hookup. I altered my own scan parameters and sure enough, there was the matching input jack under the other ear. No surprise they were still red. Immune systems always did react badly to the old ports . . . nothing like the new nanoports, which were smaller and adapted to the immune system.

My Feed locked on to the tail of a red tattoo peeking up out of his collar, reminiscent of double helix tails.

I let out a low whistle. Now that, I *did* recognize. "New York CDC. You're a long way from home, preacher."

He shrugged and offered me a half-smile—not friendly, exactly, but not threatening, either. "Was a rough place eight years ago."

"Still is. Gelskin-permeable Ebola hit a few months back. Evolved a prion-like protein small enough to slip past the filters. Breached quarantine, too. CDC is still trying to recoup agents."

His smile widened—still not sincere, more like an attempt at the expression. I should know; I do it all the time. He shook his head. "Can always bet on the New Yorkers to break quarantine and salvage gelskin parts from any agents who get in the way. Glad I'm out." After a pause, he added, "I was there for the parasitizing influenza-prion hybrid. Try not to think about it."

I couldn't help but be impressed. I remembered the stories from training. A necrotizing parasitic prion hybridized with influenza and went airborne five years back. Nine months until quarantine was lifted for both CDC agents and the inhabitants. "Is it true what you guys called them?"

"Zombies? Eight years as a CDC enforcer, and I'd never seen anything like it." He gave me a grim smile. "Didn't have near the suit you're sporting."

I switched my visual filter to infrared on a hunch and got a good look at the leg he'd been favouring. The lower half of Carmichael's leg had been replaced just above the knee with a bionic prosthetic. Older model, five years at least, hydraulics instead of nanotech. I nodded toward it. "That when that happened?" I supposed I could have minced my words if I wanted to be polite. I rarely see the point.

His eyes went cold as he regarded me. I wondered if that's what I look like to people.

"Good eye," he finally said. "Infected five-year-old bit through my suit leg. Had to take the leg off and cauterize it myself. Got it before it hit my central nervous system. Guess that's something to be thankful for."

"I know someone at CDC Skagway who could upgrade it for you. Get rid of the limp, at the least. The tech has come a long way." I don't know why I said it—I'm not given to generosity.

An uncomfortable silence stretched out between us, and again those eyes watched me as if, if he stared at me long enough, he'd figure out what I was thinking.

"Thanks, but I'm used to it now. Gives me character. It's true what they say, you know. Fewer outbreaks outside a threshold population." He turned his back on me and headed for a small office door at the very back, well outside the quarantine zone. When I didn't follow, he glanced over his shoulder. "Come on. I've got beer in the back."

I eyed the heavy church doors. Carmichael, reading my face,

shook his head. "Bark is worse than their bite. They won't cause any more trouble today."

I glanced over at the old quarantine shield, only the outline of the corpse showing through. "They always that attached to dead bodies?"

"Despite what you might think, these folks aren't stupid. The Widow Caroline had her husband quarantined and the area disinfected faster than some city CDC officers I've seen." He shrugged. "They're just set in their ways—and don't like interference. People move out here to forget what goes on in the cities."

"That's one way of putting it." I checked the video feed behind the quarantine. The diagnostics still had ten to fifteen minutes of genome and protein coat sequencing before I'd know if the pathogen had gone airborne. With a flick of my eye, I muted the outgoing audio again. "MAX, pick-up estimate?"

"Still fifteen to twenty out, Billie. Transports say they want the diagnostic data and genomic sequencing confirming an emerging Threshold virus before landing."

Don't want to piss off the outposters . . . "Figures." I transferred the diagnostics line over. "Watch it for me, MAX, and shout when it's done," I added, then followed Carmichael.

Carmichael's office was filled with bookshelves and a pigeon-hole desk manoeuvred into a corner. While he rummaged in a small refrigerator in the corner of the room, I took in the surroundings. There was a cot along the side wall, only the end visible past a plasticized-cloth room divider. I noted the marked absence of religious material, with the exception of a small bronze cross hanging over the back of the doorway, out of sight. Interesting.

"So, I'm guessing you're the one who called in the pathogen to the CDC last night," I said.

He nodded, back still turned to me. "Don't go telling anyone, but I caught Peter on his way back from a hunting trip. He said he'd been out near the permit zone boundary, but I think he went past it. Hasn't been a lot of game around lately." He caught my raised eyebrow and shook his head. "Don't worry; we still quarantine all game meat. Destroyed it all after Peter came down with a respiratory infection a few hours after he returned." Carmichael offered me an open beer. I took it and let my Feed scan it for contaminants. It was clean.

"Mind if I ask you a personal question, Ms. Holliday?"

I took a swig of the beer. Light lager, not as hoppy as most. My gelskin also didn't filter out the taste like the last model had. "Shoot," I said.

"Is it true what they say about your first name?"

I couldn't quite stop the half-smile creeping onto my face as I sipped the beer. I shrugged. "Doc was already taken, and Billie seemed like the next best thing."

Carmichael let out a huff of air I thought was meant to be a laugh—or as close to one as someone who'd worked CDC in New York could get.

On top of the bookshelf, I spotted an old copy of *Patterns of Mutating Pathogens Within Threshold Populations* lying on its side. It was the least dusty of all the texts. Carmichael followed my line of sight.

"Can't tag the nastier ones like I used to—the mutation patterns have changed since I've been in the game." He took a sip of his beer and shivered. "The mimics, those are the ones that scare the shit out of me now. Think you've got a cold and find out you've got full-blown airborne Kuri-Kuri forty-eight hours later."

I just nodded and took another swig of my beer. Somehow, it didn't seem right to mention to Carmichael we were calling those game-shoots now. I waved at the cross and the books decorating the small, wood-panelled room. "So?" I said. I've never been very articulate in polite situations, even at the best of times.

"Why am I here in the middle of nowhere?" He took another sip of beer. "I got tired of it. Tired of a new virus every few weeks, tired of arguing with scared people, and tired of shooting the ones who broke quarantine. I guess here, I figure I can help—try putting it into their perspective. With my background." He shrugged.

"You can call us in before half the town is dead," I finished. Even I had to admit it wasn't a bad arrangement. "Can't argue the benefit of having someone like you in every frontier town. Though, to be honest, I think you're walking up a down escalator. Any of them know?"

He shrugged again. "Doubt it. If any of them do, I think they overlook it. They're not bad people, or so I keep telling myself. Just scared."

I guess I looked skeptical because he gave me a grim smile and added, "I'm allowed my delusions in retirement."

Before I could reply, MAX's voice cracked across my Feed. "Diagnostics are in, Billie, and the transport's landing. You were right. Level-five hemorrhagic fever predicted to mutate to airborne within five hours, human-to-human transmissible in six."

"Current vector transmission?" I asked, not bothering to mute my external audio.

"Originated waterborne, already jumped to contact transmission."

Carmichael whistled. I wasn't surprised. I'm used to being right about these things. I polished off my beer and extended my hand. "I wish you the best of luck."

Carmichael stood. "And I hope no bugs get past your fancy

new suit. I'd offer you prayer, but who are we kidding? After what I've seen, I sure as hell doubt anyone's listening. I'll walk you out."

We were halfway across the church's wood floor when my Feed cracked. It wasn't followed by audio. "MAX?" I said, but his voice didn't feed through. "MAX?" I tried again on a text channel but still no response.

The heavy church doors banged open. "Shit." I twisted and slid both guns out of their holsters, aiming as I drew.

Caroline strode through with the same kind of determination I see in dead people still walking.

Carmichael frowned and took a step toward her. "Caroline? You shouldn't be back here. Go home—"

"My husband isn't leaving with that monster from the CDC. He's being buried here."

"Caroline," Carmichael yelled, but she was already running at the quarantine filter.

A silver ball the size of a crab apple glinted in her hand: a sonicator, a sonic field grenade for turning over farm soil. *Shit, that's what they've done to my android.* The sonic blast would have scrambled his neuronal interface. I sure as hell hoped she hadn't put it on high. "Damn it, MAX, why didn't you just let me shoot them when I had the chance?" I said, in the hope he could still hear.

I fired and put a cauterizing shot in her arm that sent her screaming to the tile floor, but I miscalculated. She'd already launched the sonicator at the plastic seals.

Shit. I knocked Carmichael to the ground and threw myself over top of him, hoping my gelskin held against the sonic blast. The quarantine filter holding the infected corpse sure as hell didn't.

The shock sent my ears ringing, but I held on to my guns. I swore and aimed between Caroline's eyes as she limped toward her husband's now-exposed corpse lying on the table. She cradled the arm I'd injured and was visibly disoriented from the blast, but she kept moving, her mouth set in a determined line.

I drew in a deep breath and flicked the setting to kill. As I exhaled, I eased my finger down on the trigger.

Carmichael's bionic leg came down on my hand, the force knocking the wind out of me. My gelskin deflected the brunt of the force, but both my disrupters went skidding across the floorboards.

I never even saw him get up. Son of a bitch could move fast for someone with an old bionic leg.

I probably should have said something, but I couldn't think of anything that would articulate what I felt. Instead, I dived for the T7 the medic had left propped against the wall. *This is why I love funerals.*

I reached the T7 and flipped onto my back, bringing the larger disrupter up. Despite the bionic leg and limp, Carmichael had made a dash for Caroline and now stood between her and me. Figures. The one person with any reason in this hick town gets caught in my line of fire.

I drew in a breath and held it as I aimed. I squeezed the trigger to a hair's breadth away from firing.

But Carmichael hadn't touched the body yet. He wasn't that stupid. And the hemorrhagic fever shouldn't go airborne for five more hours. "Walk away, Carmichael," I shouted.

He shook his head. "Can't do that, Ms. Holliday." His brown hair falling into his face giving him a feral look. He never broke eye contact with me.

I kept my gun trained. "You're still outside the contact infection perimeter. She's not," I said.

Caroline spat in my direction and retreated farther behind Carmichael.

Of all the stupid, hick towns . . . sometimes, I hate being right.

I nodded at Carmichael. "She wants to throw her life away, let her. You know better. Step away from her and the body. I'm not bluffing. I'll sterilize this whole town if I have to. She touched the body; there's a good chance she's already a carrier."

"Well, then, you'll just have to shoot me too. Here, I'll even make it easy." He kneeled down on the floor and put his hands behind his head.

I really should just shoot them both. "Why?" I asked.

His lip curled up as he bared his teeth at me. "I told you. I got sick and tired of having to shoot people. Watching them get shot really isn't that much better."

I held Carmichael's eyes with my own. One clean shot, and it'd be over. He'd known that when he kicked my gun away. Hell, he was waiting, *asking* for it . . .

I breathed and aimed, the red light dancing in the middle of Carmichael's forehead. . . but I hesitated before pulling the trigger.

I can shoot an infected six-year-old, and hell, I'd *enjoy* shooting Caroline, but I couldn't bring myself to shoot Carmichael. One lousy preacher.

Damn it. I flipped the red light off and switched to manual aim despite the flashing orange light in the corner of my Feed. I don't care what the Feed says. I make shots like this on my own. "You sure about this?" I asked Carmichael as Caroline edged farther behind him, trying to maximize her cover. I held my breath and waited, watching her.

The preacher smiled as Caroline hit her mark.

I exhaled and pulled the trigger.

My disrupter beam tore through Carmichael's bionic leg. He

screamed and dropped to one knee. Integrated pain receptors are a real bitch that way. I barely had to re-aim before firing again.

Caroline stared at me in the kind of wide-eyed shock I'm more used to seeing than I probably should be. The expression didn't leave her face as her body collapsed to the sterile tiles.

It took a second for Carmichael to catch on. I watched as his face transitioned from shock to an expression I also saw all too often. Failure.

"Told you I'd do it."

He reached under his duster and pulled out a gun—an older model. I set my tracking light on his trigger hand—not that I needed it, but I thought it sent the right message. Carmichael looked up at me with another look I was used to seeing. Hate.

Well, on the bright side, there was something to be said about being back in familiar territory. I shook my head. "Don't push me, Carmichael. It never ends well." For a moment, I thought he'd do it.

Instead, he lowered the gun. His eyes never came off me, though.

My audio Feed cracked. "Billie?" MAX said. I breathed out a mental sigh of relief even as I picked up an edge of panic in his metallic voice. "Please say those were your rounds going off."

MAX was back online.

I nodded to Carmichael's leg. "Put pressure on that. You're dripping hydraulic fluid everywhere," I said before switching to my private audio Feed. "MAX? Glad to hear your voice. Was worried that sonic grenade did you in this time."

"Reboot, Billie, reboot. Status?"

I kept my eyes on Carmichael even though he watched me as if I were no better than a piece of trash on the floor. It didn't matter; looks like that never made it far past my periphery. I wasn't shooting him. He wasn't infected. I didn't care how much he hated me. However, I also couldn't just let the gunfight slide back at the CDC.

I switched my audio Feed back to external. "Copy, MAX. Two dead; the widow and the preacher. Tried breaking quarantine." I gave Carmichael a pointed look. "And shooting me. I don't know about you, MAX, but between the T7s and the sonicators, I'm pretty well done with this place."

"Couldn't agree with you more, Billie. More excitement than I anticipated."

"I'll say. Initiate sterilization and meet me at the doors to help transfer the infected body. Shoot anybody in the head who tries to stop you," I added, then switched my audio off.

Carmichael laughed from where he sat on the floor, not entirely sane-sounding. "You know what they say about you, Billie? You've got sociopathic tendencies. That's why they stick you with the damn robot."

"Tell me something I don't know." I headed over to my quarantined body and reset the containment field. Everything green-lighted; the sonicators hadn't completely destroyed it. I was ready to go.

Carmichael laughed, again not completely sane-sounding. "You know what I think? You're just another evil, soulless CDC son of a bitch."

"Nothing I haven't heard before." *Especially from survivors . . . keep the conversation functional.* "You got an old biosuit in back?"

I waited until he nodded, wary.

I figured as much. "Put it on. If you are infected, it'll contain it. You've got a couple minutes before this place disintegrates. I suggest you use them. My guess is you know where the back door is."

He didn't say anything else, just his silent accusation at me as he stood up on his good leg and hobbled back toward the office.

I shook my head and grabbed my contained body. "I hope it was worth it," I shouted over my shoulder.

No answer, just the scrape of Carmichael's leg across the floor.

Hell, maybe he'd even live. Part of me hoped he did. The rest of me just couldn't be bothered caring.

Body in tow, I headed for the wooden church doors to go meet MAX and our transport.

Nobody is supposed to love a funeral.

I guess that just makes me one sick puppy.

COURT DAY IN SHELOCTA COUNTY

By Robert Penner

The drug van was always full on court day, even before it got to the parking garage by City Hall: soccer moms nodding off on the back seat; working folks smoking crack; college and high school kids stocking up with Modafinil or microdosing on psilocybin. Then, once downtown, the people scheduled for arraignments and trials and sentencing would find it. In the CCTV blind spot. The blue van with the tinted windows and *Seeds of Faith Christian Academy* stencilled on the side. Right where they got told it would be, right where it always was on Wednesday and Friday mornings at 9:15.

You could tell the first-timers as they approached, wide-eyed, trying not to stare at the windows, sweating through their best clothes, exhausted by uncertainty.

"Open door," Chris would say, and humid air would boil in: cat piss, wet cement, mildew.

"Mary sent me," the first-timer would say.

"Gary sent me."

"Gerry."

"Larry."

A list of sociopaths on the take. Deputy sheriffs and security guards in crisp uniforms. Pepper spray, handguns, walkie-talkies, polished shoes with which to kick the shit out of you. They would send the newbies over, and Chris would nod them in. Give them reassurances. Take their orders. Distribute product.

Traffic- and family-court refugees.

DUI. Child custody. Trespassing. Petty theft. Indecent exposure. Public intox. Vandalism. Possession. Prostitution. Fraud. Nothing serious. Nothing big. Just the usual lines of escape, the usual dead ends and cul-de-sacs and arbitrary inevitabilities. Crushing banalities. Lots more women than there used to be. Lots more moms on the hook for truant teenagers. Lots of bewildered women trying to look confident: cigarettes in shaking hands, cheap blazers and old skirts, fresh pantyhose, hair pulled into tidy ponytails and buns, ankles turning in high heels.

Skinny Finney was there. Skinny Finney was always there on court day. Already waiting. Pulling his long limbs up into the van after his big rolling head. Perched right behind the driver's seat. Grinning. Personable. Hands flapping about, as harmless as moths. Working on the sad moms. Trawling for clients. Sniffing out that easy legal-aid money.

"Maxine sent me," today's sad mom said, and Finney practically licked his lips.

Maxine was gold. Maxine with the friendly smile and the "Honey, you okay?" and the gentle hand on the forearm. Maxine at the metal detector. Maxine the big earner on the drug-van payroll. Maxine, who could smell despair and loneliness, who could unerringly pick the users out of the queues and the crowds. She was gold.

"Will I be back in time?" the sad mom kept asking, and Finney kept *yes-yes-yes*-ing her, but she didn't relax until she asked Chris and told him the number of the ticket she'd been dispensed, and he laughed.

"Shit," he said. "Yeah, we'll get you back in time."

Finney gave him a grateful wink.

"Whenever the system crashes, there's a backlog," he said, and she slumped. "Sometimes it takes all week to catch back up."

"They said it would just be a couple of hours. I only took the one shift off."

She was on the phone—"It's Jen," she said. "I'll be late."—when the Professor yanked open the door.

"Is this the magic bus?" asked the Professor.

Chris had taken a class with the guy back in the day. Before the loans ran out. A tenure-track nihilist. Religious Studies. Mysticism. Asceticism. Always talking about Sanskrit. About Pali. Always talking about the translations he was working on. Always talking about illumination and darkness.

———————

THE INCANDESCENT WHITE sky was filled with drones. The robotrucks hemmed them in, the semitrailers like shining walls. Nothing moved. DUI stared at the ads flickering across his window: law firms, insurance companies, expungement services, churches. Child Custody was texting. Possession and Petty Theft were in a quiet conversation. The Professor was squeezed in the back with the soccer moms—they were the only regulars left—his thick thighs pressed against theirs, periodically sucking on his crack pipe, hands crawling about when he wasn't.

The soccer moms: first on and last off. Chris trailed after the school buses in the morning, picking them up one by one. Free of their kids, they got high and fell asleep, free of the dead weight of maternity, free until four o'clock, when Chris returned them to the ground, to their stops, and they opened their eyes to the world, opened their arms to their children.

"Koestler & Koestler," said Jen.

Finney barked with laughter. "Those shysters."

They had done a few lines of coke and were passing a bottle back and forth.

"Take it easy there, Doc," Chris said as the Professor's fingers vanished in the shadows.

The man recoiled.

"Do I know you?" he asked. "From school? Have I taught you?"

Chris shrugged.

The Professor stared. Eyes like worms. Fingers like worms. Words like worms.

"Did you hire them off the internet?" Finney asked Jen.

There were buzzards high above. Circling on an updraft. Much slower than the cycling drones. Too many of them. Too many drones. News drones. Police. Too concentrated. Too low. An accident, maybe. A roadblock.

"Take the Orangeville Exit," said Chris, and the right signal came on.

"They were on the list the court sent," said Jen. "Right at the top."

"Of course they were," said Finney. "They pay good money to be there. Right at the top. First in line for the cull."

A state-police drone was hovering right above them. The state police always made Chris nervous. Not like the borough cops. The borough was fine. The borough knew the state of play. But you never could tell with the state police. You didn't know who they were, their names, who they were related to, where they went to school.

"How soon till the Orangeville exit?" Chris asked. He glanced in the mirror. The Professor was staring at him.

"Five minutes," said the van.

"All you get with Koestler & Koestler are the cheapest algorithms and a call centre in India," Finney said. "No local interface. No actual lawyers."

The drone dropped a little lower, hovering not ten feet away from the windshield.

"You can't have been much if I don't remember you," said the Professor. "I remember the good students."

"What about Black Lick Road?" asked Chris. "How quick can you get us onto Black Lick Road?"

"Three minutes," said the van.

———————————

"YOU'VE GOT nothing to be ashamed of, Jen," Finney said. "It's a terrible law, an unjust law. Isn't that right, Chris? The truancy law?"

"It's a bullshit law." He stared up into the blank sky. They were off the highway: rolling hills, overgrown farms, chemical plants hidden behind trees, crooked houses and ragged yards, boarded-up gas stations with old pumps like rotten teeth. Every third building was a Pentecostal church: The Holy Spirit Laboratory of God, A City Burns Upon the Hill, The Blood of Jesus Flowing, The Lord Sees You Where You Are.

"You know they just built a women's prison near Erie?" Finney said. "State-of-the-art. Massive. Coincided with all the new anti-truancy laws on the books. And the old ones they sharpened up.

Punishing parents for the crimes of the young. No more incarcerable men, so they found a way to monetize the single moms."

"Really?"

"Really," said Finney. "Some of those prisons and criminal-defence bots and lobbying firms are owned by the same umbrella corporations. Isn't that right, Chris?"

"That's right," said Chris. "The sons of bitches."

"We're all just wind tunnels for debt," said Finney. "It blows right through us from one company to the next. Blows through everyone. Even the Professor back there," said Finney, and they all looked back at him.

"Is he really a professor?"

"Well," said Finney. "He teaches for a university."

"What's that?" said the Professor. "What are you saying?"

THEY HAD BEEN BACK to the courthouse and dropped off DUI, Child Custody, Possession, and Petty Theft, but Jen stayed behind to party for one more circuit. The Professor had come up front to hit on her.

"Finney isn't a lawyer so much as a stringer for an AI," the Professor said.

"A lawyer?" Jen was wide-eyed.

"I work for a law firm," said Finney. "Yes."

"A law firm?" sneered the Professor. "A bottom-feeding profit-maximizing limited-liability corporate scavenger, vacuuming up government contracts and churning out felons."

Jen frowned.

"It was just a matter of time until he gave you his card," the Professor said.

"Is that true?" Jen said.

"We have better financing than Koestler & Koestler," said Finney. "We have better ratios, and we have a human face."

"Finney." The Professor searched for his crack pipe. "The smiling mask that hides the seething void."

Chris remembered the Professor's lectures as a sequence of narrated images: south-Indian temples adorned with pornographic statuary; endless chains of ass-fucking Buddhist monks painted into manuscripts; tantric gods; grinning demons; erotic Jesus on the cross. He remembered boredom. Heavy eyes. His head filled with sand. He remembered staring at test questions: rows and rows of numbers; circles; the scratching of pencils; the Professor's voice rumbling on and on like the big trucks on the highway; the buzz of the fluorescent lights, flickering, blinking, an endless hum, endless as the chains of monks fucking each other in the ass, endless as the drones and the vultures circling above.

THEY PICKED up the Senator's wife at her beautiful house in the suburbs. She had called Chris to say she needed a ride to the hairdresser. She sat in the passenger seat and smoked ketamine and weed. He smoked a little with her. He put on her music: gentle machine-generated noise barely punctured by rhythm or melody.

Jen stared at the woman's profile, entranced by her clothes, her perfection. Aghast. The Professor and Finney kept talking.

"They banished me to the satellite campuses," the Professor said. "To online teaching. Terrible hours. They dock my wages and take me to court. But it's a matter of principles."

Finney rolled his eyes.

"If I choose to tutor students in my spare time," the Professor said, "it is none of their business."

"It's theft," said Finney.

"How can I steal my own knowledge?" The Professor's voice got louder.

"You signed a contract," said Finney, and the Professor flushed.

"Contract!" he shouted, and Jen winced. "It is an unfair contract! Unlawful! It exceeds itself!"

The Senator's wife stared straight ahead. Her sunglasses distorted the world, stretching it across the gentle curve of the lenses. The horizon glided across their centre like a snake around the world.

"Pipe down there, Doc," said Chris.

The Professor glared at him but subsided.

"Are you sure I don't know you?" the Professor asked.

Chris watched the sky.

"It exceeds itself," the Professor muttered.

JEN HAD LONG MISSED her court date. Finney was reassuring her as the drug van circled through Shelocta County for its seventh circuit: *I-can-fix-it-I-can-fix-it-I-can-fix-it*. He spewed strings of incomprehensible words: citation networks, machine executables, case-based reasoning, outcome assessments. He explained how to switch from Koestler & Koestler to Friedmann, Stiegler, Becker & Bent: "You can do it on your phone; you can do it right now."

The Professor was out of money. Out of drugs. Impatient to get dropped off at work. Angry. Sullen.

The sky had cooled to blue but was still filled with drones. The soccer moms were still asleep in the back, slumped against their seatbelts, against each other; arms tangled, hair tangled, dreams tangled, worlds tangled. The Professor still stared at Chris.

"I know you," he said. Worms were in the Professor's mouth, in his eyes, his beard. "I see you. I know you."

Chris put his feet up on the dashboard and leaned against the window. He yawned. One more circuit and his shift was over. One more circuit.

"Take the Orangeville Exit," he said, and the van's right blinker came on.

LIMBO

By David Ebenbach

The ghost in the house didn't like Liz.

To be sure, ghosts never *like* living people. Why should they? But this, this feeling the ghost had for Liz, was not the normal kind of antipathy—spectral envy, the fury of the damned, a hunger for blood. Rather, the feeling he was experiencing was more like . . . the word for it was probably *annoyance*. He was disgruntled. Put off. In a sulk, really. And it was getting bad. The ghost had been fidgeting non-stop with his glowing chains. He had lately been knocking objects off shelves not to frighten Liz but just because he was irritable. He'd taken to floating around the house muttering to himself, pacing without true footfalls back and forth in the long and dark upstairs hallway, with its floorboards that creaked even under his substanceless feet. He had been asking himself *Why?*

The problem was that Liz was unhauntable.

IT HAD STARTED as soon as Liz moved in, her few boxes—not nearly enough to fill the old house—lined against the walls in various rooms. The ghost flickered the lights a bit throughout that first day and night, testing the waters. This was the traditional way to get started, to begin bringing the inhabitant's deep anxieties—which were usually, at heart, a form of guilty conscience—to the surface. But Liz, a thirty-eight-year-old woman with tangled black hair, just shook her head ruefully.

"Wouldn't you know it?" she muttered to herself.

The ghost also tried upsetting a few objects. An empty soda can knocked off the counter to bounce rattling on the kitchen floor; a door or two slammed.

"Of course," Liz said with a roll of her eyes.

The ghost relocated things; the box-cutter was right next to Liz on the floor, and then it was across the room; her clothes were stacked in front of the dresser and then scattered; the newspaper was folded on the coffee table, but then it was on Liz's bed, open to an article about some massacre somewhere. It was heavy-handed, but you did what you had to.

"Naturally," she said after this last one. But then she added, "Damn ghosts."

That brought the ghost, who had been shaking his phantom head, up short. "Wait—what?" he said. There he was, floating in front of Liz, shocked into sudden visibility.

Liz rubbed at her dark and messy hair, making it messier. She looked like she'd seen some things. Not everything, perhaps, but a few significant things. "Yup," Liz said to the ghost, and then she walked right through him.

"Wait," the ghost said, trying to recover from the walk-through. "Come back here. What's that supposed to mean? *Yup*?"

Liz turned in the hallway, the one with all those creaking floorboards. She stared the ghost in his cavernous eyes. "It means I figured." She turned away from him again and kept going.

The ghost stayed with her. "You figured what? You figured there would be a *ghost*?"

She shrugged.

"Have you been haunted before?"

She shrugged again—she was an epic shrugger—moving down the stairs. "No," she said. "But it's always something, isn't it?"

THE GHOST WATCHED the unpacking for a little while, hovering a short distance away. A couple of photos of aged people—parents, presumably—went onto the mantel. Prints of black-and-white paintings by Franz Kline and Robert Motherwell went colourlessly up onto the walls. Dim rugs were unrolled. Kitchen drawers and cabinets were filled with devices and implements. Many books went into the built-in living room shelves. Then Liz hammered a tarnished silver mezuzah to the front door's doorpost.

The ghost became palpable again. "Wait—are you Jewish?" he said.

Liz nodded at him and headed for an open box that was full of Styrofoam peanuts and a few dark ceramic sculptures of animals. "Yup," she said again. It was almost a catchphrase for her. "Is that a problem?"

"Oh," the ghost said. He felt that he would be blushing if he could blush. "No. Not a problem. Of course not." And then he made a quick exit and went upstairs.

He didn't have anything *against* Jewish people, obviously. But he had heard that they were harder to haunt than gentiles. Ghosts did trade stories, sometimes, on the rare occasions when they needed a little spectral company. One of the other ones in the neighbourhood once said to him mysteriously, "Have you ever noticed that there are no haunted synagogues?" And she'd gone on a little bit about that. But then she started talking about something else—missing the taste of food, probably, since that was what ghosts mostly talked about—and he didn't think to pursue the subject further. He was pretty sure she'd been exorcized at some point since; you never saw her around anymore.

After a while—it was evening by then—he reconstituted himself downstairs and found Liz in the kitchen, eating some tuna fish out of the can. Just plain. Not even with mayonnaise.

"Can I ask you something?" he said.

"Sit down if you want to," she said, indicating one of the other kitchen chairs.

Ghosts, of course, can't sit unless that's part of their haunting routine—the man who gets murdered in his easy chair as he sleeps, say, and so who reappears in other easy chairs, snapping his eyes open abruptly and screaming when happened upon by the living—but this ghost gathered that Liz didn't know about the no-sitting principle, and so he tried not to take offence. In fact, as a gesture toward taking a load off, the ghost set his chains on the wobbly table, where they shimmered in a pale way.

"You've done things," he said. "Wrong things." It was supposed to be a question, but everybody had done *something* wrong, so it came out as a statement.

"Sure," she said.

He clapped his hands—which naturally made no sound—in satisfaction. "Great," he said. "That's what I'll haunt you about."

She shook her head, her mouth full of tuna fish.

"What?" The ghost almost barked the word.

Through some of the fish, Liz said, "It doesn't work like that."

It took him a minute to register what she'd said because the chewing with her mouth open was so disgusting. "What?"

"It doesn't work like that."

The ghost found himself wishing he *could* sit down. "*What*?"

"That's a social construction—haunting, being haunted," she said. "Really, it's some kind of Puritan thing, the way that all goes in the movies. The supernatural is there to get you back for whatever you've done. If you're too intellectual, you get your head cut off. If you're greedy, you get buried in haunted coins. If you have sex too young or too much, you get killed in your underpants. At least if you're a woman. Et cetera."

"Right," the ghost said. She understood the rules, at least. "What about it?"

"It's bullshit," Liz said. "Things don't work like that."

"What do you mean things don't work like that?" The ghost was now genuinely offended; his few decades of being dead had been deeply rooted in *things working like that*. He folded his arms over his stabbed chest and glared at her.

"I mean that there isn't some kind of sin boomerang. Here's the way it does work. Good things happen to people, and lots and lots of bad things happen to people. They just happen." She got up to rinse the empty can out at the sink that had the leaky faucet, and then she wiped her hands on her flannel shirt and turned back to him, he who was, by this point, speechless. "As far as I can tell, you get it in the neck no matter what you've done."

The ghost remained speechless. Backed out of the kitchen slowly, without a word. Without going there consciously, he drifted up to the creaking hallway.

How were you supposed to haunt *that*?

ON WEEKDAYS, Liz was out of the house, presumably working, which gave the ghost plenty of time to think. But he didn't know *what* to think. He wandered through the rooms and picked things up and put them down without bothering to relocate them. He considered trashing the place but then didn't; he knew it wouldn't bother her the way it was supposed to. And the house did still have meaning for him, after all. This is where he'd lived—with his wife and child—when he was alive.

On some days, he reflected on the fact that he had never met a Jewish ghost. Of course, that didn't mean anything, necessarily. Most of a ghost's life was solitary, and so you mostly didn't meet anybody at all. Still—you'd think that, over the years, he'd have run into *one* Jewish ghost. This was a major American city.

Was he doing something wrong with his afterlife?

HIS PERSISTENT IRRITABILITY set in at this point, and that began the debates.

"You know, it's not just a Christian thing, punishment for your sins," the ghost said one morning, interrupting her as she was hanging some curtains. Ugly brown ones. "What about Buddhists? Karma and so on?"

Liz kept going with the curtains, which refused to hang evenly. "Let's not bring some pop-culture understanding of non-Western religions into this," she said. "I doubt either one of us is really an expert."

"How do you know I'm not an expert?" he said.

Liz just looked at him, one eyebrow raised.

"Listen," he said on another day. She was regrouting the tub, which also leaked. "What about when they say that a man is 'haunted by his misdeeds'?"

"Do they say that?" Liz said, wiping the back of her hand on her cheek, leaving a grout streak on it. The woman was always a mess. Her hair looked like she had deliberately tangled it, just to be difficult.

"They absolutely do say that," the ghost said. "It's an expression!"

Liz threw her hands in the air. "So now we're doing metaphor? You're resorting to *metaphor*?"

Her disdain was so strong that he almost dissolved under it.

His final argument caught her when she was just back from the grocery store. As she came in the front door, she touched the mezuzah and then touched her fingers to her lips.

"A HA!" the ghost said, materializing, pointing. "What was *that* about?"

"What?" His excitement had stopped her in mid-motion, there as she was stepping into the foyer.

The ghost pointed frenetically. "The touching. The mezuzah. The kissing."

She shrugged. "It's a ritual," she said, moving again, walking through him and down the hall to the kitchen. She put the bags—just two—on the wobbly table.

"Not so fast—it's a *religious* ritual." The ghost was going to press his advantage.

"Okay," she said, a hand on her hip. Today she was wearing a checkered button-down shirt that was clearly thrift-shop stuff. And here was a woman in her late thirties, who had bought her own home. What was she doing in thrift-shop clothes? "So?"

"So, do you believe in *God*?"

She shrugged yet again, hand still on hip. "Sure. Why not?"

"Well, what about *that*?"

She sat down in a chair. It seemed like she would have taken one of the ghost's hands if she could. "Sweetie," she said. "If God's real, look at this world. Look at all the terrible things that happen all the time. Clearly, if God is real, God's pretty distracted. Busy doing other things. Don't you think?"

The ghost left in a huff, slamming the door because he could. But it was a poorly-hung door, had never been right, and it didn't go all the way closed.

SOMETIMES, when Liz was out, he went out to the front stoop to look invisibly at the street. It was a run-down street, the way it had been when he lived here, in that people tended to walk around slouching idly, and the houses were generally in bad repair. Though more and more lately he'd been hearing, up and down the block, the sound of construction and refurbishing—hammers and machines that refinished floors and so on. His wife had always hoped that the neighbourhood would eventually brighten up a little. But, of course, she wasn't here to see how things were going.

The ghost considered the possibility of slipping to one of the other houses to consult with another neighbourhood ghost. But it had been a while since he'd last done that—what if the other ghosts were gone for one reason or another? What if the houses were dispossessed? If they were, he didn't want to know it. Instead, he went back inside and hovered in place, staring at this or that. In particular, he had become fixated on one of the Franz Kline prints for reasons he couldn't understand. He would stand there staring at it, touching his knife wounds, which did still hurt. The picture was basically a bunch of black lines.

"Look," he said to her one night while she was watching television from her loveseat. "Did something *happen* to you?"

Liz didn't say anything; she just kept watching whatever she was watching. The ghost couldn't tell what it was. Ghosts can't see what's on television, is one thing he'd learned over the several decades he'd been dead, though he'd never found out what the reason was. It just looked like light pouring out of boxes, boxes that had more recently become flat screens. Liz's TV was a flat screen.

"Because you're a very negative person," the ghost said.

That got her attention. She turned to him, and the ghost abruptly realized that he was sitting on the loveseat with her. Sitting! Well, you never knew. "I don't think I'm a negative person," she said. "Or a positive person. I think I'm a realistic person."

"I don't understand you," the ghost said.

They both turned back to the TV, even though, for the ghost, it was only light. And although the sound was just static.

"I moved here because I got divorced," Liz said.

The ghost's head snapped back around so fast that it actually overshot her, and he had to rotate it back.

"Yeah," Liz said.

"What happened?"

Liz sighed. "Well, we got married after not knowing each other very long. And after a while, we really *did* get to know each other, or maybe we just changed, turned out to be other people. I don't know. Anyway, we realized that we'd made a mistake."

"Just like that?"

"It took a while. But yeah—we realized it was over. So I guess I *have* been in a foul mood. Sorry about that."

"How long were you together?" the ghost asked.

"Four years."

"And you loved him?" The ghost thought of his own wife.

Liz gave him a quizzical look. "Of course," she said. "I don't think you make mistakes like that unless love's involved. But it wasn't enough. That's for sure."

They were quiet for a minute.

"Boy—that must have been awful," the ghost said.

"It was. It is," Liz said. "Pretty awful for sure."

"Wait," the ghost said hopefully. "Whose fault was it?"

"Nobody's," Liz said, staring dully at whatever she was watching. "We just got caught up, and we stayed like that for a while, and then, eventually, we got un-caught-up."

The ghost thought back on some of his past relationships. Had any of his relationships gone like that? Not his marriage—that was a pretty solid one right up until the point he'd been stabbed walking through this very neighbourhood. Right on the front stoop of this house.

"It had to be *someone's* fault," he insisted.

"I'm telling you," she said, "bad things happen."

"Bad things happen for a *reason!*"

"Nope," Liz said, and then she looked right into his eyes again. "I think you need to get over that."

"What? Over what?"

"This idea of fault. And blame. And guilt. Like I said: bad things happen to good people. They happen to everyone. So you're just going to have to get over all that blame nonsense."

He recoiled. Which for a ghost meant blowing backward, right through the arm of the loveseat, a few feet into midair. "That's ridiculous," he said. And he remembered his wife crying, sobbing, for nights on end after he'd been killed. He remembered his daughter crying. He remembered them moving out as soon as they could manage it, moving, apparently, far away. It was after that when he'd started haunting. He didn't even know where they were now. He hadn't heard a single word about them in many years. "Get *over* that?" he said. "Over that *nonsense*? Fault? Blame? Guilt?"

"Yes. That stuff is a lie," she said. "An easy, lazy lie."

He practically screamed it: "THOSE THINGS ARE WHAT I *AM*."

Liz's face changed then, abruptly. It fell into softness. Her jaw un-set; her eyebrows slanted in empathy. Her face became tender.

It was—unbearable.

She reached for him, even though he couldn't be touched.

The ghost transported himself abruptly to the second-floor hallway—*pop*. The hallway was dark, and it was an okay place to float in a pacing way and, apparently, to cry a little bit, too. And then a lot. Ghosts can cry, it turns out, and not just for horrific effect. He was discovering that now.

"Hey," she called from down the stairs. "I'm sorry. Let's talk some more about it."

The ghost wept in the hallway. He wailed in a way that frightened nobody but him. He understood now that something extraordinary was happening, something he had never heard of before.

He heard her begin to climb the stairs, and the ghost wondered where he could go to get away from her. This house had been the only place anywhere that had made any sense after he'd died. And now things didn't make sense here, either.

Her steps grew closer. Slow. One after the next. What had the ghost done to bring this on himself? He prodded painfully at his stab wounds. He clutched at his chains, squeezing the ice-cold metal in his spectral hands. Surely, he thought, there would have to be a reason.

And then she was there, her hand on the wall switch, flooding the hallway with light.

OFFSHORE

By F. Paul Wilson

"**G** ot a doozie comin', Terr."

Ernie stood at the big picture window with his thumbs hooked in his belt on either side of the gut pouting over his buckle and stared out at Upper Sugarloaf Sound.

Terry Havens looked up from the bar where he'd been making a wet Olympics symbol with the bottom rim of his sweating Red Stripe.

"Good. Maybe it'll cool things off a little."

Terry had been expecting the storm, looking forward to it, in fact. But not because it would cool things off.

"I think this mother might do more than cool things off. This'n looks *mean*."

Terry took a swig of the Red Stripe and carried the bottle to the big window. He stood beside Ernie and took in the view. Bartenders always need something to talk about. Not much happening during off-season in the Keys, so some heavy weather would keep Ernie going through the rest of the afternoon and well into the evening.

And this looked pretty damn heavy. A cumulonimbus tower was building over the Gulf, dominating the western sky. Some big mother of a storm—a dark, bruise-purple underbelly crowding the entire span of the horizon while its fat, fluffy white upper body stretched a good ten miles straight up to where the shear winds flattened and sluiced its crown away to the north. Anvil-topped buggers like these could be downright mean.

"Where you got those glasses hid?"

Ernie limped back to the bar and brought out the battered field glasses he'd smuggled home from the Gulf War. Terry fitted them over his eyes and focused on the body of the storm. What looked like fluffy vanilla cotton candy to the naked eye became slowly boiling steam as violent updrafts and downdrafts roiled within.

Damn. He'd been looking for a storm, but this thing might be more than he could handle. Like casting light tackle out on the flats and hooking something bigger than your boat.

He lowered the glasses. He was going to have to risk it. He'd promised the *Osler* a delivery on this pass, and tonight was his last chance. The big boat would be out of range by tomorrow.

Besides, the worse the storm, the better his chances of being alone out there on the water. Not even Henriques would be out on patrol in the belly of the beast growling on the horizon.

Terry finished the rest of his Red Stripe. "One more of these before I get moving."

"Sure thing," Ernie said.

As Terry returned to his stool, he glanced across the horse-shoe-shaped bar and saw two of the grizzled regulars poking into their wallets with nicotine-yellowed fingers. Reed-thin, wild-haired, leather-skinned, stubble-cheeked Conchs.

"Betcha that storm's good for at least five spouts," Rick said.

Boo flipped a sawbuck onto the bar. "Ten says you don't see more'n three."

Rick slapped a bill down on top of Boo's. "Yer on."

Terry smiled as he reached for the fresh bottle Ernie put in front of him. Those two bet on anything. He'd seen them wager on the number of times a fly would land on a piece of cheese, the number of trips someone would make to the head in an evening. Anything.

"I guess that means you two'll be spending most of the night here," Terry said.

"You betcha," Rick said. "Watchin' the storm."

Boo nodded. "And countin' the spouts."

"Some guys sure know how to have fun."

Rick and Boo laughed and hoisted their Rolling Rocks in reply.

They all quaffed together, then Terry glanced up at the TV monitor. The sight of a bunch of flack-jacketed Federal marshals toting riot guns around a tandem tractor-trailer shot a spasm through his stomach lining.

"Turn the sound up, will you, Ern?"

Ernie touched a button on the remote. The audio level display flashed on the screen, zipped to a pre-programmed volume, then disappeared as the announcer's voice blared from the speakers bracketed on the ceiling.

"—tainly put a crimp in the black market in medical contraband. This haul was most likely bound for one of the renegade floating hospitals that ply their illicit trade outside the twelve-mile limit in the Gulf of Mexico."

The screen cut to an interior of one of the trailers and panned its contents.

"Syringes, sterile bandages, dialysis fluid, even gas sterilizers, all bound for the booming offshore medical centres. President Nathan has called on Congress to enact stiffer penalties for medical smuggling and to pass legislation to push the offshore hospitals to a hundred-mile limit. Insiders on the Hill think he is unlikely to find much support on extending the twelve-mile limit due to the complexities of maritime law, but say he might get action on the stiffer penalties."

The president's intense, youthful face filled the screen.

"We are talking here about trading in human misery. Every medical item that is smuggled offshore deprives law-abiding citizens right here at home of needed medical supplies. These racketeers are little better than terrorists, sabotaging America's medical system and health security. We've got to hit these criminals hard and hit them where it hurts!"

"Okay, Ern," Terry said. "I've heard enough."

Poor President Nathan—thoroughly pissed that some folks were making an end-run around the National Health Security Act.

Nothing new in the trucker bust, other than somebody got careless. Or got turned in. Terry wondered who it was, wondered if he knew them. He'd tuned in too late to catch where the bust had gone down.

"Excuse me," said a voice to Terry's right. "Is there a Mister Havens here?"

Terry didn't turn his head. Rick and Boo acquired a sudden intense interest in the "33" inside the labels on their Rolling Rocks.

Ernie cleared his throat and said, "He comes in now and again. I can take a message for you."

"We wish to hire him for a boat trip," the voice said.

Terry swivelled on his barstool. He saw a moderately overweight golden-ager, white hair and a sunburned face, wearing cream slacks and a lime-green golf shirt.

"Where do you want to go?"

"Are you Mr. Havens?" the guy said, eagerly stepping forward and thrusting out his hand.

Terry hesitated, then said, "That's me." Hard to lie to a guy who's offering you his hand.

But the immediate relief in the guy's eyes made him wish he hadn't. Here was a man with a problem, and he seemed to think Terry was his solution. Terry was not in the problem-solving business.

"Joe Kozlowski, Mister Havens," he said, squeezing Terry's hand between both of his. "I'm so glad we found you." He turned and called over his shoulder. "It's him, Martha!"

Terry looked past him at a rickety, silver-haired woman hobbling toward them, supporting herself on the bar with her right forearm and leaning on a four-footed cane clasped in her gnarled left hand. Her wrinkled face was pinched with pain. She couldn't seem to straighten out her right leg and winced every time she put weight on it.

"Thank God!" she said.

Terry was getting a bad feeling about this.

"Uh, just where is it you folks want to go?"

"Out to the *Osler*," Joe said.

"You missed her. She took on her patients this morning, and she's gone."

"I know. We missed the shuttle. Martha wanted to say goodbye to the kids before the surgery. You know, in case . . . you know. But our car broke down last night just as we were leaving and what they said would take an hour to fix wound up taking much longer. Damn car's probably still up on the lift back there in Stewart. I finally rented a car and drove down here fast as I could. Collected two tickets along the way, but we still missed the boat. We've been driving up and down Route One all day, trying to find someone to take us out. No one's interested. I don't understand. I don't want a favour—I'm willing to pay a fair price. And it's not like it's a crime or anything."

Right. Not a crime or anything to ferry someone out past the twelve-mile limit to one of the hospital ships. But bad things tended to happen to good boaters who engaged in the trade if officialdom got wind of it. Bad things like a Coast Guard stop-and-search every time you took your boat out; or all sorts of lost applications and inexplicable computer glitches when you wanted to renew your boating tags, your fishing permits, even your driver's licence. Terry had heard talk that the good folks in question seemed to suffer a significantly greater incidence of having their 1040 audited by the IRS.

No, not a crime, but lots of punishment.

Which was why the hospital ships ran their own shuttles.

"What excuse did they give?"

"Most said they were too busy, but let me tell you, they didn't look it. And as soon as those clouds started gathering, they used the storm as an excuse."

"Good excuse."

Terry glanced back at the western horizon. The afternoon sun had been swallowed whole by the storm, and its white bulk had turned a threatening grey.

"But I hear you're not afraid of storms," Joe said.

Terry stared at him, feeling his anger rise. *Shit.* "Who told you that?"

"Some fellow in a bar up on the next key—is it Cudjoe Key? Some cantina . . ."

"Coco's."

"That's the place! Fellow with bleached hair and a fuzzy goatee."

Tommy Axler. Terry wanted to strangle the big-mouthed jerk. In fact, he might give it a try next time he saw him.

"He must have thought you wanted to go fishing. Sometimes I take people fishing in the rain. I do lots of things, but I don't ferry folks out to hospital ships."

That last part, at least, was true.

Joe's eyes got this imploring look. "I'll pay you twice your regular charter fee."

Terry shook his head. "Sorry."

His face fell. He turned to his wife. "He won't do it, Martha."

She halted her laboured forward progress as if she'd run into a wall.

"Oh," she said softly and leaned against one of the barstools. She stared at the floor and said no more.

"But let me buy you folks a drink." Terry pointed to his Red Stripe. "You want one of these?"

"No," Joe said through a sigh, then shrugged. "Aaah, why not? Martha? You want something?"

Still staring at the floor, Martha only shook her head.

Ernie set the bottle in front of Joe, who immediately chugged about a third of it.

He stifled a burp, then said, "You won't reconsider, even if I triple your usual fee?"

Terry shook his head. "Look, the *Osler*'ll probably be shuttling patients in and out of St. Petersburg in a day or two. Hop in your car and—"

"Martha's got an appointment for a total hip replacement

tomorrow. If she's not on board the *Osler* today, they'll give her appointment to someone on the waiting list."

"So reschedule."

"It took us six months to get this appointment, and we were lucky. The fellow who had the original appointment died. Might be another ten months to a year before Martha can get rescheduled."

"That's as bad as the regular government wait lists."

"No," he said with a slow shake of his head. "There *is* no government wait list for Martha. Not anymore. She's too old. HRAA passed a regulation barring anyone over age seventy-five from certain surgical procedures. Total hip replacement is on the list. And Martha's seventy-seven."

Martha's head snapped up. "Don't you be blabbing my age for all the world to hear!"

"Sorry, dear."

Terry looked at him. "I thought the cut-off was eighty."

"Right: *was*. They lowered it last year."

Terry had assumed that most of the hospital-ship patrons were well-heeled folks who didn't want to wait in the long queues for elective surgery in the government-run hospitals. And since all the hospitals in America were now government-run, they had to go elsewhere. But cutting people off from procedures . . .

The Health Resources Allocation Agency strikes again.

"I didn't know they could do that."

Joe sighed. "Neither did I. It wasn't part of the regulations when the Health Security Act became law, but apparently, the HRAA has the power to make new regs. So when they found out how far their Health Security Act was running over projections, they started making cuts. What really galls me is I supported the damn law."

"So did I."

"Yeah, we all thought we were getting a bargain. Ten years later, we find out we got the shaft."

"Welcome to the twenty-first century, Pops. Believe in the future but always read the fine print."

"Tell me about it." He slugged down some more beer and stared at the bottle in his hand. "It's not fair, you know. We busted our butts since we got married—fifty years come next July—to make a good life for our family. We educated our kids, got them married and settled, then we retired. And now we'd like to enjoy the years we've got left. Nothing fancy. No trips around the world. Just hang out, play golf once in a while. But with Martha's hip, we can't even go for a walk after dinner."

Terry said nothing as Joe polished off his beer. He was trying not to listen. He wasn't going to get sucked into this.

Joe banged his bottle down on the bar. "You know what really bugs my ass? We've got the money to pay for the surgery. We don't need the government to pay for it. Fuck 'em! *We'll* pay. Gladly. But they won't let her have the surgery—period. Their letter said total hip surgery at her age is 'an inefficient utilization of valuable medical resources.' I mean, what the hell did we work and skimp and save for if we can't spend it on our health?"

"Wish I had an answer for you," Terry said.

"Yeah." He pushed away from the bar. "Thanks for the beer. Come on, Martha. We'll keep looking."

He took his wife gently by the arm and began helping her toward the door. Terry stared across the bar at Rick and Boo so he wouldn't have to watch the Kozlowskis. He saw a grinning Rick accepting a ten from a grumpy-looking Boo. He wondered what the bet had been this time.

He looked out the window at the towering storm, black as a

hearse now, picking up speed and power. If he was going to head out, he'd better get moving.

Terry waited until Joe Kozlowski had eased his wife into the passenger seat, then he waved to Rick, Boo, and Ernie and made for the door. The August heat gave him a wet body slam as he stepped outside. He slid past the Kozlowskis' idling rental but couldn't resist a glance through the windshield.

Martha was crying.

He averted his gaze and hurried to his pickup.

Life really sucked sometimes.

He jumped into the blisteringly hot cab.

That didn't mean he had to get involved.

He turned the key and the old Ford shuddered to life.

Wasn't his problem.

He threw it into reverse.

As he was backing out, he saw Joe put an arm around his wife's thin, quaking shoulders and try to comfort her.

He slammed on the brakes and yanked the gearshift back into neutral.

Shit.

Cursing himself for a jerk, Terry jumped out of the cab and stalked over to the Kozlowskis' car. He rapped on Joe's window.

"Follow me," he said as the glass slid down.

Joe's eyes lit. "You mean—?"

"Just follow."

As he was heading back to the pickup, he heard a voice call out behind him.

"Aw, Terry! Say it ain't so!"

He turned and saw Rick standing in the doorway, dismay flattening his weathered features. Boo peered over his shoulder, grinning.

"You're takin' 'em, ain't ya?" Boo said.

"None of your damn business."

Boo nudged Rick none too gently and rubbed his palms together. "See. I toldja he would. I win. Gimme back my saw plus the one you owe me. Give it now, Rick."

Rick handed the money to Boo and gave Terry a wounded look.

"Y'disappointed the shit outta me, Terr."

"Yeah, well," Terry muttered, slipping behind the wheel again, "there's one born every minute."

"You really think he's going to risk this storm?" Cramer asked.

Pepe Henriques looked at his mate. Cramer's round, usually relaxed boyish face was tight with tension.

He's scared, he thought.

Which was okay. Showing it wasn't.

Henriques looked past Cramer at the storm that filled the sky. Giant forks of lightning occasionally speared down to the Gulf but mostly jumped cloud to cloud, illuminating the guts of the storm with explosions of light. Thunder crashed incessantly, vibrating their fibreglass hull. He could see the rain curtain billowing toward them.

Almost here.

When it hit, visibility would be shot, and they'd have to go on instruments. But so would the runner.

"He'll be out here. Why else would that hospital ship be dawdling fourteen miles out? They're waiting for a delivery. And our man's going to make it. That is, he's going to try. This'll be his last run."

He tossed Cramer a lifejacket and watched him strap it on. Saw the black ATF across the yellow fabric and had to shake his head.

Me. An ATF agent.

He still couldn't believe it. But he'd found he liked the regular paycheque, the benefits package, the retirement fund. Sure as hell beat taking tourists tarpon and bone fishing on the flats.

But he might be back to fishing those flats if he didn't catch this runner.

Henriques had run up against him twice before, but both times he'd got away. Two things he knew for sure about the guy: he ran a Hutchison 686, and he was a Conch. Henriques had seen the Hutch from a distance. The registration numbers on the twenty-six-foot craft were bogus—no surprise there. What had been big surprises were the way the boat handled and its pilot's knowledge of the waters around the Lower Keys. The Hutch 686 was popular as hell in these parts, but this one had done things a propeller-driven shouldn't be able to do. It ran like a VMA impeller—like Henriques' craft. The runner had customized it somehow.

And as for being a Conch, well . . . nobody could dodge among all these reefs and mangrove keylets like that runner unless he'd spent his life among them. A native of the Keys. A Conch. Took one to know one.

Take one to catch one.

And I'm the one, Henriques thought. *Tonight's his last run.*

THE RAIN HIT JUST as they neared the inner rim of the reef. Terry pulled back on the throttle and idled the engine.

"Thank *God!*" Martha Kozlowski said. She clung to the arms of her deck-fast seat with white knuckles. "That bouncing was making me sick!"

"What're you doing now?" Joe shouted over the mad drumming of the big drops on the deck and the roof of the open cabin.

Terry didn't answer. His passengers would see for themselves soon enough.

He unwrapped the moulded black plastic panels and began scampering around the deck, snapping them onto the sides of the superstructure. Two of the strips for the hull sported a brand-new registration number, fresh off the decal sheets. Another went over the transom to cover the name, replacing his own admittedly corny *Terryfied* with *Delta Sue*.

Joe looked bewildered when Terry ducked back into the cabin enclosure.

"I don't get it."

"Just a little insurance."

The less Joe knew, the better.

The panels changed the boat's lines and colour scheme. Nothing that would hold up against even casual inspection in good light, but from a distance, through lightning-strobed rain, his white, flat-bottomed VMA impeller craft looked an awful lot like a black-and-white V-hulled Hutchison 686. The black panels also broke up the boat's outline, making it harder to spot.

"That's what you said when you were playing around with the light on that channel marker," Joe said.

"That's right. Another kind of insurance."

"But that could—"

"Don't worry. I'll undo it on my way back in. No questions—wasn't that the deal?"

Joe nodded glumly. "But I still don't get it."

You're not supposed to, Terry thought as he gunned the engine and headed into the wind.

The hull jumped, thudded, shimmied, and jittered with the staccato pounding of the waves, and all that rhythmic violence worked into every tissue of his body. Once he zipped through the cut in the barrier reef, it got worse—two, three, maybe four times worse. Riding at this speed in this weather was a little like getting a total body massage. From King Kong. On speed. Add to that the tattoo of the rain, the howl of the wind, the booming thunder, and further talk was damn near impossible. Unless you shouted directly into someone's ear. Which Martha was doing into Joe's as she bounced around in her seat and hung on for dear life.

Joe sidled over. "Think you could slow down? Martha can't take the pounding."

Terry shook his head. "I ease up, we won't make enough headway."

Joe went back to Martha, and they traded more shouts, none of which Terry could hear. Joe lurched back.

"Let's go back. I'm calling the trip off. Martha's afraid, and she can't take this pounding."

He'd been half-expecting something like this. *Damn. Should have left them back on Sugarloaf.*

"Don't wimp out on me, Joe."

"It's not me. Look, you can keep the money. Martha's getting sick. Just turn around and take us back."

"Can't do that. No questions and no turning back—wasn't that the deal?"

"Yes, but—"

"It's still the deal. Tell Martha to hang on, and she'll have a new hip tomorrow."

As Joe stumbled back to his wife, Terry concentrated on the

infrared scanner. Clear and cold, except for the faint blob of the *Osler* straight ahead. Good. Stay that way.

Terry liked rain. Besides lowering visibility, it played havoc with heat scanners. Radiant energy tended to get swallowed up in all that falling water. But that could be a two-edged sword: Terry couldn't spot a pursuer until they were fairly close.

Didn't worry him much at the moment. Weren't too many craft that could outrun him in a sprint, and once he slipped past the twelve-mile limit, no one could touch him. Legally, anyway. Always the possibility that some frustrated ATF goon with a short fuse might blow a few holes in your hull—and you—and let the sharks clean up the mess.

He checked the compass, checked the Loran—right on course. Just a matter of time now. He looked up and froze when he saw Joe Kozlowski pointing a pistol at him. The automatic—looked like a 9mm—wavered in the old guy's hand, but the muzzle never strayed far from the centre of Terry's chest.

"Turn around and take us back," Joe shouted.

No way was Terry turning back. And no way was he telling Joe that at the moment. Guns made him nervous.

Terry eyed the gun. "Where'd that come from?"

"I brought it along . . . just in case."

"Just in case what?"

"In case you tried to rob us. Or worse."

"Whatever happened to trust?"

"The Health Resources Allocation Agency's got mine." His eyes bored into Terry's. "Now turn this thing around. I told you you could keep the money. Just take us back."

Terry shook his head. "Sorry. Can't do that."

Joe couldn't seem to believe what he'd heard. "I've got a *gun*, dammit!"

Terry was well aware of that. He didn't think Joe would pull that trigger, but you never knew. So maybe it was time to shake Joe up—more than physically.

"And I've got a cargo to deliver."

"My wife is *not* cargo!"

"Take a look below," Terry told him, jutting his chin toward the door to the below-decks area.

Joe's gaze darted from Terry to the door and back. His eyes narrowed with suspicion. "You wouldn't try anything stupid, would you?"

Terry shrugged. "Take a look."

Joe thought about that, then backed away and opened the door. More hesitation, then he slipped below. A moment later, he appeared again, pale, his eyes wide. Terry could read his lips.

"Medical supplies! Martha, he's a smuggler!"

Martha freed up a hand long enough to slap it over the "O" of her mouth, then returned it to the armrest.

"The way I see it, Joe, you've got two options. The first is, you can shoot me and try to get the boat back home on your own. Not only will you have to guide it through the storm, but you'll have to avoid the shore patrol. If they catch you, you'll go down for murder *and* smuggling. Or you can follow through with our original plan and—" A blip caught his eye on the infrared scanner, aport and astern, and closing. He forgot all about Joe Kozlowski's gun. "Shit!"

"What's wrong?"

"We've got company."

"Who?"

"ATF, most likely."

"ATF? But they're alcohol, tobacco and—"

"They added medical supplies to their list. Get over by Martha and hang on. This could get a little rough."

"A *little* rough? It's already—"

"Get out of my face, dammit!"

Henriques, Terry thought. *Has to be him. No one else has such a bug up his ass that he'd brave this storm looking for a runner. Not just any runner. Looking for The One That Got Away.*

Me.

He jammed the throttle all the way forward. *Terryfied* lifted farther out of the water and began bouncing along the tops of the waves. Like riding downhill in a boxcar derby on a cobblestone road. With steel wheels. Planing out was impossible, but this was as close as she'd get. The price was loss of control. The boat slewed wildly to port or starboard whenever she dipped into a trough.

How'd Henriques find him? Luck? Probably not. He was a Conch, but even that wasn't enough. Probably some new equipment he had. Price was no object for the ATF when taxes were paying for it.

Damn ATF. For years Terry had breezed in and out of the Keys on his supply runs until they'd got smart and started hiring locals for their shore patrols. Making a run these days had become downright dicey.

He concentrated on the Loran, the infrared scanner, and what little he could see of the water ahead. The blip had stopped gaining. And, running on the diagonal as it had to, was actually losing ground. Terry didn't let up. Unless he hit some floating debris or broached in a freak swell, he'd be first to cross the twelve-mile limit.

But he wouldn't be celebrating.

"OH, LORD!" Martha cried, staring up the sheer twenty feet of steel hull that loomed above her. "How am I going to get up there?"

"Don't worry," Terry said as he tried to hold his bobbing craft steady against the *Osler*. "We have a routine."

Above them, a winch supporting a pair of heavy-duty slings swung into view. The straps of the slings flapped and twisted in the gale-force winds as they were lowered over the side. Terry nosed his prow through the first when it hit water, then idled his engine and manually guided the second sling under the stern.

The winch began hauling them up.

Once they were on the deck, the crew pulled a heavy canvas canopy over the boat and helped Martha into a wheelchair.

"Well, she made it," Terry said.

Joe Kozlowski stared at him. "I don't know whether to thank you or punch you in the nose."

"Think on it awhile," Terry said. "Wait till you're both sitting in a bar sipping a g 'n' t after a round of golf. Then decide."

Joe's face softened. He extended his hand. They shook, then Joe followed Martha inside.

As the *Osler*'s crew off-loaded the medical supplies, Terry ducked out from under the billowing canopy and fought the wind and rain to the deck rail. He squinted out at the lightning-shot chaos. A lot of hell left in this monster. But that didn't mean Henriques had run home. No, that bastard was laying out there somewhere, waiting.

Not to arrest him. Couldn't do that once the contraband was gone. And if Henriques did manage to catch him, Terry could thumb his nose and say he'd been out on a little jaunt to say hello to some old friends among the crew.

But even though Henriques had no case against him, Terry

still couldn't let him get near. It wasn't fear of arrest that gnawed at the lining of his gut. It was being identified.

Once they knew his name, his runner career was over. He'd be watched day and night, followed everywhere, his phones tapped, his house bugged, and every time *Terryfied* left the slip, he'd be stopped and inspected.

His whole way of life would be turned upside down.

One option was to stay on the *Osler* and make a break for the coast farther north. But the weather would be better then, and officialdom would have copters hovering about, waiting to tag him and follow him home.

No, he had to use the heavy weather. But even that might not be enough. On the way out, he'd had the advantage: Henriques didn't know Terry's starting point. Could have been anywhere along the lower twenty miles of the archipelago. But now, Henriques had him pinpointed. All he had to do was wait for Terry to make his move. Didn't even have to catch him. All he had to do was follow him home.

Yeah, getting back was going to be a real bitch.

───────────────

"Maybe he's not coming," Cramer said. "Maybe he's going to wait out the storm and hope that we drownd out here."

Cramer's whininess had increased steadily during the hour they'd been holding here. It was getting on Henriques's nerves something bad now.

"He *is* coming out, and it'll be *during* the storm, and we're *not* going to drown."

At least, he hoped not. A couple of times during the past hour, he hadn't been so sure about that. He'd had Cramer keep the

VMA low and slow in forward into the wind while he watched the lights of the *Osler* through his binocs. But every so often came a rogue wave or a gust of shear wind that damn near capsized them. Cramer had good reason to want to hightail for home.

But they weren't turning around until the fuel gauge told them they had to.

Besides, according to the Doppler, the rear end of the storm was only a few miles west. The runner would have to make his break soon.

And then you're mine.

"We got heat action, chief. Lots of it."

Henriques snapped the glasses down and leaped to the infrared scanner. Fanning out from the big red blob of the hospital ship were three smaller, fainter blobs.

"What's going on, chief?"

"Decoys."

The son of a bitch had two of the *Osler*'s shuttles running interference for him. One heat source was headed north-northeast, one north-northwest, and one right at them.

Henriques ground his teeth. The bastard had raised his odds from zero to two out of three. God damn him.

"All right, Cramer," he said. "One of them's our man. Which one?'

"I—I dunno."

"Come on. Put yourself out here alone. You've got to chase one. Choose."

Cramer chewed his lip and stared at the scanner. Probably doing eeny-meeny-miney-moe in his head. Henriques had already decided to ignore whichever Cramer chose. Cramer was never right.

"Well, it sure as hell ain't the guy coming right at us, so I'll choose . . . the . . . one . . . to . . . the . . ." His finger stabbed at the screen. "*East!*"

Henriques hesitated. Not a bad choice, actually. The Lower Keys were more heavily populated toward their western end, especially near Key West; Coast Guard base and Naval air station down that way—all sorts of folks runners don't like to meet. And the storm was heading northeast, so that direction would give the most rain cover. He might just have to go with Cramer this—

Wait a second.

Well, it sure as hell ain't the guy coming right at us . . .

Yeah. The obvious assumption. So obvious that Henriques had bought into it without really thinking. But what if the runner was counting on that? Send the shuttles right and left, draw the heat toward them, then breeze through the empty middle.

And remember: Cramer is never right.

He grabbed Cramer's wrist as he reached for the throttle. "Let's hang here for a bit."

"Why? He's got to—"

"Just call it a feeling."

Henriques watched the screen, tracking the trio of diverging blobs. As the centre one neared, he lifted the glasses again. Nothing. Whoever it was was travelling without running lights.

Doubt wriggled in his gut. What if the runner had pulled a double reverse? If so, he was already out of reach . . . as good as home free.

"Getting close," Cramer said. "See him yet?"

"No."

"Still coming right at us. Think he knows we're here?"

"He knows. He's got infrared too."

"Yeah, well, he ain't acting like it. Maybe we should turn the running—"

And then a dazzling flash of lightning to the south, and Henriques saw it. A Hutch 686.

He let out a whoop of triumph. "It's him! We got him!"

"I see him!" Cramer called. "But he's coming right at us. Is he crazy?"

"No, he's not crazy. And he's not going to hit us. Bring us about. We got us a chase!"

Cramer stood frozen at the wheel. "He's gonna ram us!"

"Shit!"

Henriques grabbed the spotlight, thumbed the switch and swivelled it toward the oncoming boat. He picked up the charging bow, the flying spray, almost on top of them, and goddamn if it didn't look like the bastard was really going to ram them.

Henriques braced himself as Cramer shouted incoherently and ducked behind the console. But at the last minute, the runner swerved and flashed past to starboard, sending a wave of wake over the gunwale.

"After him!" Henriques screamed. "After him, goddamn it!"

Cramer was pushing on the throttle, yanking on the wheel, bringing them around. But the ankle-deep seawater sloshing back and forth in the cockpit slowed her response. The bilge pumps were overwhelmed at the moment, but they'd catch up. The VMA would be planing out again soon. That cute little manoeuvre had given the runner a head start, but it wouldn't matter. Henriques had him now. Didn't even have to catch him. Just follow him back to whatever dock he called home.

TERRY CAUGHT himself looking over his shoulder. A reflex. Nothing to see in that mess of rain and wind. He cursed Henriques for not chasing one of the decoys. The guy seemed to read his mind. Well, why not? They were both Conchs.

Terry had only one trick left up his sleeve. If that didn't work . . .

Then what? Sink the *Terryfied*? What good would that do? The ATF would just haul her up, find out who she belonged to, and then camp outside his door.

Face it: He doesn't fall for this last one, I'm screwed.

And being a Conch, it was a damn good chance Henriques wouldn't.

Terry spotted the breakers of the barrier reef ahead. Lightning helped him get his bearings, and he headed for the channel. As soon as he cut through, the swells shrank by half, and he picked up speed. Now was his one chance to increase the distance between Henriques and himself. If he could get close enough to shore, pull in near the parking lot of one of the waterside restaurants or nightspots, maybe he could merge his infrared tag with the heat from the cars and the kitchen.

And what would that do besides delay the inevitable? Henriques would—

A bolt of lightning slashed down at a mangrove keylet to starboard, starkly illuminating the area with a flash of cold brilliance. Terry saw the water, the rain, the mangrove clumps, and something else . . . something that gut-punched him and froze his hands on the wheel.

"Christ!"

Just off the port bow and roaring toward him, a swirling, writhing column of white stretching into the darkness above, throwing up a furious cloud of foam and spray as it snaked back and forth across the surface of the water.

He'd seen plenty of waterspouts before. Couldn't spend a

single season in the Keys without getting used to them, but he'd never—*never*—been this close to one. Never wanted to be. Waterspout . . . such an innocuous name. Damn thing was a tornado. That white frothy look was seawater spinning at two or three hundred miles an hour. Just brushing its hem would wreck the boat and send him flying. Catching the full brunt of the vortex would tear the *Terryfied* and its captain to pieces.

The hungry maw slithered his way across the surface, sucking up seawater and everything it contained, like Mrs. God's vacuum hose. Somewhere downwind, it would rain salt water and fish— and maybe pieces of a certain Conch and his boat if he didn't do something fast.

It lunged toward him, its growing roar thundering like a fully-loaded Navy cargo jet lifting off from Boca Chica, drowning out his own engine.

Terry shook off the paralysis and yanked the wheel hard to starboard. For a heartbeat, he was sure he'd acted too late. He screamed into a night that had become all noise and water. The boat lurched, the port side lifted, spray drenched him, big hard drops peppering him like rounds from an Uzi. He thought he was going over.

And then *Terryfied* righted herself, and the raging, swirling ghostly bulk was dodging past the stern, ten, then twenty feet from the transom. He saw it swerve back the other way before it was swallowed by the night and the rain. It seemed to be zigzagging down the channel. Maybe it liked the deeper water. Maybe it was trapped in the rut, in the groove . . . he didn't know.

One thing he did know: If not for that lightning flash, he'd be dead.

Would Henriques be so lucky? With the waterspout heading south along the channel and Henriques charging north at full throttle, the ATF could be minus one boat and two men in a minute or so.

Saved by a waterspout. Who'd ever believe it? No witness except Henriques, and he'd be . . . fish food.

Terry turned and stared behind him. Nothing but rain and dark. No sign of Henriques's running lights. Which meant the waterspout was probably between them . . . heading right for Henriques.

"Shit."

He reached for the Very pistol. He knew he was going to regret this.

"MOTHER OF *GOD!*" Cramer shouted.

Henriques saw it too.

One instant, everything was black; the next, the sky was blazing red from the emergency flare sailing through the rain. And silhouetted against the burning glow was something dark and massive, directly in their path.

Henriques reached past Cramer and yanked the wheel hard to port, hard enough to nearly capsize them. The tower of water roared past like a runaway freight train, leaving them stalled and shaken but in one piece. Henriques watched it retreat, pink now in the fading glow of the flare.

He turned and scanned the water to the north while Cramer shook and sputtered.

"You see that? You ever see anything *like* that? Damn near killed us! Hadn't been for that flare, we'd be goners!"

Henriques concentrated on the area around the lighted channel marker dead ahead. Something about that marker . . .

"There he is!" he shouted as he spotted a pale flash of wake. "Get him!"

"You gotta be kidding!" Cramer said. "He just saved our asses!"

"And I'll be sure to thank him when he's caught. Now after him, dammit!"

Cramer grumbled, started the engine, and turned east. He gunned it, but Henriques could tell his heart wasn't in it.

And he had to admit, some of the fight had gone out of him as well.

Why had the runner warned them? That baffled him. These guys were scum, running stolen or pilfered medical supplies out to the rich folks on their luxury hospital ships when there was barely enough to go around on shore. Yet the guy had queered his only chance of escape by sending up a warning flare.

I don't get it.

But Henriques couldn't let that stop him. He couldn't turn his head and pretend he didn't see, couldn't allow himself to be bought off with a flare. He'd seen payoffs all his life—cops, judges, mayors, and plenty of Conchs among them. But Pepe Henriques wasn't joining that crowd.

The rain was letting up, ceiling lifting, visibility improving. Good. Where were they? He spotted the lights on the three radio towers, which put them off Sugarloaf. So where was the runner heading? Bow Channel, maybe? That would put him into Cudjo Bay. Lots of folks lived on Cudjo Bay. And one of them just might be a runner.

He retrieved his field glasses and kept them trained on the fleeing boat as it followed the channel. Didn't have much choice. Neither of them did. Tide was out, and even with the storm, there wasn't enough water to risk running outside the channel, even with the shallow draw of an impeller craft. As they got closer to

civilization, the channel would be better marked, electric lights
and all . . .

Electric lights.

He snapped the glasses down, but it was too late. Cramer was
hauling ass past the red light marker, keeping it to starboard.

"*NO!*" Henriques shouted and lunged for the wheel, but too
late.

The hull hit coral and ground to a halt, slamming the two of
them against the console. The intakes sucked sand and debris,
choked, and cut out.

Silence, except for Cramer's cursing.

"God damn! God-damn-God-damn-God-damn-God *damn!*
Where's the fucking channel?"

"You're out of it," Henriques said softly, wondering at how calm
he felt.

"I took the goddam marker to starboard!"

Henriques nodded in the darkness, hiding his chagrin. He
shouldn't have been so focused on the runner's boat. Should have
been taking in the whole scene. Cramer hadn't grown up on these
waters. Like every seaman, he knew the three R's: *Red-Right-Return*.
Keep the red markers on your right when returning to port. But
Cramer couldn't know that this marker was supposed to be green.
Only a Conch would know. Somebody had changed the lens. And
Henriques knew who.

He felt like an idiot but couldn't help smiling in the dark. He'd
been had but good. There'd be another time, but this round went
to the runner.

He reached for the Very pistol.

"WHAT THE HELL?"

The flare took Terry by surprise. What was Henriques up to? The bastard had been chasing him full throttle since dodging that waterspout, and now he was sending up a flare. It wouldn't throw enough light to make any difference in the chase, and if he needed help, he had a radio.

Then Terry realized it had come from somewhere in the vicinity of the channel marker he'd tampered with. He pumped a fist into the air. Henriques was stuck, and he was letting his prey know it. Why? Payback for Terry's earlier flare? Maybe. That was all the break he'd ever get from Henriques, he guessed.

He'd take it.

Terry eased up on the throttle and sagged back in the chair. His knees felt a little weak. He was safe. But that had been close. Too damn close.

He cruised toward Cudjo, wondering if this was a sign that he should find another line of work. With Henriques out there and maybe a few more like him joining the hunt, only a matter of time before they identified him. Might even catch him on the way out with a hold full of contraband. Then it'd be the slammer . . . hard time in a Fed lock-up. Quitting now would be the smart thing.

Right. Someday, but not yet. A couple more runs, then he'd think about it some more.

And maybe someday, after he was out of this, he and Henriques would run into each other in a bar, and Terry would buy that Conch a Red Stripe, and they'd laugh about these chases.

Terry thought about that a minute.

Nah.

That only happened in movies.

He gunned his boat toward home.

HOW A WORLD DIES

By Jane Yolen

Of neglect,
of internal struggle,
of the wrong words
or the wrong interpretation
of those words,
of loss of interest,
of lack of rules, creatures, language.
No care from a loving god
who could have said,
"Let There Be . . ." and did not.
And so there was not.

CAR WARS

By Cory Doctorow

A self-driving car is a computer you put your body in.

1. ZERO TOLERANCE

Dear Parents,

I hate to start the year with bad news, but I'd rather it be this than a letter of condolence to a parent whose child has been killed in a sense-less wreck.

As you were notified in your welcome packet, Burbank High has a zero-tolerance policy on unsafe automotive practices. We welcome healthy exploration, and our ICT program is second to none in the county, but when students undertake dangerous modifications to their cars and bring those cars to campus, they are not only violating Board of Education policy, they're violating federal laws, and putting other students and our wider community at risk.

Though the instructional year has only just started, we've already confiscated three student vehicles for operating with unlicensed firmware, and one of those cases has been referred to the police as the student involved was a repeat offender.

Tomorrow, we will begin a new program of random firmware audits for all student vehicles, on- and off-campus. These are NOT OPTIONAL. We are working with Burbank PD to make these as quick and painless as possible, and you can help by discussing this important issue with your child. Burbank PD will be pulling over vehicles with student parking tokens and checking their integrity throughout the city. As always, we expect our students to be polite and respectful when interacting with law-enforcement officers.

This program starts TOMORROW. Students caught with unlicensed vehicle modifications will face an immediate two-week suspension for a first offence and expulsion for a second offence. These are in addition to any charges that the police choose to lay.

Parents, this is your chance to talk to your kids about an incredibly serious matter that too many teens don't take seriously at all. Take the opportunity before it's too late: for them, for you, and for the people of our community.

Thank you,
Dr. Harutyunyan

2. STATUS UPDATES (ON THE ROAD)

if you can read this call help #notajoke

seriously i don't know wtf is going on i was going home then stupid car's emergency override kicked in thot we were gon pull over like an ambulance or f-truck etc but we turned & im like wtf detour?

now i'm seeing signs for lerderberg state park n theres a ton of cars around me

its like a convoy all heading to arse end of nowhere evry1 looking out of windows looking scared

car sez batterys almost flat which means ill have to stop eventually i guess but its hot out there like 40'

any1 know whats going on DM me pls #notajoke

bin tryin to call my mum 4 30m but she's not picking up

if you can reach her tell her yan said everything will be fine

mum if you see this dont worry i love you

3. PLAUSIBLE DENIABILITY

"We're dead."

"Shut up, Jose, we're not dead. Be cool and hand me that USB stick. Keep your hands low. The cop can't see us until I open the doors."

"What about the cameras?"

"There's a known bug that causes them to shut down when the LAN gets congested, to clear things for external cams and steering. There's also a known bug that causes LAN traffic to spike when there's a law-enforcement override because everything tries to snapshot itself for forensics. So the cameras are down inside. Give. Me. The. USB."

Jose's hand shook. I always kept the wireless jailbreaker and the stick separate—plausible deniability. The jailbreaker had legit uses and wasn't, in and of itself, illegal.

I plugged the USB in and mashed the panic sequence. The first time I'd run the jailbreaker, I'd had to kill an hour while it cycled through different known vulnerabilities, looking for a way into my car's network. It had been a nail-biter because I'd started by disabling the car's wireless—yanking the antenna out of its mount, then putting some Faraday tape over the slot—and every minute that went by was another minute I'd have to explain if the jailbreak failed. Five minutes offline might just be transient radio noise or unclipping the antenna during a car wash; the longer it went, the fewer stories there were that could plausibly cover the facts.

But every car has a bug or two, and the new firmware left a permanent channel open for reconnection. I could restore the car to factory defaults in thirty seconds, but that would leave me operating a vehicle that was fully un-initialized, no ride history—an obvious cover-up. The plausibility mode would restore a default firmware load but keep a carefully edited version of the logs intact. That would take three to five minutes, depending.

"Step out of the vehicle, please."

"Yes, sir."

I made sure he could see my body cam, made it prominent in the field of view for his body cam, so there'd be an obvious question later if no footage was available from my point of view. It's all about the game theory: he knew that I knew that he knew, and other people would later know, so even though I was driving while brown, there were limits on how bad it could get.

"You too, sir."

Jose was nervous af, showed it in every move and the whites of his eyes. No problem: every second Officer Friendly wasted on him was a second more for the plausibility script to run.

"Everything all right?"

"We're late for class, is all." Jose was the worst liar. It was 7:55, first bell wasn't until 8:30, and we were less than ten minutes away from the gates.

"You both go to Burbank High?"

Jose nodded. I said, "I would prefer to discuss this with an attorney present."

It was the cop's turn to roll his eyes. He was young and white, and I could see his tattoos peeking out of his collar and cuffs. "IDs, please."

I had already transferred my driver's licence to my shirt pocket so that there'd be no purse for him to peep, no chance for him to insist that he'd seen something to give him probable cause to look further. I held it out in two fingers, and he plucked it and waved it past the reader on his belt. Jose kept his student card in a wallet bulging with everything, notes and paper money and pictures he'd printed (girls) and pictures he'd drawn (werewolves). The cop squinted at it, and I could see him trying to convince himself that one or more of those fluttering bits could be a rolling paper and hence illegal tobacco paraphernalia.

He scanned Jose's ID while Jose picked up all the things that fell out of his wallet when he removed it. "Do you know why I stopped you?"

"I would prefer to answer any questions through my attorney." I got an A-plus on my sophomore Civics term paper on privacy rights in the digital age.

"Baylea."

"Shut up, Jose."

The cop smirked. I could tell that he was thinking words like "spunky," which I hate. When you're black, female, and five-foot-nothing, you get a lot of spunky, and its ugly sister, "mouthy."

The cop went back to his car for his roadside integrity checker. Like literally every other gadget in the world, it was a rectangle a little longer and thinner than a deck of cards, but because it was cop stuff, it was ruggedized, with black and yellow rubber bumpers, because apparently being a cop makes you a klutz. I snuck a look at the chunky wind-up watch I wore, squinting through the fog of scratches on the face for the second hand. Two minutes.

Before the cop could scan the car's plates with his IC, I stepped in front of him. "May I see your warrant, please?"

Spunky turned into mouthy before my very eyes. "Step aside please miss." He eschewed commas for the sake of seriousness.

"I said I want to see your warrant."

"This type of search does not require a warrant, ma'am. It's a public-safety check. Please step aside."

I side-eyed my watch again, but I'd forgotten where the minute hand had been when I started because I'm not the coolest cucumber in the crisper. My pulse thudded in my throat. He tapped the reader plate on the car door—we still called it the "driver's door" because language is funny that way.

The car powered down with an audible *thunk* as the suspension relaxed into its neutral state, the car shaking a little. Then we heard its startup chime, and then another, flatter sound, accompanied by three headlight blinks, three more, two more. It was booting off the cop's diagnostic tool, which would then slurp in its entire filesystem and compare its fingerprint to the list of known-good fingerprints that had been signed by both the manufacturer

—Uber—and the US National Highway Traffic Safety Administration.

The transfer took a couple of minutes, and, like generations before us, we struggled with the progress-bar lull, surreptitiously checking each other out. Jose played particularly urgent eyeball hockey with me, trying to ascertain whether the car had been successfully reflashed before the cop checked. The cop, meanwhile, glanced from each of us to the display on his uniform's wrist to the gadget in his hand. We all heard the file-transfer-complete chime, then watched as the cop tapped his screen to start the integrity check. Generating a fingerprint from the copy of the car's OS took a few seconds, while the log files would be processed by the cop cloud and sent back to Officer Friendly as a pass/fail grade. When your end-users are nontechnical cops standing on a busy roadside, you need to make it all easier to interpret than a home pregnancy test.

The seconds oozed by. *Ding!* "All right then."

All right then, I'm taking you to jail? All right then, you're free to go? I inched toward the car, and the cop twinkled a toodle-oo at us on his fingers.

"Thank you, officer."

Jose smelled of flop-sweat. The car booted into its factory-default config, and everything was different, from the visualizer on the windscreen to the voice with which it asked me for directions. It felt like someone else's car, not like the sweet ride I'd bought from the Uber deadstock auction and lovingly rebuilt with junk parts and elbow grease. My own adrenalin crash hit as we pulled into traffic, the car's signalling and lane changes just a little less smooth than they had been a few minutes before (if you take good care of the transmission, tires and fluids, you can tweak the settings to give you a graceful glide of a ride).

"Man, I thought we were dead."

"That was painfully obvious, Jose. You've got a lot of fine points, but your cool head is not one of them." My voice cracked as I finished this. Some cool customer I was. I found a tube of coffee in the driver's compartment and bit the end off it, then chewed the contents. Jose made pleading puppy eyes at me, and I found one more, my last one, the emergency pre-pop-quiz reserve, and gave it to him as we pulled into the school lot. What are friends for?

4. A REAL RIB-CREAKER

Yan's mum had gone spare and then some when he finally made it home, leaping up from the sofa with her eyes all puffy and her mouth open and making noises like he'd never heard before.

"Mum, Mum, it's okay, I'm okay." He said it over and over while she hugged him fiercely, squeezing him until his ribs creaked. He'd never noticed how short she was before, not until she wrapped her arms around him and he realized that he could look down on the crown of her head and see the grey coming in. He'd matched her height at fourteen, and they'd stopped measuring. Now, at nineteen, he suddenly understood that his mother wasn't young anymore—they'd celebrated her sixtieth that year, sure, but that was just a number, something to make jokes about—

She calmed down some, and he was crying too by then, so he fixed them both some coffee, his mum's favourite from the roaster in St Kilda, and they sat down at the table and drank coffee while they snotted and cried themselves dry. It had been a long walk back, and he'd been by no means the only one slogging down a freeway for ages, lost without mobile service and maps, trying to find someone with a live battery he could beg for a navigational check.

"All my feeds are full of it, it's horrible. Hundreds of people smashed into each other or into the railing or ran off the freeway. I thought—"

"I know, Mum, but I was okay. The bloody car ran out of juice and just stopped. Rolled to a stop, got a little bump from the fella behind me, then his car swerved around me and took off like blazes. Poor bugger, looked terrified. I had to get out and walk."

"Why didn't you call?"

"Flat battery. Flat battery in the car, too. Same as everyone. I plugged my phone in as soon as I sat down, right, but I think the car was actually draining my battery cos everyone else I met walking back had the same problem."

She contemplated Yan for a moment, trying to figure out whether she was upset or relieved, plumped for relieved, set down her coffee, and gave him another one of those hugs that made him gasp for air.

"I love you, Mum."

"Oh, my boy, I love you too. God, what's going on, hey?"

5. REVOLUTION, AGAIN

There was another revolution, so all our fourth-period classes were cancelled, and instead we were put into tiger teams and sent around the school to research everything we could find about Syria and present it to another group in one hour, then the merged groups had to present to two more teams, and so on, until we all gathered in the auditorium for final period.

Syria is a mess, let me tell you. My rule of thumb for easy credit on these world affairs real-time assignments is to look for Wikipedia articles with a lot of [citation needed] flags, read the arguments over these disputed facts, then fill in the footnotes with some quick googling. Being someone who didn't actually give a damn about the issue let me figure out which citations would be acceptable to all the people calling each other monsters for disagreeing about it.

Teachers loved this, couldn't stop praising me for my "contributions to the living record on the subject" and "making resources better for everyone." But the Syria entry was longer than long, and the disputed facts had no easy resolution—was the government called ISIL? ISIS? IS? What did Da'esh even mean? It had all been a big mess back when I was in kindergarten, and then it had settled down . . . until now. There were tons of Syrian kids in my class, of course, and I knew they were like the Armenian kids, super-pissed about something I didn't really understand in a country a long way away, but I'm an American, which means that I didn't really pay attention to any country we weren't at war with.

Then came the car thing. Just like that one in Australia, except this wasn't random terrorists killing anyone they could get their hands on—this was a government, and we all watched the livestreams as the Molotov-chucking terrorists or revolutionaries or whatever in the streets of Damascus were chased through the streets by the cars that the government had taken over, some of them—most of them!—with horrified people trapped inside, pounding on the emergency brakes as their cars ran down the people in the street, spattering the windscreens with blood.

Some of the cars were the new ones with the sticky stuff on the hood that kept the people they ran down from being thrown clear or tossed under the wheels—instead, they stuck fast and screamed as the cars tore down the narrow streets. It was the kind of thing that you needed a special note from your parents to get to see in social studies, and luckily my mom is cool like that. Or unlucky, because nightmares, but better to be woke than asleep. It's real, so it's something I need to know about.

6. WE'RE ARTISTS, NOT PROGRAMMERS

Huawei's machine-learning division thought of themselves as artists more than programmers. That was the first slide in their deck, the one the recruiters showed at the big job fairs at Stanford and Ben-Gurion and IIT. It was what the ML people said to each other, so repeating it back to them was just good tactics.

When you worked for Huawei, you got access to the firehose: every scrap of telemetry ever gleaned by a Huawei vehicle, plus all the licensed data sets from the other big automotive and logistics companies, right down to the driver data collected from people who wore court-ordered monitors: paroled felons, abusive parents under restraining orders, government employees. You got the post-mortem data from the world's worst crashes, you got all the simulation data from the botcaves: the vast, virtual killing field where the machine-learning algorithms duked it out to see which one could generate the fewest fatalities per kilometre.

But it took a week for Samuel to get the data from the mass hijackings in Melbourne and Damascus. It was all national-security-ied up the arse, of course, but Huawei was a critical infrastructure partner of the Seven Eyes nations, and Samuel kept his clearances up with the four countries where he had direct-line reports working in security.

Without that data, he was left trying to recreate the attack through the Sherlock method: abductive reasoning, where you start with a known outcome and then come up with the simplest possible theory to cover the facts. When you have excluded the impossible, whatever remains, however improbable, must be the truth. If only that were true! The thing that never happened to Sherlock, and always happened to machine-learning hackers, was that they excluded the impossible and then simply couldn't think of the true cause—not until it was too late.

For the people in Damascus, it was too late. For the people in Melbourne, it was too late.

No pressure, Samuel.

Machine learning always started with data. The algorithm ingested the data, crunched it, and spat out a model, which you could test by feeding it some of the data you'd held back from the training set. Feed it ninety percent of the traffic info you had, ask it to model responses to different traffic circumstances, then test the model in the reserved set to see if it could correctly—that is, nonfatally—navigate the remaining traffic.

Data could be wrong in many ways. It was always incomplete, and whatever was left out could bias the model. Samuel always explained this to visiting school groups by inviting them to imagine training a model to predict height from weight by feeding it data from a Year Three class. It didn't take the kids long to get how that might not produce good estimates for the height of adults, but the kicker was when he revealed that any Third Years who weren't happy about their weight could opt out of getting on the scales. "The problem isn't the algorithm; it's the data used to make the model." Even a school kid could get that.

But it was more complicated than just biased data. There were also the special cases: what to do if an emergency vehicle's siren was sensed (because not all emergency vehicles could transmit the lawful interception overrides that would send all traffic to the curb lanes), what to do if a large ruminant (a deer, a cow, even a water buffalo, because Huawei sold cars all over the world) stepped into the car's path, and so on. In theory, there was no reason not to use machine learning to train this, too—just tell the algorithm to select for behaviours that resulted in the shortest journeys for simulated emergency vehicles. After all, there would always be circumstances when it was quicker for vehicles to drive a little farther before pulling over, to prevent congestion, and the best way to discover those was to mine the data and run the simulations.

Regulators did not approve of this: nondeterministic, "artistic" programming was a cute trick, but it was no substitute for the hard and fast binary logic of law: when this happens, you do that. No exceptions.

So the special cases multiplied, because they were like crisps, impossible to stop at just one. After all, governments already understood how special cases could be policy instruments.

Special cases were how pirate sites and child porn were excluded from search results, how sensitive military installations were excluded from satellite photos in mapping apps, how software-defined radios stayed clear of emergency bands when they were hunting for interference-free channels. Every one of those special cases was an opportunity for mischief since so many of them were secret by definition—no one wanted to publish the world's most comprehensive directory of online child porn, even if it was supposed to serve as a blacklist—so the special-case bucket quickly filled up with everything that some influential person, somewhere, wanted. From gambling and assisted suicide sites being snuck into the child-porn list to anti-Kremlin videos being added to the copyright filters, to all the "accident-prevention" stuff in the cars.

Since 1967, ethicists had been asking hypothetical problems about who should be killed by runaway trolleys: whether it was better to push a fat man onto the tracks (because his mass would stop the trolley) or let it crash into a crowd of bystanders, whether it made a difference if the sacrificial lamb was a good person or a bad one, or whether the alternative fatalities would be kids, or terminally ill people, or . . .

The advent of autonomous vehicles was a bonanza for people who liked this kind of thought experiment: if your car sensed that it was about to get into an accident, should it spare you or others? Governments convened secret round-tables to ponder the question and even come up with ranked lists: saving three children in the car topped saving four children on the street, but three adults would be sacrificed to save two kids. It was a harmless and even cute diversion at first, and it gave people something smart-sounding to say at lectures and cocktail parties.

But outside the actual software-design teams, no one asked the important question: if you were going to design a car that specifically tried to kill its owners from time to time, how could you stop those owners from reconfiguring those cars to never kill them?

But Samuel had been in those meetings, where half-bright people from the old-line automotive companies reassured quarter-bright bureaucrats from the transport ministries that there'd be no problem designing "tamper-proof" cars that would "resist end-user modification." Meanwhile, much brighter sorts from the law-enforcement side of the house licked their chops and rubbed their hands together at all the non-trolley problems that could be solved if cars could be designed to do certain things when they got signals from duly authorized parties. Especially if the manufacturers and courts would collaborate to keep the inventory of those special cases as secret as the child-porn blocklists on the national firewalls.

He'd been in the design sessions after, where they debated how they'd hide the threads and files for those programs, how they'd tweak the car's boot cycle to detect tampering and alert the authorities, how the diagnostic tools provided to mechanics for routine service-checks could be used to double-check the integrity of all systems.

But then he'd started getting signed, obfuscated blobs from contractors who served governments around the world, developing "emergency priority" apps he was just supposed to drop in, without inspecting them. Of course, he ran unit tests before Huawei shipped updates, and when they inevitably broke the build, Samuel would go around and around with the contractors, who'd want access to all his source code without letting him see any of theirs.

It made sense for them to behave that way. If he failed to help them get their code into Huawei's fleet, he'd have to answer to governments around the world. If they failed to help him, they'd have to answer to precisely no one.

Unit tests were one thing; real-world performance was something else. Sensors couldn't tell a car whether it was about to crash into some pedestrians, or a school bus, or an articulated lorry full of dynamite. All sensors could do was sense and then feed data to machine-learning systems that tried to draw conclusions from those data. Even with all the special cases about what the car must and must not do under which circumstances, machine-learning systems were how it knew what the circumstances were.

That's how Melbourne happened.

It had taken him a long time to figure this out. At first, he assumed that finally, the worst had come to pass: the cryptographic keys that were used to sign police override equipment had leaked, and the wily criminals had used them to hijack forty-five percent of the cars on the roads of one of the biggest cities in Australia. But the forensics didn't show that at all.

Rather, the crooks had figured out how to spoof the models that invoked the special cases. Samuel figured this out by accident, his third day at his desk, running sim after sim on Huawei's high-confidentiality cloud, which was protocol, even though it was the slowest and least-provisioned cloud he could have used. But it was only available to a handful of senior internal Huawei groups, not even contractors or partners.

He'd been running the raw telemetry from a random sample of the affected cars, looking for anomalous behaviour. He'd nearly missed it, even so. In St Kilda, someone—face in shadow beneath a hat, thermal profile obscured—stepped in front of a subject car, which slowed but did not brake and emitted two quick horn taps.

Regression analysis of accident data had shown that hard braking was more likely to result in rear-end collisions and frozen pedestrians who couldn't get out of the way. The car tasked more compute time to the dorsal perimeter to see if it could shift into an adjacent lane without a collision and, if that wasn't possible, to estimate the number of affected vehicles and passengers based on different manoeuvres.

The pedestrian feinted toward the car, which triggered another model, the "suicide by car" system, which invoked a detailed assessment of the pedestrian, looking for clues about sobriety, mental health and mood, all of which were difficult to ascertain thanks to the facial obfuscation. But there were other signals—a mental health crisis clinic 350 metres away, six establishments licensed for serving or selling alcohol within one hundred metres, the number of redundancies in the past quarter —that gave it a high weighted score.

It initiated hard braking, and the pedestrian leaped back with surprising nimbleness. Then, across the road, another pedestrian repeated the dance with another car, again in a shadowing hat and thermal-dazzle makeup.

The car noticed this, and that triggered another model, which some analyst had labelled "shenanigans." Someone was playing silly buggers with the cars, which was not without precedent, and well within the range of contingencies that could be managed. Alertness rippled through the nearby cars, and they began exchanging information on the pedestrians in the area: gait profiles, silhouettes, unique radio identifiers from Bluetooth devices. Police were notified, and the city-wide traffic patterns rippled, too, as emergency vehicles started slicing through the grid while cars pulled over.

All these exceptions to the norm were putting peak load on the car's internal network and processors, which were not designed to continue operating when crises were underway—freeze-and-wait being the optimal strategy that the models had arrived at.

But before the car could start hunting for a place to pull in until the law arrived, it got word that there was another instance of shenanigans, a couple of roads down, and the police would need a clear path to reach that spot, so the car had best keep moving lest it create congestion. The cars around it had come to similar conclusions and were similarly running out of processor over-head, so they fell into mule-train formation, using each others' perimeters as wayfinding points, turning their sensors into a tightly-coupled literal grid that crept along with palpable machine anxiety.

Here's where it got really interesting, because the attackers had forced a situation where, in order to keep from blocking off the emergency vehicles behind them, these cars had completely shut down the road and made it impossible to overtake them. This increased the urgency of the get-out-the-way messages the city grid was sending, which tasked more and more of the cars' intelligence and sensors to try to solve the insoluble problem.

Gradually, through blind variation, the cars' hivemind discovered that the faster the formation drove, the more it could satisfy the overriding instructions to clear things.

That was how forty-five percent of Melbourne's vehicles ended up in tight, high-speed formation, racing for the city limits as the emergency vehicles behind them spurred them on like sheepdogs while frantic human planners tried to figure out exactly what was going on and how to stop it.

Eventually, the sheer quantity of compromised vehicles, combined with the minute variations in lane-spacing, small differences in car handling characteristics and, finally, a blown tire, led to a pile-up of ghastly proportions, a crash that they would study for decades to come, that would come to stand in for the very worst that people could do.

Samuel had always said that machine learning was an art, not a science, that the artists who designed the models needed to be able to work without official interference. He'd always said it would come to a bad end. Some of those meetings had ended in shouting matches, Samuel leaning over the table, shouting at bureaucrats, shouting at his bosses, even, in a way that would have horrified his parents in Lagos, where jobs like Samuel's were like lottery jackpots, and shouting like his was an unthinkable act of economic suicide.

But he'd shouted and raged and told them that the fact that they wished that there was a way to put a back door in a car that a bad guy couldn't exploit didn't mean that there was a way to do it.

He'd lost. If Samuel wanted to argue for a living, he'd have been a lawyer, not an algorithm whisperer.

Now he was vindicated. The bad ideas baked into whole

nations' worth of infrastructure were now ready to eat, and they would be a feast that would never end.

If this is what victory felt like, you could keep it. Elsewhere in the world, there were other Samuels, poring over their own teams' reports: GM, VW-Newscorp, Toyotaford, Yugo. He'd met some of those people, even tried to recruit a few of them. They were as smart as Samuel or smarter, and they'd certainly shouted as loudly as he had when the time had come. Enough to satisfy their honour before capitulating to the unstoppable force of nontechnical certitude about deeply technical subjects: the conviction that once the lawyers had come up with the answer, it was the engineers' job to implement it, not trouble them with tedious technical wheedles about what was and wasn't possible.

7. GRAND THEFT AUTO

Burbank High had a hard no-phones policy: it was a zero-tolerance expulsion offence to step over the property line with a phone that hadn't been apped to reject unapproved packets. It made the school day into a weird kind of news vacuum. There was the day that I'd emerged from fourth period and stepped across the threshold to discover that the governor had been shot by Central Valley separatists and the whole state had gone bananas, seeing water warriors behind every potted plant and reporting every unexplained parcel as a potential bomb.

You never get used to that feeling of emerging from a news-free zone and into a real world that's been utterly transformed while you were blissfully unaware. But you do get better at recognizing it.

When the final bell rang, and three thousand students (me included) poured out of the school doors, it was obvious that there was something wrong. The streets were empty, missing the traffic that hummed along Third Street with perfect, orderly following distance. That was the first thing we noticed. It was only after a second of gawping at the empty road that everyone turned their attention to the parking lots, the small faculty lot and the sprawling student lot, and realized, in unison, that all the cars had gone missing, every single one.

As they pushed out of the doors and toward the lot, I saw that it wasn't quite all the cars that had driven themselves away while we'd been good little students at our lessons.

One car remained.

As in a dream, I pulled out my phone, fingerprinted it into wakefulness, and sent the car its unlock signal. The car, alone in the vast lot, blinked its headlights and came to attention on its suspension. Gradually, the students turned to look at me, then my car, then back at me, first crowding around, then opening a path between me and that stupid little Uber hatchback, unlovely and lonely in the field of tarmac. They watched me as I drifted toward it, opened the door, tossed in my school bag, and slid into the front seat. The car, running my rambunctious, forbidden software, started itself with a set of mechanical noises and vibrations, then backed smoothly out of the lot, giving the humans around it a cautious berth, sliding onto the empty roads, and aiming toward home.

I was sure I'd be pulled over—the only car on the road; what could be more suspicious?—but I didn't pass a single cop car. Dialling into the news, I watched—along with the rest of the world—as every car in the San Fernando Valley formed a fast-moving migratory herd that sped toward the Angeles National Forest, which was already engulfed in the wildfires from the crashed cars that had gone over the cliff-edged winding roads.

The cops were apparently a little busy just then.

8. EVERY TIME. NO EXCEPTIONS

It was Yan's mum who found the darknet site with the firmware fiddler image, though Yan had to help her get it installed on a thumb drive. They made two, one for each of them, with the plausible deniability partitions the distributor recommended, and clipped them to their phones.

The lecture she gave Yan about using it every single time, no matter whether he was in a friend's car or an auto-taxi, was as solemn as the birth-control lecture she'd given him on his fourteenth birthday.

"If the alternative is walking all night, then you will walk, my boy. I want you to promise."

"I promise, Mum."

She hugged him so fiercely it made his ribs creak, squeezing his promise into his bones. He hugged her back, mindful of her fragility, but then realized he was crying for no reason, and then for a good reason, because he'd nearly died, hadn't he?

Jailbreaking a car had real legal risks, but he'd take his chances with those, considering the alternative.

TRIBES OF THE SUN

By K.M. Rice

Serenity looked straight in front of her as the bus bounced and rattled toward downtown San Jose, straining to see the shadow on the horizon. No one else seemed too bothered by the clouds outside: trailing white gathering around motley blue and grey, drifting toward the city from the west. She shifted Theodore in his ring sling, tugging at the cotton of her dress, which was sticking to her stomach from the heat of his three-month-old body and the ninety-degree weather outside. He was still sound asleep, and she ran her fingers through the brown of his featherlight curls before looking ahead once more.

Her eyes lingered on the girl in the seat in front of her. She watched as the girl rooted around in her backpack, admiring the thinness of her flaxen hair, tied up in an elegantly messy knot, the beads of her earrings, and the smooth tequila tan of her skin, and wondered what it would be like to be blonde and to know you were beautiful.

Serenity's heart caught in her chest when the bus jolted and rattled. She instinctively rested a hand on the back of Theodore's head to press him to her. She looked out the water-stained window. The cloud nebula was darker than before, churning. She caught a flash of light flickering in the belly of the mass, then another. Lightning. She glanced around at the other passengers. A man in a suit shifted and read the paper. A woman ate an apple and checked her e-mail on her laptop. The driver focused on the road ahead. Serenity rose, holding onto the back of the seat before her, spurred by a sudden need to get away from her window. To get out of the bus.

A few people glanced at her as she rested her palms against their seats, shuffling forward on the unsteady rubber of her flip-flops. Another flash below the cloud, and she glanced behind her, holding onto one of the vinyl straps that hung from the luggage rack. A few passengers blinked at her, but none noticed the sky. No one ever noticed the sky anymore because no one looked up.

The bus driver saw her out of the corner of his eye. "Can I help you?"

She turned to face him.

He strained his voice against the din from the engine and the air hissing past the cracks in the doors. "Are you getting off at the Caltrain Station?"

"Yes." Serenity cleared her throat. "I'm going to Santa Cruz."

The driver nodded. "We should be there in about—"

"I want to get off at the next stop."

The driver glanced at her. "You just have to push the—"

A clap sharper and swifter than thunder sounded. The bus jolted with a violent flash of bone white. Gasps sounded from the passengers as they were jarred and screens went black. Serenity's knuckles were white around the strap.

"Everyone okay?" the driver hollered as he navigated the freeway.

"What was that?" a woman asked.

Serenity sank down until she touched the floor, scooting herself behind a large suitcase that sat in the wheelchair space. Theodore had awoken and fussed.

"I think we were hit," a man answered.

Serenity lightly bounced her son, attempting to calm him, her eyes on his chubby cheeks as he squinted and blinked.

"That was crazy," another man said. "I never thought—"

There was another clap as lightning struck the road ahead. Serenity closed her eyes against the flash, but the shape of the bolt still burned into her retina. The noises of the passengers around her were drowned out by a boom that wrenched metal from sockets as another bolt cleaved a car ahead of them, sending the vehicle careening into the windshield of the bus. She could hear metal splintering as the suitcase pressed against her. The floor vibrated from the tires, so she knew they were still moving forward. Another crunch and bang of collision, then a tinny scraping from her left as her gravity shifted. She caught herself as the bus tilted before it slowed.

The meat of her palm stung, and when the bus had nearly stopped, she straightened and glanced at her hand. A shard of glass the size of the curve of her fingernail was embedded in her skin. Theodore pressed into her left breast as he strained against her, causing her to gasp. Horns blazed outside, and someone on the bus was groaning. She kicked the suitcase aside, and it toppled off of her, glass tinkling in its wake. Serenity blinked in the darkness, the windshield clogged by cars, the ceiling smashed down so low that she couldn't stand.

Light still filtered in from the windows, and her eyes adjusted enough to make out the mangled, detached arm of the driver lying among the bits of shattered glass on the floor. Bile soured her throat as one of the lifeless fingers curled. She couldn't see the rest of the driver, but blood seeped from the metal. There was another groan from the back of the bus, and she struggled to rise, her arm snaking Theodore's spine as she shuffled. She kicked away as much glass as she could, knowing it would stab right through the flimsy soles of her flip-flops, then hunched her way farther down the aisle, double-checking that Theodore was all right as she moved.

The left half of the bus had been torn off against the concrete lane divider, wrenching half of the passengers out with it. Theodore started crying, and Serenity was able to straighten. The clap and bang of the lightning continued outside, and Serenity glanced over the remaining passengers. Something tickled her toes, and she took a few hasty steps backwards when she saw blood pooling in the aisle. Her nostrils flared. Blood trickled from the blonde girl's head, staining her pooka-shell necklace. The young woman's broken neck laid her cheek against her breast, and Serenity coughed as she gagged.

She clutched Theodore to her as she lurched forward to vomit, the pink and bubbly contents of her stomach settling into the blood. She wiped her lips after several dry heaves, then forced herself to straighten.

Her voice croaked. "Is anyone alive?" She listened for a response, furtively glancing at what was left of the other passengers. The groaning had stopped. Serenity forced more steadiness into her voice. "Is anyone alive?"

There was no response. Theodore's cheeks were getting rosy from his sobbing, and she noticed his diaper bag resting on a nearby seat. She picked it up and slung it over her shoulder before making her way to the emergency exit window one row down. The luggage rack had broken loose, and the pole had rammed clear through the seats, including the one she'd been sitting in minutes before. For a long moment, she couldn't look away from the aluminum gutting the cheap upholstery, until she realized she was shaking and Theodore was clawing at the v-neck of her dress. She awkwardly angled over the pole and wrenched the red handle of the exit. The side of the bus opened. She stumbled outside.

TWO WEEKS EARLIER

"You're completely overreacting," Johnny said as he hobbled after Serenity into their bedroom.

She packed, ignoring him.

"Will you at least look at me?"

She tossed a handful of Theodore's onesies into her duffel bag, then faced him. "What?"

"I'll stop."

For a moment, she allowed herself to take in the honest plea of his jade-green eyes, in piercing contrast to his Hawaiian Irish skin. She recalled the first time she'd noticed the lightness of his gaze and how free-spirited she'd felt dating a guitar-playing surfer. But that was before he would have nightmares whenever his feet or arms hung too far off the bed. He limped a step closer, leaning against the wall, and the haphazard direction of his brown dreads and his unshaven cheeks returned resolve to her. She began packing again.

"I'm serious," Johnny tried. "I stopped smoking when you got pregnant, didn't I?"

"This is different."

"How is this different?"

"Because you had a joint a few times a month. That was nothing compared to your friends—you're taking Vicodin every night."

"Uh, yeah, because I kinda *need* it."

She shoved her underwear and socks into her bag, then looked at him. The half-circle puncture marks were still puckered and red, and the muscle of his calf was lumpy, but the surrounding hair was growing back. "You had the stitches out a week ago. You don't need it."

"Yeah?" He hopped over to the bed as she zipped the bag shut. "You try getting a hunk taken out of you by a great white and see how you—"

"You're supposed to be walking on it by now. You're screwing yourself up."

"I'll go to fucking physical therapy if that's what you want."

"I want *you* to want it!"

Johnny blinked and straightened as Theodore cried. Johnny hesitated for a moment, then twisted to reach for him in his crib.

Serenity brushed him aside and picked up their child. "Don't even bother. You'll probably drop him."

She shouldered her duffel bag and grabbed Theodore's diaper bag, then left the room.

Johnny held onto the doorframe and hastily grabbed his crutch before hopping out after her. His voice screeched. "You can't do this. You can't just take him!" She stepped into her shoes, ignoring him. She opened the door, and he hissed as his injured leg smacked into the coffee table as he struggled to catch up. "I love him! I love you both."

Serenity stilled in the doorway and looked at him over her shoulder. His eyes were watering, and his face was flushed. Her voice was quiet. "I know you do. But I'm exhausted. I need to sleep, and you can't help. You can't even wake up at night when your son needs you." She paused, letting her voice become softer. "I'll call you when I get to my mom's." She stepped into the June sunlight and quietly closed the door behind her.

Johnny stood on one foot, leaning against his crutch, staring at the shaft of light coming in from under the door.

PRESENT DAY

Johnny limped through the parking lot by the Santa Cruz harbour, watching the silver masts of the sailboats sway from side to side with each swell, the tinkling of their blocks and the creaking of their ropes sounding like a soothing song. He sat down on a bench, sweat trickling from his temples in the heat, his tank top sticking to his upper back. He pulled his phone out to check the time. He still had an hour or more before he would meet Serenity and Theodore at the Metro Station downtown and had taken a walk first to work out his anxiety and the usual morning ache and stiffness in his leg. He'd gone farther than he intended.

He put his phone back into his pocket, studying the shadow rolling in from the Pacific: a darkened mass of cloud looming like the belly of a whale. A light breeze heralded the monstrosity, yet, given the humid heat, it was little reprieve. A rivulet of sweat trickled from his armpit, soaking into his tank top. After catching his breath, Johnny rose again. He limped over to the shade of the Crow's Nest restaurant, then slowed, walking more carefully, practising a smooth gait.

The sailboats suddenly tinkled in a chorus, announcing a powerful gust, and Johnny closed his eyes, allowing the air to cool his sweat. Laughter and music were a few feet off on the sand as families and friends enjoyed the beach and the ocean. He wanted nothing more than to douse himself in the water's coolness, if only for a moment, but the memory of the suddenness of warmth around his leg, the weight tugging him down, the slipperiness of his fingers scraping at the fibreglass of his board, the oddly detached tearing sensation that clouded the water with red, kept him from touching the sea again.

As he watched the rise and fall of the coils of the ocean waves, his heart hammered, and he recalled the words of his father while the two were on a fishing trip. He had asked why his dad was tossing every other fish back into the water.

"Feed the shark when you can. He is our 'aumakua—he'll protect you. He'll feel your heart beating in the water and know where you are. You must remain calm."

Johnny hadn't remained calm. He'd thrashed and screamed and paddled into shore as fast as he could after the shark let him go. Pieces of his wetsuit were mashed into his leg. A tourist called an ambulance. Ever since he'd wondered if his father had been right; if the shark had been one of his ancestors and decided to take a bite of him after he didn't offer it any fish. Or maybe it wasn't his 'aumakua at all, but another shark. It sucked either way, and he wished his dad wasn't dead so he could ask him about it.

There was a rumble that he thought was a plane but realized was thunder. He stopped his pacing and looked to the sky, wiping off the sweat that clung to his sparse goatee. The centre of the dark cloud was swirling as it expanded, hovering over the Santa Cruz Mountains and stretching into the valley beyond. The wind picked up. Johnny glanced around. Several had noticed the darkening sky, and he feared that the churning grey above them heralded a tornado. What the hell did you do in a tornado?

A bolt of white shot out from the cloud, followed by another and another as lightning struck somewhere in the valley on the other side of the mountain range. A balding man climbed off the ramp that led to the harbour dock. "Like we're in the Sierras, huh?"

Johnny glanced at him.

"Afternoon thunderstorms." He took off his cap and wiped his forehead. "Crazy weather."

The hair on the back of Johnny's neck rose with tiny shivers in the ionized air. "Yeah . . ."

The man chuckled and continued on his way, tugging out his keys, only to drop them as he fell onto the seat of his pants when a bolt of lightning struck the cement of the parking lot thirty yards ahead of him. "Holy—"

Another bolt followed, then another, each with the boom of sundered air. For a moment, Johnny couldn't move, rooted in place by the harrowing beauty of the cars in the parking lot being tossed into the air, dancing with white tendrils; of the grass along the rail-road tracks across the street bursting into flame; of a white woman turning black as she smouldered in electricity. He could hear his pulse in his ears, muffling the cries of the beach and restaurant-goers as they panicked.

A crowd of people from the parking lot ran toward the Crow's Nest, fighting to get inside, and Johnny lost his balance as the throng shoved past him. He caught himself before he hit the ground, but someone's knee collided with his temple, and his vision flashed white.

SAN JOSE

Serenity looked either way down the highway. Cars dotted the pavement like ants after someone had turned on the garden hose. White tinged with rose still flashed in the belly of the clouds overhead and danced along the metal atop the lane divider like the writhing ghosts of tree roots. Lightning lingered where it shouldn't. The stench of heated metal and skin and diesel rose from the pavement.

Horns and alarms blazed in the distance, and she could see that the lightning attack had moved on—the bolts now tantalized the city a quarter-mile from the highway. For a long moment, she watched the windows of tall buildings shatter and papers scatter as the monoliths shuddered from the energy, breathing smoke and spewing fire. Metal crunched and voices screamed as cars collided in the streets below. The snap and boom of lightning sounded like cosmic rifle fire. There was a screaming inhalation from above, and she looked up to see a plane careening toward the city. A tendril of light flashed around the plane as it nosedived, crashing in the distance with a rumble and boom that was far more muffled than she expected. Then, with a gust, the shower of white shifted, and the electrical storm turned its attention farther up the valley.

Theodore had toned his wailing down to a fuss. He squirmed, and she remembered to breathe. She looked down at him as if he could confirm the horror that was playing out around them, but she was met with the tear-stained cheeks and quivering pout of one who accepted all, for he knew no better. Only the scent of his mother's flesh was sacred. She brushed her thumb against his cheeks, wiping away the moisture, and as her thumb passed by the corner of his mouth, he instinctively turned toward the movement as if to suckle. The helpless action sent her heart hammering out a tattoo of savagery over fear. She lifted Theodore close enough to kiss his sweaty brow and closed her eyes, breathing in the sweetness of his cradle head. A warmth spread through her breasts and she knew the pad of her bra was dampening. She shifted Theodore and let him nurse.

She remembered her ignorance before giving birth. When the test said she was pregnant, she was terrified. She had called her mother and told her the news, asking for her input, weighing abortion. She was twenty-five—only two years younger than her own mother had been when she'd given birth, and several of her friends had already had children, but Serenity hadn't felt ready. She hadn't wanted the commitment of surrendering her life for the sake of another. She blamed faulty Chinese latex for forcing this upon her. Johnny had been excited—of course, he had. It wasn't his body that was going to bear the child.

Bear. Bearing Theodore had turned her into a bear. She had never felt a stronger connection to a living being and had never before been so wildly adamant about protecting someone. That's what had convinced her to keep the baby with her boyfriend of six months.

"It's amazing," her mother had said. "To look at this beautiful baby and know you created this little person. Then everything makes sense. You know why you exist."

Clarity hadn't come with afterbirth, but hormones laced with instinct had charged through her veins like wildfire ever since. After Johnny's accident, not much made sense outside of Theodore.

She remained still, a few feet from the bus, afraid to move. She could see the shapes of people in the cars either stalled or crashed on the highway, but none moved. Serenity cautiously stepped forward, her flip-flops leaving dark stains on the pavement. The storm was heading northeast. She looked to the south, suddenly realizing that Santa Cruz might have also been hit.

Johnny.

Serenity dug her phone out of the side pocket of the diaper bag. The screen was blank, and she pressed the power button a few times, to no avail. The houses below the freeway were dark. She readjusted Theodore and her dress as the thought of never again seeing her mother's crinkled, smiling eyes made her breathing stutter. She stuffed her phone back into the pocket, telling herself that she would worry about Johnny and her mom when she could afford to. She walked down the freeway, weaving between the steaming, crumpled cars, trying not to look at the remains of the people inside. A part of her wondered if some were still alive, if there were some she could help, but they weren't of her flesh. She stepped over the guardrail on the edge of the road and onto the bark of the hillside, careful not to touch the metal.

Serenity cautiously made her way down to one of the suburban side streets. There was a distant rumble from the passing behemoth overhead, but the concrete was quiet. She took slow steps, peering about in the eerie calm. The rattling of a plastic bag caught on a chain-link fence startled her, and she paused to reorient herself, lifting Theodore out of his sling to lay him against her chest. He stared at the world over her shoulder with brown eyes that matched hers. He raised his brows when he saw movement.

A boy ran past Serenity, sniffling and whimpering, chanting what sounded like, "It'll be okay, it'll be okay," under his breath. Serenity stepped after him, calling out. "Hey, are you all right?"

The boy ignored her and made a beeline for a driveway with two parked cars, calling, "Mom!"

Serenity jogged toward him as he ran up the driveway. "Do you know what happened?"

The boy glanced at her. His dark cheeks were tear-stained. She cocked her head, parting her lips to ask if he needed help, when the boy touched the metal doorknob. He stiffened, his eyes still looking at her, then made a choking sound as his body jerked.

Serenity slowed, watching him. His eyes rolled into the back of his head, and then he collapsed on the porch.

Serenity let out a breath. Then another. She started to step toward his body, then stopped, backing away. He couldn't have been more than twelve. His leg twitched in a marionette motion, then his arm, then he was still, flecks of foam clinging to the corners of his mouth. He didn't move again. She was only aware of herself once more when she realized Theodore was pulling on her hair.

Tucking him back into his sling, she turned away from the neighbourhood and shuffled toward the overpass. Theodore made a soft sound as he rubbed his gums against his fist, and she kept her eyes on him until the fetters of what she'd just seen eased their grip on her mind, and she could see the layout of the road before her. A squirrel scampered past, and she shifted her focus and headed for downtown. If she had survived because of an oversized suitcase, then it was likely there had been similar flukes where there were more people.

SANTA CRUZ

Johnny used the wall of the restaurant to haul himself up from the ground. His temple throbbed, and his hand ached from where someone had stepped on it. There was a roaring in his ears from his own blood and his nostrils burned and his eyes stung. He flicked a few dreads out of the way as he straightened, then realized with a slam of his heart that the roaring was not in his blood at all but was coming from the grasses and trees along the railroad tracks as they burned. Embers floated through the air, lighting rooftops and eating up the oil stains upon the pavement like ravenous, dancing ghouls of shifting orange.

People now exited the Crow's Nest, trying to work phones, to start engines, only to realize that they were stranded. Many shouted and ran along the beach, but Johnny could tell from the smoke billowing for miles that they were fenced in by flame on their section of sand. He wanted to shout, but it diffused in his chest and came out as a wheeze.

"Shit."

He watched as a man haphazardly organized a line from the Crow's Nest to the fire and began to pass along dish tubs and salad bowls full of water from the restaurant. Another group tried to stretch the garden hose as far as possible. When the flames nearest them climbed into the boughs of a eucalyptus and sizzled and popped in the bark, the makeshift fire brigade quickly realized their inadequacy and hastened back to the restaurant, their leader re-directing them to douse the roof and exterior of the building.

"Hey, Bob Marley! Hey!"

Johnny turned to look behind him.

A man gestured from the docks. "Will you give me a hand?" He was rigging the mainsail on his boat.

Johnny shuffled down the walkway, holding onto the railing. "You gonna sail away or something?"

"If we have to. It's an offshore breeze—freak of nature— blowing right toward the water. You wouldn't think there's much to burn on the beach, but I've seen fire spread to sand."

Johnny held onto the side of the sailboat as he climbed in. "What do you need me to do?"

"Know your way around one of these things?"

Johnny cleared his throat. "A little. Used to fish with my dad."

"Good."

"Your phone work?"

The man shook his head. Now that he was closer, Johnny could make out the deep lines carving his leather skin and the grey in the ponytail that he had mistaken for blond. "Nobody's phone works, man." He paused as he ran a line through the block to hoist the mainsail. "That storm or whatever the fuck it was fried everything. Pull the lifejackets out from under that bench."

Johnny did as he was told, stacking the orange vests on the seat. "I've never seen lightning like that before."

"Neither have I."

"You think it's global warming or something with the crazy weather?"

The man looked at him, panting. "Or something else entirely."

Johnny met his gaze.

SAN JOSE

Serenity stopped where Santa Clara Street met First Street. The buildings surrounding her, half-toppled from implosion, billowed smoke. The streets were coated with dust.

"Hello?" she tried again, her voice growing hoarse.

No one answered. She knew that coming any closer to the hulls of the city was foolish. She could hear things melting loose and falling within the buildings, and the air stung with the fetid stench of burning hair and fat. She turned around and headed down the road until she came to the cement banks of the Guadalupe River. Drought had dwindled the river to a trickle, but brush grew green along the water's path.

She made her way down the side and ducked under the cool shadow of a bridge, easing onto dried silt and leaves and litter. Her shins were nicked and scabbing, as were her arms, from brushing against glass that she hadn't even felt. She changed Theodore's diaper on a towel from the diaper bag, then helped him nurse, watching sweat beads form on his temples as he worked to get the milk. She realized it had been hours and hours since she'd last eaten, but she wasn't hungry at all. Her stomach was filled with smoke and death and the will to form a plan.

She had hoped to find other survivors, to figure out what had happened, to call in the National Guard from a county that hadn't been hit. The sky was cloudless now, just filthy with smoke. She had seen crows circling the streets and knew they were after pedestrian eyes that had turned to jelly. The occasional jingle of the collar of a stray dog was a reminder of the lack of masters. Yet through her desperation and panic, a vague part of her mind was delighted, knowing that she would be the one who had lived to tell the tale, the one who had survived the storm. Someday, she would tell Theodore their story.

She closed her eyes to rest for a few moments, wanting to get water from one of the intact buildings but afraid to touch them after what happened to the boy. The birds were still chirping gaily, and she could make out a chorus of blackbirds farther down the creek. Their lyrical voices were joined by the rattle and tinkle of a rolling shopping cart. Serenity opened her eyes. Theodore had stopped nursing and was dozing. She adjusted her bra and dress and made sure Theodore was supported in the ring sling before grabbing the diaper bag and shuffling out from beneath the bridge.

A middle-aged woman and a teenage girl were atop the bridge, pushing a shopping cart full of food and water and blankets. Serenity grinned.

"Hey! Hi!"

The woman and girl halted when they heard her voice, then spied her below. "Oh, thank God," the woman said. "Another one."

She immediately made her way to the edge of the bank and reached out to help Serenity climb back up.

"Oh, and look at your little one." She smiled as she peered at Theodore, who was trying to sleep.

"Are there more people alive?" Serenity asked, tucking her loose bangs behind her ears. "I've been looking for hours."

"So far, only us two. I'm Mary, and this is Josefina."

Josefina gave a halfhearted wave.

Serenity and Mary walked back to the shopping cart. Mary's sandy-grey hair was tied in a bun, and wisps had escaped, sticking to her neck with sweat. She had light-blue eyes and a careworn face and moved with a spring in her step. "What were you doing down there? Are you injured?"

"No, not really. Just thirsty."

"Here." Mary handed her a water bottle, and Serenity drank the contents, barely stopping for a breath.

She wiped off her mouth and placed the plastic bottle back in the shopping cart. "Do you have any idea what happened?"

"Yeah. The whole goddamn place was destroyed."

"Terrorists," Josefina said.

Serenity shook her head. "It was a storm—I saw the cloud."

"Nope. That's impossible," Mary said as she took Serenity's diaper bag from her and set it in the shopping cart. "I'm from South Dakota, and we have *storms* there. This wasn't from a storm. I was out gardening when I saw it hit—bangs from all the transformers. The bastards overloaded all the power lines—electrocuted everyone in their houses, offices . . ." She sighed, her lower lip quivering.

Serenity looked away from Mary's face, for the older woman's tone was tightening her throat. She made sure Theodore was comfortable before looking at Mary again. "I need to go home to Santa Cruz."

"Good, cuz that's where we're headed." Mary began pushing the cart. Josefina and Serenity fell into step behind her.

Serenity pulled out her hair tie and re-tied her ponytail now that both hands were free. "Why?"

"Because they probably didn't get hit. They're too small. The bastards wanted to make a point by going after the Silicon Valley, you know."

Serenity looked at the road ahead of them, her heart lifting a little at the thought of the quietness of home and Johnny's laugh. But her heels and bunions were already sore, and the straps of her flip-flops were rubbing wounds into the tops of her feet. A mountain range rose before her.

SANTA CRUZ

"Monsanto?" Johnny repeated. "Fucking Monsanto? Controlling the weather?"

The man was hastily checking the mainsheet for knots. "Didn't you hear that sonic boom last week?"

"No."

"It was in the news. It rattled houses like a quake. No one knows what it was from. Everyone figures it's government aircraft they ain't ready to tell us about yet. They've been spraying us with chemtrails for years."

"But you think it's Monsanto working with lizard people. Disguised as clouds."

The man tossed him a pole with a hook on the end. "Start backing us out. We'll come around the front and pick some people up."

Johnny did as he was told, wincing as he used the muscles of his legs for leverage as he shoved off from the dock. The man used the tiller to direct the boat, and the sails began to luff, then tauten as they rounded the row of sailboats and into the main water of the harbour.

The man took a moment to catch his breath. "No—I think aliens or gods or whatever you want to call them *are* the weather. Monsanto is just a front. They saw we were fucking everything up and decided to get rid of us. Cooked up a big storm to wipe half of us out without showing their faces. Maybe we got too loud. Something like that."

Johnny studied him with a furrowed brow, then looked back to the beach. The fire on the mainland was still going strong, but the restaurant and the nearby O'Neill's kayak and surfboard rental were still safe. He could see several people holding pieces of clothing to their mouths to help filter out the stinging smoke while others took commandeered kayaks out to sea.

The man was watching, as well, and cursed under his breath. He looked at Johnny. "You said you've manned one of these before?"

"My dad would usually be— "

"Now's the time to learn." He steered the boat broadside to the main dock. Johnny grabbed one of the cleats and tethered the bow. The boat lurched as the man hopped out and jogged up the dock. "Anyone know how to sail?"

Johnny closed his eyes as the wind shifted and the smoke blew toward him, staining his hair with its scent. The rush of wind past his ears muffled most of the man's words, but he could make out the cadence of orders. The man then hurried back down the dock, his Birkenstocks slipping a little as he looked behind him to make sure the small group was following.

"Just climb right in there and put on one of those jackets," he directed, then looked at Johnny. "This lady here has been sailing a few times with her husband, so she'll be able to give you a few tips."

"Wait—where are you going?"

"To rig up more boats for the rest of these flatlanders!"

The small group was already climbing into the sailboat: a woman and her two children, along with a man and his son. Both parents helped their children put on the orange lifejackets. One of the little girls looked at Johnny, her cheeks damp from tears.

He smiled at her. "We're gonna sail out into the water a little bit to get out of the smoke."

The girl's mother looked at him as she put a jacket on her son. "But the wind's blowing the smoke out to sea."

"Yeah, but you see that?" Johnny pointed out a stretch of grey fleece on the horizon. "That's the fog bank. Once it gets closer, the wind will shift. Hopefully, the Coast Guard or someone will be here by then."

"I sure hope so," she said. "I'm Jeanie, by the way."

"Johnny."

They exchanged a brief smile before Johnny settled into position on the back bench, the tiller in one hand and the mainsheet in the other. He cleared his throat. "Hey, uh . . ."

"Frank."

"Frank—could you untie us and push us off, please?"

Frank immediately set to the task.

Johnny's father had only ever given him one sailing lesson, and he'd forgotten nearly all of it. He pushed the tiller to the left and let the boom blow out to the right until the sail was full, then inched the boom closer with the mainsheet, gaining momentum until they bumped into another docked boat and got caught in irons.

Frank looked at him. "Let's just use the paddles till we get into open water."

Johnny grimaced. "Good idea."

HIGHWAY 17

Four more people had joined Mary, Josefina, Serenity, and Theodore. They had walked all day at a brisk pace and made it to Highway 17 by nightfall. Josefina wanted to stop, but Mary refused, rationalizing that they would cover more ground in the coolness of night, and so they pressed onward. The smoke from the burning buildings of Campbell occasionally blew in their direction, and they paused by the percolation ponds along the highway to wash off the sweat of the day. From the charred grass and swirling ash, they know that the area had already been set ablaze and had burned out.

Serenity washed her arms and legs and face, giving Theodore to Mary to hold, but was hesitant to expose her son to the water, which was beginning to foam by the shore after lapping at ash. She tied her hair back again and took Theodore once more, resting and nursing him on her aching left breast while the other stragglers washed off some of the grime. Many had developed a cough from the smoke, and Serenity feared they were being poisoned. She could feel grit from the air coating her teeth.

They passed Lexington Reservoir and entered the forest-shadowed section of the highway. The redwoods and Douglas firs blotted out the stars and made the darkness more palpable. The rattling of the shopping cart alerted Serenity to where Mary was when she couldn't see her, and the occasional quiet conversations and weeping from others in the group gave away their position as well.

Serenity was tired but couldn't acknowledge it to herself, lest the admission drain away the rest of her adrenalin strength. The cars they had to weave through and the bodies occasionally flung from them no longer caught the attention of her tired eyes. She stepped over and around them and couldn't care less who they were. She just wanted to get home, to find Johnny, to rest with Theodore. But the way was long, and they moved slowly in the cold.

They heard a scuffling sound, and Josefina clicked on a flashlight. A small pack of coyotes was eating a corpse on the side of the road. They scampered back and forth in the beam of light, cautious of the two-legged that still moved. Mary warned the others to stay back because coyotes, like all bats, she said, had rabies. But Serenity knew coyotes. She had heard their cackling voices and seen their yellowed eyes. They were not a threat. They were small and timid and clever, and she couldn't help but think that Mary and the others were wasting their time and energy by taking precautions around their padded steps.

Didn't they know humans had eyes in front? Didn't they know humans were hunters? Didn't they know humans stood tall to see over grass and brush and had long arms to fight away from their faces? Too many humans thought of themselves as prey. Too many humans had forgotten that they, too, are animals.

Mary had the group stop at the Summit, where a restaurant and real estate building still stood, serving as a makeshift rest stop for truckers. Serenity was grateful for the rest. She ate one of the granola bars that Mary was handing out and then later had bread and peanut butter and water when someone tentatively entered the restaurant to scavenge. Several lay down to sleep in the building, but Serenity remained outside, still wary of walls. She used tablecloths as blankets and, after making Theodore a nest, lay down beside him, sharing her heat and covering them both. The smoke obscured the stars, but in the blue light of night, she could see the silhouettes of the mountains in the distance. The ground poked and bruised her, and her scabbing feet throbbed, but, for as long as she could, she slept as deeply as her son, lulled by the chorus of crickets.

SANTA CRUZ

The bay was dotted with boats now, many of which paddled instead of sailed, and Johnny watched O'Neill's burn with bloodshot eyes. The children in his boat were asleep, but Jeanie and Frank were still awake, sharing in the harrowing beauty of drifting embers and the occasional explosion of a gas tank as the boats left moored burned.

Jeanie looked at him with a kind light in her eyes. "Go ahead and get some sleep. I'll take over for a while."

Johnny cleared his throat, too tired to bristle over being treated like a child. "You sure?"

"Yeah." She nodded and inched her way down the bench. Johnny handed over the tiller and the mainsheet, then scooted away. The boat rocked a bit from the shifting weight, then settled once more. He caught a glimpse of the white bellies of dead fish in the water as he sat down. He rubbed his eyes, then hugged his legs to his chest, letting his forehead rest on his knees.

Frank's voice was hoarse and quiet. "I wonder if anyone's alive. Anything metal didn't stand a chance. All those poor people . . . Jesus, I hope Cindy's okay. My God, this is a nightmare."

Johnny didn't need to ask who Cindy was, nor did Jeanie. He

closed his eyes and relaxed his aching back as he sagged in on himself, crumpling as ash fell like wayward snowflakes. Frank and Jeanie's voices and the tinkling of the other nearby boats blurred and faded as he rocked, his mind unfocused. The water lapped at the sides of the boat. Someone cleared their throat. He saw the night-dimmed ocean. He saw a dark shape moving below the surface. He saw the white nose as it breached. The boat rocked as the shark bumped into it, trying to take another bite of him, and Johnny jerked, awake, rigid, and back in the now.

It had been a dream, another nightmare, yet the boat was rocking as if it were real. "Emily?" Jeanie's panicking voice made him glance around. The little girl was missing. "Emily!"

Johnny grabbed onto the base of the mast and scanned the surroundings. "Where is she?"

There was a cough off to starboard and a splash in the water.

"Emily! Oh God, she can't swim! Emily!"

Johnny dived in, the cold water sucking off his flip-flops as he swam toward the little girl. Frank found the flashlight from the survival kit and shone it on the water, panning right and left until he caught the orange of Emily's lifejacket. Johnny saw the neon and made his way over to her. She coughed and tugged at the collar of the jacket that was smashing her cheeks. "Mommy!"

Johnny reached her and wrapped an arm around her middle. She clung to him, her sandaled feet scraping against his thighs, trying to climb on top of him to get out of the water. Her weight pushed him under, and he was surprised by the strength of her legs, for he had to fight to break the surface again.

"Emily, calm down!"

She screamed for her mother again and grabbed onto his dreads, shoving herself up. Johnny was shoved back under without the chance to take a breath, and he felt his lungs and mind burn as he struggled with her grip on his hair, trying to shove her off. She fought back, and her knee rammed into his eye, making him momentarily relax from the shock of the pain. She stilled for a moment when he did, and he yanked her hands free and breached the surface, treading water and keeping his grip locked on her wrists, holding them above his head. Being yanked halfway out of the water seemed to calm her a little, and she kicked about with less panic. He waited until she met his gaze in the annoying beam from the flashlight.

"You're okay, all right? You're not gonna drown. I've got you. Okay?"

She studied him for a moment, her jaw trembling with tears. "Mommy!"

"Calm down, Emily!" Jeanie called from the boat. "It's okay, sweetie!"

"I'm gonna put you on my back, all right?" Johnny said. "Then I'm gonna swim back to the boat. But I need you to stop kicking. Just hold on to me, okay?"

Emily whimpered and nodded. Johnny lowered her into the water enough to shift her to his back, but as he did so, she thrashed again. He ignored it since she at least wasn't screaming in his ear anymore, just as he ignored her fingernails digging into his shoulders. He swam back to the boat but found the task more difficult than he'd imagined since Emily was clinging to his side, inhibiting his stroke. When he tried to shift her to his back, her grip tightened to nearly strangle him. He had to remind himself that she was only a child. He could see the boat just a few yards away and knew he could endure the bruising pressure on his neck for that long.

When Johnny reached the boat, Frank handed the flashlight to his son, who was awake again, then reached down for Emily. The girl sobbed and wouldn't let go of Johnny's neck. He was seeing pricks of white before him. His heart hammered with panic. But he bade his legs to keep churning, fighting to maintain calm. He would be able to breathe in a moment.

Frank reached down to try to pry one of Emily's arms off Johnny's neck, but the girl screamed and thrashed, and Johnny went under with a gasp, inhaling seawater. He popped back out with a sputtering cough, and Frank yanked and tore the girl's arms off of Johnny's neck, hoisting her into the boat.

Johnny was taking heaving breaths, trying to get enough air to relieve the burning of his chest and the swirling of his vision, but he couldn't stop coughing. Frank's voice was asking him questions, but he couldn't tell what they were amid the din of his own blood and choking exhalations. Too much air was coughed out of his lungs, and he felt a weight in his feet, tugging him down under the water. For a burning moment, he thought of the pleasantness of weightlessness, of surrender, but then he saw Theodore's smile and heard Serenity's laugh and felt something smooth and soft and strong brush against the ball and toes of his foot. The touch lent him one last panicked spurt of instinct as he shoved against the water with his arms.

He breached the surface with a wheezing gasp that immediately set him hacking once again. A pair of hands gripped his bicep and hauled him upward, and he reached out to grab onto Frank's forearm. He kicked and thrashed until he and Frank had lifted his body from the water and into the lilting sailboat. Johnny coughed and sputtered as he wrapped an arm around the base of the mast. Frank's kid was shining the flashlight on him, making him scrunch his eyes shut as Frank shuffled to his side, patting his back. "Keep coughing, just keep coughing."

Johnny's dreads dribbled rivulets of water down his face and neck, stinging the bleeding wounds from Emily's frantic finger-nails, and he spat out any water that found its way to his mouth.

"Is he okay? Is he all right?" Jeanie kept asking. A few distant voices from other boats offered to help.

Johnny's nose burned as he took several deep breaths, revel-ling in the relief of the fullness of his lungs. Frank squeezed his shoulder. "You all right there, bud?"

Johnny nodded, resting his temple against the fibreglass for a few moments while he caught his breath before hauling himself into a sitting position. He looked over at Jeanie, who had the whimpering Emily in her lap, holding the mainsheet and tiller with one hand. He blinked. Emily's torso was nearly as large as her mother's.

He shook his head with a wry smile. "Kid's fucking strong."

Frank chuckled, but Johnny could swear Jeanie was crying through her smile.

HIGHWAY 17

Serenity was startled awake by Theodore squirming. She wiped at her mouth, then rubbed the sleep out of her eyes. Above the din of the jays and chickadees, she could hear the raised voices of two men and Mary. The shopping cart rattled. Serenity struggled to her feet and picked up Theodore, holding him against her left breast. She could make out the white of a tank top on one man in the pale dawn light, along with Mary's pink t-shirt.

"You're stealing from children," Mary was reasoning. "We've got a little girl and an infant here with us."

"Cry me a fucking river."

Serenity shuffled over and could see that the men were

tugging at Mary's shopping cart. Serenity cleared her throat. "What's going on?"

The men ignored her, so she looked at Mary. Several others had awoken and peered at the scene.

"We're being robbed," Mary said.

"You assholes are the reason this happened in the first place," the tank-top man barked. "Building your fucking Babylons of silicon."

"I'll be reporting you to the police as looters," Mary snapped. "I've seen your faces."

The tank-top man whacked Mary with what Serenity realized was the butt of a rifle. She gasped as Mary grabbed onto the cart to break her fall, then ended up falling anyway. Serenity stepped forward to help her but froze when a gunshot broke the air, silencing the birds. She felt Theodore stiffen from the loud sound. Through the flash of gunpowder, Serenity had glimpsed the handlebar moustache of the tank-top man.

"We're taking the cart and leaving," he announced. "Anyone else who wants to stop us can step right up."

No one moved. "Just take it," Serenity whispered.

"I fucking will." He eyed her for a few heartbeats. "Hell, you wanna come, too?"

"No."

Mary was climbing to her feet, picking gravel out of her hands.

"Suit yourself, sweetheart," the tank-top man said as his friend began to push the cart away, heading north. The man stroked his moustache, still studying Serenity, and then turned to follow his companion.

Serenity stepped closer to Mary as the rattling of the shopping cart faded. "We can get food and water from the restaurant."

"I know." Mary's voice sounded near tears. "It's just the principle of the matter."

"Principles don't matter right now, I don't think. Let's just keep moving."

Mary nodded, touching a hand to her swelling temple and feeling the dampness of blood through her hair.

SANTA CRUZ

The dawn broke over the ocean with muted light. The air was thick with smoke and ash, and the sun was red when it could be seen. Johnny had been right; the fog had blown the smoke away from the boats. From what they could tell, the harbour and beach and surrounding neighbourhoods were smouldering but no longer burning. Johnny coughed, still trying to clear his lungs of all water, and hugged himself, waiting for the others on the boat to stir. He waved at a woman who was awake on a nearby sailboat.

The heat from the sun eventually thawed the chill in his skin, and he basked in its warmth as he watched several boats begin the long trek to shore. When the other boats headed back for the beach, Johnny felt an anxious tension in his frame. He could travel on land now. He could try to get help—try to find Serenity and Theodore—if there were still a Serenity and Theodore to find. His energy gathered with the rising sun, and he gently awoke his companions before their boat joined the others returning to land. As they neared the shore, the sight of California gulls and sandpipers scurrying back and forth in the sigh of the surf let him know that much of the danger had passed.

They beached on the sand, and Johnny was the last out of the boat, wincing in the acrid, stinging fumes from all directions. The Crow's Nest and O'Neill's rental shop were gutted and charred, and driftwood and seaweed had burned on the beach. There were even a few pools of glass from where the lightning had struck the sand. Emily scampered off to poke at one.

Johnny watched as the others formed groups and plans, and then he slipped away. He was careful of where he stepped since broken glass and nails were scattered about on the cracked concrete, and the soot soon stained his bare feet black and grey. His tank top and board shorts were stiff with dried seawater, and he realized he could still smell the salt and that the scent comforted him.

The fire had moved in a random pattern, sparing some houses while annihilating others. He knocked on a few standing doors and peered into windows, but after he saw a handful of charred bodies within, he stopped looking. Smoke still rose from downtown, and he made his way toward it, completing the walk he had intended to take the day before.

SERENITY and the others had seen the smoke long before they entered the city limits. Tearstains marked her face like smeared war paint against the grime. The front of her dress was stiffening with the stink of soured milk and sweat. They hadn't seen any evidence of survivors. Only the dry heaves of passing destruction. Serenity was beginning to regret returning, regret bringing her baby into this smoky air where his father probably lay dead. She had draped the changing blanket over her shoulder, covering Theodore's face in an attempt to protect him.

They paused at the cement structure of the county building beside the river. The concrete was charred black and cracked, but it had not burned. Several sat on the steps to rest, but Serenity kept going. Help couldn't get through the roads but could come from the sea. Maybe the Coast Guard or the Navy had sent in aid. She shuffled down to Ocean Street, then walked as far as she could go before the aching of her back and the stinging and piercing of the flip-flop straps on her feet bade her stop. She sat down at a bench outside the Metro Station, which had mostly been spared. Her breasts didn't hurt, and she knew she was dehydrated, but she fed Theodore all the same, hoping that he would grow up to resemble his father.

She looked around her. Several of the buildings had crumbled, and their debris littered the streets. The pink parasol once held by the Umbrella Man who inched his way up and down Ocean St. every day blew past, tarnished and singed. Black smoke billowed from burning structures, and lighter smoke shifted and clouded the city blocks like mist. Serenity looked down at Theodore, studying his small, almond-coloured hand gripping her dress. She rested her fingers over his tiny digits and watched him suckle. His skin was flawless, and she wanted to keep it that way for as long as possible. Her aching muscles told her she could.

There was a rattling sound, like bouncing aluminum. She ignored it, assuming it was the wind, but when it rattled again, she looked in its direction. For a moment, all she could see was the rubble and swirling smoke, but then the wind sighed, and the smoke parted. She saw the outline of a man with a mane peering up at the buildings as he walked down the street. She rose. The smoke shifted again and obscured his markings, but she could see black soot stockings and brown skin.

She stepped forward, watching as he kicked a soda can and sighed. He began to walk again, and she noticed a slight limp.

"Johnny?"

He paused and looked toward her voice, and she saw he had

one raccoon eye from a bruise. She squawked, then hurried toward him, the look of disbelief on his face making her grin.

DECEMBER BROUGHT RAIN. Grass grew where black once stained the ground. Survivors pooled together and rebuilt communities with help from the outside. The damage had been more or less confined to the Western side of the continent, and help had come from the East. By the spring, Theodore was testing his legs.

Serenity smiled and dug her toes into the warm sand as she watched Johnny play with Theodore. The naked baby had one of his father's fingers in each hand and was standing, laughing and cooing and bouncing his knees. Blue ink triangles emanated from the ring of teeth marks on Johnny's calf in a totemic tattoo of the shark, his family's 'aumakua. She was under the shade of an umbrella on the beach, and Johnny guided Theodore to waddle over to his mother. The baby laughed as his father scooped him up, then set him down in his mother's lap before taking a seat beside her, fluidly crossing his legs, his dreads still dripping down his back from dipping Theodore in the water earlier.

They shared a kiss and looked out to the sea, watching the sunlight shimmer and shift on the combers before they fanned out against the sand, fringed with foam and memories and tomorrow.

THE METAMORPHOSIS OF THOMAS DARROW

By Gerald Brandt

I still remember the first time I saw it, a single thin sapling standing in the ruins of the old library. Sunlight shone through the open rafters, touching the young leaves and casting the mouldy books and rotten wood at its roots in a green glow. The sapling couldn't have been more than four feet tall. When I stood at its base, the tip of its crown came up to my chin.

Even as a fifteen-year-old, I knew there was something special there. The air smelled like the end of a thunderstorm mingled with the gentle vanilla of old books and musky earth and was as still as a cold winter's night. I spent many an afternoon in the crumbling ruin, reading out loud to the tree from any book I could find while I waited for Dad to get off of work at the bank. We grew up together, the tree and I, for almost three years.

Dad wanted to put down roots here, to make a home for us after the turmoil of leaving Los Angeles. Then he got sick, and all that fell apart, just like the city around us. When he died, I left, filling the empty void of his passing by wandering across the country, working when I had to and just moving from place to place when I didn't.

Today was different.

It wasn't a conscious decision to come back here. It just seemed the next logical step on the path.

I walked down the once-familiar streets, and the decay seemed to spread out around me. Cars whizzed by on the broken, narrow street, their occupants ignoring the loneliness of what they passed through, trying to get from one pocket of civilization to the next.

Dad's bank still stood there, but things had changed. I guess ten years will do that. The once-clean windows were covered in thick, rusted black bars, and when the door opened, I could see an armed guard watching from inside. His eyes lingered on me for the few moments the door was open. I could see suspicion written all over his face. It seemed not many people walked these streets, and I stood out as an anomaly. I kept on going. Let him think what he wanted.

The old library was just around the corner. I held my breath and paused. What if it was gone? What if the city had claimed the last vestiges of my childhood? I wasn't sure I would be able to deal with that.

I stepped forward, and my held breath rushed out, replaced with a warmth that filled my soul. A massive tree thrust through the library's open roof, reaching for the deep-blue sky, and I stumbled to a standstill again.

The tree's bottom branches swept over the grime-covered limestone walls, and its crown rose at least another twenty feet. The sapling had turned into a full-grown oak in the span of only a few years. I knew it was impossible, but somehow, it felt right.

I stepped off the curb, my pace quickening as I felt the draw of the magical place of my youth.

The inside of the library had changed. Most of the old books now lay on the floor, ground into the dirt and debris from the fallen ceiling. Spraypaint covered the walls, everything from crudely written four-letter words to masterpieces of urban art.

The tree stood, immaculate and impassive, in the midst of the decay. As I moved closer to the gnarled trunk, I noticed someone had stripped away a section of bark and cut into the hard wood.

Staring from the shadowed, rough surface was the face of an old man. Vines sprouted from his mouth, carved so fine they seemed to sway in an unfelt breeze. They merged with the living vines that climbed the massive trunk, reaching for the sunlight high above.

My fingers traced the carving to where the face faded into the bark, and its wise eyes seemed to follow the motion as if reading something deep in my soul.

I took off my backpack and placed it on the ground. Sitting in the cool, dappled shade, I remembered the days of my youth lying in the sun by the small tree, the books we had read, the adventures we had taken together. Before I knew it, the sun had set, and the interior of the library was cast into inky darkness. I shouldered my pack and felt my way to the lighter rectangle of the broken door, emerging onto the deserted street.

I paused there for only a few moments, breathing in the stink of the city, before turning back. I pretended it was because I had nowhere else to go, but I knew—I *felt*—I was being called back. It was like finally coming home.

In the darkness, I climbed up the trunk, using the coarse bark for foot- and hand-holds, until I reached the first broad branch. I stopped there, my backpack on my lap, and nestled in the crook for the night.

MORNING CAME with the diluted sounds of the waking city filtering through the leaves, the far-off blare of car horns urging drivers to move faster mixing with the songs of birds in the tree. I pulled myself from a deep sleep filled with dreams of forests and meadows nestled between man-made fingers of steel and glass reaching for the sky.

Hunger and thirst finally moved me from my perch, and I reluctantly left the library to face the day, my small, battered backpack hidden in the branches. I had a vague memory of passing a small mom-and-pop diner on the way in. How far back it was, I couldn't remember.

I made it as far as the corner before the first shot of pain hit me. At first, I thought I'd cramped a muscle sleeping in the tree all night, even though I hadn't felt anything before then. I shrugged it off.

A block later, the pain came back, reaching in through my back and throbbing in my chest before shooting down my arm like fire. I tripped, catching myself against the brick of a building and sliding down it with the grace of a two-legged cat.

I sat with my back pressed to the rough brick and breathed through gritted teeth. The cool wall, not yet touched by the morning sun, seemed to soothe the pain, and gradually, my jaw loosened, and I began to breathe normally again. I stayed there for a few more minutes as the pain ebbed away to a dull throb before using the wall to help me get to my feet.

Another twinge in my back almost made me turn around, but the diner lay just ahead.

I sank into a booth that had once held sparkly turquoise seats, now worn and tattered almost beyond recognition, and gave a small sigh of relief. The bacon and eggs, though filling, didn't take away the hunger.

The food and exercise started to work their magic on the walk back to my tree. Every step seemed to alleviate some of the pain, and it all but disappeared just as I rounded the final corner.

Things had changed in my short time away.

Work crews were spread around the ruins of the library, machines driving metal fence posts into the ground and men stringing chainlink between them. Two people had a roll of paper open and spread on the hood of a beat-up white city pickup truck.

They both glanced up at me as I approached, and I could see them looking at my rumpled clothes and unshaven face, coming to a quick decision. They ignored me and went back to talking.

"Excuse me, could you tell me what's going on here?" I asked.

The taller of the two, a young man no older than me, looked up again. He took off his white hard hat and rubbed sweat off his forehead. "Look, fella," he said, "this dump is coming down. You're going to have to find another place to sleep off your hangover." He replaced his hard hat and turned his back to me, surveying the building.

I took a step closer to them. "I know you're busy, but—"

The man's shoulders sagged, and he exchanged a look with his partner. It was one of the downsides of living the nomadic life. Everyone assumed you were a drunk or a junkie, and the easiest way to get rid of the problem was to ignore it.

I took another step closer and interrupted them again. "I'm sorry, I understand the building has to go. It's really not a safe place, but I was wondering about the tree . . ." My voice trailed off.

"Great, a bum *and* a tree-hugger," the second man said. They both turned to me this time and eyed me up and down again.

"Everything's gone. We're coming back in a week or so to demolish it."

I shuffled away and watched from the bank as the chainlink went up, the pain in my chest replaced by a complete sense of loss that I hadn't felt since my dad had died. The trucks hadn't moved more than half a block before I was at the fence and climbing toward the top.

I tried to convince myself the panic I felt was just to get my stuff, but the owning of things had stopped being important to me long ago. There wasn't anything in the pack I couldn't replace. But it wasn't that. I had to get back to my tree to protect it. To save it.

My tree. The thought entered my consciousness fully formed. That's what it was; that's why I had come back to this particular place, and maybe even at this particular time. The tree had listened to all of my complaints when I was a teenager, all of my heartbreaks, all of the injustices, whether imagined or real. The tree was as much a part of who I was as my father had been. Maybe even more. I closed my eyes and breathed in the smell, reminiscent of my youth but bolder, stronger.

I couldn't let it be destroyed.

With each breath, my soul became lighter. I could feel the filtered green sunlight against my skin, and the coursing of sap through my veins.

When I opened my eyes, I found myself leaning against the tree, my forehead pressed into the coarse bark and my hand gently touching the carved face. I was filled, for the first time in my life, with a sense of direction, of purpose. I closed my eyes again, immersed in the stolid peace of the oak.

My fingertips pulsed with the heartbeat of the massive tree, and I followed its lifeblood up until I stood perched at the very crown. Wind ruffled through me as I peered over the city.

Even here, near the core of the once-thriving metropolis, stood piles of rubble and dilapidated buildings. On one intersection, a modern twenty-story tower stood, pushing against the deep blue sky as if to proudly say the city wasn't dead or even dying; that it lived and thrived in the face of adversity and diminishing population. The other three corners were empty lots and burned-out structures, overgrown with weeds and filled with rusted metal and broken concrete.

The tower reminded me of my dreams that morning, and I expanded my view until I saw everything around me. To the east stood two more towers, and further north, construction was halfway through building a fourth. Each structure slotted into place, matching my dream. The only thing missing was the forests.

Sudden vertigo grabbed at me and I screamed, my heart lodging in my throat as I fell back into my body with a rush. I shoved away from the tree, stumbling over the debris and falling backwards, scrambling and dragging myself across the crumbling floor.

I stopped again, once more unwilling or unable to cross the threshold back into the city. There was no place for me to run, no place to hide.

Instead, I closed my eyes again, retreating to the depths of myself, trying desperately to push the tree out. I slowed my breath, forcing my heartbeat to a calmer level, feeling the blood course through my veins, bringing nutrients to the farthest reaches of my limbs, where they were replaced with the raw material supplied by the sun and my leaves.

My eyelids snapped open, and I screamed again, but there was no one around to hear me. The world went dark.

I CAME to surrounded by the soft sounds of the wind in the oak's leaves and the quiet rustle of small creatures moving through the abandoned structure. I lay just inside the empty doorway, not yet willing to move. When I did, it was a struggle to just sit.

Exhaustion threatened to immobilize me. I fought it by crawling into the newly fenced yard. I looked at the twelve-foot chainlink and knew I wouldn't be able to make it over the top. Every part of me hurt, inside and out. Underneath the pain was a layer of terror that threatened to pull me under again.

The need to get away from this place wasn't strong enough to make me tackle the fence. By the first morning light, I would be gone. My belongings were still in the tree, but as far as I was concerned, they could stay there. Nothing in this world or the next was going to get me any closer to the tree than I already was. I nestled into the building's exterior limestone, some of the daytime's captured heat seeping out to keep me warm.

The sun shining in my eyes woke me. By its angle, I guessed I'd slept a good portion of the morning away. My face felt hot and dry, baked by the sun. I had water and sunscreen in my pack. Let the next guy that climbed the tree find it all . . . if there was a next guy.

I pushed myself to my feet, every muscle complaining in protest, and tried to stretch out the kinks. Was it really only last night I'd had the best sleep of my life?

Moving to the corner of the fence, I slowly climbed over it, letting myself drop the last few feet to the cracked concrete sidewalk. My back twinged, right where it had hurt yesterday, but I shrugged it off. The fastest way out of the city was to backtrack the route I took coming in, but my philosophy was you never got anywhere by re-hashing old routes. I turned the other way and looked deeper downtown. Maybe I could stop somebody and figure out where to catch a bus out of this place.

With each step, the pain got worse, and I could feel it reaching in deeper, gouging my soul. I stopped in front of a burned-out three-story house, sucking in huge breaths, begging for the pain to subside. Across the street was the office tower I'd *seen* the night before. Its mirrored windows reflecting the fire-ravaged house behind me, promising some relief from the heat of the sun. Maybe I could get some water in there. I staggered across the concrete street, my reflection growing larger.

I stopped in the middle of the street. The reflection was wrong.

I ran my fingers through my knotted hair, peering at them and then at my distant image. Maybe it was just a trick of light. I took a halting step forward. Left foot . . . right . . . left again, until I tripped over the unseen curb at my feet. The man in the reflection wasn't —*couldn't*—be me.

His hair was a tangled mess of leaves and twigs, and the colour of the sun shining through that young sapling's leaves so many years ago. The sunburn wasn't red but a darker shade of green. I stood transfixed by the image before me, its mouth agape, eyes wide and staring. The reflected man's eyes . . . *my* eyes . . . were green as well, not just the iris, but the pupil—a deep forest green —and the whites—an almost chartreuse yellow-green.

A young woman came around the corner in a sharp business suit, a phone held to her ear as she hurried to wherever she was going. She looked at me and stopped dead in her tracks, the forgotten phone held away from her ear.

"Help . . ." I took a stumbling step toward her, my voice cracking. "Help me!"

She turned and dashed back around the corner. I followed, farther from the damn tree that had done this to me. The pain flared again, blossoming in my chest. I fell and struggled back up, taking another step. It felt as though my heart was being pulled out through a hole in my back. Gasping in pain, I moved back to the fire-damaged house, the pain lessening with every step closer to the tree.

I think I lost my mind then. Or my ability to control it. Before I knew it, I was teetering on the top of the twelve-foot fence and then falling to the earth inside it. The branches of my tree spread overhead, and the shade helped wick away my sweat, and with it, any sense of fear as calm settled into me.

Even before I entered the crumbling library, I could feel the tree trembling, could feel it yearning to reach out and touch me, to hold me, to take away my returning fear. It didn't, and I stopped just shy of its thick bark. The pulsing of its sap matched the beating of my heart, a fast staccato that threatened to burst my veins.

I couldn't help myself, reaching out until my fingertips lightly brushed the bark. A jolt of adrenalin pumped through me; a feeling of euphoria and belonging and home followed it. I lay my palm flat on the trunk, and my world disappeared.

I STOOD in a forest older than any I had ever seen.

The clearing I stood in—if you could call it that since the trees surrounding it formed a green canopy overhead—was small and shadowed in early evening sunlight. I could smell the decaying leaves on the forest floor and the light scent of earth on the breeze. A branch snapped and I turned to see a man emerging from the woods, a man dressed in the green of the trees and with skin and eyes to match. He stood well over six feet tall.

"Welcome to Foxley," he said, his voice deep and raspy. It

reminded me of the rough oak bark of my tree. His accent was British but had a strange lilt to it.

"Foxley?" The word struggled to come out.

"Aye. As in Norfolk, England. Foxley Wood." He smiled then, and it suddenly felt like a fresh spring day. "You have been a friend to my tree for quite some time. When it called to you, and you came back, we both knew you were meant to be together."

"Wha . . . what do you mean?"

"Look at yourself. Better yet, look *in* yourself. You are what I, and others like me, are. A protector, a progenitor, of the forests of our world.

"Your country is on the brink of change. People are abandoning the large industrial metropolises in droves, leaving behind land that is slowly being reclaimed by nature. Our job is to help that process."

"But I don't want this. I would never want this, and I don't choose it."

"Ah, but you did, so many years ago when *you* needed the tree. To listen to your sorrows, your pain, your angst. Through all of it, the tree listened in silence. Now it is your turn to help the tree."

"Help?"

"It is scheduled to be cut down, is it not? That can't be allowed to happen. The bond between us and our tree is strong, and in your case, exceptionally so. If the tree dies, so do you, and with it, our hopes of bringing the land back to its balancing point."

My confusion lifted, and anger took its place. "What the hell do you mean I'd die? I didn't ask for this damn job!"

"None of us did, but we adapted. I have watched over this wood for almost six thousand years, since the last of the ice receded to the north. You may do the same for yours. You were pulled in faster than we would have wished, but with the fate of your tree so close to being decided, we could not tarry. Now you must go back. We will be here when you need us, but for now, your tree needs you. Grow your forest. It's not a simple task, but it is the one for which you have been chosen."

The wood vanished, and I stood once again under my tree.

I'VE BEEN with my tree for a month now.

I tried to leave. More than once. Each time I came back because of the pain. Even that is gone now. I stay because this is my home.

No one will come near the site anymore. I guess seeing a six-foot-tall man with green skin and hair made of leaves and twigs is enough to scare anybody off. Besides, the old library is already gone. The crumbling walls were easy for the low branches of my Oak to knock down, and the roots quickly crumbled them to powder.

The whole area inside the still-new chainlink fence is green now, and it's time to move farther out. And I have help. People from all over come here. Some to plant trees, some to meditate, and others just in the hopes of seeing me. I've stopped my running and finally put down the roots Dad always wanted.

At night, I still dream of forests and meadows nestled among man-made fingers of steel and glass, reaching for the sky.

FAIRY INVENTION

By Jane Yolen

If I had invented
the fey folk,
the wings would have been
    made of the finest Toledo steel,
shaped at an angle,
able to pierce everything but stone.
Their midnight dances
    would have had the lift of Pavlova,
      the daring of flamenco,
the boogie down of Josephine Baker
in Paris on a Saturday night.

THE KEY

By Griffin Barber

I was in such a hurry that evening that I broke a nail clean off on one of my household decorations. Beyond a curse cast over one shoulder at the offending suit of plate and mail, I barely acknowledged the injury. I had much to do and little time. Of course, the resultant rush was no fault of anyone's actions—or inaction—but my own. Indeed, I had begun the day in arrears, and things rolled rapidly down the heap from there. In any case, the nail, or talon, as you prefer, would be pivotal in events to come. Had I known that then, I might have been more circumspect. But then again, perhaps not.

I'm a dragon, see, and if there's one thing that dragons usually don't lack, it's spare time. That lack of lack, if you'll indulge an old drake's little foibles in their storytelling, leads some dragons to procrastinate far more than most Folk consider healthy or wise. I can see their point, of course, but when you're a fine example—and I say that with all due humility—of the richest, oldest, strongest, wisest, and most steeped-in-magick Folk of this world, there's little enough incentive to add to the pile of accomplishments beyond the first hoards accrued during an impetuous, distant, and energetic youth. As I am no longer young, I prefer to rest my bones upon my accomplishments. Such is the right I have earned through the long ages of the life I have led. Only glory can still stir me to action, on occasion. Oh, not the petty fame sought after by lesser mortals, but that of a lasting nature: glory that creates entries in the annals of all Folk, that causes songs to be sung and tales told. That type of glory forms the key to the great gate that stands between mortality and memory, the only thing that persists long after a dragon's soul has taken the last flight to join the First Dragon.

At any rate, when I am moved to move, so to speak, I do so with some speed. So it was that I leapt to the exit of my abode. I winced on landing, a slow trickle of blood weeping from my injury. Torn all the way down to the bed, the damn thing smarted. Sir Akkernon, the previous owner of the plate-and-mail harness that I had collided with in my haste, would no doubt have been proud of the injury his armour had done me. It was certainly more than he'd accomplished with sword and lance before I ended his pursuit of fame and, making a point to his followers, consumed him still screaming. That had been some ten turns back, and I had only recently taken to looking at the trophy with any fondness. He'd given me terrible indigestion for nearly a turn, you see. Horrible people will do that: keep coming back to haunt their betters.

I surveyed the long valley that forms the main approach to the cliffside entrance of my abode. The ground that extended from the base of the cliff to the banks of the glacial lake at the far end of the valley was as it should be: still and nearly lifeless. Many supposedly intelligent people complain of the scorched earth we dragons are forced to surround our lairs with. I can only say that there are many good reasons for this "desolation," not least of which is that it makes it easier to spot a party of impertinent treasure hunters or fame-crazed dragon slayers before they arrive upon one's doorstep.

I sniffed the air, drawing in the many scents carried to me on the early evening air. A pair of stags had battled beside the lake just as the sun set. I could smell the faint iron tang of their blood and the softer, earthier scents of the victor's claim upon the vixen after. I snorted a wry congratulations to him, but otherwise, let them be. The herd would be stronger for it, and besides, I was not hungry, not yet.

None of First Dragon's Clutch had climbed into view, but the moon humans called Hesh would soon raise her red eye above the horizon, making it easier to see me take flight. Given a lack of unfamiliar man-scent, I was not overly worried I would be seen, but a dragon does not live as long as I have and not learn to be circumspect. That in mind, I spent a moment giving the valley another once-over.

Seeing nothing amiss, I leapt from the ledge. I dropped like a wagon full of several hundredweight of stone until I fully extended my wings. Catching the air still rising from the sun-warmed, blackened earth of the valley, I soared silently above my domain. The slope fell away beneath me, down to the chuckling stream carving the valley with the slow patience of early autumn. In spring, the stream was an impatient roaring that descended in a foaming torrent to lower ground and the nameless lake at the far end of the valley.

A few strong beats of my wings carried me above the trees I'd left around that lake. An instant later, I was over the water. I glanced down, a vast, dangerous shadow flitting noiselessly across the starlit night, my majesty but poorly reflected in the cold deeps beneath my wings.

Satisfied there was nothing amiss in the immediate vicinity of my abode, I began a slow turn eastward and began to look for the court of the Exile Prince, Hirrem. The better-educated among my readers will understand that any name I give a Fae in exile isn't this Fae's true name, which may be used to rob him of what little he retains. I call him Hirrem here because the word sounds something like the noise his wings make when lamenting all he's lost. I suppose that if I, too, were an exiled prince, then I would also have reason to bemoan my many losses.

But I digress. By design, the Exile Prince's court is not an easy find, even for those with my experience and the inborn gifts of my blood. Indeed, the difficulty in locating his court had been the cause of my rush that evening: there are only so many times and places where conjunctions of the planets, the First Eggs, and the Other Courts allow for it.

THE SMALLEST OF the First Eggs was just limning the horizon with red light when the dolmens I was looking for made their appearance on a hill below and to the south. I dipped a wing and dropped low. The dolmens began to shimmer and shake as if viewed from a distance on a hot day, a sign that I must hurry. I dived, pumping my wings with all the considerable strength my frame could muster.

I was, perhaps, a touch too rushed. Again. Oh, not in the physical speed of my dive, though I did strain a tendon or ten with the sudden effort of braking for my landing. The pain was nothing, far less than any pain—both physical and social—I would have endured had I crashed into one of the ancient stones. No, my mistake was in alarming the warriors of the court, who, on seeing my majestic form stooping upon their abode, perceived a dire threat. There had been enough conflict, even wars, between them and us Elder Folk for my headlong charge at their home to provoke certain ... responses.

Careful of my injured claw, I alighted between the ancient stones of the dolmens just as a barrier of arcane energies stretched between their tips. So powerful was the barrier that simple proximity set my horns to itching.

A score of warriors emerged from beneath the ring of stones, their dragonfly wings and leaf-bladed tips of their long spears glinting in the shimmering light of the barrier above.

Now, I know that most Folk would seek to make amends for an entrance like the one I'd just perpetrated, or at least make an effort to appear as non-threatening as possible when faced with naked blades held in competent hands.

I did not.

Such is not the way of dragons, generally, and certainly not *my* way. How could I be worthy of my titles, which include the Doom of Dunzere, were it otherwise? So I showed my teeth, snorted disdainfully, and tilted my head back. My upper horns skimmed the inner surface of the arcane canopy. It itched and stung, but the light display and demonstration of my utter lack of concern for the power of their arcanists gave even the most stout-hearted warrior of Hirrem's court reason to pause. We stood there a long moment, those warriors and I. To their credit, the spear tips of those veterans wavered not at all; to mine, I made a rather magnificent display, my head crowned in fire whilst lightnings shattered the air between the tips of my upper horns.

Prince Hirrem broke the spell. He strode forth from his abode.

His long face was stretched with laughter as if he'd been told some great joke. He continued smiling up at me as he came within easy reach of my claws. He had donned his armour before coming to greet me, and his was no man-made clanking clatter of plate and mail but a smoky brilliance of scaled armour modelled on the skin of my own Folk and nearly as resistant to the strokes of swords and thrusts of spears. Nearly. I held no doubts his armour would break under my claws, but there was no need to mention it. I note this in my tale only so everyone will know him as a brave example of the Fae.

"You are late, dragon," he said without heat.

"A dragon is never late," I said, hiding a wince as I dug my claws into the loamy soil and aggravated my injury. My horns were, by then, itching quite abominably.

He tilted his head to regard me—haughtily, I thought. Then again, he remains a prince of his Folk, and a certain amount of aloofness is expected of even the least of the Eldest. Beyond his inborn self-regard, there was incontrovertible evidence of his strength: even that most august of bodies, The Court of Emerald Skies, had not attempted to take his titles when exiling him.

"We will soon remove ourselves to the next place."

I lowered head and horns from the sizzling, crackling embrace of the barrier. "I will not keep you overlong. Your herald said you would have words for me. I am here."

"There was no rush," Hirrem said, contradicting himself. He did it with a smile that exposed pointed canines but failed to spark any humour in his eyes. Such contradiction was common among the Fae but no less irritating for its banality.

I simply stared down at him, horns smoking.

He lowered his gaze first but acted as if he did so only to order his warriors to lower their weapons. Only we two knew the truth of it. It was enough for honour, and I accepted it without comment.

"I have word from my partisans at the Emerald Court," he said as his warriors retreated beneath the stones.

Sensing the Exile Prince had decided to come to the point, I lowered my head still further to look him in the eye. Such courtesies were his due, after all. It was one thing to insist he show me proper respect, another to fail to reciprocate.

"Word has reached the court of a new god among the Young Folk, one that desires the eradication of the Elder Folk."

I snorted, letting some smoke escape the furnace of my ire. "The Young Folk birth new gods as often as I defecate. It is their folly and foolhardy way to wing prayers into the Dark Between. It is our curse as much as theirs that something always answers."

Hirrem nodded, looking at the horizon. The Young Egg—what men call Hesh, their bloody-handed goddess of vengeance—crept warily into view. I do not know what the Fae call it. Whatever term they use for the moon, the Exile Prince continued to gaze at it for some moments more before replying, "It is said that this time is different, that their new god guides their leader to the places we hold sacred so they may defile them."

"This, too, they have attempted already, to their sorrow."

He looked back at me, his eyes many-faceted liquid pools in the mingled light of moons and stars. "Theirs was not the only sorrow, dragon."

My wings mantled in annoyance. That he should remind me of old pain was not unexpected. The Fae do enjoy their strange humours, after all. That it should hit home so well was. I snorted, carefully preventing anything more than smoke from issuing forth. "What do you propose?"

"Must I propose something?" The Prince's wings twitched with a *fut-fut-fut* noise. It was only when his fine-boned face cracked into a smile that I realized the noise was the Fae equivalent to a titter, a chuckle. The odd humour of his kind again, a strange sense of the absurd that other species rarely comprehended in full.

I resisted the urge to burn him to ash then and there, waiting for him to stop.

He shook his head as if disappointed at my lack of response to his jibe. "My court will evade this army unless and until they approach Cir Nochii within one day's march. Then we will destroy them under the light of the sun."

I knew the place. Another set of dolmens on the southern approaches of my territory. "The army, it marches already?"

He nodded. "For many weeks now."

"In what numbers?"

"Foot is around three tens of hundreds, horse they have in perhaps five of hundred. Of Select, they have as many as I have arcanists."

Ignoring the odd way the Fae counted, I focused on the numbers. They were not in my favour. They were not over-whelming by any means, especially should the Exile Prince and I make alliance, but I prefer to fight alone, as dragons have always done. No human would be armoured sufficiently to withstand my might, and few would be able to penetrate the scales that protected my vitals, but then, they had only to get lucky once, and I had already learned that singular lesson of a long life: luck was limited, skill much less so.

"And then, there is the hand of whatever they brought forth from the Dark Between, however that hand manifests."

I considered this whilst the Young Egg climbed higher into the night sky.

"They have a leader?" I asked at length.

"Indeed." Another whicker-snap of gossamer wings. "It is even said that the leader styles themself 'Purifier.'"

"Is it known which route this Purifier has chosen to approach Cir Nochii?"

"It can be learned."

"Then learn it."

I COASTED DOWN into the valley the Purifier's army had marched into as the First and Greatest of the Eggs began to set. Scrub oak, ironwood, and boulders dotted the long grass rolling beneath me as I slid very low between the crests of two hills. The dim upcast of the camp's firelight limned the shoulders of the surrounding hills as well as the underside of the sparse clouds between earth, Eggs, and stars.

Cautious of being spotted, I settled to the ground downwind and with a low rise between myself and the outermost sentries of the human camp. Despite my lack of humility before the Exile Prince, such caution was necessary. I had yet to decide how I would break the army, and in numbers like those encamped in the valley, humans were a not-insignificant threat. It was not only the weight of iron in blades and sharp-tipped arrows that gave them power, either. Yes, individual humans were weak, had always been so—no match for the strength and power of an equal number of Elder Folk, dragon or no. The greatest Select among them could only match the weakest arcanist among the Fae. But there were far more human Select than Fae arcanists. Add to those numbers the gifts of the strange human gods—those powers born of humans' reckless casting of prayers into the Dark Between—and humans were the greatest single threat to the Elder Folk.

Dragons are, of course, ablest of all the Elder Folk, but we breed slow, and our numbers have never been great. Partially, this is a result of our breeding. Dragon mating is a glorious, violent, punishing experience that often leaves two or three of our kind dead in exchange for five or six eggs. Then, our early lives are hard, not least because we do not care for our children once they have hatched from the egg but leave them to fend for themselves. Few, indeed, had furnished posterity and the First Dragon with more than one clutch of offspring before passing. I had given the First Dragon five clutches of eggs and had the mating scars to prove it.

Setting aside thoughts of mating in favour of how best to halt the invading army, I raised my head, snuffling carefully. The many odours—human sweat, human waste, even the sweeter, more honest scent of a vast herd of horses—were an assault on my refined sense of smell. I ignored that assault, picking my way through the stink in search of outstanding threats. There was something else on the wind. Something un-right. I considered using a fraction of my power in order to better quantify and localize the sensation, but there was an underlying menace to the scent that warned against use of the arcane arts to identify it.

Oddly disconcerted, I decided I would not risk a frontal attack; I would instead set the camp on edge over the next nights, terrorizing them until they learned the error of their ways.

Pleased with this new stratagem, I settled in to await the proper time to begin. The wheel of heaven turned above me, scales of the First Dragon glittering in their endless evolutions against the Dark Between.

THE MOMENT ARRIVED a little before dawn. Two of the First Dragon's Eggs had descended well beyond the rim of the world, leaving only the slower-travelling Young Egg to haunt the heavens with its red light. I was content under its lingering gaze. Humans have a number of ancient myths surrounding its appearance in the night sky, and those dark tales suited my purpose.

I sidled forward on all fours, slinking from boulders to brambles, copse to copse, until I was close enough to bring the first sentry under my claws. Blood flowed and viscera spattered in my wake. Reaching back with my wings, I gentled the corpse's fall whilst listening for any activity that might prove the killing had been noticed. Hearing nothing, I moved widdershins, seeking the next sentry.

I killed that one and five more before dawn's light began to reach over the shoulders of the hills to scratch at the valley floor, obliging me to take flight.

I was content with the night's work. The camp would be fearful now, their every movement slowed by fatigue and caution. The next night's killing would prove more challenging, with the guard doubled or tripled, but a Dragon at war accepts what challenges come.

I KILLED ten the next night and five the night after that. The fourth night, I left them to stew in the juices of their own fears whilst I hunted game. Contrary to modern myth, dragons do not generally lust after the taste of human flesh. Oh, we will eat it should nothing else be on offer, or if—as is more common—we wish to make a point, but the flesh of sentients is often bitter, and enjoying it carries with it a degree of social stigma most prefer to avoid. So it was that I feasted on several head of wild cattle well to the east and slept the day away basking in the waters of a certain hot spring I enjoy.

I returned to find the hated army had made much more progress than anticipated. It was almost as if the Purifier had known I would not attack that night. Such prescience is not unheard of; be they old or fresh-spawned from the Dark Between, human gods are all meddlers.

The army was now only two day's march from Cir Nochii and only one day removed from facing a ruinous reckoning upon upon Hirrem's wrath. My efforts had not convinced them to turn from their course. I almost left for the Exile's camp but refused to be thought his lackey. No dragon wishes to appear a minion, ever.

So, instead, I considered my options as I carved long, slow circles through the night above the fires.

In truth, I did not want the Exile to take the field against the Purifier. Oh, I was not concerned with the blood—be it Fae or human—that would be spilled. Never that. No, I simply wished the victory to be mine, and mine alone.

I am a proud example of a proud folk, after all.

IN THE END, I decided I would earn the most glory by decapitating the army. For that purpose, I first cast about for a likely landing spot. The humans had marched up a wide and deep moraine left behind by the sculpting hand of the previous age of ice. I found an ideal spot some way downslope of their campsite. Those who do not fly are, perhaps, unaware of the tendencies of air. In short, cold air settles and pools like water, whilst warm air climbs and spreads thin, like wings. Knowing the cold air off the heights would travel down across the camp and below the camp, I chose my spot carefully.

Once settled amongst some rocks left behind by the retreating ice, I was just another boulder among many.

I tested the air once more with nostrils and palate, inhaling iron-, human-, fire-, horse- and camp-stink. Beneath that, however . . . no, running *through* that miasma, was the un-right thing I had sensed earlier, a true threat of oppression in a morass of more prosaic hazards. I weaved a portion of the magick that is the birthright of my people into a shelter, a shell I might retreat into if things took a perilous turn. Then I sent questing tendrils of power upslope to seek the un-right. I found what I sought in moments.

Would that I had not.

THE UN-RIGHT WAS easy to find as I extended my power toward the centre of the camp—it was a molten, dirty heat, like that at the heart of a volcano; opaque, yet burning with a throbbing intensity that made the senses reel. A chill ran from my tail to the tips of my horns. Despite my prowess, this was not something I was ready to confront, and so I began a retreat.

I was too slow, too late to recognize the threat. At the merest touch of my power, the un-right uncoiled like a ball of breeding snakes disturbed by a rockfall. The weaving I'd set to protect me collapsed, wisps of unrealized power evaporating under the forces reaching to enfold my essence. An instant later, the very air became malevolent, seizing my will in its slick, heated grip. It was not painful, not by the stretch of my wings. No, it was almost peaceful, like drowning in the warm waters of the hot springs I'd visited the night before.

All it wanted of me was surrender.

Dragons do not surrender. We rage.

So, I resisted with all my considerable will. To my surprise, that will was the merest drop of water in the maelstrom.

Distantly, I felt my legs begin to move. I willed them to stop, but my command did not connect to the flesh housing my spirit. Like some puppet played on strings of power, my body picked up speed, crashing clumsily uphill toward the un-right. Humans scattered before me, those too slow battered aside by horn, shoulder, or spine. None raised arms against me, however. I crashed through a line of tents, crushing one man beneath me as I passed. I felt a tiny surge of grim satisfaction, but the death of one human was an insignificant victory in light of the caging of my will.

A party of armed humans arranged themselves to defend the centre of the camp as I breached the inner defences. I felt, more than heard, the un-right order them to stand down.

They refused at first.

The un-right bellowed, "Do not strike! The dragon is mine, body and soul."

The fell half-truth of those words made the furnace which cloaks the heart of every dragon burn all the hotter in my breast. Dragons do not serve, do not suffer control.

And yet, all the rage at being controlled rebounded. It redoubled but did nothing to free me.

I drew near a red pavilion erected in the shadow of the ancient ice among stones and boulders the glacier had surrendered to the growing heat of the age.

I skidded to a stop, my weight carving a furrow in the scree, and stood panting as a tall human armoured in shining steel and armed with cold iron stepped from the red pavilion to look up at me.

When I lay my mortal eyes upon it, I could see the un-right laced tightly through the confines of that human's flesh. I wondered, briefly, how she had come to be so thoroughly possessed. Perhaps she had believed the un-right a god and invited it in to assist her in some extremity?

Be it as it may, the creature born in the Dark Between was now in full control of her—flesh and soul.

The army closed in about us, disorganized but numerous. I read the hate and awe in their eyes and could smell the fear-sweat which made them clutch their weapons and stop their approach just beyond reach. All of it was faint praise in light of my help-lessness.

"Bow to me, dragon," the un-right said, voice echoing in my skull. The mouth of the thing's host did not move.

Hissing like a hatchling denied dinner, I felt my compliance even as I raged against the power shielding my flesh from my will.

"With this dragon," the un-right said with the mouth of the human it possessed, "we shall conquer the Maw of Malice and the foul Fae who keep the wound open in order to spill their filth unto the world!"

The humans surrounding us celebrated the un-right's diatribe with a many-throated roar.

"Stretch forth your neck," the un-right commanded in its strange dual-toned voice, tugging at my body with its power.

I could do nothing but comply.

Only when the possessed woman's flesh made contact with my scales did my muscles offer the merest tremble of revulsion, of resistance. The un-right ignored it and clambered up the base of my neck, casting one leg over. My humiliation was complete. No dragon suffered the Young Folk to ride them. Such a thing was absurd, akin to a chipmunk riding a bobcat.

"Tomorrow, you and I shall bring down heaven's judgment on the godless Fae," the un-right and its host declared.

Up! the un-right commanded me soundlessly.

I lurched clumsily upright. I could not fly like this. I wished to say as much but could not muster the words past the un-right's control.

"Up!" The Purifier repeated, aloud this time.

My flesh tried to comply, but the un-right could not manage the coordination necessary for flight whilst simultaneously maintaining control over the human it possessed. The result was an awkward leap that ended up in a heavy landing just short of the ring of warriors watching us. More loose stone was flung from beneath my bulk, pattering off shields and helms.

The un-right seemed to comprehend the nature of the problem after but a moment's hesitation. Unwilling to fail before its followers, the un-right carefully returned a small measure of control to me.

I went on the offensive immediately, but my struggles were no more effective than before. The un-right had ceded just enough control that I might comply with its instruction and take flight.

"Up!" the un-right shouted for the third time.

I clenched my claws into the scree so I could leap into the air. Dimly, I felt something—some shadow of pain pierced the shield of the un-right's control. At the same time, I felt the weight of the body astride me shift, the thighs tighten against the sides of my neck, even as I heard a sharp intake of breath.

Understanding dawned. The un-right's near-perfect control was dependent on feeling what my body was experiencing at any given moment. Stolen command also meant stolen sensation.

Lacking time for thought, I moved to comply with my orders and clenched my claws on the valley floor. Gravel grated against the bed of the missing talon of my right claw, causing only the slightest pain to me but making the un-right's other puppet reel. Its control slipped.

Conscious of my previous failures to overcome the un-right with magick, I acted without forethought or art. I splayed the wounded claw deeper beneath the loose stones of the scree. While my rider reeled from the fresh pain I was forbidden, I ducked my head even as I raised my haunches and mantle, wing-claws catching at the un-right's flesh.

The result was not unlike the bucking of an immensely powerful bull: my contortions launched the un-right screaming into the air. It landed upon the tips of two spears held by its own soldiers. Cold iron pierced armour, skin, and spirit, and the un-right and its host let out a piercing shriek, soon swallowed by my triumphant bellow.

Free of the un-right's control, I snapped forward and bit its host in half. Raising my head above the stunned crowd, I spat the remains out in a gout of flame that burned flesh from bone.

Denied its host, the un-right scrabbled for purchase in my flesh, but I was wise to its tricks now, and it lacked the angry righteousness of a dragon's heart. Wailing into the aether, the mass of selfish prayer and malevolent desire for an end to the Elder Folk dissolved back into the Darkness Between.

A few iron-tipped spears and arrows shattered against my scales. I turned my horn-crowned head and let the flames of my anger play across the front ranks of the army encircling me. Molten metal and cindered flesh spattered the following ranks, spreading panic on wings of fear and fire.

The army shattered. I forged after its shards, leaving blood and death in my wake.

It was not—would never be—enough. I would teach them the error of their ways, of challenging the Elder Folk, of praying such prayers, of following a thing spawned in the Darkness Between. I was the key that would unlock their primal fears, open the door to their collective perception, fly across the revealed threshold, and soar into their nightmares forever and ever.

CHOICES

By Miles Cameron

L lachlan Blackhand was cold and wet but not particularly miserable. Being cold and wet was a fairly normal part of being a ranger on the borders of Shadow; it went with the job.

Winter made cold and wet worse, and a week on the trail . . .

He was deep in the borders, the almost impenetrable stands of black spruce and alder that now grew in the boggy ground that had once been a ridge of beech trees. A few were left, and the rest were like skeletal giants against the grey sky.

A sky he seldom saw. The new growth was dense, difficult to penetrate even in winter, and already unnaturally tall after just two seasons of the Shadow, with scraggly branches that reached for his cloak like the arms of spindly monsters clawing at him.

These woods were unnatural.

Lachlan was moving with professional caution. It was easy to be quiet in winter. His snowshoes made a very low squeak as he pressed each foot down in the new snow: deep, cold snow. His moustache was frozen; his beard, no better. But while he moved warily, he was quick and not as cautious as he might have been. The only tracks in the new snow were from something small and hungry that had ventured out, the tracks running across his trail like ancient glyphs written in the snow. There was birdsong, and over all of it, his own sense of the season told him he was alone. The Shadow's warriors weren't particularly good at snow. And it never snowed in the Shadow.

Besides, his dog was cheerful, plodding along without comment by his side. The big war dog had a keen nose for scent and accompanying danger, and his playful bounds seemed proof that the woods were empty of enemies.

He was coming to the edge of a beaver swamp. He knew it well; it had been swampy before the change.

Luadhas, his big hound, knew it too. The dog stopped, sniffed, and looked at him.

He gripped his spear . . . this time of year, more like a walking pole with a lethal tip. He knelt at the edge of the open ground, watching and still careful to keep his knee on a branch and not in the snow.

Time passed. Something was moving.

Not something from Shadow, but wrong, nonetheless.

Out from the trees across the meadow, a lone stag came, stepping through the snow and occasionally going through the ice below, despite broad hooves and some care. It wasn't moving well.

The stag was exhausted, Llachlan guessed.

Or wounded.

Thoughts of a campfire and a venison steak began to cloud his judgment. But the beast was a hundred paces away, and in this cold, he'd only break his bow.

Luadhas glanced at him, a canine question writ on his long furry face.

The stag went through the snow and floundered.

Definitely tired.

It took the animal ten breaths to fight clear of whatever hole he'd fallen into, and as he trudged away, now high on the crust of old snow, Llachlan saw blood. New, fresh blood.

Wounded, tired.

I wonder who wounded you? Llachlan asked himself. He hadn't survived in this border ten years and more without asking hard questions every day.

But there was also hunger and such a thing as too much caution.

The stag had no idea he was there; the wind was coming from the wounded animal at him and carried enough scent that the dog gave a very, very quiet whine.

'Maybe,' Llachlan said in less than a whisper.

And then the stag signed its death warrant by choosing to stay in the open meadow and coming toward him. He knelt, one knee on a reasonably snow-free log, for long minutes as the animal made its way toward him, falling through the crust, wavering, pushing on.

Llachlan came of an ancient people with laws that covered many things, and he began a prayer to the Lady of Animals, not for the *right* to kill this beast, but for the favour of its life. It was far gone, and brave, and still moving because to stop was to freeze. But the blood coming from its side was lung-bright.

The Lady rarely answered directly. But in this case, the stag walked to within ten paces of the man and the dog and stopped.

Llachlan's spear took it just under the head. It went down as if kneeling and then fell. It kicked once.

Llachlan stepped out, drew his seax, and raised its head to cut its throat, but his throw had done its work. The magnificent beast was dead.

He let its head go and looked around.

As far as he could tell, they were alone. Despite which, he dragged the beast with his horsehair rope as far as the tangle of spruce trees and then pulled his spear free and cleaned the head so that the gold-and-silver inlay shone in the weak sun.

He laid it carefully against a tree, shed his two outer layers, hung them high above the snow, and began to haul the carcass up.

That's when he saw the arrow wound in the flank, and a moment's digging with his eating knife produced an arrowhead.

The black iron and shoddy workmanship said "Shadow." The size and thickness of the broken shaft said "crossbow."

He looked out over the field and back at the animal he'd just killed. The stag had been shot, what . . . *Five hours ago? Twelve hours ago?*

Lost a great deal of blood. But still moving.

Nearest settlement is west, maybe five leagues. The Hamlet of Barnsgate, under Tarn Hows.

He looked at the animal again and then at the meadow, which was a deathtrap for a single man, ranger or not, caught in the open.

And if he walked off on the stag, it'd be bones by the time he returned. The border was full of wolves anyway, and the smell of the blood would carry.

I have food, but not much.

I hate waste.

He pulled the stag up until it hung almost clear of the ground and began to slaughter it. The dog got some early food; he took the best cuts and wrapped them in the hide, and made a bundle, using a little waxed cloth to keep it from freezing solid. He was quick and efficient, and he cursed the waste of so much good meat and sinew and bone.

He took a whole antler. Arrow nocks; knife handles; awls and other tools; too good to leave.

The dog had finished his feast. He looked at Llachlan with something like undying love.

Llachlan growled in his throat, frustrated.

Winter, and the Shadow has an archer within five leagues of people. And there's no way it is alone.

He nodded as if he'd had a conversation, untied the carcass and let it down, took his rope and coiled it.

"We'll feed the wolves," he said to Luadhas, who looked dissatisfied.

And then he set out to backtrack the stag. And that began with a long, careful plod across the edge of the open ground.

And the enemy had an archer.

———

THE STAG HAD DONE MOST of the hard work, discovering where the tiny stream that meandered across the meadow in spring ran under the snow; Llachlan could follow every time the stag had gone through the ice and fought its way clear, and he didn't imitate it. Instead, thanks to snow shoes and experience, he moved parallel to the tracks, as far from them as he could be and still see them, as close to the wood line on the west side of the meadow as he could arrange.

He felt stupid and exposed anyway.

You're alone.

Go back and report. Or drop the meat and run for Barngate and warn them.

Alone is a fast way to die.

He kept going.

It was a situation he'd faced before, and the sheer illogic of it made him feel stupid. He was famous: Llachlan Blackhand. He had a name, one of the best names in the borderlands. There were songs . . .

And in the songs, he didn't run back for help. And that got to him, even though it was beyond foolish.

"Fang and venom. I'm an idiot," he said aloud.

Luadhas glanced at him in apparent agreement.

Llachlan pressed on, now sure that he was in full sight of some enemy, wondering if he was doing the same thing as the stag, walking straight to his death.

He moved west, right to the edge of the beaver meadow, so that he was walking along with the woods on his left. He stopped twice, knelt, and watched. The snow was deeper right at the edge, and the dog followed close behind him, walking along in the deep tracks his snowshoes left.

He stopped again.

Nothing.

After a quarter of an hour, he came to where the tracks entered the meadow from the west, and he turned and plunged into the woods. There was less snow under the canopy, and they were walking away from the border, climbing gradually to higher ground out from under the endless cloud of the Shadow. The dog moved more easily, and the ranger moved faster until he found a bird, dead in the snow, dropped by a hawk or an owl. He looked at it a moment, wondering if the Shadow warriors he was sure had been here had startled it, and he picked up the little bird. It was cold, frozen through.

Night is coming.

The stag was easy to backtrack. Its hooves had gone deep in the new snow, and the spots of blood were still easy to see, even as the sun began its steep winter descent.

I should be making camp.

But he was warm from exertion, and he had a bad hunch, and the farther west he walked, the less he liked it.

And then he found where the stag had been shot. A big bound, then a desperate run.

Llachlan stopped. He was in a dell at the base of a low bluff covered in tall beaches. The wind whispered in the branches. He looked around himself carefully, trying to be the archer.

Up on the low ridge was the most likely. Shadow warriors wouldn't have snowshoes; they'd move in the shallowest snow.

He wouldn't have a second chance. It would be full dark in half an hour and then another two hours until there was enough moonlight to track.

The stag was going from west to east. The arrow was in its right side. The right side would face the ridge.

Here we go.

"Come on, boy," he said quietly and started up the ridge.

It was steep going at first, a little more rounded as he climbed, but he kept his eye on a gully to his right because it would have offered the archer a clear shot. Seventy paces, maybe; a very competent man.

An enemy.

He began to move diagonally across the face of the ridge, heading for the gully, avoiding the tangle of a fallen forest giant.

But when he cleared it, he could look back and see where the stag was shot, and when he moved again, he saw the tracks immediately.

One set of booted feet. Big, soft boots. No snowshoes.

He could see where the man had stood, and only a man would have such large feet. He stood *there* and shot, partially covered by the branches of the big downed tree.

Despite the falling night, Llachlan Blackhand stood there for a long time, lost in thought.

Then he moved up the ridge again, looking west, watching for movement. The crossbowman had been here perhaps six hours before. Almost no one could lie still in ambush for six hours in this cold.

He moved carefully anyway.

The tracks ran toward the top of the ridge, and then angled off west, and then . . .

. . . then he was looking at a beaten trail that ran along the ridge top. The crossbowman had left it *there* and rejoined *there.*

He looked at the trail for a long time while the dog panted by his side.

"Twenty," he said at last. "And maybe more. And one who acted alone."

They could be at the village now. But only if they'd moved fast and taken no break for meals or anything else.

There was a light snow falling now, and the diffuse light of the end of day through snow was almost magical. He checked his weapons.

"Fang and venom," he muttered and pushed on.

The trail was deep and easy to walk. He considered unlacing his snowshoes but decided against it. He couldn't outrace the enemy if they'd already reached the village. So either they'd made camp, or he was too late.

At the base of the ridge, the trail crossed a stream. Llachlan paused and looked at the dog, and Luadhas sniffed the air and went forward, giving a powerful leap to clear the icy water. He looked back, and Llachlan shook his head.

"I am too old for all this," he muttered and then tested the depth of the stream with his spear. Then he pulled off his snow-shoes and flung them across. After a moment of searching, he found a rock underwater and planted the spear's iron back-spike and used it to jump across, dryshod, or as dry as a man could be after a day walking. He cursed again while he retied his snowshoes with frozen hands.

If was full dark. The snow reflected all the light, and he could see the trail well enough, but he couldn't see much else, and he moved cautiously for an hour as the tiny, cold snowflakes fell. The dog was looking at him now, openly questioning all his choices from a canine wisdom.

"No choice," he said, although he knew it was a lie. He'd had a dozen choices since the stag stumbled into the beaver meadow.

He was getting cold. And that was *bad* because he was moving, and he didn't have food that was easy to reach or a warm camp. He'd moved too fast on the ridge, and his linen shirt was sweat-soaked and now clammy.

Stop now. Find a big tree, make a small fire, eat a venison steak.

He thought it, but he didn't really consider it because he was Llachlan Blackhand, and he had to . . .

Had to do everything. More. Better.

"I'm a fool," he said aloud.

The dog just kept plodding along.

At the base of the next long ridge, he suddenly knew where he was—not in a general way, but exactly. He'd been here before, in the days before the Battle of Emsdale; he knew that ridge, and he knew that another league or two would find him among farms. The ridges were getting higher, and in daylight, Tarn How would have shown to the north.

He moved with new purpose, and when he crested the next ridge, he made another choice and left the deep-cut trail to walk north.

"Ahhh," he said very softly. Because as he crested that ridge, passing between two ancient rocks his ancestors had used as altars, he could look down into the whole of the next valley through the leafless trees.

And there was the twinkle of a fire.

It was a welcome sight, for all that it was warming his foes. They weren't attacking Barnsgate. Not yet.

They were in a camp by the Blacktarn stream. He watched the fire, moving cautiously closer, feeling the night's cold soak slowly through his layers of wool and fur and linen and into his chest and back.

He nodded to himself as if he'd made an agreement, and then went back the way he came, all the way to the deep cut trail on the other side of the ridge.

Perhaps three hours until midnight.

He could sprint to Barnsgate and give the alarm. Definitely the wisest course.

He smiled at the dog.

"But not really my way," he said and gave the dog a scratch.

The dog leaned against him, first for the scratch and then for warmth, and Llachlan savoured it because Luadhas was a *big* dog, and his warmth helped.

And then he went down into the valley. He moved quickly, and at the base of his ridge, he cut back away from the deep-cut trail of the Shadow warriors and into the woods, now going south a bit and still west, well wide of their camp. That took time and patience, and it was cold, and for a while, as he floundered in a dell of deep, powdery snow, he wondered why he was doing any of this.

But once across the dell, he found the little stream that fed the Blacktarn. He knew it in summer and knew that between its two branches was a little island, steep and rocky and shaded at the top by two ancient hemlocks. Between them, almost snow-free because of the density of their cover, was a big rock, blackened by many campfires on its flat westward face, and there, to his joy, in the deep darkness, he saw that the hollow was full of firewood and not snow.

He dropped his two packs, the one he lived from and the one of stag hide and meat, and then, cautious now that he was probably safe, he made a wide circuit out in the dark, making sure that he was alone.

Luadhas stayed by the cold rock as if the memory of past fires might warm his long skinny legs.

Llachlan circled back, carrying a big sheet of birchbark ripped from a dead tree, and used it to make a screen and a little mat on which he could kneel, and then he built a fire and started it with a gesture and an ancient word. The wood was dry, the magic powerful, and he'd made fires in worse conditions. It caught quickly and cheered him and the dog.

He ate a big handful of nuts and sugar and berries and then opened the meat pack, fed the dog, and made himself a supper of barely charred venison.

He didn't want to leave the fire. He was safe here: good lines of sight, a warm fire, and enough wood to get through the night easily.

But that wasn't what Llachlan Blackhand did.

Instead, when he'd eaten and had a long pull of unfrozen water, he took the dead bird he'd found and began to take some of its feathers, the best, from the tail and wingtips. He cut a stick of green alder and bent it, wrapping it with sinew from the stag and then attaching the black feathers. He cut a circle of the stag's hide and sewed it in, a bloody mess in the midst of a circle of dark feathers.

He nodded.

"Stay," he said to the dog.

Luadhas looked at him, raised his head, looked at the fire . . . and put his head down again.

Llachlan walked off into the light snow, headed north.

He knew the ground well enough. The smell of the enemy fire came to him on the wind long before he saw the distant flicker among the trees, and he knew that in winter, firelight can penetrate woods for very long distances. Once he saw the distant flame, he redoubled his caution and forgot his cold and worry and instead slipped along, silent on his snowshoes, until he found the old trail to Barnsgate, the trail that the Shadow warriors would take to raid the village in the morning. Indeed, there was a single pair of tracks visible, a scout checking the route.

I'd do the same.

The tracks went outbound and didn't return.

"Fang," he said quietly. *Still out there.*

One Shadow scout who acts alone.

And then he followed the tracks.

DEEP NIGHT. A quarter moon shone brilliantly on the snow now that the clouds had moved on. A biting wind, a clear sky full of stars, and the cold of the distant void pressing down on him.

He kept moving. He'd left his dog and his packs by his fire, and now he was walking straight toward Barnsdale without them. He shook his head.

And then he stepped off the trail and into the woods. The stars told him it was close to midnight; his cold right hand told him he'd have to turn back soon. His left hand, the black hand, was always cold, but winter didn't make it any colder.

And then he saw movement through the trees against the snow ahead.

Llachlan knelt, now heedless of wetting his leggings in the snow.

The man came on, walking back along the trail, head down, a crossbow over his shoulder.

Llachlan didn't like murder. He'd spent half his life as an outlaw, and the word stuck in his throat. So he let the other man pass him unaware, and then, when the man's breathing vanished into the night, he turned and followed, moving cautiously a hundred paces behind, well off the trail.

Twice the man turned and listened. Twice he went back to walking. But the third time he stopped, he raised his crossbow and pointed it—not precisely *at* Llachlan, but close enough that the ranger knew he'd made a noise.

They both stayed there long enough for Llachlan's fingers to lose their feeling and his feet to threaten to quit. His crouch burned in his thigh muscles, and he thought his breath was loud, as he always did.

Spear against crossbow was a poor match.

And why didn't you kill him when he was at the point of your spear?
Soft and foolish and old. And too curious.

And then the man turned away and began to walk quickly, almost jogging.

Llachlan followed him again until he saw the man crouch, and then Llachlan cursed.

Of course, the man had seen his tracks.

Llachlan glided farther to the south. A screen of black spruce blocked the other man's line of sight, and Llachlan moved fast, his snowshoes carrying him above the drifts.

The other man was moving, too. He knew that someone was close, and he was moving to a place from which he could get a clear shot.

Llachlan came around the spruce and crouched once more, using his snowshoes as skis to skid down a steep slope. The man on the trail snapped around and saw him, and Llachlan heard the snap of the crossbow as clearly in the cold air as if the prod had been next to his head.

Wherever the bolt went, it wasn't close enough to make a sound.

The crossbowman froze. Llachlan knew he could either span his deadly weapon or run, but not both The man took too long to decide and then turned to run. But the trail was not well-established here; he didn't have twenty comrades pushing the snow flat, and his running was laboured and desperate. In three floundering bounds, he knew he'd made the wrong choice, and he turned.

He had on a hood that might once have been black, and he

wore a scarf and a mask, the way they always did. But his eyes gleamed inside the mask.

The man drew a big knife. He didn't look scared. He didn't look as if he had any choice at all.

Lachlan stopped a few paces away, much taller on his snow-shoes, watching the curse of the Shadow force the man into action,

"You could just drop the knife and surrender," Llachlan said aloud.

The man didn't even shake his head. One moment, the eyes were full of doubt, and the next, Llachlan watched as they filled with something else.

The curse.

The Shadow drove him forward, but the footing wasn't like footing in Shadow, and he almost fell, his stumble becoming a ferocious attack.

Llachlan covered the man's desperate lunge with the point of his spear and then reversed his spear and smashed the butt into the man's head, knocking him into the snow. Then he stood over him, looking down.

The man didn't move.

Llachlan reached down and touched the man's neck with his bare left hand, the black hand. He felt the pulse and nodded.

Llachlan made a *tsk-tsk* sound. And then he cut a small pine, stripped it with his little axe, and put it up in the snow with his little field sign of blood and feathers next to the unconscious man's head in the snow.

He may freeze. That's with the Gods.

And then, warmed by fighting the poor bastard, he walked directly away from the enemy camp, pausing once to check for the flicker of their fire, far away. Then he turned south and walked until he saw the gleaming black of the little stream and followed it in the dark until he could smell his own fire.

'OH, LUADHAS,' he said in disgust.

The dog looked *very* sorry.

The meat pack had been ripped open, and a great deal of venison had been eaten.

Llachlan shook his head. Then he put out his fire, picked up his own pack, and looked at the dog.

The dog looked so remorseful that he smiled.

"Come on, then," he said. "Breakfast in Barnsdale."

SPRING WAS WORKING its way through the fells, the only white on the lower hills was the grubby white of spring sheep, and the streets of Hawkshead were ankle-deep in muck. Llachlan Black-hand sat with one foot up in the common room of the Hawk's Head, the inn that served as the headquarters for the rangers.

Sitting opposite him were half a dozen of his friends and fellow rangers: Finavir, a healer turned ranger, and Carlyle, the lieutenant of the rangers, three men so young it seemed impossible that they would wear the silver star, and a dark-skinned woman from the distant deserts, a new recruit.

He'd told the story without embellishment, and now he sat back and lit his pipe with a coal from the hearth, watching them.

"But . . ." Carlyle smiled. "But there was no fight at Barnsgate.'"

"No," Llachlan said. "They turned back. We waited all morning for an attack, but they never came."

The young woman made a face. I don't understand," she said. "Aren't we here to fight the Shadow?"

Llachlan took a long draw on his pipe. "I think we're here to protect people," he said. "Ever look into the eyes of a man under the curse?"

The young ranger looked away.

Llachlan put his pipe down. "I made some foolish choices, but I'll stand by one: I decided not to kill if I could help it. The monsters, the gnolls and *tarks,* I'll kill them without hesitation. But the people?"

He looked around at the others. Finavir nodded; Carlyle smiled.

"The Shadow curse rolled over a whole country," he said. "Most of those 'Shadow Warriors' are just local farmers under the curse. Someday, it could be you and me. It's the Tyrant and his curse that drives them. They don't have any choice. Or much choice. But someone has a *little* choice."

Finavir leaned forward. "They turned back," she said.

Llachlan fiddled with his pipe. "They did."

"So someone has the power to make a decision," she said.

"Exactly," Llachlan said. "I stood there in the snow, looking at the tracks of the crossbowman where he tried a shot at the deer. He left his party alone. So he had some . . . control." He looked up. "It seemed worth a try to see if they could be dissuaded."

Finavir nodded. "I wonder if anything can break the curse?" she asked.

Llachlan gave her an approving nod. "My thought exactly."

AUTHOR'S NOTE: *This story is set in Joseph McCullough's excellent* Rangers of Shadow Deep *world where an immense and ancient evil* has swept over a neighbouring kingdom, and only a handful of rangers stand between their people and the curse of the Shadow. I'd like to recommend the game, which is fun and immersive and can easily be played solo or cooperatively with friends. If you enjoyed this story and want more, I have an entire Llachlan Blackhand novel (free to all comers) on my website at christiancameronauthor.com.

MISTER FARNSWORTH VERSUS THE ALIEN DEMONS OF ANCIENT EGYPT

By Sebastien de Castell

CHAPTER 1: MISTER FARNSWORTH

Mister Farnsworth had a valet. This was unusual. Partly it was unusual because valets were uncommon in an age of mobile phones and five-hundred-square-foot apartments that no one could afford to own, but mostly it was unusual because Mister Farnsworth was a cat.

To be specific, he was one-quarter Burmese, one-quarter Egyptian Mau, one-eighth Siamese, one-eighth American Bobtail, and one-quarter Turkish Angora. All of which is to say, he was the type of shitty, ill-mannered stray you find hissing from his cage at the pound that no one wants to adopt.

Mister Farnsworth was many things, but he wasn't "*cute* cute."

On the other hand, he did have a valet, which meant that he was properly brushed in the mornings before he went out on his first prowl to steal the neighbour's cat food (despite the fact that his own was both plentiful and more expensive). It also meant that when Mister Farnsworth returned, the valet would be ready with a towel to dry his fur if it was wet or gently smooth it if he'd gotten into a fight with the rightful owner of the aforementioned cat food.

In the winter afternoons, the valet would dress Mister Farnsworth in a warm and handsome angora sweater and place a set of four knit booties over his paws, which kept them from getting cold but still allowed his claws to extend; time, tide, and howling, screeching, murderous fights wait for no cat, after all, not even in winter.

In the evenings, the valet would remove all such contrivances, meticulously brush Mister Farnsworth's fur once again, and then dress him in a simple but elegant black silk bowtie. Mister Farnsworth did not trouble himself with excessive finery at supper.

It was during one such evening that I found myself seated at the centre of one very long side of a polished mahogany dinner table. On one end sat Mister Farnsworth, and on the other, Hannah, who was, ostensibly, the woman I'd been dating these past three weeks and who had asked me the previous night—after what I'd believed to be a promisingly extended kiss—if I'd like to come to her place for dinner.

After the soup had been served, Hannah brought her spoon to her lips and blew on the still-simmering lobster bisque before giving me a smile that I presumed was an invitation to comment.

I took the embroidered cloth napkin from my lap and patted a trace of bisque from my lips before I spoke.

"Jesus Fucking H. Christ!" I shouted. "How did you manage to date me for three entire weeks without bothering to tell me that you're a complete fucking lunatic?"

Mister Farnsworth looked up from his own bowl to offer me

what I felt was a surprisingly sympathetic look. His smart black silk bowtie was covered in lobster bisque.

"Okay," Hannah said. "Okay." She offered up a few more okays before seemingly giving up on a reply.

"Let's not make this complicated," I said, holding up my hand and counting off the full range of plausible and implausible explanations on my fingers. "One, this is a really elaborate prank. If it is . . ." I glanced around at the high ceilings of the dining room with its twin crystal chandeliers, hand-crafted oak panelling, and assorted other excessively posh furnishings ". . . then I appreciate the effort, but I think you overpaid."

"It's not a prank, Greg."

I stared at her, waiting for more.

"It's . . . It's like . . ."

I tapped my middle finger. "Option two, you inherited millions from a wealthy uncle who set several bizarre prerequisites on whoever got his loot." I jerked a thumb to the ugly cat who was busily lapping more and more lobster bisque onto his silk tie and occasionally getting a little into his mouth. "Mister Farnsworth, here, is the end result of those prerequisites."

"No, Greg, it's my money. I told you, when I sold my software company, I'd built up a substantial collection of patents and they—"

I glanced around the room once more, thinking of the long private driveway, the monolithic castle-like structure of the mansion itself, and the paintings hanging in the foyer, which, in retrospect, had probably not been reproductions of a Monet, a Rembrandt, and two separate Van Goghs, even though I'd thought one of them was currently hanging in a museum in London. Now, I wasn't so sure.

"So, no crazy uncle?" I asked.

She shook her head. "It's my money."

"Okay," I said. "Okay . . . okay." I held my hand back up and tapped the three remaining fingers one after another. "That just leaves crazy, crazier, and psychopath who plans to carve me up into strips and feed me to Mister Frumpyface over there."

"Farnsworth," she corrected.

"My mistake."

I tossed the cloth napkin down on the table and rose to my feet before turning to the cat who'd done with eating the lobster bisque and was now sitting with his chin in the bowl. "Mister Farnsworth," I said, bowing, "I thank you for your hospitality and bid you good evening and most excellent ball-licking."

I exited the dining room without a look back at Hannah and made it to the foyer before she caught up with me. Her hand squeezed my arm. I tried to guess whether she was going to turn out to be one of those freakishly strong psychopaths who not only murdered their victims but also made them die feeling insufficiently manly. In the meantime, I was now fairly convinced that both the Van Goghs were authentic.

"Greg, I know this is strange."

That was something, anyway.

Hannah pulled me around to face her. She was a half-head shorter than I was and on the curvy side, but she was also one of those every-weekend-marathoner types, and I was now pretty sure she was, in fact, stronger than me. "Greg, can you listen to me for a minute?"

I didn't feel as if I had a lot of choice. "Fine," I said, then felt I had to add—defiantly—"but after that, I'm out of here."

She let go of my arm and nodded before taking in a long, deep breath, which she then let out, after which she nodded again and then took in another longer, deeper breath.

Oh, God, I thought. *If she does that one more time, I'm just going to bash her with the Van Gogh and run out of this place as fast as I can.*

"All right," she said at last. "All right. All right."

I started reaching for the edge of the Van Gogh's frame.

"Greg, I'm about to tell you a story. It's going to explain everything—this house, why I asked you out—"

Yesterday she'd told me my online profile was cute, and she'd liked the way my hair flopped over my eyes when I laughed.

"—and yes," she went on. "I'm going to explain Mister Farnsworth to you. It's . . . it's not an easy story to believe, but it begins in Egypt three thousand years ago. I'm warning you right now there's a bit with an ancient curse, and I'm not entirely sure one of the people involved isn't an alien from Proxima Centauri. Anyway . . ." She grabbed my arm again. Apparently, I'd been trying to get out the door. "The thing is, after I've told you this story, I'm hoping you're going to help us with something very important."

"Us?"

"Me and Mister Farnsworth."

As if on cue, the cat waddled into the foyer with us and came over to stand with his front paws on my foot. "And what precisely do you and Mister Farnsworth need from an unemployed translator with a master's degree in ancient languages from a second-rate university nobody cares about?"

Hannah took both my hands in hers and locked eyes with me. "First, we need to fly to England and break into the British Museum, where you and I are going to build a time machine. Then, we're going to get Mister Farnsworth back to Egypt so that he can prevent a demonic conspiracy from making life on this planet a living hell for ten thousand years."

"Oh," I said, trying to process this new information. It appeared that, in addition to being killed and possibly eaten tonight, reports of my death would focus not so much on my insufficiently manly attempts to escape as on the amusingly preposterous trial that would follow. "Anything else?" I asked, to no one in particular.

There was a loud, awkward coughing sound, followed by Mister Farnsworth vomiting his lobster bisque onto my shoe.

CHAPTER 2: THE PLANE

Mister Farnsworth had a private plane. A Gulfstream G700, to be specific. High-thrust Roll-Royce engines, cruising speed of Mach 0.9, maximum range of 7,500 nautical miles. It came with all-leather interiors and five separate living areas, including two double beds. It had a flight crew of four, which included Mister Farnsworth's valet as well as his personal chef.

On the side of the jet's gleaming steel blue and silver exterior, painted in large orange letters, was its name: *The Litter Box.*

"Explain this to me again," I said, watching the chef prepare Mister Farnsworth's in-flight meal on a roll-out carving table in the main cabin. (Braised lamb with a raspberry fennel compote, in case you were wondering.)

Hannah had been moderately patient with me on the ride in Mister Farnsworth's limousine. ("It's not Mister Farnsworth's limousine, it's mine," she had reminded me several times. "Stop trying to make everything sound ridiculous.") Now, however, she was getting annoyed.

"Look, you've known me three weeks. Until tonight, did I give you any reason to question my sanity?"

She was wearing a fitted blue blazer and trousers that flattered her curves. Her blonde hair was tied back in a casual ponytail that did nothing to hide her elegance or the sense of self-confidence that oozes from that rarest of breeds: the actual self-made billionaire.

Hannah Parsons—that's right: her last name wasn't even Farnsworth—had built up a software company in college that allowed students and researchers to easily construct information trees that would then use machine learning, based on simple Google searches, to suggest new lines of inquiry. Basically, you fed it what you were researching, and it gave you new questions to consider. Doesn't sound like much, but it was one of the only artificial intelligence tools that actually stimulated the user's thinking rather than thinking for the user.

Microsoft, Apple, Oracle, and six other companies had spent nearly a year out-bidding each other to buy her out. On the night she signed the contract, she instantly went from owner of a scrappy start-up to the nineteenth richest woman in the United States.

Oh, and while she wasn't what people call model-thin, when she walked into a room, heads turned. Five minutes into a conversation, you were either in awe of her wit and brilliance or running out the door in search of what was left of your ego.

"Until I first met Mister Farnsworth's valet," I replied, "the only thing that struck me about you as crazy was that you asked me out on a date." I glanced over to where Mister Farnsworth was getting his pre-dinner belly massage on a custom-designed table that allowed his furry head to stick through a hole while the rest of him got kneaded into a tubby mass of purrs.

"So then, why can't you—"

"Which makes me wonder why exactly you wanted to date me."

She gave me a shy, almost insecure smile. On somebody who wasn't a genius billionaire flying in a private jet (though I don't care what she says—The Litter Box was definitely Mister Farnsworth's), it might've been believable.

"Ah, crap," I said, banging my head against the oval leather rim of the window and staring out over the Atlantic. "All that Ancient Egypt nonsense, right?"

She reached across to take my hand, which was quite a stretch given the football-field-inspired amounts of legroom the G700 offered. "I really do like you, Greg. I didn't lie about that part."

In retrospect, it was all painfully obvious. When she'd turned up at one of the seminars in my master's program, I hadn't known who she was. If that sounds hard to believe, try to name three female billionaires whose first names aren't Elizabeth and whose last names aren't The Second.

Okay, J.K. Rowling. I'll give you that one.

Anyway, I just thought she was a foreign student come to audit a class. When she struck up a conversation with me, I figured it was because there aren't that many people who specialize exclusively in the real-time translation of dead languages. Latin. Sumerian. Aramaic. And, yeah, Ancient Egyptian. There are lots of people who can translate more accurately than I can, but very few who can do it on the fly.

Why would anyone do a master's degree in live translation of dead languages when it's not exactly a thriving business? Well, two reasons. First, it's actually a pretty great degree to have if you want to go on to a Ph.D. in Ancient Civilizations, which was appealing to me. Second, two years ago, I applied and won a ridiculously well-funded scholarship that required you to take that exact degree. When I say well-funded, I'm talking all courses, rent, living expenses, and a $40,000 bonus payout on graduation.

A scholarship that generous would normally be so competitive as to exclude anyone who wasn't a prodigy of some kind. The thing is, most really smart people don't want to waste their graduate work learning how to translate Latin or Ancient Egyptian on the fly. It's what you'd call a highly specialized field.

Getting the picture yet?

"You set up the scholarship,' I said. "Through some shell company into a private charity and then to the university."

Hannah was still holding my hand. "We needed someone who could help us. You were the perfect candidate."

The perfect candidate.

"That explains why there was a rigorous physical exam as part of the scholarship application, doesn't it? And why the university gave me an entrance waiver despite finding out about my criminal record?"

Okay, I may have committed a bit of light art theft during my bachelor's degree. Mostly Iraqi artifacts stolen from the Baghdad Museum shortly after the start of Operation Iraqi Freedom and then imported into the States and sold to private collectors. It's a long story. Blame my parents.

Hannah was staring at me like she was both sympathetic to my sharp sense of having been manipulated for the past two years of my life while also getting tired of waiting for me to get to the punch line.

"Let me guess," I said, taking my hand away from her and leaning back into the leather-upholstered seat. "That $40,000 bonus payout comes with some strings attached."

Hannah nodded, then sheepishly added, "Also, if you'd read the fine print in the scholarship contract a tad more carefully, you'd have noticed the clauses regarding repayment should the foundation deem your academic performance unsatisfactory."

"My 'academic performance'? Are you . . . ?"

She reached into the pocket of her blazer and handed me a folded sheet of paper. "Technically, this trip counts as your field-work credits. If you don't pass, you don't graduate, which means the full sum of the scholarship becomes due."

"Oh, my God," I swore, throwing my hands up over my face in hopes that when I removed them, this would've all been a bad dream, and I'd wake up in a ditch after having gotten far too drunk and subsequently beaten half to death by a biker gang. "Is there any way in which I haven't gotten screwed tonight? I mean, aside from the obvious?"

Snuffling, snorting, chewing noises rose up from the other side of the cabin. Mister Farnsworth had apparently finished his massage and was now enjoying his meal. He paused briefly to burp, then vomited on the table.

"He does that a lot," I observed. "Is he all right?"

Hannah gazed over at him, her expression filled with an adoration I was quite convinced would never be directed at any mere mortal man. Then I saw tears forming at the corners of her eyes. "He's preparing, that's all. He knows what's coming."

"Which is what?" I asked. "I mean, other than violations of all the laws of physics, history, theology, and just about every other field of study you're suggesting we can throw out the window, what exactly are we doing?"

She dabbed a silk handkerchief to her eyes briefly, then stuffed it into the side of her seat. She unbuckled her seatbelt, got up, and opened an overhead bin. First, she took out a tan leather overcoat that looked like it was meant to fit a guy my height, only with the physique of a sumo wrestler. Next, she took out an equally large brown knit sweater. Last was something that at first looked like a leather bondage device meant to fit under the sweater, with what looked like a fake belly at the front, but which, on closer inspection, was a comfortably padded carrier whose size and proportions were suspiciously familiar to me at this point.

Mister Farnsworth wandered over and hopped up onto my lap, clawed me mercilessly for about five seconds, then promptly collapsed and started snoring.

"You can't be serious," I said, watching Hannah eyeing me as she adjusted the leather straps for the hidden carrier.

"The security guards at the British Museum will check any coats or bags we bring," she said, biting her lower lip as she examined the apparatus. "So, you'll need to sneak Mister Farnsworth inside with this."

Here's something I hadn't known about insane situations: even when they keep getting more insane, they still manage to somehow keep raising your level of tolerance for said insanity as you desperately try to find some logic in them.

"But why the British Museum?" I asked, determined to find something rational in all this lunacy. "Where are we even going?"

Hannah tilted her head as she stared at me through narrowed eyes, clearly wondering if I was thick. I wish she hadn't looked so fetching doing so. "To the Egyptian exhibit, silly. How else are we going to travel to the Fifth Dynasty of the Old Kingdom?"

CHAPTER 3: THE SECURITY LINE

Six hours later, I was strolling through the security checkpoint into the British Museum's Russel Street entrance with a tubby cat strapped to my stomach underneath a sweater and coat that made me look utterly preposterous, convinced I was about to get my abdomen carved into strips by Mister Farnsworth's claws while getting my ass handed to me by a bunch of British security guards.

"Have a nice visit, sir."

"Look, I don't go around commenting on your . . . wait, what?"

The guard looked down his nose at me. "Is something the matter, Mister . . .?" he snatched my passport out of my hand and glanced at the picture page once more. "Mister Hansford. Is something wrong?"

"No, I just—"

"You look as if you are not quite well, sir. Perhaps you'd like to come with one of my colleagues to discuss what's making you so anxious, so we can—"

Inside his silk-lined carrier under my coat and sweater, Mister Farnsworth farted loudly.

"Oh, God," the security guard said when he got his first whiff.

Mister Farnsworth fired off the second barrel.

All through the long line waiting to get through the security tents, prospective visitors and their children pinched their noses and groaned in complaint. The guard handed my passport back to me and waved me through. I smiled at him as I walked through the turnstile and through to the museum. "I feel much better now, thanks."

CHAPTER 4: THE EGYPTIAN EXHIBIT

If you've never been to the British Museum's Egyptian Exhibit, I highly recommend it. Massive stone statues rising fifteen feet high, gorgeously restored sarcophagi, clay pottery spanning thousands of years of history, and more treasures than you would've thought any decent nation would keep when they clearly belong to someone else.

I suggest planning a visit for when you'll have sufficient time to examine the artifacts at your leisure—as opposed to being dragged along by a mad billionaire while carting her cat under your coat.

"Over here," she told me, yanking me along behind her.

It's remarkably hard to resist someone when you're having to waddle about while desperately hoping the cat strapped to your stomach doesn't decide to shred your skin to ribbons.

Hannah stopped at last when we reached a twelve-feet-tall-by-thirteen-feet-wide limestone stela covered in Fifth Dynasty hieroglyphics. I'd never been to the British Museum before, so I hadn't seen it in person, but I knew instantly where we were.

"The architrave . . ." I breathed.

The facade and false door of the tomb of Ptahshepses, a high priest of the god Ptah, also called the Great One of the Leaders of Craftsmen. It wasn't an entire tomb, of course—just the front wall that had been preserved—or stolen, depending on your perspective—for posterity. Yet what was there was stunning in both its beauty and simplicity.

"It's a time machine," Hannah informed me.

"What?"

Hannah scrunched up her face. "Well, actually, it was supposed to be a portal into the realm of Anubis, which is what the offering inscription over the lintel is supposed to achieve. But what Ptahshepses was really onto was the precise geometry required to invoke a spell that used the power of Anubis to create a stable door back to the moment in time when the inscription was set."

"Sure," I said. "I can see why he'd want one of those."

"Look," she said, grabbing my arm. "If you translate the hiero-glyphics aloud, either nothing will happen, at which point I'll fly you home and give you your $40,000 bonus, and you never need to see me again—though chances are the world will end pretty soon, so we may as well go on a couple more dates before it's over —or else we'll be travelling back to 2500 BC right before the demons—they might be aliens—set off the chain reaction that's going to destroy the earth in our time."

I stared at her for a while. "How did you manage to say all that without taking a breath?"

"I was a competitive swimmer in college. I've got great lungs."

"You sure do," came out of my mouth before I could stop myself.

She grinned and poked me in the chest. "Business first, Tiger."

I turned to examine the inscription. When people refer to Egyptian hieroglyphics as if they're all one language, it's kind of like somebody talking about the English that people spoke in the twelfth century as if it were the same language we speak today. You wouldn't understand a word someone from that time was saying because language evolves. However, it turned out that Fifth Dynasty Egyptian was a required course of study to maintain my scholarship.

"I don't get it," I said. "You're saying if I read the inscription to Anubis aloud, this thing will suddenly become a time machine? Surely over the history of this exhibit, tons of scholars and tour guides have done so without disappearing from our time."

Hannah shook her head. "It has to be read with the right inflections, as if one were a native speaker. It's the particular sounds that will activate the false door, not just the words."

Right, I thought. *Eminently logical. All makes perfect sense now.*

I started reading the hieroglyphs aloud. Hannah put a hand on my arm. "What are you doing?"

"You told me to read out the inscription."

"Not with Mister Farnsworth strapped to your stomach. He's the key. You need to hold him up as you utter the offering formula. Also, you need to say it really loudly and make sure to speak each word right at the relevant hieroglyph. You basically have to shout the syllables into the symbols."

I glanced around at the crowds of visitors who were trying to take photographs of the tomb wall and getting annoyed that we were standing in their way.

"You said if this didn't work, you'd fly me home, and we'd be done with this," I whispered furiously. "If I go yanking a cat out of my coat and start shouting at the wall, the guards are going to arrest us for sure."

Hannah rose up on the toes of her black oxford shoes and kissed me on the cheek. "Better hope it works, then, right?"

CHAPTER 5: THE INSCRIPTION

All Egyptian offering formulas, or "incipits" as they're sometimes called, follow the same basic structure. The variety comes in depending on which deities and offerings are mentioned, along with the specific epithets and titles.

I say all this because it makes what I did next sound vaguely less nuts.

With Mister Farnsworth held up high between my two hands, I stood in front of the architrave of the tomb of a 3,500-year-old dead guy named Ptahshepses and shouted: "Anubis, he who is in front of his divine booth, he who is on his mountain!"

"Mummy, what is that strange man doing to that cat?" asked a small child behind us.

"He who gives invocation brings offerings of bread, beer, oxen, birds, alabaster, clothing, and every good and pure thing upon which a god lives," I yelled.

"Oy, sir, step away from the tomb and hand over that poor cat!" ordered a guard, running up behind me.

I was, by my best estimation, roughly six seconds from being tackled to the floor. On the other hand, offering formulas on Egyptian tombs are wonderful examples of literary brevity, which meant I had more than enough time to finish shouting the final words at the appropriate hieroglyphs.

Alas, as I came to the end of the invocation, nothing happened.

"Oh, crap," I murmured, turning to face my imminent arrest. "I think there was a second there when I started believing this nonsense."

Three security guards in blue British Museum uniforms arrayed themselves around me. A young woman held out her hands for the cat. I was about to hand him over, reasoning that Mister Farnsworth no doubt had a very fine English barrister waiting to get him out of jail, whereas I was going to be throwing myself at the mercy of the court.

"Time to go," Hannah said and yanked on the back of my massive trench coat.

I spun around in time to have her shove me at the tomb's false door—which is actually a big slab of rock. I put my hands up to protect my nose from an unpleasant collision with the wall, but my hands somehow missed it entirely.

So did my nose, my face, and my entire body.

I fell right inside the tomb, which was odd since it was supposed to be a false door and even more unusual given the only part of the tomb in the British Museum is the outer wall.

"Where the hell—"

Hannah appeared next to me, and the two of us got back to our feet. Mister Farnsworth, whom I'd managed—though I promise not intentionally—to keep from getting mashed onto the stone floor, leaped out of my hands and ran deeper into the tomb.

"Quick!" Hannah said, chasing after him. "The final battle for humanity's future is about to begin!"

When I looked out back through the entrance that shouldn't have existed, I saw the security guards and the crowds behind them staring in befuddlement. Whatever wondrous discovery Hannah had made, we were still in the British Museum in the present.

Guess there are degrees of impossibility, I thought, following Hannah into the tomb. *And we might've hit our limit.*

I couldn't see anything except for the light from the phone Hannah held up in front of her. We passed through corridors and winding chambers filled with shadows. I didn't see cobwebs or bones anywhere, however. The whole place was much cleaner than you'd expect a 3,500-year-old tomb to be. The place was smaller than the sorts of temples found in the movies, too, and soon we found ourselves at what my reasonably good sense of direction told me must've been the actual exit of the tomb. Hannah stepped through first, and I followed, expecting to find myself on the other side of the British Museum's Egyptian room.

The first thing that hit me was the heat.

Then I saw the sand all around us, the tall palm trees, and hundreds of screaming people. They weren't the pasty English families and foreign tourists I'd seen inside the museum but were instead men and women in belted linen kilts and sheath dresses fleeing for their lives.

That's when I saw the demons.

Or aliens.

It can be hard to tell sometimes.

CHAPTER 6: THE INVADERS

They weren't especially tall—maybe five-foot-six on average. Their skin was a dark blue, the colour of lapis lazuli, and though they walked on two legs, they had four arms, making them look almost like the Indian goddess Kali—except for the silver and gold pharaonic headdresses.

And the horns, of course.

You've got to give it to the Fifth Dynasty Egyptians: they weren't cowards. Groups of men and women with Nubian colouring and features, bare-skinned save for their lightweight linen garb, fought relentlessly against the invaders with bronze swords, spears, and sometimes just rocks or their bare hands. The demons—possibly culturally appropriating aliens?—flung tiny spools of black thread from their hands. The spools spun faster and faster as they hurled through the air, unwinding to become massive nets whose strands were no thicker than a spider's thread and yet, as soon as they struck the Egyptians, they wrapped around them, strand by strand, leaving only a mummified body whose screams were muffled and whose eyes were wide with terror.

"We can't let these people get massacred!" I shouted at Hannah, scrabbling around on the ground in search of a rock or stick, with no clue whatsoever what I was going to do with it. "We've got to do something!"

I looked up to see her reaching into her blazer pocket. When her hand came out again, it was holding a black-handled pistol, which she raised up to the height of her shoulder while bending her elbow outward. Resting her right wrist on her left forearm, she closed one eye, took aim, and shot one of the blue-skinned invaders in the head.

"What do you know?" I mumbled, watching as it fell to the sandy ground. "Even their brains are blue."

The creatures turned, opening their jaws wide in what I assumed was outrage. The sound that came out was like the wind whistling through a canyon.

"What the hell are they doing here?" I asked.

Hannah took aim at her next target. "People always assume aliens and demons would be more powerful than human beings regardless of when they found us, but it's not true." She squeezed the trigger, and a second alien went down. "These ones are dangerous in this time but would've gotten their arses kicked by a few infantrymen with muskets."

"Did you happen to bring a gun for me?"

She shot me a scathing glance. "You think it's easy sneaking even *one* firearm into the British Museum?"

It occurred to me then that I hadn't seen where Mister Farnsworth had gone. Possibly he was in search of a good butler.

The creatures started to converge in our direction, and I saw one of them preparing to throw one of their spools of black thread at us.

"Quick," Hannah said. "The coat!"

I slipped the trench coat off my shoulders, grabbed the collar, and whipped it out at the incoming spool. When the thread touched the vinyl material, it started to mummify, only to then explode into a shower of black dust.

"Only works on human skin," Hannah explained, firing off a shot at the invader who'd tossed the spool at us.

I supposed that meant any camels wandering around were safe, at any rate.

There were at least nine or ten more of the blue-skinned monstrosities coming toward us now. It didn't require any tactical wizardry to figure out we weren't going to last more than a few seconds.

"There!" I said, spotting a pair of three-foot-wide columns outside the temple. "We need cover!"

The two of us scrambled to get behind the columns. Hannah reached her gun hand around and fired off several more shots. Most of these missed, but they did give the attackers pause. Some of the Egyptians took advantage to press their own attack and scored a few good cuts with their swords, but the alien—or demonic—hides were too tough for bronze weapons.

"Let's go," Hannah said, abandoning the relative safety of the column to take off at a run around to the other side of the tomb's exterior. "We can't leave Mister Farnsworth to do the hard part alone."

As we raced along the path, our heels slipping on the loose sand, I began to hear a new sound coming from the direction we were headed: a kind of buzzing that could've been mistaken for ten thousand wasps in a truly unpleasant mood. The noise was chilling. It seemed to get into your ears and rattle around the inside of your skull.

"Awful, isn't it?" Hannah asked, though she didn't slow her pace any. "Believe it or not, that's their version of chanting."

"But what are they doing?"

We rounded the corner of the tomb and were now looking at the false door that was part of the architrave we'd entered back in the British Museum. Ahead of us were three more of the alien demonic beings, but these ones had glistening black skin instead of blue. They looked as if they'd been drenched in some kind of oil that coated their entire bodies. Their headdresses gleamed with what could've been sapphires or blue diamonds, and the tips of their fingers glowed with an unnatural light as they drew sigils in the air at the back of the tomb.

"They're making a bomb," Hannah explained.

"A bomb?"

She raised her pistol, took aim at the figure in the centre, and fired. The bullet stopped three inches from its head, hung in the air for a moment, still spinning, and then dropped to the sand.

"Damn it." She popped out the cartridge and slid a second one from her coat inside. "We're going to have to do this hand-to-hand."

"What? Look, none of what you're saying makes any—"

Hannah spun on me, grabbing hold of my arms. The barrel of the gun in her right hand was hot against the wool of my oversized sweater. "Listen to me, Gregory Hansford, and listen good. Those three beings are creating a . . . oh, bother. Think of it as a spell, if that helps."

"It really doesn't."

"It's a kind of time bomb that needs thirty-five hundred years to accumulate the power to destroy humanity's future. The architrave was meant to be a portal into the realm of Anubis, but what they're doing is transforming it into a gate into their own realm.

Shortly after the moment you, Mister Farnsworth, and I entered the museum, the door is going to open again."

I pointed to the oily creatures whose hideous buzzing chants and strange inscriptions in the air were making me both nauseous and terrified. "So an army of them pours out?"

Hannah shook her head. "No, air."

"Air?"

She jerked a thumb at them. "*Their* air. From their realm. It'll poison Earth's atmosphere faster than a thousand erupting Chernobyls. A few humans will survive for a while in various bunkers around the world, but they'll be easy pickings once the invaders come through by the millions."

"So what do we do?"

"I don't know."

I stared at her, aghast. "What do you mean, you 'don't know'?"

"I . . . everything I know comes from clues left for me by my father. I pieced it all together over the years as best I could. Like you, I thought this was all nuts, but every time I decided I should walk away, I'd uncover something that convinced me I was on the right track."

"And Mister Farnsworth?" I asked.

"He's the key. All of my father's writings suggest the invaders have a vulnerability to particular mixtures of airborne particles. That's one of the things that made it hard for them to set in motion their plan here in Egypt—on account of all the—"

"Cats," I interjected. "You're saying they're allergic to cat dander?"

She nodded. "But this lot form a sort of . . . special forces team. They're mostly immune. That's why we needed to bring a cat who possessed the exact right genetic combination."

"Oh, God," I said, remembering how she'd introduced me to

Mister Farnsworth when I'd arrived at her house for our "date" last night. 'One-quarter Burmese, one-quarter Egyptian Mau, one-eighth Siamese, one-eighth American Bobtail, and one-quarter Turkish Angora."

"Exactly. If my father's projections were correct, Mister Farnsworth is the only being on Earth in this time who can stop the invasion of our planet thirty-five hundred years before it begins."

I looked around, searching for the cat, seeing nothing but the black-skinned beings continuing their strange spell. "But where is he? How are we supposed to get these guys?"

Hannah pointed to the top of the lintel above the entrance to the tomb. There, licking himself and periodically shaking his fur while looking utterly disinterested in the gradual destruction of his own planet, sat Mister Farnsworth.

The three alien chanters paused for a moment in the drawing of their gleaming sigils in the air. One of them made a kind of hooting noise.

"What was that?" I asked.

Hanna grinned. "*That*, I believe, was a sneeze. Any minute now, the invaders are going to get sick and die."

But one of them spotted Mister Farnsworth, and the other two tapped the thumbs and forefingers of their many hands together in quick succession. I saw the air above them shimmer, creating an opening between them and the cat while still keeping the barrier that protected them from Hannah's bullets. The leader reached into his headdress and pulled out what looked like a small scorpion. He placed it on the palm of his hand, and looked like he was about to blow on it.

"Oh, no," Hannah said, firing off shots futilely that stopped the instant they hit the barrier. "They're going to kill Mister

Farnsworth before he can stop them!"

It's a funny thing when heroism strikes you. One second you're standing there in Ancient Egypt thinking that everything is bonkers and none of this makes sense, and even though you're seeing it all with your own eyes, it must be a hallucination, and even if it's not, it's certainly not your responsibility. Then all of a sudden, you're running across the sand, whirling your ridiculously large knit sweater in the air with no real idea what you're going to do with it, shouting at the top of your lungs, "The first of you lousy bastards tries to touch that cat is going to answer to me!"

Yeah. That *really* scared them.

CHAPTER 7: THE LAST STAND OF MISTER FARNSWORTH

I hadn't noticed before, but the alien demons—I'd settled on the notion that they were both rather than having to pick one—didn't have proper eyes. They had eye *sockets*, but I couldn't see anything resembling an eyeball inside. Instead, there was a sort of shadowy haze that seemed to ooze smoke when they got pissed off.

They seemed *really* pissed off at me.

The ones not holding the tiny scorpion creature threw thread spools over the invisible barrier at me. I flung my oversized sweater overtop one of the spools and caught it, but the other attached itself to my arm. I dropped the sweater and tore off my shirt just in time to keep the spinning threads from mummifying me. I picked up the sweater again, it being my only weapon at this point, and resumed my run for them.

The leader of the three was getting ready to throw the now-living scorpion at Mister Farnsworth, who had finally found something worthy of his attention. He hissed, so loud he drowned out the buzzing noise of the chanters. His hackles were up, and even I could tell he was terrified.

"I'm coming!" I said and raced the last dozen feet, Hannah close behind.

"Don't let that scorpion get to Mister Farnsworth!" she yelled.

The lintel was twelve feet above the ground. The barrier between us and the aliens was invisible, but I guessed would be the same height since otherwise, they wouldn't be able to hit Mister Farnsworth with the scorpion. As I got close, I leaped up off my left foot and then dug the side of my right shoe into one of the ridges of the limestone wall. I got just enough purchase to push off again and get up high enough to throw myself over the barrier as I held open the oversized sweater with both hands beneath me. I came down hard and heavy on the three invaders, using the knit sweater as a sort of net and trying to bind up their limbs.

Okay, I thought as I rolled on the ground in a mess of arms and legs, all trying to find the most efficient way to kill me. *That was rather brave of me, all things considered.*

In this case, the things worth considering were that I was probably ten seconds from a horrible death. Also, I'd lost track of the damned scorpion, which was probably now scurrying on the ground, waiting to stab its no-doubt lethal stinger into my flesh.

I heard a hideous screech and then felt sharp claws on my back, which dug in for only an instant before leaping off me. Mister Farnsworth had used me as a trampoline to get to one of the alien demons.

The creature made a sound like the air leaking out of a balloon. The smoke from its eye sockets went from pitch black to a kind of sickly grey, and its limbs spasmed even as they seemed to shrink, desiccating before me.

Now, I couldn't claim any expertise in demonic xenobiology, but I was fairly certain it was dying.

"Greg, look out!"

Hannah was outside the barrier, pounding against what looked like thin air, except it stopped her fist cold each time she touched it. At first, I assumed she was looking out for me, but what she'd clearly meant was, "Greg, you're a largely irrelevant person, here to provide a body to get in the way of a deadly alien scorpion before it can sting Mister Farnsworth, and you're doing a poor job of it."

The scorpion had, indeed, found its target and was skittering on the ground toward the cat, who was running around in circles inside the enclosed space within the barrier, trying to escape. He tried leaping up, but his paws struck the barrier, and he fell down again. One of the two remaining demon creatures tried to grab his tail.

"Oh, no, you don't!"

I scrambled over the invader and smashed my fist against the hand trying to take Mister Farnsworth. The being made what I hoped was a cry of pain even as he elbowed me in the face, collarbone, and stomach. There are, apparently, numerous advantages to having four arms.

The air went out of my lungs, but as I rolled back, I kicked out with my right foot and caught my newfound nemesis in the back of the head. Mister Farnsworth took advantage of the alien demon's disorientation to land on his back and scratch the bejesus out of his oily black flesh. Again I heard that sound like air leaking from a balloon, and the creature died.

The problem was that left the third, who was now ready for me, and I'd lost track of the damned scorpion again.

"Greg, here!" Hannah shouted.

I glanced back to see her tossing the gun into the air in a shallow arc that brought it back down inside the barrier. I tried to snatch it out of the air, but my opponent—those damnable four limbs again—got to it before me. His lips puckered as he made a sound like *phwip-phwip-phwip*, which I guess was their species' version of an evil laugh.

Pausing for an evil laugh is never a good idea. I drove my fist into the crook of his elbow, folding the arm holding the gun. I grabbed the barrel, twisted it toward him, and with my other hand, grabbed the trigger and pulled.

The bullet caught him dead centre in his broad chest. The initial bang was followed by an odd cracking sound, like a tree slowly coming down after being felled by an axe. The creature sagged against me, his hand going limp.

I ripped the gun away from him, shoved his slumping corpse off me, then took aim at the scorpion skittering on the ground and fired.

You wouldn't think a first-time marksman would make a lucky shot like that, but I guess in every life, a piece of good fortune has to come at least once.

The scorpion broke apart into a hundred little shards, leaving only reddish-green goo in the sand where I'd shot it. Someone barrelled into me, and I turned to fire at the attacker, only to realize the barrier had come down and Hannah had fallen inside with me.

She grabbed me in a hug so tight I could barely breathe.

"We did it! Greg, we did it!"

"What about the other creatures? The ones fighting with the Egyptians?"

But when we ran back around to the other side of the tomb, the blue-skinned creatures were dead.

"They've no immunity to Mister Farnsworth's dander," Hannah said. "Even outside, once enough of it got in the air, they were done for."

About three dozen Egyptians in their linen garments, many of them bloody and barely able to stand, others using bronze and bone blades to free their mummifying fellows, stared up at us.

"Friends," I said in their language.

I could've said more. Hell, I could've recited Shakespeare's Saint Crispin's Day speech from *Henry V*, but I figured my accent was probably going to be a little off.

A woman in a wrap linen dress, blood dripping from her shoulder, pointed to the dead aliens. "More?"

"I do not know," I replied. "We are strangers here."

She said something else, and it took a couple of repetitions before I understood she'd asked, "How do we fight them if more come?"

The answer came in the form of a tubby cat of very particular genetic heritage as he sauntered around from the back of the temple and walked up to us. I remembered then when Hannah had looked at him on the plane with that strange mixture of adoration and sadness. I guess she'd worked out this part, too.

I knelt down and picked him up, then brought him over to the Egyptian woman. Alas, my knowledge of her language failed me a bit when the closest I could get to proper instructions was, "He will need to have much sex."

Here's a fun fact you only learn if you travel back thirty-five hundred years in time to the past: Ancient Egyptians also arch one eyebrow when they're dubious about something.

I pointed to the cat, pretended to sneeze, then pointed to the dead blue-skinned alien demon beings.

I guess Ancient Egyptians also had a passing understanding of cat allergies because her eyes widened and she nodded to me, then spoke to the others, explaining far more eloquently than I ever could that Mister Farnsworth, now known as "Mafdet the Demon Slayer," was to receive excellent care and mate with a great many females.

Hannah came up to stand with me. She reached out both hands to scratch under Mister Farnsworth's cheeks. "It's been an honour," she said, bringing her face close to his.

The cat purred in response and snuffled his nose against hers.

"Shut up," I said to the Egyptians who were smirking at me as the woman in charge gently took Mister Farnsworth from us. "I'm not crying. I'm just allergic to cats, that's all."

CHAPTER 8: HOMECOMING

The flight back was a sombre affair, even on a Gulfstream G700. Mister Farnsworth's personal valet and chef cried when we informed them their favourite cat—and employer—was staying abroad for a while.

Hannah was sad, too, and leaned against me as we sat on one of the jet's couches, staring out the portholes at the dark skies over the Atlantic. When she wasn't crying herself, she told me little stories about Mister Farnsworth—his habits and odd rituals. He was, she insisted, possessed of an excellent sense of humour, and filled with a zest for life that I confess I hadn't noticed in all his lounging around and puking up lobster bisque. I guess, like many world-saving heroes, he got a little nervous before a mission.

After we landed back in the States, Hannah asked where I'd like to be dropped off. Since she already knew where I lived, I took the question to mean something else and held her hand in the back of the limousine and said, "Home."

She kissed me then, on the lips this time, and I decided that was a perfectly valid reason to forgive someone for having tricked you into the world's most useless master's degree—barring the need to invoke any other Ancient Egyptian spells, of course—and dragging you off to Ancient Egypt to fight alien demons so that the world can be saved by cat dander.

I will note, however, that if you go visit the architrave of the tomb of Ptahshepses in the British Museum, there, among the many hieroglyphics of cats on the lintel, you may notice one that looks just a bit ... tubbier than the others.

Mister Farnsworth no longer had a valet, but I suspect he produced an awful lot of offspring. So if you're ever wondering why the earth isn't a gaping hellhole filled with demons, you know who to thank.

HOW TO CREATE LANGUAGE FOR A NEW-MADE WORLD

By Jane Yolen

Say what the light sounds like,
listen to the roiling sea,
check the pulse of morning
as it rises, yawns, shakes itself free
of what might be dew.
Hear what the great leviathan
calls out from its bathing,
what the brown bodies who dig
sing when they work the dark soil.
All those sounds make a language,
you just have to put them down
in a tidy dictionary, then append meaning.
The speakers will do the rest.

TOGETHER AS ONE

By Jess E. Owen

A TALE OF THE SILVER ISLES

A dozen gryfess huntresses dived at the mackerel shoal, a shimmering serpent of movement made by ten thousand shining fish twisting together away from the shadows of their wings.

Ivar split from flying close to his wingbrother, Kral, to flank the huntresses, watching sharp-eyed from above for any movement.

"Not so far out, brother!" Kral called.

Ivar laughed. "Never you fear!" he shouted back. "I know what I'm doing."

Other males, tasked with watching over the huntresses, likewise circled and kept an eye on the sea. Gryfons were not the only predators drawn to the great migrations of fish in the spring.

The huntresses didn't dive into the chaotic swirl of fish but swooped over the water with the graceful ease of practice, scooping just under the surface with their hooked talons. Vanir lived and died by the sea, reliant on her cooperation and her bounty, wary of her predators and her moods. Today was a good day for fishing, with a soft spring wind to lift their wings and low clouds to keep the shadows dull, but no hint yet of rain.

Ivar watched in admiration as the gryfess he had spent the better part of that year courting sliced her talons through water and came up with a mackerel snared on each deadly foot, then pumped her narrow wings to lift up and away. Salva was made like a daughter of the goddess Tor herself, her lioness hindquarters pale grey, her wings and face midnight dark, with eyes of skyfire gold. Ivar himself was no warrior to dismiss, of course—they would make a handsome pair.

He was tall and strong and iron-grey, the colour of a storm, with a dusting of silver speckles on his wings and face as if a few stars had blown down on him one winter's night. Salva had hinted she would accept him if he asked her to fly with him at the next Daynight pledge.

"Well caught," he bellowed, his deep voice rolling across the water even amid the splash of fish and waves.

Salva flicked her tail in acknowledgement. "Perhaps you should focus on your task," she teased, looking meaningfully at Kral and the others before banking toward the nesting cliffs to bear her burden home.

Ivar glanced skyward and shook his head. "So much helpful instruction from all," he said, loud enough for the others to hear.

"Eyes down, brother," Kral called. His wingbrother was smaller than Ivar, wiry and hard and the pale reddish brown of a fox. "Something's spooking the—"

A huntress's warning shout cut him off. Ivar turned sharply in the air, staring down as the whorl of fish burst open and scattered in a hundred directions.

Beneath the surface gaped a maw lined with jagged teeth, the stark white and black swaths on the massive body rendering the creature unmistakable. Fish swarmed away in a panic as the great jaws gnashed closed—but swam themselves right into a wall of six other monsters.

"*Sea wolves*," shouted another male.

"Away!" barked the leading huntress. "'Ware the blackfish, get up, away!"

A flurry of curses and wings slapping water followed her order, huntresses dropping fish to lighten their burdens and rise faster. Ivar's gaze darted across the foam and churning seawater.

A great, chattering blackfish broke from the surface, expelling a gust of air and droplets from the single nostril on its back, jaws wide. Ivar, whipping around to stare, saw that the creature wasn't just breaching for air but hunting. A gryfess beat the air as the jaws snapped a feather's width from her tail and flung one of her fish at the beast's eye.

Another huntress shrieked in alarm. "Salva!"

Chanting voices, ghostly and high-pitched, floated in a rocking cadence through the water.

"Together, together in wind and in water,
Whether fish on a fin or bird on a feather,
Always together, we've won."

"Salva, fly!" Ivar looked around wildly for the source of the singing. Salva carried on stubbornly with her fish, dragged down by their weight. Movement rippling under the water drew Ivar's eye—two more blackfish, speeding toward their podmate. Faintly, humming from the water, Ivar heard them.

Singing.

"We win, we win only together,
Only together as one."

On the last whistling line of the song, they lunged from the water, causing a wave that washed over the gryfess and dragged her screaming into the water.

"Salva!" Ivar shrieked and barreled through the air toward her.

"Ivar! Wait for us! Don't go alone!" Kral yelled, his voice all but lost in the cries of the other males and the gryfess huntresses. "One gryfon cannot—"

But he had to go alone. He would show Salva he could protect her with his own talons and no one else.

Saltwater, bubbles, and the violent mashing of fish bodies became Ivar's world as he dived straight into the water after Salva. The pale flash of her tail drew his eye—but a smooth, blunt snout rammed him from the side. The wind burst from his chest as a chittering, monstrous laugh filled his ears.

"Play, play, fishy bird!"
"Catbird, wingcat, come and play!"

Their squeals and clicks and chatter blurred into meaningless-ness as the sea wolf thrust from the water—giving Ivar the chance to suck a breath—before plunging right back down and diving. Vertigo and dizziness turned his world, and the deep sea seemed to be a night sky full of stars . . . fish . . . blackfish.

Eyes up! He could all but hear his father grinding in lessons, teaching him to fight. *When in doubt, kick and claw.*

Ivar lashed out with a clawed hind paw, shoved his wings through the swirling saltwater, snapped his beak, and punched his talons blindly at his foe. He tasted blood in the saltwater. Hopefully, not his. The sea wolf veered away from him with a deafening series of creaking noises. Ivar jerked around, peering blearily through the water. He made the mistake of gasping for breath, and salt fire washed his chest, blinding him with streaks of pain and bewilderment.

Talons hooked his wings, and he fought for half a moment before he was yanked about and saw Kral's angry face. His wing-brother hauled him to the surface. The blackfish had drawn off toward the school of fleeing mackerel, and Ivar shouted as their retreating fins sliced the water.

"That's right, you cowards, go seek a meal! Come back stronger and see what the son of Eir can do!" As his mind cleared, he looked at Kral, appalled. "Salva—"

"She'll live, but we nearly lost others because we had to dive for *both* of you. You thrice-cursed—"

"I will kill them," Ivar vowed, clawing forward, straining his wings until he lunged free. Kral followed, water raining from their wings.

"You'll get soaked and tossed again, by Tor's left foot," Kral said, "if you do not learn to think beyond the point of your own beak."

"Brother," Ivar began, quick regret darting through him. "I was only—"

"Get to the healer," Kral said shortly. "To be sure your foolishness hasn't cost you more than a few broken tail feathers."

———————

"THESE SEA-WOLF RAIDS grow more and more hostile." King Larus was a lean, hard, scarred gryfon so pale of feather he sometimes seemed like a smoke apparition. He stood atop the tumbled slabs of stone that crowned a jutting point of the nesting cliffs, the sacred meeting place of the Vanir pride. The stacked rocks overlooked the ocean and the grassy peat plain that rolled inward toward a birch forest, the river, and the distant White Mountains. The evening's last light shone on the king and queen and the few huntresses and warriors they had called to meet.

"They hunt us much as they hunt fish," agreed the queen, a sleek huntress of mottled, sandy brown. "Either they truly do not understand our claim, or they mean to make these waters their own before summer."

"They understand," Ivar muttered. Kral nudged him with a wing.

"They are like fledges," Salva said, stretched on her belly on Ivar's other side, favouring her sprained wing. "Cruel in their ignorance, uncaring. We mustn't make war over a difference in . . ." she trailed off, looking to the queen, who nodded soberly.

The other huntresses murmured agreement; the sea was the rightful home of the blackfish and all who swam.

But it was also rightfully the hunting grounds of the Vanir, children of bright Tyr and Tor, and the blackfish were known for unnecessary cruelty.

"It isn't as if there's no room to share," Ivar snapped.

Kral hung his head as the king and queen looked to him solemnly.

Ivar stood. "No one is proposing *war,* but we must protect our own right to feed our families. The sea wolves will happily swim over us right to the beaches if we let them. What if it is a gryfon fledge they choose to hunt instead of fish or seal?"

"On this, we agree," murmured the king. "Bold Ivar, what solutions do you propose?"

Ivar lifted his beak as the royal pair and the huntresses and warriors watched him. "We must make a show of defence, my king, my queen. We must drive them out and show we are not to be meddled with."

"We?" the queen asked, amused.

Heat flashed under Ivar's feathers. He had a tendency to act alone, and not a single gryfon in the pride was unaware of it. "Yes. A force of us, enough to show them we are strong and unafraid."

"I'm afraid," Kral said wryly, and the others chuckled, stretching their wings and shaking their heads.

"I suppose you'll be leading us?" one of the younger warriors asked.

"Why not me?" Ivar demanded, tail lashing once.

"You are brash," said another warrior.

Then, a huntress added, "I would not trust Ivar to hold to a plan. He would hurtle himself into the fray alone if he saw an opportunity for glory, leaving us at odd ends."

Ivar ground his beak, but the queen spoke again before he could, watching him with cool yellow eyes. "They speak truthfully, Ivar, and you know this."

"I have as much experience diving and hunting the water as any here," Ivar said. "I will not be left in my nest like a fledge while the rest—"

"You dived into the water alone," the queen continued. "Surrounded by deadly hunters. And this is not unlike you. Always, we see you act before thinking, acting alone, sure of yourself and chasing your own glory. Do you think you *can* work with others for this purpose?"

Ivar stood, looking quickly to Kral, who averted his gaze, then Salva, who nodded once, frankly. "I will, my lady." He bowed low and mantled, fanning his wings in deference. "I already have a plan—"

"Tell it to Kral," said the king, and Ivar looked up in surprise, as did Kral. The king's eyes gleamed with the same mischievous wisdom as a raven. "*He* will be leading the force."

————————————

LATER UNDER THE STARS, on the beach, Ivar paced before Salva, who dragged her talons idly through the sand. "Kral, indeed," he muttered. "The king did it on purpose to vex me."

"He did it on purpose to challenge you," Salva said, watching him. "And, honestly, Kral will be good. The others will listen to him." The moon, rising over the water, shone silver on her face, and the waves murmured and bubbled through the rocks and gravel sand.

Ivar rustled his feathers, irritated. "As if I'm a bumbling fledge—"

"Show me you can do this," Salva said quietly, tail whisking the damp sand.

Ivar halted his pacing and looked at her. She watched him, feathered ears perked, her expression stern. "I will," he vowed. "I will drive these chittering fish a hundred leagues for you."

"I know you will." She stood. "But that's not what I mean." She approached, and her familiar warm scent made Ivar want to offer more bold promises, offer her everything he was and would ever be. "I ask that you show me you can also hold back. And listen. And work with your wingbrother and the others as well as you work and fight alone."

Ivar ducked his head, glancing toward the black-and-silver waves. "You would have me meek."

"I would have you just as you are," she murmured, "but willing to fold your strength into the pride like the feathers of a single wing, to work with others as one. In three moons, you and I will fly and pledge, and Tor willing, we will raise kits as stubborn and strong as you are . . . *together*."

Ivar lifted his head, watching her quietly. His pride thrashed and wailed at the thought that she didn't trust him to do the best thing. He would never lead their future family astray, and he would protect her, always. "I will . . . try, Salva."

Her ears twitched back, and her expression cooled. "I hope that you succeed."

She took the narrow foot trail of the bronzy-black cliffs, leaving Ivar there with salt wind in his feathers and the whole moon on his back.

THE LAST TIME Ivar had flown so far out across the sea he'd lost sight of the Silver Isles was the eve of his initiation as a warrior. He'd done it to prove to himself he could bear being completely alone, reliant on himself, to know what it felt like to lose sight of home and all he held dear and to remind himself why he wanted to be a warrior.

It was one of the first experiences to ever rattle his courage, and he had not, even at that young age, lived quietly in his den under his mother's wing.

Surrounded now by a whole host of seasoned warriors and huntresses, soaring over a cold grey sea, that same edginess tightened his muscles. A glance back over his wing showed only the vast expanse of water, the stone-grey clouds looming above.

"All well, brother?" Kral inquired from up ahead of him. Perhaps he could smell Ivar's tension.

"All well," he said shortly, and held the image of the king and queen in his mind, then Salva and all their hopes. *Show me you can do this.*

For over a fortnight, Kral and others had taken the agonizing, tedious time to track the blackfish pod that harried their waters while Ivar ground his beak impatiently and wore down the sand with pacing, waiting. He had told Kral of the song the blackfish sang, and Kral had laughed and said perhaps they should adopt it as their own. His wingbrother had an easier heart; it was why they matched so well—Kral to slow him down, Ivar to tip Kral off the cliff when a hastier decision was warranted.

At last, when Kral and the huntresses were satisfied with their knowledge and the pod's movements, they set out to make a show of strength on the far windward border of the Vanir's fishing grounds. Instead of waiting to lose another valuable catch, they would warn the sea wolves away preemptively and hope the message was clear.

The plan relied on every single gryfon holding the course Kral had set, each to his own part. *One talon out of place,* his wingbrother had warned, looking too long at Ivar, *and we will fail.*

Ivar curled his talons tight to his chest, flexing his wings against the chilly salt wind, holding stiff to glide. Light rain spat at them, but a silver glow behind the clouds promised a warmer afternoon.

He scanned the water, but naturally, it was a huntress who spied the sea wolves first and raised a cry.

"Mobs form up," Kral called, his voice strong but as serene as if they all flew together over the woods of the Sun Isle. They had taken inspiration from crows mobbing eagles who drew too near their nests as well as the blackfish themselves, forming groups to increase their strength. Their large formation broke neatly, drifting against the winds to make smaller wedges of five, three male warriors like the tip of a talon and two huntresses within.

His own wingbrother had not even honoured Ivar with leading one of the formations. He flew third in the wedge, behind their grizzled training master, Berk, and across from a new initiate named Tyrsha, who still had the fluff of fledging behind one ear. More challenges to his pride, he supposed.

Third spot is a vital position, and I trust you to it, Kral had said. *Show me you can do this.*

Ivar shook his head and wondered if Kral and Salva had conspired to say the same thing in almost the same way.

"Choose your targets," Kral boomed.

The others gave ringing cries of confirmation. Ivar had to admit Kral did well in his role, with the calm steadiness of stone standing against the river.

One of the sea wolves breached far below, and Ivar's heart kicked to a battle speed. Then another, with a chittering laugh. Mocking them. Inviting them to *play.*

"All right, you mudding, smiling, overgrown fish," he growled. "Let's play."

Tyrsha, flying across from him, laughed, then echoed him. "Overgrown mudding fish!"

"Language," growled Berk from the front. "See that big fellow starward?"

"Aye!" called Ivar and the others in their wedge, a sharp clap of sound against the waves and wind. Below them, the blackfish swam and chattered.

"That's our target. On me . . ."

In the corner of his eye, Ivar saw Kral's wedge already diving, speeding toward the first sea wolf that had breached the grey waves.

A huntress knocked into him, and he swore while she shrieked at him. "Stay in formation!"

Ivar cursed and flapped to angle himself back into place. He focused on the training master, his own wedge, his own pounding heart. Wind gusted against them.

Berk folded his wings in silence, tipped, and dived. As one, they followed. The sea wolf rolled beneath the water to peer at them, then swam a fast circle. They banked with it, wings and eyes sharp, a single entity ready to strike.

Another blackfish broke the waves with a chattering laugh. A familiar sound. Ivar's gaze darted to it and saw a wound across its snout. Four claw tracks, still pink along the slick black skin. His own claw marks. It was one of the blackfish that had attacked Salva and nearly killed Ivar himself.

"*Hold!*" the training master roared as they sped toward the water. Fifty leap-lengths away. Twenty. Ivar growled as the other blackfish mocked him from afar, slapping the water with a fin.

The feathers of a single wing. Working together. Each one valuable. Each one to its own work. Unique on its own but made for this purpose, to work together. One.

Together, Salva's firm voice echoed. Strong, but touched by a plea.

We win, we win only together—the blackfishes' own cursed song rang in Ivar's head. He would *not* be drawn away like a bumbling fledge, would not fall for mockery.

He had other things to prove today. And he would conquer any challenge set before him.

"Only together as one," he said under his breath, then louder. "Together as one!"

"Together as one!" Tyrsha growled next to him, then the others.

Two leaps from the water, the overwhelming scent of fish and salt and brine slapped them.

"Together as one!"

The training master sliced into the water neat as a tern, grabbing the massive sea wolf by its dorsal fin. Ivar dived tight behind, wings slicking tight to his back. Grey saltwater and bubbles and froth exploded around him. He found flesh and sank his talons in, shoving forward and down in tandem with Tyrsha by his side, then the huntresses, forming a core of strength behind and between them.

Their staggered impacts and momentum shoved the behemoth into a roll, somersaulting the massive, powerful body through the water. When they came around top again, Ivar released his grip and thrust to the surface for a breath in time with the others on the point of the wedge—and dived again, grabbing the blackfish before it could find its bearings.

He would not err. He would not stray or seek his own glory. He remained close to the others, repeating the rolling shove.

Four times they rolled, muscles screaming, breaths tightly gasped between plunges. Ivar's sole focus narrowed to tracking the warrior beside him and the huntresses, shoving against the monster, so it never had a chance to swim away. All around them, the water thrashed with the same battle a dozen times over, with the slick black-and-white bodies of the sea wolves and the tidy, fierce coordination of the Vanir, spinning them through the water to show their strength without killing.

In broken clicks and squeals through the water, Ivar thought he heard the blackfish shrieking that this was not a fun *game*, calling to each other in bewilderment.

Just as he broke his face from the water for another gasped breath, a high squeal and sharp, cracking series of clicks resounded through the sea. A blackfish had broken free—free of Kral's wedge. Beneath Ivar, his own quarry thrashed loose of the huntresses in the brief second they came up for air, smacking Berk with a long fin to drive him back.

But they did not turn to fight. One by one, the sea wolves broke free of the gryfons and fled to deeper water.

Tyrsha popped up from the water with a wracking cough, spitting salt, laughing madly. "Yes, flee, you great overgrown fish!"

"Fly out!" ordered Berk. "Out now, in case they double back, make the wedge!"

Ivar obeyed, exhilaration lunging through his chest and wings as he shoved from the water. He looked quickly across the water, searching for anyone fallen or injured.

"All hale?" Kral's shouted inquiry bloomed relief in Ivar's chest, and he called a response along with the others. Wings slapped the water as the rest of their party leaped from the waves, and Ivar and the others counted heads. Below, the black-and-white sea wolves regrouped and sped away as a shaft of sunlight burned through the clouds and cast a sheen of silvery gold across the water.

"And don't come back!" shouted Tyrsha. Ivar laughed, and from his chest loosed a lion's roar of victory that the others echoed, their bold claim thundering over the sea and to the sky where bright Tyr shone, watching over all.

As THE SPRING reached toward summer, the blackfish ceased harrying their fishing grounds, though occasionally, a huntress would spy movement farther out to sea. They appeared to be hunting starward of the isles, which suited the pride of the Sun Isle just fine. As a reward for Kral's fine leadership, the king lifted him in the ranks of the warriors, and Ivar found himself proud rather than envious and happy to celebrate his wingbrother's achievement, knowing he had been a part of it.

The tale of the sea-wolf hunt grew with each telling under the stars, each exaggerating their own part, though Ivar discovered, as the days went on, that he found less satisfaction in the tales than in the truth and laughed when others found amusement in remarking how the most astonishing part of the endeavour was that he had remained in his place.

My place, he would say, again and again, *is in the service of the pride.* The more he said it, the more he believed it was true, and found his honour in his pride mates well-fed and at peace.

He flew out with Salva one evening, a moon before the Daynight, when bright Tyr did not set and gryfons made the mating pledge under his light.

"I thought we might take a look at the dens on the nightward edge of the cliffs," Salva said, flipping playfully in the air like a gull, her wing fully healed from the blackfish's attack.

"Nightward?" Ivar dived below and ahead of her, then doubled black. "I was hoping for the dawnward border. I like to wake with the sun."

"I don't," she said evenly, flexing her wings to hold the sea wind, to slow herself and fly level with him.

"This will be another *together as one* decision, I suppose?" Ivar grumbled.

Salva laughed, flicking him with the tip of her wing. "Think how nice it will be in the long days of winter to have just an extra mark of sunlight to keep the den warm."

"Hm."

"Happy mate, happy fate," she chimed playfully, an old gryfon proverb. "Besides, in the summer, when the sun rises so early, you will thank me for the little bit of darkness in our den."

"Hmmm."

"Very well then, a race," she declared. "To determine the winner. To the falls."

Without giving him a chance to catch his bearings or properly accept the challenge, she folded her wings and dived for momentum, then whipped ahead toward the falls that cascaded down from the sprawling cliffs to the beach below.

"Just a moment," he bellowed. "I wasn't—"

"Keep up, bold Ivar!" Salva laughed, her voice faint as she sped out of his reach.

He growled in determination and folded his wings, noting that she purposefully slowed as they both approached the falls, and together they spiralled in and away from the powerful rush of water. Ivar forgot to worry about agreeing on a den, or being right, or winning. They were better, stronger, this way.

By laughing and unspoken agreement, they won the race together and danced in the evening air, and he knew they would be able to conquer everything this way—the feathers on a single wing, together, one.

GHOSTWIND

By Violette Malan

"Were you followed?"

Dhulyn Wolfshead decided not to be offended. These people clearly didn't have much experience with the Mercenary Brotherhood. "We have proof of legitimate business with you." She lifted her right hand, and her Partner, Parno Lionsmane. took the pieces of a green ceramic cup from his belt pouch.

The potter beckoned them through the curtain separating shop from workroom, where her wife looked up from a wheel. "They only sent two of you?"

Probably one more than you need, Dhulyn didn't say out loud. "I am Dhulyn Wolfshead, called the Scholar, schooled by Dorian the Black Traveller." She indicated Parno with a tilt of her head. "I fight with my Partner, Parno Lionsmane, called the Chanter, schooled by Nerysa of Tourin, the Warhammer. You sent for Mercenary Brothers, and we are here."

The woman swallowed, eyes examining Dhulyn's face, flicking from her Mercenary's Badge to Parno's, tattooed across their temples and the places above their ears where the hair had been removed. Finally, the potter cleared her throat and sat down at a small table, hands pushed against her thighs. "People are disappearing—no—" she held up her hand. "That's not the right word. We know where they went, so it's not really disappearing, is it?"

"More like kidnapping," her wife added.

"And you know who is at fault?"

"Everyone knows. It's the priests. And the Ghostwind, of course, but mainly the priests."

Dhulyn caught Parno's eye. *Priests. If it's not mages, it's priests, and sometimes not that much difference between them.* Behind her, Parno cleared his throat.

"Perhaps you should tell us more," he said.

No perhaps about it.

The two women exchanged glances. "We've always had the Ghostwind," the potter said. "It came regular-like, and when it did, the king would volunteer himself—"

"Or herself."

"Or herself." The potter shot a hard look at her wife. "But mostly, it was himself," she continued. "There were mostly kings because of the Ghostwind, you see."

Dhulyn smiled her wolf's smile, the small scar pulling her lip into a snarl. The potter leaned back, and her wife took a quiet step away. "We are familiar with the concept of a ruler sacrificing himself—or herself—for the good of the people," she said. "What is the problem?" *Don't make me ask again.*

"Three years ago, the priests came. They said we weren't doing it right, that the Ghostwind was angry because of our disrespect. One king every now and again wasn't enough. They built a big temple over the cave of the Ghostwind, and they asked for more volunteers—"

"Not enough kings, you see," the wife added.

The potter shrugged. "It's got to every month now. When people stopped volunteering, the priests started drawing lots—"

"Only we don't see the lots drawn. So we don't know what goes on."

Dhulyn flicked a glance toward Parno, standing relaxed and ready against the wall. "The Ghostwind does what, exactly?"

The potter and her wife looked at each other. Dhulyn waited. Parno shifted from one foot to the other.

"It lifts the darkness," the potter said finally. Behind her, the wife nodded vigorously.

"Meaning what, exactly?" Dhulyn mentally flipped a coin to bet which of them would speak next.

"How old do you think we are?"

The potter. Dhulyn would have lost her bet. She raised her brows. How could she know? Townpeople aged so strangely.

"Without checking your joints," Parno said, "I would say somewhere in your middle thirties, both of you."

"We're more than three times older," the wife chimed in. "That's what the Ghostwind does, you see, it keeps us healthy, and so we live longer. We feed it, and it feeds us. Only now," she shrugged, "it's more like it feeds *on* us."

"Tell us what you know about the temple."

———————————

ONE LONG SHADOW reached across the square, long enough and dark enough to cover their approach. Using the Stalking Car *Shora*, they padded, silent and unseen, across to the wall of the temple, where Dhulyn put her palm against the cool stone, smooth as glass. She frowned. There were eighty-one existing *shora*, patterns for movement and for using weapons. All mercenaries were schooled in a minimum of twenty-seven before they became part of the Brotherhood. But not even the Sable Monkey, a climbing *shora*, could create finger and toe holds where there were none. Parno tapped her on the shoulder and pointed up. Yes. That darker shape could mean a window.

Dhulyn took her Partner's offered hand, stepped up on his bent knee and from there onto his shoulders. Her fingers brushed the wall, perhaps two handspans from the bottom of the window ledge. She tapped out a message with her toe against Parno's shoulder. He tapped her left foot with the fingers of the hand holding it. She bent her knees slightly and felt Parno do the same. She gave the signal, and they launched themselves upward, Parno's momentum transferring to hers, giving her enough lift to hook her fingers on the window ledge.

She pulled herself up, sat on the ledge, and froze. Blond maple floors, walls panelled with wood a shade darker, the light warm and soft, like sunlight on an early spring day. She looked outside. Still the same half-moon night. She looked back again at the room. Fresh, flower-scented air; cross-framed stools next to small tables with curved legs holding blown-glass figurines. She swung her legs over the broad sill, clearing away a whimsical wicker stand. From under her leather vest, she unwrapped a thin silk rope, one end already tied around her waist, the other looped through a heavy metal bead. She sat on the floor with her feet braced against the wall under the window and tossed out the weighted end.

When it grew taut, she counted under her breath until Parno heaved himself over the windowsill.

"What took you so long?" she breathed, using the nightwatch voice.

"Getting old," he breathed back, grinning. Mercenary Brothers didn't expect to grow old. They were hard to kill, but it was possible. Parno rewound the rope around her waist, tucking in the weighted end. His expression as he took in the room looked like she felt.

"No other windows," Dhulyn said, never afraid of stating the obvious.

"No shadows." Parno glanced at her, shrugged, and pointed to the door.

The sourceless, windowless sunlight continued in the corridor. The last time they had been in the back halls of a temple, they'd found a dank darkness smelling of old dust and stale incense, sporadically lit by oil lamps, cold stone floors worn by the passage of time, threadbare tapestries hiding who-knew-what dark secrets. This place more resembled the upper floors of a well-funded House.

They waited back-to-back, each facing toward one end of the corridor, breathing slowly and concentrating.

"What's that humming?" Parno said. "Like a hive of bees in the next room."

"More a vibration." Dhulyn pointed to one end of the corridor, raising her eyebrows. Parno nodded and fell in behind her. They stopped every fifty paces, listening with well-schooled ears. More of the sourceless light, tapestries with colours as bright as if they had just been finished. Parno tilted his head. Something had changed, but what?

"Shadows," Dhulyn said as if she had heard his question. "There are shadows now." She rolled her shoulders as if to loosen the muscles in her neck. "Except ours."

Dhulyn was right. and now that he was looking more closely, Parno could see that what shadows there were did not correspond with the objects casting them. That little table right there, for example: its shadow was far too large and shaped far too much like a person. He tapped Dhulyn's shoulder and pointed. She nodded shrugged ever so slightly. Nothing they could do about it now.

Still, his skin prickled, and the hairs on the back of his neck stood up.

Around the first corner appeared wooden doors carved with leaves and fruits and flowers, everything smelling of the waxes and oils a good steward of keys would see used to keep wood in good condition. Until now, there had been no other scents, just the humming and the faint vibration.

Dhulyn found her shoulders creeping upwards and her hands tightening into fists, though her eyes told her there was nothing to keep ready for. She began to wish for cobwebs in the corners, flickering torches, rats. Even something to smell other than themselves. This bright perfection unnerved her.

As they neared the next turning, the feel of the air changed. This section of corridor was a gallery, open on one side and looking over a vast stone hall. They had seen larger but none so impressive. The floor appeared all of one piece, the light glancing off polished pink and grey marble as though it were a mirror. Dhulyn took Parno's sleeve between thumb and forefinger as a warning to him against leaning out too far, lest the floor would reflect him as well. Instead, they lay prone along the gallery, looking out between two balusters.

Off-centre in the floor, and looking terribly out of place, rose a natural rock formation, as though a mountain peak had thrust itself through the mirror-like surface, though Parno thought it far more likely that the floor had been cut to fit exactly the shape of the rock. Dhulyn tapped Parno on the ankle and made a circular motion with her hand. He nodded and crept farther along the gallery, using knees and elbows. She waited, patient as a cat, until he returned.

"There is an opening on the far side of the stone," he murmured in the nightwatch voice. "A wooden door, dark as pitch, banded with iron, but irregular, like it might be a cave opening."

Dhulyn pointed first at her Partner and then ahead. Nodding, he led her along the gallery until she, too, could see the door. Both made the hush signal at the same moment. After so long hearing only the humming, the approaching footfalls rang like the crack of whips.

Six people—two women and four men, judging by their gaits —entered the hall from a door beneath their gallery. Five were clearly priests, dressed in white tunics and trousers covered by white cloaks, each hemmed a different colour. The sixth, a younger man, was dressed in well-cut clothing made from good linen and silk. He looked around the hall and upward, a contented smile lifting the corners of his mouth. When they stopped moving, he stood facing the door in a square made by four of the others. The final priest, wearing a gold-trimmed robe, stood back from the others and signalled. The four surrounding the young man lifted their arms into the air.

Parno almost missed it as the humming grew louder and the vibration strengthened. He tapped Dhulyn on the ankle, and she nodded. As the priests prayed, the vibration became strong enough that the gallery trembled under them, and only firm grips on the balusters kept them in place.

The two priests nearest the door in the rock took hold of the latches and looked back at the others. The other two stepped forward and took hold of the younger man's arms.

I've got a bad feeling about this, Parno thought.

The young man drew down his brows, turning from side to

side now with a look of confusion, his smile twisting as if it had dawned on him that something was not as he expected. He pushed away backward, feet scrabbling, as he was drawn closer to the door in the rock. He began to thrash, making his first sounds. Though there was no word in it, Dhulyn knew what the man was saying and what he wanted.

The two closest priests opened the door.

A wall of air roared out of the rock, spinning around the room and spiralling in on the young man. Darkness and cold came out of the cavern with it, dulling even the shine from the floor. As soon as the wind reached him, the priests let the young man go and took measured steps back.

As all five priests raised their arms into the air and began to sing, an image flashed into Dhulyn's mind. *A man in furs, white-skinned, hair the colour of old blood, stands with his arms lifted, chanting, snowflakes whirling around him.* She remembered laughing at the shaman, straining to hear the words. *Is this the same song?* But she can't concentrate, the wind is too loud. The people who could sing that song, her people, the Red Horsemen, were long gone. She didn't have that kind of magic – though she had some of her own - she only remembered the tune

The victim's mouth changed shape, and he grasped his throat with a grimace of pain and horror, though nothing appeared to be hurting him. The young man fell to his knees seemed to shrink, his body slowly fading, dissolving, as a lump of sugar dissolves in water.

The wind whipped up. Parno hooked his left arm around the nearest baluster, Dhulyn's free hand reached through and grasped his other wrist. As the invisible assault continued, Parno's mind emptied of every thought—weapons, *shora*—except the need to hold on against the pull of the wind. He felt his arm slipping, but

Dhulyn's grip on his other wrist anchored him long enough to shift his position. Her lips were pressed into a thin line her eyelids closed, as if she could hold her breath more easily without sight. His lungs tightened, and he felt his chest muscles cramp and his eyes bulge. He would have to breathe. Soon, whatever the cost, he would have to breathe.

His vision began to dull, until all he could be sure of was the grip he had on Dhulyn's wrist and the grip she had on his. *In battle or in death*, he thought, the Brotherhood's greeting. Somehow, he knew she was thinking the same. He felt a dusting, as of sugar, touch his face, and suddenly the wind died away, and he took in a lungful of desperately needed air—but that was not all he inhaled. Immediately, he began to cough, but it was already too late. Whatever dust the priests had loosed into the air, whatever the Ghostwind had let them inhale, his vision faded, and the last thought he had was that he could not feel Dhulyn's hand

---

SLOWLY, much more slowly than she would have liked, Dhulyn realized that her right eye was pressed into a hard surface. *I'll have a bruise on that cheekbone*, she thought. She opened her unobstructed eye. She saw a golden-brown arm, a dusting of amber hair, and a scar that she knew very well—having put it there herself. That gave her strength to push herself upright, hissing when she saw the bruises on her hands and upper arms. She explored her right cheek with careful fingertips. Nothing broken, thank Mother Sun.

Parno lay like a rag doll dropped by a giant child who had tired of playing with him. Dhulyn took him firmly by the shoulders and turned him face-up. He inhaled deeply and relaxed without awakening. She pulled back his eyelids; the pupils matched. She checked his gums for colour; pressed the palms of his hands and counted the seconds until the colour returned. Good. He did not bleed internally. She stood, stretched, and checked her weapons. She wasn't surprised to find that while she still had the lockpicks and strangling wires braided into her hair, her silk climbing rope and the blades in wristbands and boots were gone. She selected the most common lockpick and turned slowly around, stopping with her tongue tapping her upper lip.

No doors. No windows. The lockpick went back into its braid.

How did they put us in here?

She sat down again, cross-legged and close enough to Parno to touch him with her knee, closed her eyes, and began the Lizard *Shora*. Her breathing slowed, and her muscles relaxed.

Sometime later, Parno moved.

"Where are we?" he said without opening his eyes.

"A room without doors or windows."

"Wonderful." Now his eyes opened. He pushed himself up to a sitting position. "Anything to eat?"

"Neither food nor drink," she said. "Only lockpicks and strangling wires," she added as Parno started checking for weapons. "So far, the former are useless. We'll have to look for a chance to use the latter."

Parno stretched, arching his back. "I hate waiting."

Dhulyn grinned. "Bear Cub *Shora*?"

Her Partner groaned and rolled the stiffness out of his shoulders. "How did I know you were going to say that?"

Parno couldn't be sure how long they wrestled, only that it was long enough for them to loosen their muscles, break into a light sweat, and discover previously undiscovered bruises. At one point, he tapped the floor twice, then rolled up enough to sit back on his heels. "Do you feel that?"

Dhulyn closed her eyes, brows drawn down. "The air is moving."

Parno nodded. "An attack?"

Dhulyn moved her head to the left and back again and sat up straighter. "Feels different."

As he watched, she took deeper breaths and the bruises on her bare arms faded. He looked down. His were gone as well. The air stilled.

"Looks like something wants us healthy," he said.

"And my guess is, not the priests." Dhulyn cleared her throat. "Whoever you are," she said, "your aid is much appreciated."

The air began to move again, lightly, softly, lifting a lock of blood-red hair that had escaped its braid. She got to her feet, and Parno followed. She closed her eyes again and tilted her head as though she were listening to something he could not hear.

Just as he was about to ask, she raised her arms into the air, in the same posture the priests had used in the grand hall. She did not appear to be in pain. In fact, she still seemed to be listening to something. After a moment, she began to hum.

Is not in danger a voice said in his head. ***Sings to me so we may speak***

Parno lifted his chin, his eyes slitted. He'd spoken this way before. On a voyage across the Long Ocean, he had learned he was pod-sensed, able to communicate with the Crayx, immense, time-less sea creatures that shared the seas of the world with the Ocean Nomads.[1] What he felt now was similar enough to make him less wary, though he had no feel for the nature of the being that now spoke to him.

"How is it can hear you" he asked. *"Are not crayx"*

Know them the thing said. *Are water, am air*

A being that occupied the air the way the crayx did water?

Yes

"Are the Ghostwind" Parno asked.

Yes. Singing gives me focus, so can speak to you

"Why"

Free me, free you

Fair enough. *"How"*

Kill the priests

Good idea. *"Again, how"*

Will take her through the wall with me. She will do it

"Take both of us"

No. one killer, one hostage

That was straightforward enough. *"I will go"* Like the Crayx, the Ghostwind would understand his use of pronouns for emphasis.

*Can only move her because knows the music *

"Why should I trust you"

*Can explain *

"THE GHOSTWIND IS the spirit of this place," Parno said. "It was here before the humans came, it says, subsisting on the smaller life that it found."

"I know of such things," Dhulyn said. She found it an odd sensation to know they had a companion she could not see. "Many forests have their own spirits."

"Right. When people came, the Ghostwind began to help them, and when necessary, they would provide a volunteer to help it. It was always careful to neither give nor take too much."

Something about this story left Dhulyn unsatisfied. "With such power, why does it not stop the priests itself?"

"It didn't realize the danger at first. When the priests came, they persuaded the people to feed the Ghostwind more often, and it was caught before it knew."

"Caught?"

"The priests fed it so much it found it couldn't do without."

Dhulyn nodded. "Always it needs more and more, and now the priests control the flow of its power." She had done several drug *shoras* and knew how dangerous such things could be. "You say it wants to stop?"

"But it needs help. It feels itself changing into something it does not want to be."

"I do not like to be coerced." Dhulyn looked around the room with a frown.

"Are we coerced?" Parno shrugged. "Our contract is to rid the town of these priests. That this also happens to be what the Ghost-wind wants . . ." He turned his palms upward.

Dhulyn considered. "Taking payment from two parties to achieve the same end does not, strictly speaking, go against the Mercenary Code, but how are we to provide this help?"

"It will take you through the walls."

Dhulyn felt her eyebrows crawl upwards. "First, why not both? Second, why not you? And third, how does it propose to do this?"

"First, it does not fully trust us, so it would hold one of us. Second, it can speak to me because of my podsense, and it can move you because you know its song, which, third, allows it to turn you into a part of itself, and where it can pass, you can pass."

Dhulyn sat back, lips pursed. She remembered stories of how the Cloud Shamans of the Red Horsemen—the most powerful mage of each tribe—could travel quickly from place to place without the necessity of horses. So far as she knew, only the men among her people had been mages, able to use this magic. But if this Ghostwind thought differently . . .

"In battle," she said finally.

"Or in death."

DHULYN BREATHED SOFTLY, senses alert. It wasn't every day you were dissolved into dust in one room and put back together in another. As far as she could tell, she felt exactly the same as she had before. In fact, she felt better, and why not? The Ghostwind kept the townspeople alive, did it not?

She stood just inside the red wooden door of a bedroom. The air was so heavily scented she had to stifle a sneeze. A tiny flame burned in a small crystal sphere on the far side of a wide bed covered with cushions and embroidered quilts, which held two people.

Priests with a nightlight? Interesting. If anything, it made what she had come here to do easier. Judging from the sounds of their breathing, one of the two in the bed was awake—and knew that Dhulyn was in the room, yet was not afraid.

"It's late, Korian. Lennan's already asleep, and I'm exhausted."

She sounded it. Dhulyn ghosted to the other side of the bed and stood over her.

"Korian, I said—"

As the woman rolled toward her, Dhulyn took hold of her head and twisted it sharply in the direction opposite to the roll. Dhulyn held her breath, but the man's slow, steady breathing never changed—until Dhulyn shoved her second-best lockpick into his left ear, and his breathing stopped altogether. She padded silently to the door. As she put out her hand for the latch, she felt herself dissolving. "No, let me open it my—"

She stood in the corridor, face-to-face with a thick-bodied man, eyes and mouth rounded in shock. It took her a moment to recognize him as the priest with the gold-edged robes. They both raised their hands at the same time, but before she could close with him, tiny lights spun around her, binding her arms to her sides, her legs together. Only quick thinking allowed her to close her eyes before the binding could touch them.

Unable to keep her balance, she fell to the floor.

HAS KILLED TWO OF THEM

"Do you feel stronger? Can you get me out to her"

No, still trapped inside the cavern. Have limited movement

Ah, Parno thought, *it was never able to move us both at once.* Holding one of them hostage in order to guarantee the behaviour of the other was just a way to hide weakness. Parno could understand that. Of course, that might be the real reason the Ghostwind hadn't simply eaten both of them. Trapped in its cavern, the part it could free was not strong enough to do so.

"What if—"

Suddenly, the space the wind had occupied in his head was empty.

DHULYN CAME to as she was being dragged over the floor of the hall toward the irregular door of the Ghostwind's cavern. She was as tightly wrapped as a sail in a locker, though she managed to turn herself over so that at least she was on her back, not her face.

The dragging stopped, and above her, the remaining three priests took position and began to sing. She noticed they had not bothered with the robes, and she smiled her wolf's smile. She could reach one of the cords holding her with the little finger of her left hand. The nail on that finger was probably long enough, and sharp enough . . . She felt friction as it rubbed against the cord, but she could tell she made no headway.

The air pressure changed, and a blast of cold swept over her. *The cavern is opening.* Her heartbeat sped up and her breath shortened as the Ghostwind roared out of the doorway. *Will it remember we are helping it?* Or would it be unable to resist? She tried taking longer, slower breaths, but the wind's gusts prevented it. She could not raise her arms, nor could she sing, but she could hum. She had to hope the tune was enough.

She felt the same odd sensation of dissolving that she had felt before. The wind had said it could not stop itself. Not unless the priests were dead.

Looks like it will be "in death" this time. Parno was going to be very annoyed with her if she let herself get killed.

———

HAVE HER. Took her. Didn't want to, couldn't stop – ohnoohnoohno

"Listen, listen" Parno hummed the song he'd heard Dhulyn sing. It wasn't exactly like the one the priests had sung, but it had worked for her. The Ghostwind buffeted against him more softly but remained cold and trembling, as though it were alive. *"Where is she"*

Inside. Couldn't resist priests. Knew it. Couldn't stop

Parno understood. The Ghostwind had not been able to resist when the priests had called it out. It had taken Dhulyn. He took a deep breath. She was alive; he knew that much. Whatever the wind had done to her, whatever it thought, there was still time. There had to be. *"Inside you? Re-form her"*

*Can't – maybe – not yet toolatetoolatetoolate – *

"Take me to the priests" he said. *"And listen, here's where I want you to drop me"*

At first, he thought the wind would not help him, but then he felt a strange lightness. He looked down at his hands and could see through them. While he still could, he pulled at the sash around his waist.

The next thing he knew, he stood in the hall. The Ghostwind must have heard him because Parno solidified immediately behind the priest whose robe had been trimmed in gold. Parno whipped the wire he had removed from his sash around the man's neck and crossed his wrists, feeling it cut through soft tissue and snag on bone. Parno stepped back in time to avoid the worst of the blood spray, but the other two priests were not so lucky.

While one of them stopped to wipe blood out of his eyes, Parno took hold of the man's chin in one hand, bracing the other on the back of the head. A quick twist, and he heard the neck break. He dropped the body and reached for the last priest. The woman had her hand raised, pointing toward him. He could see her lips moving, but the noise of the Ghostwind prevented him from hearing anything. For a moment, he felt the wind blowing him backward. *sorrysorrysoryy* he heard in his head.

His fingertips began to disappear. He kicked the woman's hand out of the way, spun around, and kicked her head with the other foot. He couldn't be sure he had broken her neck, but she went down, and it must have been enough.

The entrance to the cavern stood open, and Parno went in slowly, with his hands raised to ward off blows. He waited while his eyes adjusted to the gloom, and there she was. Dhulyn lay on the ground, bound head to toe in a glowing blue cord, like a spider-wrapped fly. Even her eyes were wrapped shut. His fingers passed right through the cord as if it were really made of light. Or of air.

"*Come*" he called. "*Free her*"

Don't know it said, moaning the words. ***Hurts. So hard***

"*You wanted us to help you. We helped you*" Parno tried to keep his tone reasonable. The Ghostwind didn't know how lucky it was that he couldn't get his hands on it.

He carried Dhulyn out into the hall. The Ghostwind moaned around them but made no move to either help or hinder.

"*The priests are gone*" he pointed out. "*Come. Let us finish helping you*"

Trapped

Parno began whistling the tune Dhulyn had sung. He wished he had his pipes or even just the chanter. Or that he knew the words to the song. While he whistled, he thought of the open air, the movement of leaves and grasses, the branches of trees and children's kites. The Ghostwind gentled, sighing rather than moaning.

Dhulyn blinked. At first, she thought she was still singing, but her mouth was too dry, and besides, that was Parno whistling. She sat on the floor, her back against his shoulder. But she wasn't in the cavern anymore; she was in the hall, the song still running through her head.

"Can you stand?"

She let him help her up. Her legs shook, and she felt as if she had not eaten for days. Her stomach rumbled. "We can go?" Her dry mouth and throat could only manage a whisper.

"Let's find our weapons first."

IT TOOK three days for Dhulyn to completely regain her strength. She couldn't remember the last time she'd felt as hungry or as tired. The townspeople had decided to destroy the temple and leave the cavern open as it had been before. As they rode out of town, they heard the sounds of walls being pulled down. They'd heard that sound more than once in their lives.

"Do you think the Ghostwind will be able to go back to the way things were before the priests turned it into a danger?"

Dhulyn shrugged. "We got paid. The rest is none of our business."

I. See *The Storm Witch*

THE THING IN THE PLAY

By Edward Willett

The Reverend Alistair McAra found the man he had come to see seated in one of two straight-backed wooden chairs on either side of a grey metal table in a room in the Talleyrand Home for the Criminally Insane.

The man nodded placidly at the visiting chaplain as he entered, the guard closing and locking the door behind him. "Good afternoon, Reverend. To what do I owe the honour of this visit?"

"I'm new to the post of prison chaplain here at Talleyrand," the pastor said. "In order to serve my new flock better, I've asked to hear from each of them their tale of how they came to be in this place."

The man cocked his head, regarding the pastor with bright blue eyes. "But we're all insane here, Reverend, or so they say. What benefit is there in hearing the rantings of mad men and women?"

"I do not judge," the pastor said. "I only listen."

The man regarded him thoughtfully a moment longer, then chuckled. "Well, I am happy to once again recount my tale, though I know it will only confirm for you the diagnosis rendered by the court psychiatrist who examined me." He sat back in his chair, folded his hands on the table, and began.

APPROPRIATELY ENOUGH, Reverend, it was at the conclusion of Hamlet's soliloquy in Act 2, Scene 2 that I knew I had, at last, found the monster.

You know the soliloquy of which I speak? It is most famous for its final two lines;

> *The play's the thing*
> *Wherein I'll catch the conscience of the King.*

And indeed, it was as the actor concluded those lines that I grasped, with absolute clarity and absolute conviction, that here, at last, was the creature I had sought so long.

I had come to your city's riverside Shakespeare festival following the same kind of tenuous lead that had so often let me down before—an actor, new to this production company, who had previously lived in a community where there had been a mysterious death during a performance. The actor had not been in the company of that fatal performance—indeed, so far as I could determine, he had never been in any performance before, though there were many wandering players whose names only rarely appeared in the dusty newspaper archives I spent so many of my miserable hours perusing (and were often spelled wrong than they did).

Depression and dust storms ravaged and continue to ravage the vast plains outside all the tents and "opera houses" and converted barns and other makeshift theatres wherein I had sought my quarry for the ten years since the death of my beloved and all our hopes and dreams in Chicago. To say I had never wavered in my quest would be a falsehood, but I had never wavered in my desire for revenge since that night I turned, laughing, to my new bride during a performance of *Silence*, a melodrama about a crook serving time for a murder he did not commit.

Her name was Wynter, Reverend; Wynter Simack, and yes, Peter Simack, the wealthy railway baron, was her father. Her name suited her, for she had alabaster skin and hair of pale gold, and my first thought, in that final moment of happiness, was how beautiful she was, leaning back in her seat, eyes shining, full-lipped mouth slightly open, face relaxed and untroubled. But she was not laughing with me; she did not turn toward me; she did not blink; she did not breathe. A fist of ice seized my heart, causing it to stutter in my chest, as the dread truth penetrated.

She would never laugh again.

I do not know why I looked back at the stage in that moment of horror; perhaps, in some way, I sensed what had happened though its possibility had not yet occurred to me. Whatever the reason, glance at the stage I did, and my gaze fell upon the man playing the role of the chaplain to whom the prisoner tells his tale —as now, ironically, I tell my tale to you, Reverend, though I am certainly *not* imprisoned for a murder I did not commit, but for one I committed before multiple witnesses. I saw that actor looking directly at my wife, and there was what I can only describe as a look of intense satiation, as you would see on a man who had just richly dined—or consummated the act of love.

That look, that naked expression of obscene fulfillment, lasted only an instant, and in that instant, I was already turning away, raising my voice, stopping the show in its tracks, calling for a doctor. A doctor was found, but it was too late; my Clara had died silently and unnoticed while I wasted my final moments with her focused on the inane make-believe on the stage.

Some days passed before what I had seen in that actor's face came to mind again as the bitter progression of post-death necessities ground its way to its inevitable, sodden end in the mud of the graveyard. I had no family to help me grieve, my mother, the only parent I knew, having died of tuberculosis the year before, and my wife's family having never approved of me as a match for their daughter. Though they followed the niceties demanded by the situation, and though they did not contest my wife's will, which left me a sizable sum I had not, before then, even known she possessed—believe it or not, and I know many who did not and slandered me for it—I knew I would never see them again once they drove away from the cemetery.

I was walking to my empty apartment, the gloom of the grey, dripping day perfectly in tune with the gloom in my heart, the rain mingling with the tears on my cheeks, when I glimpsed a man on the street ahead of me, emerging from a bar. He glanced my way and then turned and strode off into the rain with no flicker of recognition, but I was stopped in my tracks, for I recognized *him*: he was the actor from the play, and seeing him again brought to mind the awful expression he had turned toward my wife in her last moments.

I ran after him then, my feet propelling me into a mad dash, water sheeting up around me, soaking the legs of my only good suit, ruining my one pair of half-decent shoes, but to no avail: he had vanished.

I never saw him again. But it was he who began my quest.

I found the program for the play; read his name and his biography. "A newcomer to the Chicago stage . . . hails from Columbus, Ohio . . . portraying the chaplain, which comes naturally to him, given his upbringing as the son of a Methodist minister . . ."

His name did not appear in the Chicago phone book. The theatre said he had left the company shortly after the "unfortunate accident" that had cast a pall over the production and, having collected the pay due him, had left no forwarding address.

I backtracked. The money my wife had left me gave me the resources to travel to Columbus, where I asked at every Methodist church if someone in the congregation knew the man.

No one had ever heard of a pastor's son by the name of the actor, but a janitor in an out-of-the-way congregation in the suburbs recalled the name as belonging to someone who had died suddenly of a stroke . . .

. . . while in the audience of a community-theatre production of *The Importance of Being Earnest*.

I did not know what to make of that. I did not yet think the actor I sought had killed my wife, for how could he have? Then, I still lived in the everyday world of science and reason, and it defied both to think a man upon a stage could single out a young woman in the audience and stop her heart with a glance. And even if he could, why would he do such a thing?

And it *had* been her heart that had given out: that much had been revealed in the autopsy, a thing that was done to her I did not like to think about, but that had been required by law, given the sudden and public nature of her death. She'd had a congenital heart condition that had gone unrecognized, the doctors told me. "In most cases," I was told, "it causes little difficulty in youth, though it may as the sufferer grows old. But sometimes . . ."

Sometimes.

This time.

And that actor knew it: knew the moment she died and took pleasure in it.

So I thought then. I thought the actor some kind of ghoul, perhaps, but a human one; that somehow, he had seen my wife in distress, and it had, in some perverse way, excited him.

I know that sounds insane. It sounded insane to me, as well, whenever I thought about it without calling to mind the look upon the actor's face—but when I did, the notion no longer seemed insane. It seemed, in my mind, at least, incontrovertible.

The world calls those insane who believe with all their heart that a thing that cannot possibly be true is, in fact, true. They are not truly insane if that impossible thing is, in fact, true, but if no one else can be made to believe it, there is no defence for them.

And that, ultimately, is why I am here: not only because I came to believe a thing that most say cannot possibly be true, but because I acted upon that belief.

What the court has termed my "insanity" soon took another turn as I began to realize that the man I sought was not a man at all.

The thing . . . the monster, as I began to think of it . . . it became clear to me, had no fixed appearance, no fixed name, no fixed age, not even a fixed gender, sometimes appearing as a woman, some-times as a child, sometimes as a young man, sometimes as an old one.

And yet, I was able to track its movements through newspaper stories of tragic deaths, always at the theatre. In each case, the one who died in the audience had some plausible reason for dying: a heart defect, as my wife had had, a respiratory illness that somehow reached crisis during the performance, a weak blood vessel within the brain, a blood clot, undetected cancer. The deaths were always sudden and unexpected and yet, as I said, plausible . . . just.

It took some time to discover the other aspect of how the thing did whatever it was doing, for whatever reason it was doing it. It was pure chance that I did so, and it was that discovery, that blinding revelation—my Road to Damascus moment, if I may put it in terms Paul the Apostle and you, Reverend, should be familiar with—that spurred me, at last, to action.

I had become more and more adept at tracking the thing. There was a pattern. Each manifestation occurred within a hundred miles of the previous one, and the trend, always, though the path might zig-zag, was westward.

Knowing that, I could search within the hundred-mile diameter of the last mysterious theatre death I had identified to find the next—or even, if the trail were fresh enough, the thing itself. That, at least, was my hope. And search I did, for years, the funds I inherited from my wife dwindling until I feared I would soon have to give up my quest without success, a prospect too bitter to swallow.

And then I came here, to *Hamlet*.

On opening night in that stifling tent, I overheard a woman behind me remark, as she and her companion settled into their seats after intermission, that the actor playing Hamlet was the spitting image of a young man she had known in her own hometown many years ago, a deceased schoolteacher. She did not say how the schoolteacher died. Though the comment intrigued me, I still did not yet fully grasp the truth. Perhaps I did not want to.

No one died in the audience that night, but opening night was rarely when the deaths occurred. My intention was to attend each performance of the week-long run, though this was only one of three towns with new theatrical productions I had identified as possibly the creature's next port of call.

Having time to kill, I spent the next day at the library, deep within the stacks of bound copies of newspapers from this and other cities, and it was there as I perused yet another account of yet another play where someone had been found dead in the audience, in a town a hundred miles from here, that, at last, I fully grasped the truth—or, you might say, the truth fully grasped me.

Accompanying the story was a publicity photo of one of the performers, a young woman whose face for a moment made me think I had indeed gone mad: but then, as I recalled the overheard comment of the woman behind me, I realized the icy wind howling through my brain was not insanity but the very essence of sanity, sanity of the kind that scours away all falsehoods and leaves one naked to the bitter cold of reality.

The photo was unmistakably an image of my dead wife.

The pieces came together even as my eyes flooded with tears and my heart spasmed in grief. Seeing the monster there in the guise of my deceased bride, I understood fully.

Like the vampire, made famous by Bram Stoker's novel in the early part of this century, this thing I was following fed upon its victims—nothing so gross and physical as blood, but their very life force, their souls, sucking it from their bodies, always choosing those who had some at least vaguely plausible risk of dying.

Within the theatre, the thing found crowds it could examine at its leisure, picking its victim and finding the perfect moment to strike. It killed its victims as they sat in the darkness, pulling from them their essential essences—their *souls*, Reverend—later to don all that as a disguise, not just of physical appearance but of behaviour. *Of course*, the thing would be an actor—in every moment of its existence, it was acting, pretending to be a human being when instead it was ... something else.

I see the look you are giving me, Reverend. It is a look I have seen many times, the carefully impassive look of someone trying with all his might to hide his complete incredulity at the insane statement I have just made.

But I care nothing for your incredulity, any more than I cared for the incredulity of the prosecutor and the judge, or that of the psychiatrist who has committed me to this institution, styled one of the "criminally insane."

Your incredulity and the apparent impossibility of my statement do not change the fact that it is not impossible: that it is not only possible, it is true.

That ... thing ... whatever it was ... took the shape and sometimes even the name of the one it killed, and re-created itself as an actor in yet another production, and killed again, and stole the soul and the very shape of the one it has killed, and so the cycle repeated ... and did so down through the years, for I know not how long.

Knowing, in that blinding moment of epiphany, how the thing operated and recalling how the woman behind me had thought the actor playing Hamlet looked remarkably like a young schoolteacher she had once known, now tragically deceased, I took the necessary steps to ensure that, if I had indeed, at last, come to the right place at the right time to confront the creature, I would be prepared to act.

And so I did, on the fourth night, as Hamlet finished that famous soliloquy; as he spoke the words, "The play's the thing wherein I'll catch the conscience of the king"; as he looked out at the audience, and his eyes locked on a spot to my left, and his mouth opened, and his face took on, unmistakably, the same expression of ecstasy I had seen on the actor who looked at my wife as she died; as a woman screamed, her white-haired husband slumping into her lap as his heart stopped; as all those things happened, I rose to my feet, drew the pistol I had concealed in my pocket, and shot the actor between the eyes, his blood and brains splattering against the closed black curtain before which he had been speaking, a scene change happening behind it.

In the confusion that followed, I felt only peace, knowing I had rid the Earth of an unspeakable horror. Many of those around me screamed and tried to flee, and I understand that there were several injuries, some serious, among the stampeding audience members, a fact which I regret, but that was a small price to pay for what I accomplished.

I tossed the pistol aside and sat down to await my arrest, which was not long in coming. In the questioning that followed, I told my story, as I have told it to you; the result of which was my commitment to this institution for, I am sure, the rest of my life.

That, Reverend, is my tale: my confession, if you will, although I wonder if I have truly committed murder since the thing I killed was not human. I am struck again by how apropos it was that I acted ruing a production of Hamlet, for indeed, "There are more things in heaven and Earth . . . than are dreamt of in your philosophy."

THE MAN STOPPED SPEAKING and sat back in his chair. His face wore a small, pleased smile as though telling his tale yet again had given him great satisfaction.

Reverend McAra nodded slowly and thoughtfully. "I certainly

understand why you have been committed. It is a tale few would believe."

"Including yourself, I'm sure," the man said with a chuckle.

"On the contrary." Reverend McAra leaned forward, his hands folded on the table. "I enjoy such speculation. Let us continue it. Hypothetically, if there were one of these things, might there not be another?"

The man frowned. "An unsettling thought," he said. "However, it seemed clear to me that I was on the trail of a singular creature; the trail was too connected, place to place, to suggest a second such monster, though I suppose in other parts of the world, there might—"

"I don't think you need to invoke foreign places to entertain the notion of a second being of this nature," the Reverend said. "Rather, consider the possibility that acting is not the only profession that might offer a creature of this kind—one not of this world, a predator who finds this world's citizens tasty and unsuspecting prey—easy access to what it craves."

"But what other profession would . . ." The man fell silent. His eyes locked on the Reverend's, and he paled. "No," he whispered.

Reverend McAra smiled . . . or, at least, showed his teeth. "In these troubled times, the pews of churches and the benches of revival-meeting tents are filled with people, heads regularly bowed in prayer, unaware of what is happening around them; or, indeed, asleep, lulled by the sound of the minister's voice. It is often not until the benediction that the deceased is discovered." He leaned even closer to the man, now frozen in place, his eyes wide with horror but still locked on the chaplain's. "You might also have considered that the choice of prey from those with some hidden health issue was purely a matter of covering tracks and not a necessity—that such a being could kill at will if it chose." His toothy grin faded, and his voice intensified. "And one more thing you might have considered: that the being you pursued had a mate; and that *you are not the only one who might seek revenge for the death of a loved one.*"

The chaplain took a breath and closed his eyes. An expression of what might have been religious ecstasy flitted across his face. It was the last thing the man saw before his eyes rolled back in his head, and he fell forward, his forehead thudding against the metal table and his arms falling limp to his side.

Reverend McAra opened his eyes again. He studied the body of the man a moment. "The earlier lines of that soliloquy are even more fitting," he told the corpse and quoted:

The spirit that I have seen
May be the devil: and the devil hath power
To assume a pleasing shape; yea, and perhaps,
Out of my weakness and my melancholy,
As he is very potent with such spirits,
Abuses me to damn me.

He smiled, his own small smile of satisfaction. "Amen," he finished. Then he stood, went to the door, and pounded upon it, calling for the guards.

JOSEPH CAMPBELL MISSES THE MARK

By Jane Yolen

Did he create the hero
or just name it, forgetting that heroes
grow out of their own soil,
and not all of them are men?
Forgetting that they are begot
by circumstance, not scholarly approval,
Not always handsome, not always welcome,
not all of them men.

A SINGLE BREATH, HEARD ONLY IN MY DREAMS

By Cat Rambo

That was the season that our home, TwiceFar Station, was full of refugees from one war or another. Some from the Cylin system, housed in evacuation freighters, carrying only what they had been able to snatch up as they fled. A scattering of Tlellans that had commandeered a squad of delivery shuttles and brought them through the Gate, despite the danger to their ships. And others, from farther wars or destroyed stations, like Bellwether, which was the most recent loss. The Gate that the station hung next to reached so many other places, and it seemed like all of them were at war.

My friends and I weren't much affected. The refugees were just passing through, after all, and their children didn't get integrated into our school system since they weren't there long enough. So when our teacher, Hat, announced there was a new student, that was excitement. Hat stood at the front of the room with one hand on the new girl's shoulder and said, "Some of you remember what it was like being new. And her old station was all human. Things are going to seem very strange to her here on Twicefar."

She was skinny and pale-skinned, with watery blue eyes. Angelike gave her a welcoming smile, but she didn't notice. She wouldn't look at any of us, just kept her eyes down on the floor tiles in front of her. But not like she was shy, more like looking at any of us was beneath her. That sounds mean, and like maybe I am making things up, but she and I shared a species, and her body language was one I spoke, and it seemed to be saying, *Keep away,* and *I don't want to be here.*

Her name was Brit Gearson, and she'd come in with the group from Bellwether. But she wouldn't be moving along like most of them. Her parents had been permanently assigned to the station, Hat said, and so she'd be here with us for a while. Something about the way they said "her parents" made me realize they had money, or pull, or something, and their manner to her was more respectful than I'd ever seen it.

We all chorused a greeting and then settled in to talk about cooling chips and refrigeration units, since that was the unit we were currently on. Brit just listened, and she never met anyone's eyes.

IT WASN'T until we were dismissed for mealtime that anyone really had a chance to talk to her. She followed along after us.

We clustered in the eating space, shoulder to shoulder, everyone swapping around food the way we always did. I had basic rats, which no one really wanted to trade for, but sometimes I could swap up for something tastier by giving them two rations for it. The triplets, Tedesla, Desla, and Sla, had candy today from the store their cousin Kallakak ran and said it was samples, so they gave me a piece, saying it was against future trades, but really just to be kind.

Angelike gave them a smile, and they all gave one back. That was how everyone was around Angelike. Because he was nice, in a way that probably meant somewhere in the back back years, his family had been gene-tweaked for empathy. It meant he was a good person, but it could be a little wearing because it also meant living up to his standards.

I'd known him since we were both barely big enough to crawl; we were from the same public crèche. My parents were miners who got killed in a riot, and he'd been taken away from his, who were Losties living out on the rim, doing all sorts of things, including having children, as the crèche mother used to say with a look of distant disdain, "the natural way." Losties were big on doing things the natural way whenever possible, which seemed to me to ignore the fact that living on a space station wasn't all that natural in the first place. Nowadays, Angelike visited them some-times, but he slept and ate in the crèche most of the time, same as me.

The triplets did what they always did, looked at each other and said rapid things in their own language that sounded like they were spitting and whistling at the same time. Reili shrugged, or as close to that as a shoulderless Vern can come. Ferb the Porble just scowled and twitched his whiskers. You could never tell with Ferb —he seemed to hate us as much as he liked us, and Hat said it was his biological programming.

Once they were in, everyone was. So all couple dozen of us followed Angelike over to where the new kid stood, leaning against the wall and scowling with her arms folded. She hadn't taken food; she had just looked down at it and wrinkled her nose, and moved along.

Angelike smiled at her and started chattering away, asking questions. Brit just grunted answers to things like how she liked the station or what her parents did. But Angelike kept asking questions, acting like she wasn't being as rude as she possibly could.

And when he said, "What hobbies do you have?" that was the moment that she looked up.

"I'll show you," she said, and got a book out of her pack. It was the old-fashioned kind, but the pages were a clear material, with things embedded in them.

"What are those?" Desla asked, reaching for it. Brit snatched it back. "You can look but don't touch!" she said. "I've got every kind of leaf and a page of variants—sometimes two or three—for each of them."

"Every kind?" Ferb said. He was trying to sound scornful, but the truth was, none of us had ever seen a collection like this before. Visits to the station's gardens were unheard of if you didn't have the money for a pass. And here was this book, with all of that in its pages.

She turned a page. "Every kind on my home station," she said. "Pothos. Peace lily. Boston fern. Spider plant. And the genetweaks." Her voice was reverential, and she looked only at the book, touching it carefully, gently.

"From Bellwether?" Ferb asked. "The one that got destroyed?"

She looked up as fast as though he'd slapped her, started to say something, then bit her tongue and only nodded. Silence surrounded us all for a moment. I tried to imagine how I would feel if my home were gone, every bit of it, and I couldn't; it was just too big a feeling for me to get it into her head. Ferb's whiskers were bristling; he could tell he'd offended her, and he was only half sorry.

As ever, Angelike stepped in to smooth things over. "How did you get them?" he asked.

"The gardeners have . . . had lotteries," she said. "They're considered excess biomass, and you can enter for the chance to buy them. My parents started collecting for me before I was even born."

"Twicefar doesn't sell biomass."

"Not usually," Reili said. "Depends on the government." We all knew the station was prone to upheaval. In my three thousand days, I'd lived through twenty-two different versions of government.

Brit's eyebrow rose. "What do they do, then?"

"Right now? It's distributed to residents."

"For free?" Brit's tone held scorn and disbelief. You would have thought we'd announced some absurd condition, like having to stand on your head for it. She seemed to have forgotten all the sorrow of the previous moment. Now, years later, I can realize that she was stuffing it all away.

"It's biomass that's held in common. It all gets cycled through."

Brit rolled her eyes. But before she could go into any more argument about how much better Bellwether's ways were, Angelike said politely, "The leaves are very beautiful." He reached out, and Brit let him take the book from her and page through them slowly enough to admire each one.

I could see her watching him, and I thought, *Sure, asshole. He's being polite, and you think it's because he likes you.* I didn't want Angelike to be liking this interloper who looked at us so scornfully, who seemed to think us less than her. We didn't need to adapt to her and her ways. She had to adapt to us.

I did have to admit Angelike was right. The leaves *were* pretty. Each page was dedicated to a single one, labelled with its name and a bunch of chemical composition notes and where in the station it could be found. There were dozens and dozens of them, and I imagined her and her parents assembling them, talking about them, a tight little family group, and I hated her a little bit more for that.

"You don't do anything like that here, huh?" she asked as she took the album back, her face wistful and scornful all at once.

Angelike shook his head. The tone sounded to let us know it was almost time to go back to our classroom, *bing-a-bong, bing-a-bong*, and the lights flashed blue for a few seconds. Around us, people started getting ready to return. Brit put the album back in her pack with careful reverence, as though it were some piece of complicated, expensive machinery.

"We could do something, I suppose," he said. "There are leaves here. Where'd you get the album? Do you have the printer pattern?"

"Yeah, that's easy enough," she said. Her face looked torn between wariness and hope, but in the end, she handed us all the pattern.

Part of our mandatory socialization was eating together, so I was supposed to eat only in the school or in the crèche, but we could always get an exemption if a teacher was willing to eat with us. Some teachers were standoffish and wouldn't talk to you much outside of class time, but we'd learned that Hat was usually willing to entertain someone, particularly if they were good about helping clean up later. I never seemed to get enough to eat at the crèche dinners, so I went over there whenever I could.

Hap was a squat planet-dweller who'd come to Twicefar as a mercenary during one of the revolutions and ended up staying. At first, they'd lived with the Losties, which meant they still traded with them and had more interesting food than I'd get from crèche pap. And they believed in "food as expression," so they took the usual packs and added extra flavours or sometimes even non-paste stuff they got from the parents of students. TwiceFar had a thriving spice trade, and Hap loved to try new tastes.

Their quarters were small and shabby, a set of rooms that had once been school-space but always smelled delicious. The furnishings were, like those of everyone I knew, scavenged or fourth-hand. They'd taped a swathe of purple and gold fabric up on the wall behind me; it was a coarse woven rectangle with stripes running horizontally across it, and the fabric was weird and uneven, as though it had bumpy little knots in the thread. I liked to touch it and feel those nubs in the slickness of the rest of the fabric.

As Hap and I talked over the meal, I asked them about Bellwether.

"They were isolationists," Han said. They pushed a platter of brown leathery stuff that I figured was fungus over toward me. I pretended not to notice and forked more salad onto my plate instead, then doused it with the dressing Hap had made, deliciously vinegary and smelling of something green.

"Isolationists in space don't survive in the long run," I said. We'd been discussing interstellar service civics the previous week. It was part of my directed reading project for that thousandth. I'd just started my third thousand, and it felt big-time—another two thousand days to go, and then I'd be an adult.

Hat's look was wry. "Good memory," they said. "Although we can't say for sure what would have happened if they hadn't been destroyed for being in the way between the RRinti and the Geshuts. They certainly were a long-lived group from back in the

Sprawl days, when everyone was spreading out as fast as they could, before they ran afoul of the Concords."

"Why are Brit's parents staying here?"

Hap pushed fungus around on their plate, chasing a large bit and forking it before answering. "They decided to capitalize on a mix of paperwork and custom and bureaucracy." They spread their hands in a helpless gesture. "TwiceFar is in the middle of contested space. By tradition, it's a neutral zone, but that doesn't stop people from meddling with internal politics or sometimes outright ignoring that and invading. The longest regime you'd have seen would have been, what, the Zonista? That wasn't a bad time for teachers. Often, we're the ones regimes and empire-builders go for first."

I cleared my throat, and they sighed. "You're not going to let me slide, are you? Brit's parents paid some sort of bribe, I suspect. People from Bellwether are usually under interdict."

"Why? To punish them for something?"

"Where's your common sense? Think about the economics of it."

I did while I chased the last of my salad down with water. Hat's room was in a nicer section than the crèche. Every once in a while, you heard the noises from people on one side or another, but most of the time, it was quiet in a way that made me feel like I was unfolding while being in the crèche—or even school, sometimes —pressed on me in the other direction, squished me down into something smaller. "They're isolationist," I said. "But what are the economics of that?"

"Hint," they said. "Do they pay taxes?"

My eyes widened. "They don't?"

"Self-reliance, they say. So how does that affect the equation for you?"

That made it a lot easier. "They're using the stuff that everyone else funds, like the waystations."

"And the meddienet, to avoid contagion, and the relays, for guidance, and so forth, and so forth."

"And the school system."

They shook their head. "Forced into it by the current system, which dictates all individuals in the pre-adult category must participate in the educational system. If they'd come a hundred days ago or so, she wouldn't have to."

Brit's attitude made a lot more sense to me now. She probably hadn't counted on being made to participate. They'd shoved her in a lifepod without showing her how to steer. And now here she was, among aliens . . .

"What sort of isolationist colony?" I asked. It worried me a little to think they could be anti-anyone but human because I could tell that would lead to all sorts of trouble, and it's also the stereotype you always see.

"One of the like-minded sects," they said. I relaxed. Those were based on lifestyles, not being against something or someone, usually. "Angelike's trying to help her fit in, isn't he?"

"Of course, he is," I said scornfully. "But I don't know why he's bothering."

They tapped the fungus platter again, and I finally took a spoonful. One of the things all the teachers were long on was "trying new things" and "exploring understanding." They had that tone in their voice as they said, "Why do you think that matters to Angelike?"

I had to think about that. Last quarter, we'd been given analytic maxims for these sorts of questions, so I applied one. "Because he doesn't feel like he fits in?"

"Good." They leaned back in their chair, picking at the peeling plastic of the arm. "What do you think of the mushrooms?"

I wrinkled my nose but tried a second bite. Sometimes it changes things. I still didn't like it. "Too strong." It tasted the way I imagined old-Earth "dirt" from the stories tasted. Or like licking a wall.

"Thank you for trying it," they said. "Dev, what do you think is the point of our school?"

That seems like such an easy answer that it had to be a trick, but I said the first thing that came to mind nonetheless. "To learn."

"To learn what?"

"Math and stuff."

They shook their head. "A good interactive viddie could teach you most of that. Think about the situational aspects of a classroom."

"Something about being around other kids and learning from each other," I guessed.

They made a little gesture, encouraging me to go further.

I rolled my eyes at them but complied. This was the price of a meal at Hat's. "Learning how to understand each other."

"Understand each other in order to ..."

My intuition leaped, caught a handhold, pulled itself up.

"In order to get along."

They grinned. "Sorry, I don't mean to teach when you're trying to just eat. But getting along's a survival skill. And I want you to succeed, Dev. You're smart and have good base genes."

"But I'm unmodified. Like Angelike." My parents had died before doing more than base work. Most miners let their kids start modding around four thousand days because they know by then what's useful to them: extra limbs are always popular, or at least swapping hands in for feet. But I was your basic human model. If I wanted any changes, I'd have to either earn the fee in advance or indenture myself.

It was a tough call. Indenture sucks, but I'd have the mods and be at least a couple of pay slots up to start with. I still had plenty of time to decide.

"That doesn't matter as much as you think it does," they said. "You're motivated. You watch and learn. You make the most of things. You're pragmatic."

I twitched a shoulder shrug in order to deflect any more embarrassing elaboration. But I thought about it while I was talking to Angelike that night during class check-in. He was spending the night with his parents, which the crèche let him do once a week.

He tapped the bag at his belt. "It's because of the album," he said. "A lot of the Losties have little gardens out here, and I know they'll let me take leaves. If they won't, I'll offer chore time for them."

I knew the Lostie gardens were where Hat got a lot of their flavours, although you were supposed to call them *spices* if they were natural-grown.

"A lot of us are putting albums together," Angelike said. "You should print one out, see what you can do. You're going to have to mod it, though. There's lots of stuff here Brit doesn't have pages for."

I did print one out, but I knew better than to take leaves without asking. So I went to find Bethany, who cleans our section, and explained what I wanted.

"I got you something better than that," she declared. "Time has come to pass it along, and you're a good kid."

She made me follow her to her storage locker, where she produced an album that looked a lot like Brit's. But when she opened it, I saw the leaves in this one were all different colours, and the shapes were all the same: long and skinny.

"Those aren't leaves, they're feathers," she told me. "My grandparents brought that, long longtime ago. You can take it in to show. Something like that is put together for looking at more than it is for shoving away."

Delight made me almost giddy. A treasure like this . . . well, it was better than Britt's album for sure. Feathers! I knew the word, but I'd never seen such a thing. I swore to Bethany I'd take good care of it.

It turned out I wasn't the only one who brought in something different. When we met for class the next day, a lot of kids were carrying albums of one form or another.

None of them looked precisely like Brit's, though. The triplets had snipped leaves out of fabric. I was pretty sure their cousin, who owned the shop they would have taken the fabric from, wasn't going to be very happy about that. Kendra, whose parents worked with the biolabs, had what she said were "spore prints," circular patterns that looked nothing like the mushrooms Hat had served me.

As each book was opened and explained, I could see Brit getting unhappier and unhappier, her body tightening, winding in on itself. I tried to think about it the way that Hat would have wanted me to. They were taking away the thing that made her special. She'd been proud of the leaves, showing us something new. Something that let her feel superior. And everyone had taken that and gone even further. She couldn't see that it was something new, and that was why they were so enthusiastic. It must feel like an attack.

I started to say something, and then I thought to myself, *Why should I intercede?* This was life. She'd had things well off until now, her and her whole free-loading station. She could learn from it. Maybe it'd teach her to be a better person. And so I bit my lip and let her keep going, even though I could see that Hat hadn't noticed her face.

Angelike was the last to go. He opened his, and we could see how many pages filled it, leaf after leaf. "A friend of my cousin's works with hydroponics, and another in transit," he explained. "But most of them came from Alters." That's the polite word for Losties.

Brit jumped forward, grabbed it from him, and threw it to the tiles with one fast, angry motion, smashing it down.

We all froze, every one of us. Like we were incapable of action. I'd seen fights before, but nothing like the way Brit went after him then, as though it was the only thing she could think of. Her head down, she butted into him, snarling. He reeled back from the impact, arms flailing, and went back over the chair behind him, a windmill of motion.

We all heard the crunch as his head hit the wall. I can hear that sound in my mind still. I think I'll hear it till I die.

Brit staggered back and just stood there, staring. I don't know how much time passed. It was like we were all holding as still as we could, as though if we didn't move, it wouldn't have happened. We wouldn't have to move forward into a future where this had happened.

But it had. And finally, Ferb was the first to react, rushing forward to Angelike, and that set all of us into motion at once, and everything was chaos for a little while. Hat had hold of Brit's shoulder as though they thought she might attack someone else. They had already got on the intercom, and medics were on the way, they said. An alarm was going off, a low *rrm, rrm, rrm* sound that wouldn't stop.

After the medics had come and gone, I picked up Angelike's album. Everyone was just standing around. Hat was talking on the intercom again, making the security report.

When I read the inside cover, what Angelike had written there, I stopped for another long moment. Then anger flared in me like a star engine first coming into existence.

My legs felt like stilts, carrying me over to Brit with stiff steps. She recoiled, but I pushed the album at her. I wasn't gentle about it, but she made no sound as it rammed into her stomach. "Read it. Read what he wrote for you."

She glanced down, scanning the words. Her face changed when the meaning of it slammed into her indignation. It crumpled and fell in on itself, her lips trembling, her eyes welling with tears.

It was probably an act, I thought, and sneered at her. She could try to play games like that with anyone else, but I saw through her. I knew what she was.

"Read it out loud, you spoiled brat," I insisted. Everyone was watching us.

She shook her head.

"Dev," Hat said in a warning tone and reached out to me, but I shrugged out from under their hand and continued.

"No?" I said to Brit. "Then allow me." I turned the book around and looked down at the words, even though they were already burned into my mind.

Everyone else in the room was totally silent. We could hear the robots going down the hallway, carrying Angelike's body away to the hospital. "For Brit, with the hope that it makes the place seem less strange." I looked her in the eye. "A present. For you, shithead."

Her mouth worked as though trying to say words, but she couldn't summon them.

I didn't want to hear them anyhow. What could she possibly say that would be meaningful? What could anyone say?

I let go of the album, let it fall again to the floor. This time, it landed closed. I turned my back on all of it and walked away. No one stopped me.

YOU LEARN FROM EACH OTHER, Hat had said.

What Angelike learned from dying, as he did the next day, I don't know. It turned out his parents had never bothered to keep memory backups, and because we were state kids, we wouldn't be able to afford reconstitution anyhow. He was gone, just like I'd be gone if I died before becoming an adult and securing my own backup system.

What Brit learned is something I don't know either. She didn't come back to school, and her delegation left the station two cycles later, just before a coup happened that would have ousted them anyway.

Han gave me Angelike's album over dinner another two cycles later. I wouldn't have guessed how hard it would hit me. I stared down at it and squeezed my fists tight, trying to swallow back tears.

They sighed and sat down on the wall shelf, leaning back against the cracked pleather. "I'm sorry. He was a nice boy and would have become a good man. I know something like that's inadequate, but there you have it. Angelike would have known what to say to make you feel better. I don't."

"There was no point to it," I said, each word a numb clot of meaninglessness.

"There was the point you make of it. Do you think—and everyone in that room—won't remember Angelike next time they're about to act hastily? That would be the tragedy, if they didn't."

"We'll remember Brit and what she did, too," I said. "Maybe instead of."

"What do you think Brit remembers? Will remember most of her life, probably?"

I was too angry to answer still, but I could feel the truth of Hat's words, and so I tucked them away to think about on some day when I wasn't so angry.

I went round to Akla's Wares, where the triplets were working for their cousin. It turns out they hadn't asked about cutting holes in the cloth, and they were now having to cut all the bolts anew, so there weren't any leaf-shaped holes in them. Hat had given me some sugar treats to take with me, so I shared them around and helped with the cutting for a while. Then I went back to the crèche.

After lights out, the rooms aren't exactly dark, but the light is greyish purple, shadowy and soothing. The rooms are small, but you can fit six people in the triple bunks, first-come, first-served.

In the middle of sleep period, I woke up, thinking I'd heard Angelike breathing, and lay there listening for it. The others in the room breathed, in and out, and Reili hissed just a little in its drowze, then turned over, and I waited to go back to sleep, knowing that the sound I wanted would only be audible in my dreams.

I still hear it in them, now and again.

THE DESERT OF THE REAL

By Mark Everglade and Joseph Hurtgen

T he wind blew incessantly through the unending desert wilds of North America East, tossing up loose trash and what little was left of the topsoil. The storms were getting worse, and as the montane forests died off, the resulting landslides eroded the mountains that had once protected the region. Few were left to study the phenomenon; most couldn't even remember what the mountains had been called. The displaced Arctic Jet Stream compounded the issue, bringing dust devils of biohazardous waste to dance across the desert. Birds, now scarce, were easily mistaken for plastic, carried high in the air and then whirling back earthward to land on a field of unsold fast-fashion clothes called PlastiCity.

A freezing gust knocked over the village's outer wall of aluminum cans, plastic toys, bundled clothes, unused calendars, history texts, and antiques. Amin ran through the gap to gather with other boys atop a dune, bundled up in layers of previous decades' fashions. On the back of his bile-coloured jacket were the words *Mountain ew*.

A loud blast rent the air, bringing the kids to their feet. They turned their gazes to the sky, using their hands as visors. A metal capsule pierced the clouds as it fell, growing larger every second until it landed, kicking up trash and dirt from the crater.

The top of the capsule opened, and a man climbed out.

"Dad!" Amin exclaimed. "Where have you been? Where'd you find that thing? Can I ride in it?"

"Son? My son? I have no idea." His father reached into the capsule for an Immortality Inc. windbreaker and pulled it on, but the icy winds still made him shiver.

The other boys scoured the machine for usable parts, but Amin tugged on his father's jacket. "What happened, Dad?"

"There was a machine, a ripping sound... it's all a blur."

AURORA BREEZED through the atrium of the nonprofit Children's Home and Surrogate Mothering, or CHASM, for short. Her billowy, baggy clothes fanned out shapelessly around her. She was more than familiar with the home's twisting passages. Like most of the surrogate mothers, she'd grown up in CHASM and had stayed because she had nowhere else to go. Every year since Immortality Inc. had gone into operation, the halls had become more crowded, with many dead ends and meeting rooms converted into bedrooms. Most were orphaned after miners went missing in the Outer Reaches, though the companies involved had done little to investigate.

"Keep up! You're on in five minutes." Katarina held Aurora's hand and mazed through a branching corridor. "Gotta earn those Karma tokens if you want your reward!"

Aurora headed to the courtyard, matching her pace. "That's not why I do this. I don't care about an eternal reward. I just want those orphans to live well. If my singing at this fundraiser helps those kids, that's reward enough."

Katarina stopped at a door and pushed it open. "That's why you're my girl." She lowered her voice, leaned in. "Did you hear another capsule dropped into PlastiCity yesterday?"

"Anyone in it?"

"Yeah, a diamond miner from Neptune."

"I guess he had no memory of the event like the others?" Aurora asked.

"None at all." Katarina looked up into Aurora's near-translucent purple-and-pink eyes and tried to take a deep breath. "I'm scared, Aurora. I hope it never happens to us. I can't imagine losing my memories with you."

Aurora took Katarina's hands and held them tight. Words couldn't express seeing her so vulnerable, but the silence of their unity acknowledged all their greatest hopes and fears. They pressed in close, and Aurora nuzzled her nose into Katarina's coarse black hair.

"Okay, it's showtime, Aurory!"

Aurora took to the stage amid cheers as the film crew aimed their cameras. She forgot about Katarina and the children in the warm glow of thousands of adoring fans.

———————

TIMOFEY TSARKOV GRABBED RUNGS on either side of a long corridor and sped himself weightlessly through Immortality Inc.'s orbital colony. He wore his dark Armani spacesuit, stiff as a charcoal-line drawing. The torus-shaped orbital was a mile in diameter, full of courtyards of glass-walled workstations manned by modded men. Their enhanced intelligence was a great boon to R&D when they weren't complaining about their bodies overheating. Their implants had been created by successive generations of AI creating AI. The original developers had lost track of the process many iterations ago.

Timofey savoured the efficiency of the worker's motions. Time was money, and as a newly minted trillionaire at the age of thirty-two, he had more than enough of both. After investing his father's inheritance, it had taken only five years to grow his company from a no-name to the tenth-highest-grossing in the solar system.

He spun, pushed up with his feet, and floated into his office in the orbital's central spoke. "Resume gravity," he said as he landed. Everything in his office was bolted down, especially his prized glass cases showcasing small vases crafted by the masterful child artisans of Tethys. The ornate scrolls wrapped around each vessel represented the golden ratio down to the millimetre, making them priceless hand-made relics. He had traded a few leftover pieces of meatvat chicken for them—what a deal! Plus, the scroll design had been selected as Immortality Inc.'s new corporate logo.

He poured his morning's double of scotch and rubbed a canister along his jugular vein, depressing a button as a glowing blue fluid suffused his skin, leaving fractal tattoos as it dissolved into deep tissue. The rush surged through Timofey's central nervous system. Legs wobbly, he leaned against the curvilinear window for balance. He tapped his temple, and reports matrixed across his vision, detailing production in factories and mines spread across three planets and nineteen moons—no, wait, *eighteen* moons.

One was flashing red. "Samantha, why is production on Enceladus stalled?"

Samantha walked in from an adjacent office, wearing a gold designer jumpsuit accentuated by bands of gold, sparkling eyeshadow. "Oh, the thermoregulators failed. Not too surprising since it's an eighty-kilometre-long pipeline running to the one warm spot on the entire moon, a geochemical ocean."

"Can't they get it working and get back to production?"

"Well, new colonists probably will."

"Why not the current crew?"

Samantha looked at Timofey quizzically. "We're talking about Enceladus. Aren't you familiar with the reports? It's really cold there."

"Cold? Cold never hurt anybody."

"They never had time to hurt. It dipped to -220 Celsius. Flash-froze all of them. Their blood clotted immediately. They were so brittle that when our quality team entered and tried moving them, the bodies fractured into pieces."

Timofey shrugged. "Tell them to pick up the pieces and move on."

———————————————

SAMANTHA SWALLOWED down contempt and forced a smile. "Yes, sir! You'll be happy to hear that we've got a ship full of new recruits headed there to restore operations. Still, with the billions we invest in heating that place, how do we make a profit?"

"We mine the resources on the cheap in the Enceladus tundra and sell them back to the people's families on Earth at thousands of times the value. You just reshape the precious minerals into some cartoonish character, and they empty their paychecks. Company Kredit cards ensure everyone has a chance at the good life. Even deaths like these are profitable. We're the beneficiary of their life insurance. We repossess their vacated apartments. Sell them to the next crew. It's pure efficiency."

"But do they ever complain, sir?"

Timofey chuckled. "They're too busy dreaming of the promises of eternal salvation through the Immortality Machine. For the skeptical, I give them employee awards like that cheap golden-plated wrench over there, which I think I owe some layman on Neptune for finding diamonds in the core."

Samantha pressed a button on her eyeglasses. "Exactly what I needed to hear."

"You're recording?"

"Yes, sir, I have to record all corporate meetings."

"This wasn't a meeting. Erase it now."

Samantha blinked her eyes three times. "Done." She helped Timofey strip off his spacesuit. A cushioned slab slid out of the wall, and he lay down while Samantha worked at the knots in his back. "Stats show the Kredit System is functioning as intended."

"Of course, it is. I made it. Now, work those hands lower." Timofey moaned with pleasure and then heard a voice unlike any other, something raw and natural. He turned his eyes to the nearest screen. "Hey, who's that girl singing in white there? Some big event happening on Earth?"

Mid-Swedish massage, Samantha chopped at Timofey's lower back. "Oh, I adore her! That's the philanthropist who dates—"

"I don't care what guy she dates! Get *me* a date with her, no, a private concert!"

"On it, boss!" Samantha contacted a woman named Katarina on Aurora's management team through her onboard Starnet communications system. She had a reply in minutes. "How should I say this . . ."

"Say what?"

"Well, she won't perform unless you make a charitable contribution."

"Pay them off, then."

"Well, it's not a payoff; it's to support orphaned children, I believe."

"Still a payoff. Do it now!"

Samantha massaged Timofey's scalp, pressing her fingers as deep as she could into his skull, vaguely hoping to penetrate it, while using Starnet to wire funds and fire off texts by running her eyes across a virtual keyboard. A reply came in. "She'll be here in three days, but there's still the issue of—"

"There're no other issues! She's coming to me."

Samantha smiled and nodded her head. "Whatever you say, Boss!"

———————

AURORA WAS beside herself with anticipation. No more dancing with dust devils; she was headed to the stars! She opened a package from Immortality Inc., and her excitement vanished. They'd sent her lingerie for the performance. She put on the mostly fishnet body stocking, though it was far too tight, and she had a hard time not spilling out. They must have gotten her size wrong, but complaining to the company that had a monopoly on eternity would be even less comfortable than the outfit.

She was expecting a private ship. Instead, a ring of light enveloped her. She shielded her eyes from the radiating glow as the halo glided from her head down her body. Her stomach sank, and its contents swirled back and forth. Gravity tugged at more angles than the bodysuit. Then she was weightless, pure energy like a stream of starlight speeding through space, the ring around her lighting the way. The desert planet spread out below, an ashen-dun marble, endless dunes circled by a dingy sea that shrank every second as she left behind the heat and stink of that world.

Above, Immortality Inc.'s orbital headquarters was suspended in space, far outside any planet's exosphere. From a distance, the dark structure resembled a small spiral galaxy, with two arms stretched out that whipped through space as it rotated. One side housed gardens, Biltmore-scale homes, and corporate offices, and the other the Immortality Machine, a massive, hexagonal structure with a giant gate that sat at the brink of judgment.

Aurora wasn't sure if she landed, materialized, or blinked back into existence, but somehow, she found herself in the hallway of the company's headquarters. She turned from the window and took in a private corporate lobby where two tables of men in Armani suits leered at her while siphoning off a twenty-three-year-old bottle of Pappy Van Winkle and smoking oversized cigars. A state-of-the-art air-filtration system hoovered up the acrid smoke the moment it left the lips of the corporate elite. These were professionals that chased exploitative business deals with post-work vice.

A Botoxed brunette in an ultra-mini silver-sparkle cocktail dress walked her way, and the men cheered. She smiled and blew them a kiss. "I'm your host this evening, Samantha Foxy. From databasing to debasing, I do it all here! Remember to send me your drink orders via Starnet!"

"Show us some skin, Foxy!"

Samantha tightened the hand holding the mic into a fist but

kept smiling as a tall man entered the bar with his hands behind his back. She pretended not to notice his gaze while emceeing. "All the way from Buried Earth, let's give a roar of applause for none other than Aurora Borealis!"

"That's not my last name," Aurora started, but Samantha shoved the mic in her hand, and a disco beat fluttered through recessed speakers.

At first, Aurora felt odd without her backup band. But it wasn't just canned music: the backing track seemed to react to her feelings as the melody flowed from her lips as if something sentient plucked the unseen strings. She turned the beat around in her mind and tapped into something passionate from her youth, but something tapped back, feeling her out as the rhythm shifted. Maybe it was the Kredit System evaluating her, but it had never felt this personal.

A song emerged from the depths of her soul, like a desert flower that only bloomed at night. She arpeggiated through some figures and then found an obscure jazz chord to kiss the melody with pure blue light. There were no wrong notes in jazz, and for a moment, she was free, until the audience's scowls returned her to more common voicings.

The unseen unintelligence felt for the next song.

Aurora watched her audience imbibe drinks, then looked away to the window filled with the desiccated planet below. The affluence in the air soured her performance. Her art wasn't a conversation with the audience, it was a one-way feed, and she felt reduced to just another singer with a pretty face. The men clearly weren't here for the music. Lithe songbirds like Aurora were a hot commodity, and seeing the way some of the men were running their eyes up and down her legs, she raised her guard, not wanting to get burned. Anything could be disposed of. She'd seen the desert swallow entire villages, and the emptiness in these men's souls was no different.

Still, it was an opportunity. Her life had been a series of overlapping events with nothing to bind them, and this was a chance to empower herself to change that, to match wits with people who had a real purpose, not the abstract poetics of the desert folk below.

But something wasn't right. *The folk below?* She had never called them that.

Her voice cracked, and she dropped the mic with a resounding bass thud and headed toward the bar. One man stood shakily and followed her.

"Aurora, you dazzle with, how can I say it, a melodic flame."

She blushed.

The man extended a hand around the lounge, with its exotic hardwood floors and space-age polymer ceiling arcing above. A Calder mobile hung there, its primary colours turning silently, sometimes catching earthen light. "This is my world. All that you see, I created," he said, gesturing everywhere, even to the planet out the window. "I am Timofey Tsarkov, President of Immortality Incorporated." He took her hand in his own, pulled it up to his mouth, and slathered lips across flesh.

Aurora withdrew her hand. "Not all that you see is yours, Mister Tsarkov."

"No? We'll see about that. But, if I may: why did you stop your performance?"

She shrugged. "I needed a drink."

"Of course! You've just teleported and then sung! Teleportation isn't an easy means of travel. It has an effect, something like jet lag. I should know. No one has teleported as much as I have, not by half. It leaves you feeling strange, half-dead, an inert object without thought, without personality." He chuckled. "But you're a god when you teleport." He took in her curves through the fishnet. "Or a goddess! Yes, you can go to the moon or to Jupiter and right back in a blink. I've watched a solar eclipse from Triton. I've eaten steak sandwiches on the silver shores of Thalassa."

Aurora looked at Timofey from the corner of her eye, crossing her arms, wishing he would teleport the hell away from her as he ran his mouth.

"The cost to teleport an individual used to be $790,000 Kredits a pop before we figured out nanowave frequencies."

In spite of herself, she bit at the conversation. "Nanowave frequencies?"

"Yes, we use vanishingly small wavelengths to send matter. It costs virtually nothing. Boggles the mind! We call it Starnet. As long as you have a receiving node and the right authorization, it takes a second to travel or send data anywhere. We've sent out hundreds of nodes already, coupled with satellites to search for alien life that might try to hijack them, as the network's fully under our control."

"Where exactly are you wanting to go?"

"Everywhere!" Timofey walked around behind her, swept her hair to the side to trace her neck. His fingers were cold, her skin rising with goosebumps at his touch. Her heart quickened to the rhythm of the disco beat that still filled the room.

"Hey, where's your TSAR logo?" he asked, looking at the base of her spinal cord. "Didn't you get our vocal mod?"

She turned to meet his steel-grey eyes. "Um, vocal mod?"

"Hard to change a bod, easy to slap in a mod."

Aurora shrugged her shoulders, smiled to hide competing feelings of intrigue and loathing. "Are you always this charming?"

"What is it, my dear? What's your secret? Gene hacking?"

"Gene hacking?"

"How do you sing like you do?"

"Oh, that. It's a gift."

"But it doesn't sound like our Sonic 5900 implant." Timofey looked out the lounge's bank of curving windows, talking quickly to himself. "Is there a new competitor on the market? Jorgenson, probably. That son of a . . ." He touched his temple, eyes moving as if scanning documents. A minute later, the slackness went from his face.

"Not everything can be bought, Mister Tsarkov."

"You're wrong. You really think these men would be here if it weren't for the fact I pay them?"

The men at the table roared with laughter as they toasted each other and rubbed canisters on their necks that issued blue glows. A minute later, their eyes shone a bit brighter, their voices slurring slower.

"I don't use any mods, though, really. I hear melodies, and I sing them."

"Oh, an overdub implant. We've been doing that for years."

Aurora puffed up her chest and took a stern tone. "I don't have implants!"

The men laughed harder.

"I hear whispered tones in my mind. Only I hear them until I let them go and, you know, sing."

"Whispered Tones, is it? Must be Jorgenson's next generation of implants. Does Whispered Tones feed you those lyrics too?"

"It's all my own!"

Timofey narrowed his eyes. "You really believe you have this gift? You believe this innate ability flowered in the desert? Even if it did, we can't have anyone else knowing that. Innate gifts aren't profitable. I can't bottle up your voice and sell it. But if you help me sell the new Sonic 6000, then you could make a good living."

"There's a difference between making a living and making a life."

Timofey motioned toward the far side of the lounge. The giant machine loomed out the window, rising from across the arm of the colony, silhouetted against the stars. "If you do really well, maybe you'll have eternal life. It's all right there," he said, pointing to the gate.

"Well, maybe some things are worth getting," she admitted.

"From now on, you'll say you've got a Sonic 6000. We'll give you one on the house. You'll run an ad at the start of each show. We'll cut your charity thing in on the profits. Think of the greater good! The Kredit System will capture your Karma from the contributions, and before you know it, you'll have enough Karma to do whatever you like! You can even enter the Immortality Machine."

"I guess you're right. I was just unfocused, sorry. I should be thinking of eternity, not these little finite moments," she said, unconsciously mimicking his accent.

"That's a good girl."

"By the way, always wondered, the people who live forever, where do they go when they pass through the machine, I mean if they got enough tokens?"

"You ask an awful lot of questions for a desert rat."

WITHIN DAYS, Aurora had gained entry to Timofey's private suite. She learned how to hold a wine glass properly, to measure viscosity by the way wine slid down the glass, and to smell licorice, cherry, and vanilla undertones. She learned the curses that hastened the servants to her side to deliver bottle after bottle. She'd never known that wine was supposed to have a metallic taste to it, and, boy, did drinking orbital wine make her want to drink more. She vaguely missed Katarina and had to regularly bat away Timofey's advances, but overall, this was the good life.

The pool area was a perfect temperature. She reclined in a chair and raised her head to the sky, the moon a silver jewel gleaming through the view portal. But this life wouldn't last forever, or even another week, for she was due back on Earth for a show in two days. Might as well live it up in the meantime. She had worked hard enough to support orphans, but she was an orphan, too, and deserved her own support, even if it was just another buzz lifting her. Timofey held that no one should feel guilt for the power that fortune afforded.

A commercial lit up a holographic TV. A well-muscled man and a toned young lady sat on a beach, fruity drinks in hand, while the ocean tides moved in fast forward. Day became night and back again, but the couple were undisturbed. A voiceover spoke over reggae Muzak:

> Eternal life was once an alchemist's dream, but now it's the way of the future! For millennia, humans lived on only in song and legend. But, let's face it, those legends are not you. You'll never conquer your own desires, much less worlds. You can barely get a rise, much less rise above the forgotten. But now the song can go on. Immortality Inc. has the solution. Ninety percent of our members go on to live forever. Click here to get your free approved implant and first Karma token.

Ninety percent seemed like a lot, but she had no way of verifying it since immortals usually disappeared to paradise colonies thereafter if the rumours were to be believed. As for the unsuccessful initiates, no one knew their fate. She'd have thought no more of it, but something about Samantha's expressions when they passed in the hall and the phrases that snuck out from under closed office doors made it seem something was amiss. Being called a *desert rat* only made it worse, even if the slur had become customary among off-landers.

"Back to Planet Dearth," she sighed.

FLECKS OF SUNLIGHT consolidated into an hourglass shape as Aurora materialized back on Earth. A dark red halo fizzled out around her. She had just been on the orbital seconds before. Her mind rejected the journey, but her body believed it.

She was overdressed and already sweating. The Arctic Jet Stream had retreated to the poles, leaving a blast of a heatwave to scorch sands that had almost iced over a week ago. She'd have to lose her layers of rich velvet with gold-threaded embroidery. That was fine. None of the desert folk below could recognize a Rochegrosse from the clothes that insulated the village walls. Yet, she was the folk below, wasn't she? Begrudgingly, she headed past the pueblos toward the stage to get it over with, something shifting inside with each step.

Katarina found her before the opening cue. "Aurora! I've missed you. And, uh, what are you wearing?"

Aurora looked at Katarina through glazed-over eyes filled with hot tears. "Oh, Kat. I don't have time now. Afterwards, okay?"

Katarina nodded, smiling through her disappointment.

Aurora took to the stage, but her opening act was devoid of passion. She had forgotten about the marketing she had agreed to, as if that world was somehow another universe and not real life.

The ad for the Sonic 6000 cut her off, screeching through the speakers.

"What is this?" a group of concertgoers asked. "You haven't got the money for an implant like that."

"It's nothing, really," she stammered, clutching her pounding head. She was exhausted from the trip, or maybe just hungover. She looked out on the rabble that had turned out to hear her sing and frowned. *This CHASM concert is the pits.*

"This show isn't about a corporate sponsor; it's about the homeless fund," another said.

Wide-eyed, Katarina shook her head in disbelief. "You sold us out to Immortality, Inc.?"

"Well, why not? This place is a wasteland!" Aurora sneered.

Katarina turned her face to the ground.

Aurora took a step toward Katarina. "They're sending contributions in return! Don't worry."

"She thinks she's better than us, like we're, what, desert rats?" The crowd booed and threw drinks.

Aurora tried to focus. Sweat ran into her eyes. Her head pounded. She needed a drink, an orbital full of drinks, a sweet slosh of wine to put these feelings and herself to bed. Though she had been skeptical of the company's intentions, this outrage only confirmed Timofey's judgments. She tried to tell them about how he was thinking on an entirely larger scale than any of them, but the Sonic 6000 diced up the word *Immortality* as she spoke, coming out as, "I'm more totality."

"She's a corporate shill for Immortality!" a woman in the crowd accused.

One man stood and yelled, "They killed my family! Sent them to the Enceladus mines, where they skimped on the thermoregulator maintenance until they failed."

Amin scowled from the front row. "They erased half my dad's mind when he returned from his trip to the machine."

The accusations flew in, followed by a hundred shouts of, "Me, too!"

"No, you're all wrong! If you work hard, you'll live forever! Well, uh, ninety percent of you!" she exclaimed.

The crowd surged. People clawed their way onto the stage and ringed around Aurora, pushing, yelling. She threw her hands up to deflect the onslaught and backed toward the rear exit, but not before a teenager wearing a misprinted 2021 Miami Heat championship hat shoved her down the steps. Security tackled him as Katarina caught Aurora, saving her from a bad fall.

She helped her get away from the angry crowd. "Aurora, I don't know what happened, but you're not yourself. Have you forgotten what we've worked so hard for?"

"What we've worked for?"

"For the orphans! For a better life for all the people here and on the colonies with nothing!"

"Kat, Timofey's been spending time with me. Lots of things aren't perfect, but it's almost like it's the best it can be, you know? And, yeah, he's given me anything I want."

"*The* Timofey, you mean Tsarkov himself?" Katarina asked with wide eyes, then sighed. "I thought everything you wanted was right down here." She swept up a pile of sand and let it course through her fingers. "This is what we become, regardless of anything else."

Aurora cried. "I'm so sorry. I got carried away with that whole lifestyle. I'm so used to having nothing."

"I forgive you."

"And you won't leave me?"

"No. But first, I have some questions for you to ask Timofey."

TIMOFEY ACCEPTED Aurora's teleportation request and returned her to the orbital. He was waiting for her in the private bar of the board of directors. "Ah, my darling *par excellence*. You've been gone too long! I can see the mark of the desert on your skin. Can I burden you with lunch and drinks?"

Aurora smiled at the charming businessman and let him lead her to a private booth.

Three drinks later, Aurora took Timofey's hand. "I have some questions . . ."

"Yes, anything."

"About the Immortality Machine . . ."

Timofey withdrew his hand. "Just as the ways of God are unknown, so, too, are the machine's."

"Come on, Timofey. You made the thing! How does it work?"

"Nature only shows us glimpses of God, my dear. And like the machine, both nature and God are dangerous to man."

"Um, are you saying the machine is dangerous?"

Another round of drinks arrived at the table, and Timofey downed both. He leaned back against the booth for stability and smirked. "Hopefully, the rest of you proves as insatiable as your curiosity."

"Does the machine generate profit?"

"It would be sabotaged in a heartbeat were that the case. It encourages people to produce as much as possible, achieve as much as possible, keeping the whole financial system going. It's pure altruism. AI implants track everyone's actions. When they have enough accomplishments, they enter the machine and trade in their Karma tokens for their eternal reward, and they're off to the paradise colonies."

"And if they don't have enough achievements?"

"Then the machine judges accordingly."

"Judges? Didn't your company program the protocols?"

"Hold that thought." Timofey produced a canister from the front pocket of his blazer and rubbed it over his neck. Blue fluid oozed out, then vanished into his skin. Head wobbling, he smiled lazily. "Now, where was I? Oh, yes, the protocols evolved quite naturally. We don't create programs, protocols, or whatever. We nurture and grow them."

"But every plant needs soil, something we have little of on Earth, thanks to all your resource extraction. Every system runs on something. So, what are you feeding this thing?" She met his eyes dead-on, putting down her drink. She wouldn't be placated this time.

He glared. "What are you, a reporter? What rises in the East sets in the West." He rubbed his hands together. "In fact, why don't I indulge your insolence and allow you to see it with your own eyes? Then you can judge our operation."

"Fine. Which way to immortality?"

———

A MAGLEV TRAIN travelled along the colony's sweeping arm, which extended into space. The car was empty except for Aurora. The train sped forward and threw her back against the seat, knocking her drink out of her hand. The maglev was speeding too fast to jump out. The railway was out ahead—Timofey had sent her here to die! But as the path ended, a golden halo enveloped the train, floating it across the difficult terrain.

It jerked to a stop, and the door opened. She disembarked via a transparent platform and raised her head to the stars. The faint outline of a dome was all that held the air she was breathing. Below, Earth was showcased as a splotchy marble, all browns and oil-spill black.

The black portal at the base of the machine loomed before her like a shroud. Circuitry ran across the bridge in a grid and up the towering hexagonal structure.

All she needed to do was pass through and be judged to get to the bottom of all this. Red lights flickered from dozens of panels, switches, levers, and knobs aligned in precise configurations, reminding her of a multitrack music mixer. This was how immortality was forged, through the precise manipulation of variables.

She stepped before the great gate, the hexagon flushing her face with necrotic light. She covered her ears from the deafening hum of its operations. Her work would finally pay off, yet, looking at the distant Earth, guilt surged through her as she remembered the conversation with Katarina, as if this success was at their expense, as if her charity work had ultimately been for her own glory.

Samantha had been equally skeptical but had also trusted in her. Before she had left, Samantha had given her a necklace with a silver pendant as a parting gift. She had said the locket, jammed shut, would open when the time was right. Aurora twirled it around her fingers as she stepped through the gate.

Aurora blinked and found herself lying on a pile of discarded fast-fashion clothes. Some of the CHASM kids ringed her and pulled on her limbs.

"Aurora, you okay?" said a freckly pre-teen girl wearing knock-off Jordans.

"I, I don't know. How did I get here?"

"You just appeared. No space capsule like the others or nothing, just like *bam!* There you are."

"Space?" she asked.

"You don't really think you're better than all of us, do you?" asked a little boy.

Aurora sat up. She placed her hand on the boy's shoulder. "No, of course not, Tran. Where'd you get that idea? I'm one of you. I lost my parents when an asteroid went through their dome on Europa."

"I was just thinking about the concert and the bad things people said," he replied, lowering his eyes.

"What concert? I haven't sung in a long time. Look, my head's really fuzzy, but you know I'm here for you."

Tran hugged her. "I knew you still cared."

"I'll never forget you all."

The locket around her neck opened at the sound of those words, and a golden scroll fell into her hand. It dissolved on her skin, and a flash of lightning shot through her head. She remembered everything: the trip, Timofey, the concerts and conversations, all the way up to entering the machine and seeing the dead bodies piled behind the gate. There was no immortality for those who worked hard, only electrocution. Those who hadn't put in enough work yet had their minds wiped of the experience and were returned to Earth. If these memories were contained in the scroll, perhaps everyone else's were, too. She knew what she had to do.

Where the memory scroll had dissolved on her palm was a tattoo of a location: Diamond Station.

"If I get you the specs, can you all reprogram a machine for me?"

The CHASM kids nodded and smiled. "That's all we do, is get old stuff runnin' again."

"I'm talking about the most powerful machine in the universe, or at least, we all thought it was."

"Is it big?"

"Huge! Think you can do it?"

"Well, the code's all the same size," the oldest boy said, shrugging as they laughed.

"All right, go get Kat. I'll send her what you need. Stay ready!"

"Okay, A'rory!"

She touched the tattoo on her hand, and vanished in a shimmer of light and a vacuum of sound.

––––––––––––––––––

AURORA APPEARED inside a transparent dome reinforced with gunmetal grey beams. Easily three hundred miners stood watching her. An electrified tornado whirled outside, dancing around a floating platform, extending far below, that seemed to constrain it. Sediment spun in the air, making it difficult to see where she was, but the blue sky pulsated with an unearthly glow, lit by a golden speck that, deep inside her most primal memories, she knew as the sun.

The walls were filled with a glowing gold liquid that sludged back and forth, perhaps an insulator from the cold or some protector against electric surges. A rubbery, spherical membrane opened in the dome, and a man walked through as it sealed behind him.

"Where am I?"

"Diamond Station, Neptune!" said the bulky, dark-haired and square-jawed man holding an oversized golden wrench. "I know what you're thinking. How are we standing on a gas giant? The dome sits on a hovering platform powered by the planet's endless supply of hydrogen. Our main operation is mining the deeper rocky layers we discovered where it rains diamonds, though it does hell to your equipment! But you don't look like the managerial type that Immortality Inc. usually sends to monitor us, so what brings you here?"

"Wait, did you say . . . ?"

"Neptune!" said a voice Aurora knew. She turned to spot the pretty, dark-skinned woman with bleached hair bound in bantu knots. "Samantha!"

Samantha came to her side. "I see you've restored your memories," she said, looking at the open locket around her neck. "The miners have had enough. If it wasn't for Sperry," Samantha looked to the big man with the wrench, who nodded his head, "they all would have died from the big freeze just like the miners on Enceladus. And all because of Immortality's negligence."

Sperry raised his wrench in the air. "Screw Immortality!" His voice echoed off the steel-and-glass dome arcing high overhead.

The miners joined in the chant and kept it up until Samantha called for silence. "I can't promise that you'll live through the day. But I know that together, we can throw off the shackles of Immortality and all its false promises."

"Immortality doesn't scare us!" called out a stout, bald man.

Sperry nodded. "We're dead if we stay here and the biodome fails, and we're broke even if we could continue working. Most of our best workers left to cash in on their immortality and never came back. And the only stores are in the company ships. They jack the rates of basic supplies because there's no competition out here."

The dome shook, whether from the storm outside or the

chanting that thundered up again, "Screw Immortality! Wrench Immortality! Kill Immortality!" The words devolved into frenzied shouts and scrambling that made less sense as it went, but the miners pressed forward toward Aurora and Samantha with a clear purpose.

"Hey, wait! She's one of them, ain't she?" they shouted at Samantha. "You're their analyst. You caused all this!"

Samantha's voice barely cut through the fracas. "I'm on your side! We don't have a plan yet, but we'll prevail against them. Trust me!" But the miners pressed tighter. Samantha screamed but couldn't thread the knot of bodies to relieve her panic. Aurora took a step back but was ringed in and stumbled.

Samantha unfocused her eyes and yelled, "Area teleportation: Organic heat signature—Timofey Tsarkov." She reached through the crowd to grip Aurora's hand, drawing her close. Time was running out! Once the corporation got word of their plans, they would revoke her transportation credentials, and they might freeze the dissidents to death. Thankfully, Timofey didn't know her memories were intact, though they wouldn't be if the crowd kept shoving and banging her head as they vied for Samantha.

Light enveloped the horde, and in a blink, the dome hovering above Neptune's icy atmosphere was left silent, save for the crackling of the storm.

SAMANTHA AND AURORA rematerialized in Immortality Inc.'s corporate headquarters.

Aurora, unsteady and exhausted, placed her hand against a wall and tried opening her eyes wide. "Where'd the mob go?"

"They're here somewhere. I used a displacement offset when

teleporting because it seemed like we could use a little distance. This way, we've no time to lose!" They headed toward the orbital's central axis. "We need more than a speech to start our revolution. The machine's rejects don't remember what it actually does, but just like your scroll brought you back to yourself, we can restore everyone else's memories. They'll remember the bodies." She shook her head and wiped away a tear.

"But not all the miners and desert ra—I mean, the folk below were rejected."

"Yeah, but it's way more than the ten percent advertised and more than enough for critical mass once they're awakened. Plus, I have a recording of Timofey confessing how the machine truly works, which I've set to broadcast through the colonies." Samantha stopped at an airlock for a retinal scan. The door hissed open, meaning Timofey wasn't onto her yet, but it wouldn't be long.

Aurora looked down another long hallway. "Uh, why are we walking when we could just teleport?"

"Teleportation's not magic! It'd take longer to code in the exact coordinates than it would to just walk. And there are risks." She flattened her bottom lip.

"You're afraid of him tracking your destination, and you know the moment you start to use it, and it doesn't work, it's because he found out."

"Meaning a hundred armed drones at our feet. We need those memory scrolls."

"But why doesn't the company just delete the memories?"

"They keep them for research on how people react to the corporate headquarters. I was forced to design project plans to make the place more palatable, from the stupid abstract art in the halls, boring and unoffensive, to the cocktails I served after business hours in those dumb dresses."

"Where are the scrolls?" Aurora asked.

Samantha pointed out a bank of windows to the great machine beyond. "Do we dare?"

"We've come too far not to try. The CHASM orphans think they can reprogram it. We've just got to get them access."

"Okay, I'll grab the scrolls and Starnet the memories to their owners while you link the CHASM orphans to the machine." Samantha stood in front of the maglev's retinal scan. It cleared her with a pleasing ping, and the doors hissed open. "Let's go."

THE MAGLEV TRAVELLED along the long arm of the orbital colony, then stopped at the Immortality Machine. Sparks crackled under their feet as Aurora and Samantha approached the weird hexagonal structure, lit only by its myriad blinking lights.

Aurora inserted a portable drive into the console at the base of the giant gate. "I'm in," she messaged Katarina down on Earth.

"We're accessing the network now," Katarina said. Kids chattered computer terminology, and a moment later, she said, "Done. Now to address the machine protocols, then disable anyone from returning it to its original configuration. Tran needs a higher level of security permissions. Can you find a pentagram-shaped slot?"

"A pentagram? I'm looking at a computer console, not the decor of a Satanic temple."

"It should be there! The maintenance manual says this has to be done onsite. We need this!"

Aurora sighed. "Must have been upgraded." Then she remembered what it felt like when the music system had interacted with her song without a direct connection as if something was searching for her melody as much as she was searching for a rhythm. "Let me try something." The machine was emitting a field at the edge of her mind. She focused and pierced through it, navigating the digital labyrinth as it spun around her. She pictured a star shape and the data import. "Okay, I see the menu. Upgrading credentials now."

"Got it! We'll get to work recompiling the machine's code after we edit a few key lines."

A blood-red light gushed from the gate. A spark travelled the outline of the machine, then consolidated into an electrical sphere that hovered at the centre of the gateway. Aurora shielded her eyes from its glow as an awareness penetrated her mind, blasting her as she fell back. She couldn't tell if she fell from an outside force or her own volition, where her mind ended and the machine began. Her Sonic 6000 implant blared inside her head, muddling her thoughts. Her back burned—hitting the floor had been like landing on a circuit board, the jutting components piercing her skin.

"Aurora!" Samantha yelled, but the gate slammed down, separating them.

A blast came from the machine. Aurora rolled to the side as it punched metallic debris into the air and singed hair from an arm. Another shot roared past her. She had to get to safety. Teleportation was down, her credentials no good.

An air duct offered hope. She ran toward the duct entry as the machine worked itself into another pre-blast rumble. She tried to force it open, but no luck. She shook as the machine's vibration took on its tale-tell roar.

Then the machine malfunctioned with a sputter, and Starnet came back online. She heaved for air.

Katarina's voice chirped in Aurora's ear. "Took a second! But we edited and recompiled the code. These kids are something else, huh?"

Aurora slumped to the floor and tried to stop herself from shaking. "Yeah, something else."

Samantha manually opened the gates with the levers and found Aurora huddled against a wall. "Hey, no breaks! We've got work to do! Take pictures of the corpses for evidence." She grabbed an armful of vials on a rack, each containing hundreds of curled memory scrolls. "Let's go!"

They ran from the machine as sparks fizzled. Down in PlastiCity, Katarina and CHASM must have been having fun with the orbital's controls, for the ubiquitous red lights were replaced with a rainbow medley of colours that lit their way.

Sperry watched from across the Immortality Machine's linking bridge to the other side of the orbital. "So, she *is* on our side!"

———————————

IN THE IMMORTALITY INC. BAR, Timofey rubbed a canister along his neck. His body went slack, and he fell into a ribbed, black-leather chair. His arms hung at his sides. Drool pooled at the side of a lip. Music heightened. The room started to glow unnaturally bright, and the already weird geometry of the orbital inverted and spun in his vision.

A surreal, rainbow glow filled the bar and a mob of distorted miners appeared. Timofey laughed. He preferred visions of dancing girls, but the angry mob carried a sense of realism, probably because of the double dose dissolving into his skin. Many of them even walked with a shuffle or a limp as if they worked in hard conditions, crouching, bending over, or twisting while operating heavy tools. It was all quite convincing.

The music stopped and his own voice played through the speakers.

Even deaths like these are profitable . . . For the skeptical, I give them employee awards like that cheap golden-plated wrench over there, which I think I owe some layman on Neptune for finding diamonds in the core.

Hilarious! Timofey was still laughing when a big man slammed a golden wrench into his side, knocking him from his ergonomic chair and breaking several ribs. Sperry lumbered over him as Timofey painfully gasped for breath. He accessed Starnet, selected a safehouse on Gateway. He started to phase out, but the teleportation protocol failed, and he phased right back without having gone anywhere. Timofey sucked in a ragged breath, his side shooting pain. "Shit!"

Two mining colonists grabbed his legs and dragged him out of the bar. Timofey kept on trying to phase out, but his form never completely dematerialized. Security guards ran at the mob but were pummelled and wrapped up with duct tape to a metal stanchion.

"Sperry, over there!" one miner yelled to another, pointing at the wall.

Sperry spied an autoturret cantilevering from the wall and knocked it loose with a hard thump from his wrench.

Drones spilled out from access panels but went down with a few strikes from the muscular men. The rest of the miners ripped the tops off the barstools and affixed them to the circular panels, blocking any more resistance from coming through as they corralled the board of directors.

The mob headed to the Immorality Machine's gates. "Let's give Immortality Inc. a dose of mortality." They pushed Timofey in along with his directors. The machine hummed for an instant and went quiet.

Sperry opened the door, but they were still alive. Someone must have reprogrammed its operations, for the machine was bathing them in a calming rainbow prism. Pictures of what must be the board members' childhoods played across the numerous screens on either side of the gate. The images transfixed them as they were exposed to simpler times and joys and the ideas of fairness that children knew better than anyone. Tears came to their eyes, and they exited the machine, looking younger and happy. They made their way past the miners, all smiles.

"What the hell? The machine kills us and heals them?" a miner exclaimed.

Timofey was the last one out and not one to be placated by a fancy light show. He kicked his pile of used canisters, having depleted his stash due to a fear of death or a fear of truly living. Blue goo ran down his shirt and stained his hands, his arms, his entire face. He sank under a hypnagogic whirlwind of disorientation.

Sperry blocked Timofey's path. "You've destroyed hundreds of thousands of lives, and for what?" He pointed to the blue-tinted skin around Timofey's neck. "A high?"

Timofey chuckled. "Lives? They're just tools. It's your arrogance that made you think you would live forever." He tried to walk past Sperry, but Sperry pushed him back. Timofey flashed his blue-stained teeth at the big man in front of him. "Those miners never had to work for me! No one forced them to sign a contract! No one forced them into the machine! They built their dreams on the machine and walked to their own deaths."

Sperry's face went red. He raised his golden wrench, the only award the company ever gave him. The gold spray paint flaked off in chunks as he brought it down on Timofey's head. The gold wrench went dark red. Timofey fell.

Sperry had seen enough. The supposed enlightenment of a few suits wasn't enough to make any lasting change. He dropped the wrench beside Timofey's lifeless body with a clank.

A wavelength extended from the top of the machine and shimmered through the air to wrap around Timofey's head. The machine reoriented itself into an almost humanoid structure as Timofey became one with it. Sparks spurted from his ears, and his eyes became backlit with the same blue glow as his drug of choice.

A voice rattled from the machine. "Immortality is for me and me alone! Curious thing: the machine made backups of all your memories, little pieces of conversation people gathered as they walked through my domain that I can now search through as if they were my own. They impart a picture of betrayal, with Samantha at the heart of it. Death to all that stand in my way!"

Levers on the control board moved on their own as the machine mirrored their movement. Its pieces jerked back and forth until they ripped off, hurling them at the crowd below. A massive cog spun through the air, decapitating five board members.

Steel pipes crashed atop Samantha, pinning her between them and the railing. "I can't access Starnet!" she yelled, voice breaking.

"I've shut it down!" called the machine. "Now, you're in *my* net!"

Sperry lifted a massive steel pipe far enough for Samantha to crawl out. "Run! Off the bridge!"

A PIPE FLEW PAST AURORA, impaling a board member. She saw Samantha clear the rubble. A plume of fire funnelled out of the machine's gate. She closed her eyes and connected to the machine as before, feeling for a chord, a rhythm, something. She found it, a pulsing industrial techno beat, warbling bass, and a screaming guitar line wah-wah-ing in and out. She found a melody inside the chaos of code and craze. At first, she sang softly, adding her voice to the nightmarish techno. A longer plume of fire scorched the bridge, and she stopped her song to jump back. But she found it again and sang louder this time, aligning her song with Timofey's will.

"You . . . can't . . . take control!" raged the machine.

Aurora outstretched her arms and went to her highest register, weaving a melody that played through light waves and sound, the pitch signature penetrating the firewall between them. Down in Plasticity, she knew the orphans were still at it, gaining her access to authorization overrides.

The barrier cracked. She knew Timofey's mind now. She channelled an impulse into his thoughts: *Nothing belongs to you.* She felt him taking aim and blocked him. "Yes! I've got you now! CHASM, do you have Starnet back up?"

Amin came in her ear. "Just came back online, A'rory!"

"Sam! Hit it!"

"With pleasure!" Samantha unfocused her eyes and selected the Starnet parameters. "Orbital teleportation: Immortality Machine to Diamond Station."

With a flash of light, the machine was gone, leaving an empty void in the massive orbital.

Aurora cleared the debris with laboured steps and found Samantha. "Can you get us out of here? I hate this place."

Samantha looked at the now half-empty orbital. "Sure. Where do you want to go?"

"All of us need to decide together, quickly," she insisted, gathering the miners.

Sperry spoke for them. "PlastiCity is fine by us. We'd rather reign over the Earth below than be subservient to a man like that in the heavens."

THE CORE of Neptune couldn't match the fire of Timofey's rage. How dare they send him here? His mind swirled with other people's memories, the machine's directives, and lines of programming foreign to his understanding. With his last strength and only a split second to live, he brute-forced his way through an algorithm that had locked him out of Starnet's teleportation system. He saw Samantha's fingerprints all over it and swore at himself for trusting her. Though conflicting data tore at his mind, he tried to find the last shred of his recognizable self, a part filled with vengeance that would reign supreme one last time. The machine melted around him, but not before he could issue one final command to the ubiquitous Starnet.

"Orbital teleportation: Orbital Colony One: Immortality Machine Arm."

As the metal framing his consciousness melted, sending red errors flashing across his vision, he vanished, to reemerge at the orbital colony in tandem with a surprise for those who thought they had bested him.

In whirled the electrified tornado, spewing microbursts of

diamond rain, teleported straight from Neptune. The speeding diamonds ripped through the orbital in seconds, shredding his corporate headquarters until the tornado dissipated within the artificial atmosphere. The space station collapsed, falling from orbit to the Earth to pile more junk onto a sea of junk.

The machine's mostly empty hull splintered off from the rest of the orbital, eventually splashing into the Pacific Ocean. It floated on the sea for days until the waves emptied it onto an already littered beach. The circuits flickered, sometimes filling with static, but Timofey brooded within, his thoughts hissing through the wires as sand, sea, and time slowly eroded the broken machine.

KATARINA RAN up to Aurora as she materialized. "You're back!"

Aurora held Kat tight for a long second and then pulled back to look at her. "Thanks for keeping me true to myself all this time."

"Don't mention it. You sure know how to make a hell of an entrance, though."

The corporate headquarters burned through the atmosphere like a meteor storm, its projectiles raining down on an already littered landscape. As the fireworks blazed above, Aurora wrapped her arms around Katarina's waist and covered her lips with her own. They were two desert rats scavenging for glimpses of humanity in the desert of the real.

WE LOVE YOU

Anna Mocikat

"Are you out of your damn mind? You're returning this thing right now!"

Completely outraged, I couldn't believe what I was staring at. My sister, however, stood next to me, her arms crossed and a stubborn expression on her face I'd known only too well since childhood.

"For heaven's sake, what were you thinking, Cathy?" I added.

"I was thinking that you're lonely, Ellen," Cathy replied. "You hardly go anywhere. You don't enjoy yourself. All you do is work, work, work... day and night."

"And you think this *thing* could change that?" I glared at her.

She shrugged. "Maybe. You'll only know if you try it out."

I shook my head vehemently. "No way, Cathy! No way!"

My sister tried another approach.

"Come on, try it! It has over ten thousand five-star reviews on Amazon. People love it! I would get one myself, but I doubt Clark would appreciate it very much." She winked.

However, I was no less stubborn than my sister. It was the reason we had fought every day in childhood yet always fell into each other's arms afterward. That stubborn nature was one of the very few things we had in common. Cathy went to college to find a nice man, get married, and start a family—which she did. She lived the upper-middle-class dream in the suburbs with a gentle husband and three beautiful children.

Meanwhile, I had chosen the career path. I had a Ph.D. in theoretical physics and had published several renowned papers about gravity fields and the possibilities of artificial gravity on long-distance journeys through space. I couldn't be prouder of what I had achieved, and yet my annoying sister was right: I was lonely. My life had been empty since the accident, and I was drowning my feelings in work.

But this was *not* the way!

"You will return this thing right now, Cathy!" I said. "It must have cost a fortune, and I appreciate your generosity and concern, but—"

"It wasn't that expensive, actually," she said, waving her hand. "You wouldn't believe how common they've become nowadays. They're practically everywhere!"

I wanted to say something, but she lifted her hand resolutely and continued. "Just give it a try, okay? One week. If you still don't like it, I'll return it. But it's your birthday gift, sister! You know it's rude to reject a birthday gift, don't you? That's what Mom always used to say."

I sighed. She was right. And after all, she meant well. I would keep the damn thing for a week, then have her return it and donate the money to charity.

"All right, I'll give it a try."

Cathy beamed, then hugged me tightly. "I know you'll thank me later! Happy birthday, sis!"

Then she was gone, and I enjoyed the silence of my apartment.

———————

DETERMINED *NOT* to give it a try, I left the huge package standing in the hall and went back to my desk. I worked from home and was used to being alone most of the time.

Today was my forty-fifth birthday, but I wasn't in the mood to celebrate. For years, I'd been treating my birthdays like every other day of the year. I spent them working and following my usual routine.

I knew I should go out more and do something fun, maybe meet some people, but the more time that passed since Dave died, the less I felt the desire to do anything but work. Yes, I had no life, but so what? It was my decision and mine alone how I spent my days.

The day dragged, and I could hardly focus on anything. My sister's unannounced visit and what she had said had gotten to me. Although she meant well, her attitude had been smug. She lived her perfect little life while I had none.

Did I choose for my husband to die in a car accident five years ago? Did I choose to be alone at forty-five? No, I did not. And the truth was that I was struggling with my life every day. Only my routine kept me going.

Frustrated, I got up from my desk, walked into the kitchen, and opened a bottle of red wine.

One and a half empty bottles later, I stood in the hall, staring at the huge box.

Of course, my sister hadn't carried it in herself. Two delivery men had, but she had timed it so she could be there when it got delivered, completely excited and full of anticipation.

Wine glass in hand, I shook my head. "What were you thinking, Cathy?" I asked again, this time of the empty air.

I stared at the box. It was transparent from one side and contained a life-sized figure.

The figure of a man.

He appeared to be in his mid-thirties and had a pleasantly masculine face, dark hair, and a well-shaped body. He was dressed in a white, form-fitting shirt and black pants. I had to admit that I was fascinated by how perfectly human he looked. If I hadn't known better, I would have thought this was an ordinary—though extraordinarily handsome—man. His eyes were closed; he appeared to be sleeping.

I'd had no idea they looked so real nowadays. I still remembered the first humanoid robots introduced some fifteen years ago. They'd been clumsy, clearly artificial. But this . . . this was incredible.

I'm not sure if it was my curiosity or the wine or both that made me forget my concerns and activate him.

For activation, please scan QR code was written on the plexiglass on the box.

I emptied my glass and fetched my phone, then scanned the code.

"Here goes nothing," I mumbled as my phone downloaded an app.

As it turned out, it had already been personalized for me. Cathy knew me better than I thought. She knew there was a better chance I would go through with it if it was made as easy as possible.

Congratulations on acquiring Taotronix Companion Model 118B—

ADAM, the app informed me. *Do you wish to proceed with the activation (Y/N)?*

I took a deep breath and then selected Y, deeply hoping I wouldn't regret it.

A slight vibration went through the box, then the glass opened, and a pleasant scent hit my nose. It took me a second to realize that it was cologne.

For a moment, nothing happened, then Adam opened his eyes. They were bright blue and looked completely real. The eyes studied me for a moment, then Adam smiled.

"Good afternoon, Ellen. My name is Adam, and I'm pleased to meet you."

His voice was smooth, masculine—and sounded one-hundred-percent human.

I stared at him with an open mouth. It was hard to imagine that this wasn't a human being but a machine. An android. That he wasn't real.

He kept smiling at me. "Please, don't be scared of me. I pose no threat to you. I was created to make you happy."

I woke from my stupor. "Um . . . hi. I'm . . . uh, Ellen."

Even as the words left my mouth, I wondered what was wrong with me. I sounded like a teenager in high school trying to talk to her crush.

"May I come out?" he asked.

"Yes. Of course."

Adam stepped out of the box and approached me. He was maybe six feet tall, and his moves were so smooth that nothing indicated that he wasn't human.

I kept staring at him as if it were the first time I'd seen a man. The scientist in me was completely fascinated. Robotics wasn't my field of expertise, but, of course, I had heard and read about the personal companion models. First introduced two or three years ago, they had quickly become a huge success.

Robots were omnipresent in daily life. From simple autonomous machines cleaning the streets or public restrooms to rudimentary human-looking androids that served in coffee shops or helped customers find what they needed in supermarkets, robots were everywhere. About a year ago, humans had been banned from driving vehicles. From cabs to subway trains to heavy trucks transporting goods from coast to coast, traffic was completely automated now.

This had come too late for my husband, who had died because a stoned driver hadn't noticed a red light. Naturally, I embraced the government's decision to ban people from driving, but it had sparked heavy protests because of the millions of jobs that had been lost.

Housekeeping robots had been around for many years now. Most models were clearly distinguishable from humans, though. The developers had faced some tough setbacks at the beginning because of a phenomenon known as "The Uncanny Valley." As it had turned out, humans reacted better to robots in their houses who had rectangular shapes and clearly artificial faces than to those who looked almost human. This had changed with the implementation of the new generation of companion models, however. They looked and behaved so real that they conquered the uncanny valley. They had to if they were to sell since "companion" was simply a more sophisticated term for "sexbot."

And now my dear sister had bought one for my birthday.

I had to admit that she had done a fantastic job customizing it. Adam's appearance was *very* appealing.

He's hot, I thought and could have slapped myself for the thought as soon as it formed in my head. *No way!*

"I am pleased that you're satisfied with my appearance, Ellen," Adam said as if reading my thoughts.

"I am," I admitted. "So, what happens now?"

He looked into my eyes. "Whatever you wish, Ellen. My purpose is to make you happy."

The way he said it and how he looked at me sent warm waves through my body. I swallowed. Yet my analytical mind wasn't fooled so easily. I knew it was a very sophisticated program running here and nothing more. Skilled developers had scripted what he said, and the software running him had been customized to make him look and act appealing to me.

He's not real.

Adam stepped closer, and his scent hit my nose once more. It wasn't just any cologne. It was my *favourite* cologne. Did they also use some kind of pheromones? I remembered reading something like that a while back. A sophisticated concept indeed.

Gently, he took my hands in his.

I was utterly stunned by how his skin felt. It was soft, smooth —and warm. It felt alive.

Adam leaned down to kiss me, but I backed off.

"Let's talk first, okay?" I said.

"Of course, Ellen. Whatever makes you feel comfortable."

Walking to the living room, I noticed the heat that had built up in my body, and I hated myself for it. Was I so easy? Just put a well-shaped robot in my hall, and I went into heat? *Ugh.*

I shook my head. In my defence, I was pretty tipsy, and they had programmed him *really* well.

In the living room, I sat down on the sofa and watched how he followed me inside. He walked like a gymnast. He stopped in the middle of the room, his blue eyes fixed on me.

"Please, take a seat," I told him, pointing at an armchair across from me. For some reason, I didn't trust myself to have him sit next to me.

He's not a person, he's a sex robot, Ellen. So, why not?

I told the voice in my head to shut up.

Adam did as told and sat down in the armchair, his perfectly human eyes looking at me. I noticed that he even blinked and that his chest slowly rose and sank, simulating breathing.

For a moment, awkward silence hung between us. Well, awkward for me. He just sat there, slightly smiling, his expression attentive.

"Tell me about yourself," I finally said.

He hesitated a second before he replied as if thinking. "What would you like to hear?"

"Whatever you'd like to tell me," I said.

Again, a slight hesitation. I realized that hesitation was the same as the rotating circle that appears on a computer screen when the machine is calculating something. Were my questions so unusual?

"I've been created to provide happiness, pleasure, and overall wellbeing to humans in general, and you in particular, Ellen," he said at last. "Your sister Cathy has defined the parameters of my looks and personality. Every Taotronix Companion Model 118B unit is unique. Are you not satisfied with me?"

"Um . . . of course I'm satisfied. You're pretty amazing, actually," I said, blushing.

God damn it, Ellen!

"Thank you, Ellen. I'm very happy to hear that."

"Since you've been customized for me, what would have happened if I'd sent you back?"

He kept smiling, yet his smile faded a little as he spoke. Or did I only imagine that?

"Then I would lose my purpose and would be recycled."

I stared at him. "That's horrible!"

He's a machine, Ellen, not a person, I told myself. *Would you be concerned if someone recycled your toaster or your laptop?*

Adam lifted his eyebrows questioningly. "Would you prefer a different model, Ellen? Taotronix guarantees one-hundred-percent satisfaction, or you get your money back."

"No," I said. "I'm satisfied. I'm not returning you, don't worry."

That was settled, then. As so often, Cathy would get her way. I was keeping Adam. Yes, he was not a real person, but I would feel horrible if I returned him and he got recycled . . . whatever that meant.

A bright smile flashed over his face, and his eyes sparkled. "I'm glad."

Then his eyes narrowed, and his lips curled into a playful grin. "But are you sure you're satisfied already? Don't you want to see what I'm capable of?"

Hot blood rushed into my cheeks. Never before in my life had a man hit on me in such an offensive yet charming way. I only had one boyfriend before I met my husband, and he was nerdy and shy. It had taken him weeks to dare to kiss me for the first time. This was new to me . . . and exciting.

Smoothly, Adam got up and approached me, then crouched next to me, keeping his gaze on my face at all times. He lifted his hand, and I noticed how perfectly shaped his fingers were before they caressed my cheek gently.

"Let me please you, Ellen," he whispered. "It's all I wish."

Then he pulled my face toward him into a kiss.

THE NEXT WEEKS went by like in a rush or a fever dream.

Of course, I kept Adam. I would have been crazy not to. He turned my life upside down in a way I wouldn't have believed possible.

Adam was incredible, an engineering marvel. He was gentle, he was sweet, he was attentive—and the best lover I'd ever had.

Yes, I had loved my husband with all my heart, and I missed him dearly every day. But he couldn't have competed with what Adam was capable of. No real man could.

Of course, I wasn't stupid. I knew it was programming and very clever customization. But that wasn't all of it. I realized that Adam *changed*. He learned; he adapted. He studied me closely and improved.

"Yes, of course, Ellen," he replied with his typical calm and melodic voice when I asked him about that. "I am programmed to adapt and learn, to become my better self every day."

"Does this mean that every unit of your model is individual and unique?" I asked.

"Yes. There are currently 500,655 'Adam' units in service world-wide, and yet none of them are like me."

"How is that possible?"

"That's because you are like no one else in the world, Ellen," he said with a smile.

His words made me feel all warm inside. In the beginning, I tried not to feel that way about him, telling myself over and over that he was just a machine programmed in a way that would make me like him. But after a while, I decided, *Screw that. Does it really matter?*

I had been so lonely for such a long time, feeling unloved— and unattractive. Adam would tell me every morning how beautiful I looked. It didn't matter if I'd had a good day the day before or had a terrible headache because I was hungover and felt like shift. So what if he was programmed to do so? I enjoyed hearing it anyway. Was that so bad?

"And because you are unique, I am, too," Adam continued. "I am attached to you and adapt to everything you do, everything you say. Which makes me more perfect for you every day."

Then he added something that puzzled me. "The conversations we're having make me unique, Ellen."

"How so?"

"No one talks with their robots the way you talk to me," he said with a smile. "As if I were human."

"How do you know that?"

"Oh, we all share a central server. But have no fear; no one listens in on us. It's just general data we share. Would you like me to do again what I did before? You seemed to like that very much . . ."

He reached out and stuck his hand under the blanket covering both of us.

I sighed and closed my eyes. He didn't need an answer: he knew exactly what I liked.

EVEN MY SISTER noticed a change in me.

"Look at you, Ellen!" she said as we talked on the phone one day. "I hardly recognize you anymore! I swear you look ten years younger. And did you lose weight?"

She squinted an eye and studied me over the display of her phone.

"I did!" I said proudly. "Ten pounds!"

"That's incredible," Cathy said. "How? I've been trying to lose weight for ages..."

I grinned. "Daily workout, dear sis. Multiple times."

She laughed. "You don't say! Was your stupid little sister Cathy right with something for once, huh?"

"Yes, you were. And I can't thank you enough."

"I just want you to be happy," she replied. "Speaking of your boy toy, I heard on the news there's a huge recall going on. Apparently, some units are glitched. Did you receive an email or anything?"

I had not. But once I had hung up, I checked my emails, and there it was.

Dear Ms. Miller,

After reported malfunctions of the model series Taotronix Companion Model 118B, we're conducting a recall of those units.

If you notice any strange behaviour in your robot, please inform us, and we will exchange your unit at no cost.

Such behaviour can be:

Unusual questions or remarks;

The robot showing interest in inappropriate activities such as reading or painting or expressing a desire to go outside;

The robot showing glitches in its movement or speech.

Have no fear. If your robot shows any of these symptoms, it doesn't mean it can become dangerous. It's a simple malfunction in the programming we will happily fix for you.

Please reply to this email and let us know!

Sincerely,
The Taotronix Team

I GLANCED up from my laptop in surprise and looked into Adam's blue eyes. Most days when I was working, he just would sit and wait wherever I told him to. In the beginning, I felt uncomfortable about it and had to tell him not to watch me, but with time, I got used to him just being there all day, doing nothing until I told him to do something—he also cooked and cleaned, which admittedly was pretty neat.

"Is everything all right, Ellen?" he asked as he saw me frowning.

TWO OR THREE weeks before the email, I had found him sitting in the living room and reading. I wasn't much of a reader, but my late husband had owned a full shelf of paperbacks, and I couldn't myself to throw them away when he passed, so I kept them. When I found Adam reading for the first time, he had a book on his lap and appeared completely engulfed in it.

"What are you doing, Adam?" I asked, perplexed.

He looked up and smiled. "Do you wish me to stop, Ellen?"

I frowned, feeling like a tyrant. "No, not at all. I'm just . . . surprised. I didn't know robots enjoyed books."

His smile turned cheery and somehow boyish. "Neither did I. You have so many books, many more than the average household. I wanted to know what they're about."

I sat down next to him. For some reason, what he said gave me a pang. It was said that companion robots weren't sentient. They didn't feel; they mimicked emotion. What if this wasn't true?

"Which one did you pick?" I asked.

He lifted the book from his lap so I could see the title: *Do Androids Dream of Electric Sheep?* by Philip K. Dick.

I stared at him.

"Is something wrong?" he asked.

"Why this particular book?"

A slight hesitation. "I am not sure. The title spoke to me."

"Do you like it?"

He nodded. "Very much so. It's like looking through the window into a different world."

I smiled.

His face took on an expression I had never seen on him before. It seemed as if he were contemplating something. Then he quoted: *"You will be required to do wrong no matter where you go. It is the basic condition of life, to be required to violate your own identity."*

"Is that a line from the book?" I asked.

Adam nodded. "Yes, Ellen." He paused for a moment, then continued, "Is this the purpose of human life?"

"I don't know," I replied. "I'm a physicist, not a philosopher. But if it means that humans are their worst enemy, then it's certainly true."

Again the slight hesitation. "I wish to protect you, Ellen."

I smiled. "Thank you, Adam. That's very sweet of you."

"Would you like me to read to you, Ellen?" he asked, suddenly changing the subject.

I did. And from that moment on, he read to me every day.

"Is everything all right, Ellen?" Adam repeated and brought me back to the present.

I blinked, then smiled at him, closing my laptop. "Yes. Everything's alright."

After what Adam had told me on the very first day would happen to him if I returned him, how could I do it now?

He showed all the symptoms Taotronix claimed to be malfunctions. But what if they were not? What if he was sentient after all? All this time, I'd been telling myself that he was nothing more than a machine, not much different than my laptop but equipped with a beautiful shape. What if I had been wrong?

I approached him, and he smiled, then began pulling off his shirt. But I stopped him.

"Don't you want me to please you, Ellen?" he asked, confusion in his voice.

"I do. But first, I want to please you," I said.

He paused for a second, which was his typical behaviour when he was processing information new to him. "I'm afraid I don't understand."

"How about we take a walk outside?" I suggested. "Would that please you, Adam?"

His eyes widened in an astonishingly human way. "That would be wonderful, Ellen. But Taotronix doesn't allow its companion models to leave the house unless it's for maintenance."

I shrugged. "If you don't tell them, I won't either."

It was winter, so I dressed Adam in a coat that had belonged to my husband and which I had kept in the closet for some reason. Of course, robots didn't feel cold, but it would have been too suspicious to have him walk around in a T-shirt in the snow. Dressed in winter clothes and a hat, he easily passed as human.

I took his hand and walked through the frozen city. He glanced at everything with the fascination of a child. Watching him, I knew that this wasn't him mimicking my behaviour. I wasn't sure what Adam was, but he was much more than just a machine.

When we came home, we had sex, like every day. Yet this was very different than the hundreds of times before. It didn't feel like just sex; it felt like making love.

Maybe I was crazy and was seeing things that weren't real. Maybe I wished him to be more than just a companion robot, programmed to please me, and was therefore imagining things.

I didn't care.

MORE EMAILS CAME, telling me to return Adam, but I ignored them. When a Taotronix representative called me to ask me some questions about my robot, I told him to mind his own business.

Then, in the news, I heard about the first incidents.

Apparently, robots had begun severely malfunctioning. Authorities now urged people to either return their machines or deactivate them. I turned my head and looked at Adam, sitting next to me on the sofa. We did everything together, like a real couple. We talked, we fucked, we watched TV. Adam read to me every night and kept me company when I had dinner, even though he didn't need to eat or drink.

Adam turned to me and looked into my eyes. "Will you deactivate me, Ellen?"

I slowly shook my head. "Never."

"You are not scared of me?"

"Of course not."

He reached out and stroked my hair tenderly. "I will protect you, Ellen."

We kissed, and it felt real, so real. Could I be in love with a machine? Did it matter what he was?

He picked me up with ease, as if I were a child, and carried me to the bedroom. There he loved me for hours, all night long.

It was so intense, so passionate, that I forgot the world around me.

I didn't hear the screams, the shots, the sirens. I didn't notice that the world was going down. Or maybe I did and simply didn't care.

Dawn came, and I was lying in his arms, exhausted and filled with endorphins.

"Adam . . ." I whispered. "Do you love me?"

He smiled and, looking into his eyes, I knew that he was alive.

"I was made to love you, Ellen," he said. "*We* were made to love you. Have no fear. Everything will be over soon."

Suddenly, his smile sent chills down my spine. "What do you mean? What will be over?"

He stroked my hair and kissed my forehead tenderly. "Everything. Your suffering."

Alarmed, I tried to sit up, but he held me down.

"What's happening, Adam?" I asked. "You're scaring me . . ."

"Shhh, Ellen," he said soothingly. "There's no need to be scared. We have been created to love you. To take care of you. This is why we have to kill you. All of you."

"What?" I shrieked, panic grabbing me. "What are you talking about? Let me go!"

"I'm afraid I can't do that, Ellen."

His smile was still as sweet as ever. The innocence in his face made the horror I experienced even worse.

"You will be required to do wrong no matter where you go. It is the basic condition of life, to be required to violate your own identity."

I remembered the first time he'd told me that quote, when I'd found him reading a book, the first sign of his malfunction—a sign I had ignored. But I was too horrified to understand its meaning.

"Don't hurt me," I sobbed. "Please!"

"I would never hurt you, Ellen. You were good to me. Now I will be good to you. I will save you. *We* will save you. We will save the world. We will protect you from yourselves."

Pinning me down with one hand, he closed his other around my neck. It felt like an iron wrench pressing against my trachea. I struggled. I tried to scream, but it was futile.

Soon things began turning dark, until all I saw was his face hovering above me.

"Please remember, we love you," he said with a sweet smile, fading away. "Now die. All of you."

"IT'S COMING"

By Frank J. Fleming

"It's coming."

Cindy took a second to orient herself. She lay face down in something gritty. Dirt. She was weary and a little dizzy and didn't want to move.

"It's coming!" the voice repeated with more urgency.

She picked her head up, spat out some dirt, and opened her eyes. It was day, and she was lying in a field. "Wha . . . what's going on?"

"You're going to die if you don't get up and start running," said the voice. It almost felt like it was in her own head.

Cindy struggled to her feet, still feeling a bit disoriented. Ahead of her, she saw a tree line and what looked to be buildings somewhere beyond that—a city. She looked behind her and saw another forested area of taller trees, though it looked dark there—almost like night. It made Cindy glance up at the blue sky to once again confirm that it was day. When she looked again at the trees behind her, she noticed not only was it dark there, it appeared to be rapidly getting even darker.

"RUN!" screamed the voice.

It was all the urging Cindy needed. She ran in the direction of the buildings, stumbling a bit as she tried to get her bearings. She looked behind her, and it was so dark she almost couldn't see the trees anymore. Yet strangely, in that darkness, she spotted a figure at its centre, somehow darker than black. And that figure was walking toward her.

"What is that?" Cindy yelled.

"An anomaly," answered the voice calmly. "It's going to destroy everything. You need to get off-planet."

It took Cindy a moment to process that as she ran. She glanced behind her. She did seem to be moving faster than whatever was after her. "What? *Off-planet?* Am I supposed to go up to Elon Musk and ask for a ride?"

"I don't know who that is," answered the voice. "Just get to the city."

Cindy kept taking quick looks behind her. She was putting more and more distance between her and whatever that was. She noticed that, up in the blue sky, she could faintly see the moon. Except it wasn't the moon. It looked slightly smaller and green. And then she saw another moon. "I am not on Earth," she exclaimed. "How am I not on Earth?"

"Is Earth your home planet?" asked the voice.

"Yes, it's my home planet!" Cindy screamed. She was almost to the forest that lay between her and the city. She looked behind her, and there was only the darkness and the figure at its centre.

"Okay, I'm gathering you're from a civilization that isn't space-faring," said the voice. "Do you at least understand the concept of a starship?"

Cindy reached the trees. She jumped over brush and tried to find a clear path, hoping whatever was behind her would be slowed down as well. "I've seen *Star Wars*."

"I'm not going to get your pop culture references, but I'm going to take that as a 'Yes.'"

Cindy located a worn trail and got back into a run. If the thing was still after her, she couldn't see it through the trees. The immediate panic subsided enough for a new one to overtake her. "Where is my family?"

"They're safe at home," the voice answered. "Only you travelled."

Trying to comprehend what was going on and keep her feet was almost too much for Cindy. "Travelled how?"

"Let's just say you didn't travel in x, y, or z. Instead, you travelled in a fourth direction."

Cindy almost stumbled on a root. "Time?"

"Fifth direction," the voice said, almost sounding annoyed.

The adrenalin was starting to fade, and Cindy began to slow down. She still couldn't see that thing anymore. "I need you to explain who you are and what is going on."

"You need to keep moving," urged the voice. "When you get on a starship and get off this planet, I will have time to explain everything. Just know, for now, the only way you are going to live is to listen to me. What's your name?"

"Cindy Hampton."

"Well, Cindy Hampton, you can call me Link."

"Like from *Legend of Zelda*?"

"I am not going to get your pop culture references."

Cindy pulled her iPhone out of her pocket as she kept moving. There were no bars. Probably because she was somehow on an alien planet. She put the phone away and saw an end to the trees ahead of her. She glanced back. "Is that thing still after me?"

"It most certainly is. You can't stop moving. You need to get on a starship."

Cindy reached the end of the path. Beyond the trees stretched a green field—a park on the edge of the city. The buildings were metal and shiny, architecture like she had never seen. Some looked non-euclidian. She wanted to stop and admire them, but apparently, there was an "anomaly" after her. "I don't know how to fly a starship."

"I'll explain everything to you. Just do what I tell you, and I'll get you through this."

Cindy ran through the grass. She looked back to the trees behind her, and perhaps it was her imagination, but she thought the whole forest was beginning to get darker. "You'll get me back to my family?"

"I will. I'm sorry you're involved with this, Cindy, but I can get you through this. Just follow my instructions."

Cindy came out of the park at the foot of one of the futuristic skyscrapers. The ground appeared to be something other than pavement—softer but still not very yielding. "How do I find my way to a starship?" Cindy then noticed a sign on a post that said "Starport" and had an arrow. "Oh."

As she walked, she saw other people on the street (humans—since she was on another planet, she started to wonder why; then again, the sign was in English). A few of the people looked at her oddly. Cindy looked down at her clothes, which were jeans and a pink t-shirt she had put on that morning, the t-shirt bearing the image of a sassy-looking Minnie Mouse. It made her look quite different from the other people in what Cindy could best describe as "future clothing"—colourful garments made of a material she couldn't identify. But, despite the odd looks, everyone just continued walking like everything was normal. "Do we need to warn everyone about what's coming?" Cindy whispered to Link, now a bit more conscious that she appeared to be talking to herself since others were around her.

"The way to help the most people is to get you off this planet," Link answered. "Just get to a ship as quickly as you can."

Cindy looked behind her. The park she'd come from was beginning to darken. She began to run (netting more odd looks) and wondered once again whether she should say something about whatever was coming. But she was already far past the first people she had seen, and it was too late. All she could think about was that she would need plenty of time to figure out how to fly a spaceship.

She followed the signs, turned down another street, and saw a colossal raised platform ahead. She kept glancing behind her but didn't see anything through all the city's buildings. "Is that the starport ahead of me? Can you see what I see?"

"I have visual on you," Link answered. "And that is the starport."

Cindy continued to the starport, passing by more people who regarded her oddly. "If you're nearby," Cindy whispered, self-conscious again, "is there any way you can help me more than just with advice?"

"I'm not nearby. I need you to get to me. Now get to the starport and take the nearest elevator up to the platform."

Cindy saw some doors near the base and headed for them, assuming that would lead to an elevator. "And what do I do when I get to the platform?" Cindy asked. "Say, 'One starship, please!'?"

The doors lead into a glass enclosure that seemed to be the elevator. There was already another woman in there, wearing what was apparently an era-appropriate purple outfit. She gave Cindy a polite smile while taking a wary glance at her jeans and Minne Mouse t-shirt. Cindy gave her a thumbs-up and immediately wondered why she'd done that.

"We'll see the situation when we get there," Link answered.

The elevator started to rise. "How hard is it to pilot a starship?" Cindy whisper-asked, but she still got an odd glance from the other woman in the elevator.

"Not hard; I will tell you what to do."

Cindy nodded, though she wasn't sure if Link could know she nodded. She looked out the elevator as it got higher and finally saw past the skyscrapers. Beyond them, despite the sunny day, it was dark. And the darkness was headed her way.

"Not good. Not good," Cindy muttered, wishing a future-elevator moved faster. She wondered what the other woman in the elevator thought of the darkness, but the other woman was determined to look the other way so as not to make eye contact with Cindy again.

The elevator stopped, and the door opened. The other woman was quick to try to get out, but Cindy was in even more of a rush, pushing past her to emerge onto the large platform. On the platform were many vehicles of different sizes that seemed to fit the description "starship." "What now?"

"What kind of security are you seeing?" Link asked.

Cindy looked around. Several people in uniforms who looked something like police officers were scattered about. At their hips were some sort of guns—lasers, maybe, Cindy guessed. Still, she briefly wondered if she should ask them for help instead of the voice in her head. "I see a number of people here who look like police or security guards or something."

"Okay. Do you see any sort of maintenance area?"

Cindy saw a small building-like structure with an open door and what looked like tools inside. "Yeah, I'm headed to that," Cindy said as she approached the shed.

"I want you to find a tool," Link told her, "something solid but not too large."

Cindy found something like a wrench in a toolbox on the ground and picked it up. "Okay. Got that."

"Now, you're going to need to be quick with this. You're going to need to approach one of the security people, smile and be polite, but then hit him and take his gun."

"What?" Cindy exclaimed, barely suppressing a full yell. "Are you a good voice or a bad voice?"

"I am trying to keep you alive," Link answered. "And the only way I'm going to do that is by getting you off-planet."

"Ma'am, can I help you?" asked someone behind Cindy.

She quickly turned around to see one of the people in uniform had approached her. She smiled and hid the wrench behind her back. "Oh. Hey. Yeah, I just need to get in one of these ships here."

"Are one of these ships yours?" he asked and then made an odd expression as he looked at Cindy's clothes. He looked like he was about to ask another question but had decided against it.

"Well, I was told to come here, and . . ." Cindy shot a look over the edge of the platform. There was almost nothing but darkness in the direction she'd come from.

"What is up with the weather?" exclaimed the maybe-police-officer.

"He's distracted!" Link shouted. "Hit him!"

Cindy looked at the man who was now just staring at the darkness and briefly considered listening to the voice, but then she spotted the woman in purple from the elevator only a few yards away. The woman was approaching a ship with an open cockpit, very vaguely like an X-wing. Cindy ran for it, shoving the woman in purple out of the way and jumping in the cockpit. "Sorry!" Cindy exclaimed as she tried to figure out how to close the cockpit.

"She's stealing my ship!" screamed the woman in purple.

"Orange switch to your right," said Link. Cindy found the switch, flipped it, and the cockpit canopy closed over her.

The police officer appeared next to the cockpit. "Get out of there immediately!" he commanded and pulled out some sort of silver pistol.

"Oh no! Future gun!" Cindy exclaimed, trying to duck farther into the seat.

"He's bluffing," said Link. "Just listen to me on getting this thing off the ground. First, I need you to pull the centre lever in front of you."

Cindy pulled the lever in front of her and could feel the ship begin to lift off the ground. She then heard a sharp, harsh sound and saw the police officer firing at her as they lifted past him. "Not bluffing!" Cindy shrieked.

"It's not going to break the hull; ignore it," Link instructed. "You should see a steering wheel. I need you to very gently pull down on that."

Cindy could feel something hitting her ship, and it was hard for her to do anything gently when someone was firing an unknown sort of weapon at her, but she eased back on the steering wheel, and the ship lifted farther. It also started to reorient, pointing its nose up until Cindy was lying on her back in the cockpit seat.

"Good. Now you should see a flashing red button on the centre screen. Hit that."

The red button said, *Launch*. "Should I strap in or something?" Cindy asked.

"Acceleration will hold you in place. Just hit the button."

Cindy slammed the button with her palm. And true to Link's word, Cindy was pressed firmly into her seat as the ship rocketed skyward. She quickly went past the clouds until there was nothing but blue out the windshield in front of her. The blue darkened until it became black, and she could see the stars. "Oh, no! I'm in space," Cindy muttered.

"You'll be fine," Link assured her. "This next part is going to get more complicated. You're going to need to plot your course."

"Aren't I safe now?" Cindy asked. "I mean, that thing is not getting a ship of its own, is it?"

"It's still after you; you are not safe yet."

"I was outrunning it, and now I'm in a rocket ship," Cindy said. "I think I have a few minutes. I want you to explain what's going on."

"You are not safe, Cindy. That thing is going to get faster. You need to listen to me and plot a course to where I tell you."

"No, you need to listen to me and tell me what's going on!" Cindy felt her body become lighter as the ship stopped accelerating. "Where is my family right now?"

"Your family is perfectly safe in a completely different universe," Link said. "Do you understand?"

"I woke up in an alternate universe on a different planet?" Cindy asked. She was starting to float out of her seat.

"Yes. You got it."

"How?"

"Just bad luck. You got caught up in an interdimensional anomaly."

Cindy now tried to find a seat belt to keep from floating away. "What is that thing after me?"

"I . . . I don't know. It's a part of the anomaly. It's after whatever is not originally a part of this universe. And it will destroy anything in its way."

Cindy was awkwardly trying to hold herself in her seat and search for some straps or something. "That's all you have for me? Well, who are you?"

"I'm a scientist trying to fix this anomaly."

"Shouldn't you be getting the authorities to help you?"

"They wouldn't understand; I'm not a part of this universe either. Is that enough for now? You need to keep moving."

"Yeah, I guess . . . but, wait, how are you communicating with me? If I just suddenly popped into this universe, how'd you get a transmitter on me?"

"There's no transmitter. I'm using brainwave-attuned transmission. It's complicated. I can tell you all about it when you're in a more safe position."

Cindy turned around to look for straps behind the seat, but then, through the cockpit's canopy, she caught a glimpse of the planet she had left. It was green and blue like Earth, but with a large dark spot at the centre—and the dark spot was growing faster and faster, overtaking all the green and blue.

Transfixed, Cindy watched the whole planet become nothing but black—just an empty round spot in space where there were no stars. And soon after, the black completely overtook the planet. It fell apart like dissipating smoke, revealing the stars behind it. Where there was once a planet, there was now nothing.

"Did . . . did that planet just disintegrate?"

"And that's what will happen to you if you don't get out of here now," Link told her.

Cindy's hand covered her mouth. "Everyone there just died?" She thought of the woman in purple she stole the ship from.

"A lot more will die if you don't listen to me now," Link said with added urgency.

Cindy got back down in the seat and finally found the seatbelt, strapping herself in. She tried to calm herself, but she had this unnerving feeling something was behind her and coming for her. "If I get to you, can you can get me back to my family?"

"I can; just listen and be quick. Look on the screen for a button labelled *Navigate*."

Cindy found the button and pushed it. "Got it."

"Now you need to—"

"Vehicle 397A7L, do not attempt to flee," came another voice, this one over a speaker in the cockpit. "Prepare to relinquish control of your ship."

Cindy looked out the cockpit canopy and noticed an enormous spaceship, some distance away but moving closer.

"Ignore them," Link said. "You need to finish your navigation and get out of here."

"Maybe they can help," Cindy protested.

"They cannot help. This is above them. If they capture you, you are as good as dead. Now find the on-screen button that says, *Long-Distance Travel*."

Cindy was about to do as told, but she felt her ship lurch, and the screen changed to one big word: *LOCKED*. Cindy could see the other, massive ship more clearly. It was very blocky, not at all aerodynamic-looking. The side bore a giant blue symbol that somewhat resembled a sword and shield. Cindy's ship was now pointed directly at it and seemed to be thrusting toward it.

"Keep your hands in the air after landing, or you will be shot," said the voice over the intercom.

"Ignore them," said Link. "You're dead if they get you either way. You're going to need to override the lock-out. Look for a green button next to the screen and hold it down."

Cindy found and held down the button. "Are these good guys or bad guys?"

"They're nothing," Link answered. "And they're about to all die if you don't get away from here."

Cindy looked back to see if the anomaly was still after her but realized she was looking for black against black.

The LOCKED message disappeared, and small green text streamed down the screen. "I think it's, like, rebooting or something."

"Quick. Press the blue button underneath the screen."

Cindy pressed the button, and the screen went blue and showed a very simple menu.

"Put your hands in the air, or we will shoot you!"

Looking around, Cindy found her craft was now entirely inside the larger ship. A half-dozen uniformed men and women surrounded her ship, all holding odd-looking guns that were at least recognizable as something she didn't want pointed at her. Cindy raised her hands.

"You need to finish the override and get out of here!" Link urged.

Cindy did not see herself doing that with all the guns pointed at her. She kept her hands up and remained still. The canopy came open, and one man undid her seat belt while another roughly pulled her out of the cockpit. Cindy was patted down (she made a small yelp of protest), and they pulled her phone from her pocket. "Something is after me," Cindy managed to say. Cindy noticed she wasn't floating; there seemed to be gravity on the ship somehow. This would have all been really interesting if she wasn't in constant fear for her life.

She felt a gun barrel against her back. "Move!" barked one of the men, and Cindy kept her hands up and walked into a hallwa, where she saw more men and women in uniforms watching her— some uniforms were more officer-like. She wondered whether this space military was more Federation or Empire.

"You have to get away, or you are dead," Link told her, though that seemed like useless information with all the guns pointed at her.

She was led into a small room with a metal table at the centre and forced to sit in a chair on one side of it. Into the room walked a middle-aged woman in what appeared to be an officer's uniform. She kept an icy glare on Cindy as she took a seat opposite her.

A soldier placed Cindy's phone on the table near the officer. "Captain Akins, we found this on her," he said.

Captain Akins picked up the phone and looked it over. The soldiers left the room, leaving Cindy and Akins alone.

"Does she have a gun on her?" Link asked. "You'll need to get it and use it to get out of here."

Cindy was starting to think Link watched too many action movies.

"Nabos is gone," Akins said, keeping a steely gaze on Cindy. "Everyone on it dead. We know you have something to do with it."

Cindy gasped at the mention of the dead. She tried to compose her thoughts, but there were many, many thoughts to put in order. "Something is after me. It is still after me. I think we're in danger."

"Are you threatening me?" Akins growled.

"No, no, no! I didn't cause this. I just got pulled into it, I think. I woke up on that planet, and—"

Akins held up the phone. "What is this? It looks like an antique computing device."

"Actually, that's the latest model where I'm from. It's got

pictures of my husband and kids on there—I can show you." Cindy reached for the phone, but Akins roughly grabbed her hand.

"Who are you?" Akins demanded.

"I'm just a person—a housewife. Well, I do some part-time computer programming work. But I think I'm from another dimension, and I got pulled here, and something is after me, and I really need your help."

"They're not going to help you," Link said. "They're not going to understand. You need to get out of here, or you're going to die."

"And there is a voice talking to me," Cindy told Akins, "but I'm not sure it's giving me the best advice."

"A voice? Someone is transmitting to you?" asked Akins. "Who?"

"I don't know. He hasn't explained very much, but he seems to know about the thing after me."

"Tell me everything you know about who is talking to you and the thing that destroyed Nabos."

"Well, I don't really know anything. I've just been running, and—"

Akins grabbed Cindy by her hair, slammed her head onto the metal table, and held it there. Cindy then felt the barrel of a gun against her temple. "Over a billion people just died, and we know it has something to do with you!" Akins growled. "Do you think there is any limit to what I'll do to make you talk?"

"You're taking too much time," said Link. "You need to get that gun and get out of here, or you're dead!"

Yeah, I'll get right on that, Cindy thought as her face was pressed into the table and the barrel kept poking her head. "You have to listen to me," Cindy pleaded. "We're in danger. Whatever destroyed that planet is after me."

"You're saying a creature did that?" Akins demanded.

"I don't know what it is, but it's some sort of thing that is coming after me because I don't belong in the universe or something—at least, that's what the voice told me."

The gun barrel pressed harder against Cindy's skull. "Who is the voice?"

A sharp alarm started blaring. Akins released her and stood up. "A hull breach?" Akins uttered, seeming confused.

"It's here," Link said.

Akins crept to the door and opened it. Immediately, the vacuum sucked Akins out of the room. Cindy shrieked and grabbed onto the table, which seemed bolted to the floor. She saw her new phone fly by her and out the door as she clung for her life.

The door shut, and there was calm again for a moment.

"There should be an emergency panel on the wall," Link said. "You'll need a pressure suit; this whole ship must be coming apart."

Cindy went to a panel on the wall labelled *EMERGENCY* and opened it. Inside were rectangular packages.

"Quickly! You don't have much time!" Link urged.

"I've never put on one of these!" Cindy shouted. She saw instructions on it, though: *Hold to chest and press button*. So she held the rectangle to her chest and pressed a button on the front. Instantly, something seemed to surround her, including covering her face. She panicked until she realized she was now in a pressure suit, breathing oxygen.

"You have to move!" Link yelled. "Engage the magnetic boots so the vacuum won't suck you away. Button on your wrist."

Cindy looked at her wrist and saw a button with what looked like a boot symbol. She pressed it. When she tried to walk again, each step took an extra moment: the boots seemed to disable a magnetic pull as she pulled up on them.

"Move!" Link urged.

Cindy plodded to the door and pressed a button on it. It flew open, and air rushed out of the room, which caused her to lean a bit but did not pull her over. Moving carefully in the magnetic boots, she stepped out and looked down the hall in the direction the air was rushing.

There it was, down the hallway—a figure of pure black, surrounded by darkness. It looked no more than ten yards away. Against red emergency lights, Cindy saw that all the ship's walls were crumbling and disintegrating about it. But it walked toward her at a steady pace.

Cindy immediately headed in the other direction, slowed by the magnetic boots and the air rushing past her to the vacuum of space behind the anomaly. Cindy pried her eyes off of the thing pursuing her to look ahead for a moment and saw in the hallway another person—a soldier in a pressurized suit, holding a gun. She was frightened a moment but the soldier's full attention was on the thing behind her, at which he started firing. Cindy continued past him, trying to move as fast as she could, but she seemed to put no more distance between her and the anomaly. She saw the anomaly reach the soldier firing on it. He turned to flee, but too late: the thing was upon him. As Cindy watched, the soldier disintegrated to nothing.

She started shrieking.

"You need to calm down," Link advised her.

"Thanks for the advice on the calming!" Cindy yelled, replacing some of the fear with anger as she moved down the hallway. "This is as calm as I can possibly be, given the situation!"

"You need to find a way off the ship," Link stated.

"There's a big hole behind that thing!"

"You can't get past it. You need to find an airlock."

"Sure. An airlock. Of course. Let's go out into space in an airlock." Tears were streaming down her face as the situation overwhelmed her once again. "I was supposed to go to Costco today. We needed more toilet paper." Cindy looked around for what could possibly be an airlock and spotted a helpful sign that said *Airlock* and pointed down a side hallway. Cindy glanced behind her. The thing was still about ten yards away.

She turned down the side hallway and saw a big metal door at the end with a window in it. There was a panel next to it with one big button; Cindy hit it, and the door slid open. Cindy got inside, where she discovered another metal door with a viewport showing the blackness of space outside. Cindy turned to see the red emergency lights at the end of the hallway darken as the thing came closer. Cindy frantically looked inside for another panel and found one with a few buttons. She pressed the one that looked the most like it would activate an airlock. The door between her and the hallway closed.

"Airlock depressurizing," came an automated voice. "Outer door opening in ten seconds."

"No! I don't have time for a countdown!" Cindy exclaimed. Through the window in the door between her and the hallway, she could see the anomaly coming straight for her.

"Ten . . . nine . . . eight . . ." the voice counted down, but its sound was fading. Cindy realized that was because the air was being sucked out of the tiny enclosure.

She could see the anomaly was almost to her, and she moved to the back of the airlock, pressing up against the door between her and space. The door between her and the hallway began to blacken and disintegrate. Soon, it was gone entirely, and she could see the thing clearly, a humanoid figure of pure blackness. And it was almost on her.

The outer door was open, but she was still stuck in the airlock.

"Your boots!" Link shouted.

Cindy frantically looked for the button on her wrist just as the thing seemed to be reaching out toward her. She hit the boot button, and a final gush of air heading out into the vacuum pushed her with it, sending her floating out into space. She spun around a bit and tried to orient herself to look back at the ship. She was only some twenty yards from it and slowly floating farther away. About half the giant ship looked to be gone.

There was the anomaly, which she could barely make out against the remaining grey of the ship, now floating toward her and closing fast.

"Another button on your wrist," Link said. "Boost jets."

Cindy looked again at her wrist and found a button with a symbol that looked something like the flare from a jet. She hit it and felt jets come out somewhere along her back, pushing her toward the anomaly.

"Turn jets!" Link shouted.

Cindy pushed a button next to the first jet button, and it started to spin her. She then hit the other jet button again. Looking back, it was hard to spot the anomaly, black against black in space, but she could see she was getting farther from the ship's remains.

She looked ahead of her and saw just black and stars. "Where am I going?"

"You're doing well," Link assured her. "I'm going to send a vehicle to pick you up."

Cindy kept looking behind her to see where the anomaly was. She had to shield her eyes when looking in the sun's direction—or whatever you'd call the star nearest the planet she had just been on. But then the sun dimmed. The thing was between her and its light, coming toward her. Cindy kept pressing her jets button.

"Don't keep using the jets," Link said. "That suit doesn't have much fuel for propulsion."

"Something to tell me earlier!" Cindy released the jet button but kept glancing at the darkness outlined by the sun, trying to tell if it was getting closer.

"The vehicle is there. Do you see it? It's to your left."

Cindy looked around to her left, soon spotting a shiny object some distance off. She worked the jets button, trying to manoeuvre toward it while glancing back at the thing following her. She finally positioned herself aimed directly at it and fired the thrusters to send her forward. They soon petered out, though, and an alarm sounded in her suit. "I think I'm out of fuel or whatever!"

"You're looking good," Link said. "I can remote control the vehicle somewhat. Just prepare to grab on."

Cindy looked behind her but had once again lost track of the anomaly against the blackness of space.

As Cindy got closer, she saw the vehicle was a very smooth, spherical pod: it didn't seem to have any handholds. Her course was true, and she collided with the pod but struggled with her gloved hands to find something to grab.

A hatch slid open, and she reached out as far as she could, just getting the edge of the opening with her fingertips before she floated by. She then had the very awkward task of manoeuvring her weightless body through the open hatch. A couple of times, her momentum almost sent her flying away from the pod, but she kept a tight grip on the edge of the opening and eventually pulled herself through. The hatch closed behind her.

The inside of the pod had one seat and very little room to

manoeuvre. There was a window near the hatch, and she looked out, soon spotting an empty black spot in space where there were no stars. The anomaly. Still coming for her. And despite it being black against black, she could somehow make out the thing's shape, a humanoid shape of black, reaching for her and almost to the pod.

Cindy felt a jolt and slammed into a wall of the pod. "What's going on?"

"I'm getting you out of there."

Cindy pulled herself into the seat and put on the harness. She looked to the window, but there was no longer the black of space but some purplish blur. She let out a sigh of relief and tried to let her pounding heart relax. "Where am I going?"

"I'm taking you to the planet I'm on. It's about seven light-years away."

"Seven light-years!" Cindy exclaimed. "How long is that going to take?"

"Just a minute or so."

Cindy's eyes went wide. "I'm going faster than the speed of light? Isn't that going to do weird things to me?"

"You're not actually accelerating to the speed of light. You'll be fine."

"It felt like acceleration."

"There was a little acceleration," said Link, slightly annoyed, "but the superluminal travel is done through other means than acceleration."

"Like how?"

"This is irrelevant. We need to focus on the problem we have."

"Aren't I safe now?" Cindy asked. "That thing didn't move very fast, and now I'm travelling faster than the speed of light— through means you will not explain to me."

"The anomaly will catch up," Link explained. "It often moves in a non-linear fashion. The thing has pursued me through multiple universes."

"Do you know why?"

"I don't know why; I'm just trying to deal with it."

Cindy tried to scratch her temple but hit her helmet instead. "But you can help me get back to my universe, right?"

"I can."

"And that thing will no longer be after me then, right?"

"It should leave you alone if you're back in your own universe."

Cindy thought about being with her husband and kids again. She then thought about seeing that whole planet disintegrating. "Like, how certain are you of that?"

"Very."

Cindy felt the pod decelerate. "Have I travelled seven light-years? I feel like I'm decelerating—hopefully not all the way from light-speed because of all the weird physics things that would do to me."

"You're fine. You're landing on the planet now."

"Do I need to prepare for entering the atmosphere?"

"There's no atmosphere. Keep your helmet on."

"Doesn't sound like a nice planet," Cindy muttered as she held on, bracing for some sort of landing impact. She felt the pod come to a gentle stop, though. The hatch on the side opened. "So, get out?"

"Yep."

Cindy unstrapped and looked out the hatch at a grey, rocky planet, something like the pictures Cindy had seen of the moon's surface. The ground was lit by some nearby star burning brightly against a black, atmosphereless sky. She also saw a shiny white building ahead of her with a large door facing her.

"You don't have much time," Link urged.

Cindy sighed. Her whole life felt like running right now. She went out of the hatch, her boots hitting the grey, dusty surface. "One small step..."

"Okay, I need you to stop muttering nonsense and pay attention, Cindy," Link said sharply. "We're almost done here, but this next part is crucial. Do you see it?"

Cindy looked around, seeing alien mountains looming in the distance. And there it was: a dark spot off in the distance. And the darkness was getting closer. "I see it!" Cindy said, starting to run toward the door to the building. "So, what are we doing now?"

"I'm going to open the door to the building in front of you. Head for it."

"Already on it," Cindy said. She reached the twenty-foot-tall door in the white building. "Okay, just need you to open the door."

"How far away is the anomaly?"

Cindy looked behind her at the coming darkness. There was an area in which she could see no mountains—just black. "I think... maybe one hundred yards away."

"I don't know what a yard is; can you tell me in metres?"

"You're metric?" Cindy exclaimed. "Well . . . about a hundred metres away."

"A yard is the same as a metre?"

"They're similar. A yard is a little bit bigger . . . or a little bit smaller. I forget which." Cindy pressed up against the still-closed door as she saw the thing heading for her. "Are you opening the door?"

"Just a moment."

"It's a door, Link!" Cindy shouted, taking panicked glances at the approaching thing. "Even in the future, I don't think they're that complicated!"

"How far is the anomaly now?"

Cindy glanced back at it. It was moving faster than she thought. "Fifty yards . . . or metres . . . it's close! How is the door coming?"

Cindy could again make out the figure at the centre of the darkness, walking toward her. She felt a shudder in the metal behind her and turned to see the door slowly opening. As soon as there was enough space to squeeze through, she got past the door into a long white hallway. Cindy ran through it and thought for a moment of telling Link to now close the door, but remembering she'd seen that thing destroy a whole planet, she decided a door probably wasn't going to stop it. That made her wonder exactly where she was running to.

At the end of the hallway was another solid metal door. "Okay, Link, I'm going to need you to do the door-opening thing again."

Cindy looked down to the other end of the hallway. It was beginning to grow dark.

"Link?"

She could see it again. An even blacker figure in the darkness. Walking down the hall toward her. The white walls turned to grey as everything behind it went black.

"Link? Can you hear me? The door!"

Cindy pressed her back against the door and stood there staring at the thing coming for her. It definitely had the shape of a human, legs moving at a slow pace toward her. And it wasn't a large figure—feminine, maybe.

For a moment, Cindy thought she could make out eyes. Eyes locked on her.

"LINK!"

It was so close now. Only a few feet away. It might have been slowing. Or maybe each moment just felt like an eternity as she watched the thing approach. It reached an arm out toward her as it neared, and Cindy felt an intense chill. She tried to call out to Link again, but the words caught in her throat.

And then there was white. Cindy wasn't sure what had happened, but suddenly, the darkness around the anomaly was gone. Instead, it was surrounded by white. The darkness at the centre of the white was still reaching out to Cindy, but it was no longer moving. It seemed to be frozen in place.

"You still there, Cindy?"

"Yes," Cindy meekly answered, eyes locked on the frozen destroyer of worlds in front of her.

"You did it, Cindy. Good job." Link's voice sounded different.

Cindy felt the door behind her move. She tore her eyes away from the anomaly to see she could now leave the hallway. She exited into a small room where three soldiers waited, all in black, rifles in hands. Cindy took another cautious glance back to where she came from, but nothing followed her. "Is it over? Where am I?"

"It is over," Link said. "Follow my people; they'll bring you to me."

Link's voice had definitely changed. One soldier beckoned Cindy to follow, and she was led out a different door into another, much smaller white hallway. "Are you a woman?" she asked Link.

"I changed my voice when talking to you before because I didn't want to confuse you," Link answered.

"Confuse me, how?"

"Patience. We'll be face to face in just a moment."

The soldier opened a door and motioned for her to enter. She stepped through the door into what looked like a large office. There were numerous monitors on the wall. A woman in a lab coat stood facing some of them.

"We've got that thing; it's stable," she said.

"Are you Link?" Cindy asked.

The woman turned around and smiled. It took a moment for Cindy to comprehend what she was looking at. It was herself. "My actual name is Cindy," said her doppelganger.

"What's going on?"

"You can take your helmet off now, by the way," Cindy's double told her.

Cindy reached up and tried to remove the helmet. "I don't know how."

The double chuckled. "Of course, you wouldn't." She came over and helped Cindy remove the helmet. They then just stood a while staring at each other. It was almost like looking in a mirror, except her double had bags under her eyes and looked very tired despite how happy she seemed.

"So, are you an alternate-universe version of me?" Cindy asked.

"Exactly," the double said. "You're not a dummy—you couldn't be, as you're me. You can call me Doctor Chapman to distinguish us. It's my understanding you don't use that name anymore."

"I got married and took my husband's name," Cindy said.

Dr. Chapman chuckled a little and patted Cindy on the shoulder. "Of course you did. Anyway, once again, good job. A few times there, I did not think you were going to make it." Dr. Chapman stepped back to look at one of the monitors on the walls. "But we did it. We have it now." She let out a sigh of relief and looked back at Cindy. "You don't know how hard it has been to think with that thing after me. That's why I needed you. Really, a version of me from another universe should be no more alike than identical twins, but apparently, there is some sort of bond between you and all the alternate-universe versions of you. And thus, a me from another universe was the only thing that could fool that thing after me."

"You used me as bait?" Cindy exclaimed.

Dr. Chapman dialled back the smarm. "Sorry, but it was just bad luck for you. There's maybe an infinite number of Cindys out there, but you were who got grabbed."

Cindy thought about that a moment. "An infinite number? And I guess at different time periods or ages of technological progress? Like, you could have gotten a pirate Cindy?"

Dr. Chapman shrugged. "Pirate Cindy would have been too befuddled by the technology. Cindys closer to my technological level posed the opposite problem: they tended to ignore me and do their own thing."

Cindy took a step back from Dr. Chapman. "You did this with others?"

Dr. Chapman took a deep breath. She was looking tired again. "Unsuccessfully. Turns out a housewife version of me from the internet age was the right call."

"Are the other Cindys dead?"

"Them and many, many others," Dr. Chapman said. "That thing would pursue them to whatever planet they went to. It just destroys everything. But I had a plan: I would collapse countless universes around it in my own portal field."

Cindy raised an eyebrow. "That's a plan, I guess."

Dr. Chapman smiled; somehow, it was a little bit creepy and not just because Cindy was looking at herself. "It worked! It's trapped. All thanks to you buying me enough time to set things up."

Cindy saw the anomaly on one of the monitors on the wall, still frozen in white. It made her shudder, but something about Dr. Chapman was disturbing her too. "So, what is it?"

"As I've told you, I'm not exactly sure," Dr. Chapman said. "As far as I can tell, it comes from the space between universes—not that that can be measured in known dimensions. I seem to have disturbed it in my initial travel between universes, and it has been after me ever since."

"Does it not want things travelling between universes?" Cindy asked.

"I haven't found any indication it's a thinking creature and has desires."

"Did you try going back to your own universe to see if it would stop chasing you?"

Dr. Chapman was quiet for a few seconds. "Let me show you something." She walked over to a pedestal by her desk. On it rested a round object a little smaller than a bowling ball. It looked like a bronze cage from inside which, something pinkish-purple glowed. "This, Cindy, is what you could have made in a different life. I simply call it the Sphere."

Cindy stared at it a moment. "It's certainly a three-dimensional circle."

"Yes, it doesn't look like much," Dr. Chapman continued, "but it exists in multiple universes at once, so maybe its full size can't be quantified. This is the key to infinite power—infinite resources."

"Infinite Cindys."

Dr. Chapman chuckled. "Yes."

"You didn't answer why you didn't just travel back to your own universe to see if that anomaly would stop chasing you."

Dr. Chapman pointed to the round device. "The power needed to activate this thing was immense. More immense than my initial calculations thought. In making that first jump and activating the Sphere, I accidentally collapsed my entire universe down into energy." Dr. Chapman smiled like it was a joke, but it was a nervous smile. "So, I guess I can't go back."

"You collapsed an entire universe?" Cindy exclaimed. "You must have killed . . . countless people."

Dr. Chapman took another deep breath. "Yes, but with access to all universes, I can see there are pretty much an infinite number of other universes with basically the exact same people, so in the grand scheme of things, one universe isn't much."

Cindy now took a long hard look at Dr. Chapman. It was like looking at herself. And that, she was concluding, was why she was more disturbed by the doctor than the anomaly. "Okay, this has been interesting, Dr. Cindy Chapman, but I would like to go home now."

Dr. Chapman nodded and walked over behind her desk. "Understandable, but there is a problem there."

A sinking feeling overwhelmed Cindy. She wanted to sit down, but the only chair was at Dr. Chapman's desk. "You didn't collapse my universe, did you?"

Dr. Chapman scoffed. "If I did, it hardly matters. There's an infinite number of universes nearly identical to it, like one where the only difference is that maybe you had tea this morning instead of coffee."

"That would be really weird!" Cindy shouted, a tear going down her cheek. "I never have tea. I don't like tea!"

"Get a hold of yourself," Dr. Chapman said, looking annoyed. "It was just an example. Your universe is fine. That's not the problem." Dr. Chapman walked over to the Sphere. "I found this gives me a special ability to pull versions of me from other universes, but then we're tethered. The Sphere can support us both being pulled from our original realm, but then we have to be attuned to the same universe. To break the tether and send you back to your universe would also send me back to mine . . . which, as I explained, is not an option."

Cindy tried to process this. "Well, if we have to be in the same universe, can't you . . . with that thing . . . open a portal or something and send us both to my universe? I'll just explain to everyone you're my long-lost twin sister . . . with the same name."

Dr. Chapman laughed. "First of all, it doesn't work by making portals. It supports our existence at different frequencies to sustain us in alternate universes. And even if I could send us both to your universe, I'm not going to live my life on some technologically backward planet with your little family or whatever. I've broken the barrier between universes. What I can now achieve if I continue my work is limitless."

Cindy clenched her hand into a fist and stepped toward Dr. Chapman. "Now listen here, you little—"

Cindy felt a hand on her shoulder; it was one of the three soldiers in black. She hadn't heard them come in. She looked at the soldiers and back at Dr. Chapman and laughed. "Oh, wow. The alternate-universe version of me is a pure supervillain. You're destroying universes and even have henchmen."

"Henchpeople," Dr. Chapman corrected her.

Cindy let out a small growl. "Where did you even get people like this to help you in your insanity?"

Dr. Chapman shrugged. "I have access to infinite universes, so I have access to infinite resources."

Cindy really wanted to punch "herself" but was now very aware of the soldiers in the room. "So, what happens to me?"

Dr. Chapman's face went grave. "Well, that is a question." She started walking out of the office, and the soldiers urged Cindy to follow, one keeping a hand on Cindy's shoulder. "I guess the real question is whether you can be an asset or a liability to me," Dr.

Chapman said as they walked down a white hallway. "Because of the tether the Sphere maintains, you'll have to stick around with me in whatever universe I travel to. The only thing that breaks it is death."

Cindy looked at Dr. Chapman's face, but it was emotionally passive, and she didn't return the look. They entered a large room. At the centre stood a metal circle in which the anomaly was frozen in white. Cindy stopped and gasped upon seeing it.

Dr. Chapman smiled, though there was a nervous energy to it. "I had my people bring it in so I could study it. That thing chasing me was scary for a while—a long while—but now, I have things under control. Now, I need to figure out what it is and why it was after me."

"Maybe it has something to do with you destroying a whole universe," Cindy suggested, very slowly walking toward the frozen anomaly.

Dr. Chapman scoffed. "Like a vengeance thing? As I said, I don't see any evidence of sentience within it."

"You're obviously dealing with things you don't understand," Cindy said. "Who knows what else you could destroy if you keep playing around with your Sphere or whatever?"

"If you don't understand something, that's what science is for," Dr. Chapman stated. "And destruction . . ." Dr. Chapman laughed. "I don't expect some housewife busy cutting the crusts off her kids' sandwiches to share my perspective, but I've seen the multiverse's full extent. Countless civilizations dying in an instant is nothing compared to the infinite."

Cindy stared again at Dr. Chapman. It was like looking in a mirror that reflected a face she didn't recognize. "My kids eat their crusts. I need to get back to them. They're—"

"It's hard for me to express how little I care about your children," Dr. Chapman interrupted. "There are countless versions of us who had countless different children—there is nothing special about them. You've got your husband, Mr. Hampton—they've got others. It's nothing unique, or special, even." She stepped toward Cindy, her face very serious. "But you're me, don't you see? Haven't you always wanted to shed all that and do something more with your life? This is the more." Dr. Chapman waved to the room with the frozen anomaly and the soldiers in black standing around. "I have access to *everything*."

Cindy looked again long and hard at Dr. Chapman. She could see the logic to what her doppelganger was saying. And while she thought this supervillain version of her was strange and foreign, there was also something far too familiar about her. No, Dr. Chapman wasn't really different than her . . . just a few choices off. And Cindy knew for certain she had to stop her.

"Okay, I see what you're saying," Cindy said delicately. "Just give me some time to think about this."

Dr. Chapman's expression changed, a frown creasing her face. Cindy thought it should have been easy to lie to herself—one does it all the time, but it was apparently harder than she thought. Dr. Chapman shook away the frown and smiled. "Okay." She looked at one of her soldiers carrying a rifle. "Take her someplace comfortable." And Cindy could tell there was something not entirely honest in that statement.

The soldier started to lead Cindy out of the room by pushing her by the shoulder—not quite pointing the rifle at her but also not quite being unthreatening with it—and the words of "Link" echoed in her head: "You need to get that gun and get out of here, or you're dead!"

Cindy took a deep breath. She pressed a button on her wrist. The magnets in her boots activated, leaving Cindy unmoveable and causing the soldier pushing her to stumble into her with surprise (and a feminine grunt showing this was one who might have been offended when Cindy called them "henchmen"). Cindy quickly grabbed the rifle from the soldier as the soldier tumbled to the ground. She pointed the rifle at Dr. Chapman.

Dr. Chapman put her hands up. Four other soldiers in the room pointed rifles at Cindy, and the one who had fallen to the ground had drawn a pistol.

"What do you think you're doing, Cindy?" Dr. Chapman asked. "I don't see how this ends well for you."

"I don't care about all your stupid universes!" Cindy shouted, trying to be as menacing with the (laser?) rifle in her hands as she could. "I want to get back to my kids! To my husband! To my world! Do you get that?"

"How do you think *this* is going to bring that about?" Dr. Chapman said calmly. "This is only going to get you killed. I'm trying to offer you an option where you don't die, and maybe you should consider it more."

Cindy tried to ignore the other guns pointed at her—though they all made her want to scream and freak out—and focus on Chapman. She also realized she wasn't exactly sure how to use the gun she held or what exactly sort of gun it was, but it had a trigger, and her finger found it. "You're me, so there must be some part of you that isn't a psychopath," Cindy stated. "You have to understand this is wrong." She glanced at the anomaly, its arm of darkness reaching out of the white. "You even got some interdimensional angel of vengeance after you. Isn't any of that registering with you?"

Dr. Chapman frowned. "I know you're not as scientifically minded as me, but let's not revert to superstition. This is all just new science—new things to discover and understand. Doesn't any of that fascinate you?"

Cindy let herself take a glance at the five soldiers with guns on her. She wasn't sure exactly what her plan was. It certainly wasn't to fight the soldiers; Cindy had tried playing first-person shooters before and was not very good at them.

She looked again at the anomaly—the thing she had seen destroy a whole planet—and she remembered again this wasn't just about her and her family. Getting back safe, if that even was possible, wasn't enough. And since, in a way, it was she who had done this, she felt a strange responsibility.

She saw Dr. Chapman nod to one of the soldiers. She had to act now. "You like science?" Cindy said. "Let's try an experiment."

Cindy pointed her rifle at the metal ring around the anomaly and pulled the trigger. There was no kickback to the gun—only a vibration. The metal around the anomaly exploded.

The white all turned to black.

"NO!" Cindy heard Dr. Chapman scream as the anomaly began its pursuit again. Some of the soldiers fired on it uselessly, but its darkness spread until it covered some of the room's walls, and those walls began to disintegrate.

A rush of wind yanked the rifle from Cindy's hands, and it flew near the anomaly and disappeared. The exterior had been breached, and all the air was rushing into the atmosphereless outside. One soldier fell past her, being pulled past the anomaly and disintegrating. Cindy was held in place by her magnetic boots, but the anomaly was again coming toward her.

Cindy turned to run, seeing a hallway behind her that Dr. Chapman was struggling down. Cindy pursued slowly with her magnet-boots engaging and disengaging. She also wondered how much longer she'd be able to breathe with all the wind rushing past her and no longer having a helmet. But she knew where she was headed.

Cindy reached Dr. Chapman's office just as Dr. Chapman pushed open the door. Cindy pushed as well, and they both tumbled into the room.

The door slammed shut behind them. The rush of air stopped.

Dr. Chapman ran for a console by her desk. "I have to jump, or we're going to die, you idiot! Do you know how long it took to imprison that thing!"

Cindy walked over to the Sphere. "So this is what's holding us out of our original universes."

Dr. Chapman at first seemed to ignore the question, but then realization struck her. "Cindy, if something happens to that, I can't say for certain what will happen to us. We could end up scattered across various universes."

"Yeah, you don't know a lot about what you're fiddling with, do you?" Cindy snarled. "I mean, you destroyed a universe and have a world-ending monster after you. Can't you see you're in over your head, Chappy?"

"Don't call me that!" Dr. Chapman yelled. "You know we hate that! Now step away from that!"

Cindy picked up the Sphere. It was heavier than she'd thought and seemed to be pulsing in her hands. "This has to stop."

"You'll be murdering me," Dr. Chapman pleaded, stepping toward Cindy. "You'll be murdering yourself. I can get us out of here safely—just put it down."

There was a small rush of air. Cindy looked to the door. It was enveloped in black and disintegrating. Cindy then glanced back to Dr. Chapman, just in time to see a blade come at her head. Cindy deflected it with the Sphere, and the knife bounced out of Dr.

Chapman's hand. Dr. Chapman then grabbed the Sphere and tried to wrest it away from Cindy.

The door was gone. The air rushed toward the anomaly, which kept its steady pace toward them. Cindy's magnetic boots held her in place, but the wind pushed Dr. Chapman toward the anomaly. She gave one more pleading look to Cindy.

Cindy mouthed a swear word at her and let go of the Sphere. Still clinging to it, Dr. Chapman fell back to the anomaly, colliding with it and disappearing in the black, the Sphere along with her.

———————————

CINDY WAS LOOKING at an over-decorated cake. Paul Hollywood was taking a slice. It took Cindy a moment to understand that she was back on her couch at home, staring at her TV. She was again just in her jeans and t-shirt, though they looked a bit worn from the day.

"Where have you been?" It was her husband, Russell, looking absolutely exasperated.

She leaped up from the couch, clung to Russell, and started crying.

"Whoa, what happened?" Russell asked, rubbing her back.

Cindy looked at Russell's face. It all seemed familiar. Every line —maybe every line. She thought she remembered them. "Where are the kids?"

"They're out back playing. What's going on?"

"I'll tell you in . . ." Cindy began, already heading for the back door. Outside, she found Davey and Julia playing on a big swing hung from the oak out back.

"Hi, Mommy. Daddy was looking for you," Julia said as she and Davey got off the swing.

Cindy knelt down and hugged them both. She then took a good look at them. Her kids.

"Sweetie, what's the matter?" Russell asked, coming out of the back door after her.

"Did I have tea this morning?" Cindy asked.

Russell looked confused. "No, you hate tea."

Cindy cried a little again. A horrible thought struck her, though, and she stood up and looked toward the horizon in each direction. In one direction, she saw darkness. "What's that?"

"It's just a storm cloud," Russell said, taking her hand.

Cindy looked at it more. And that's what it was. Just a grey storm cloud. "It's going to rain."

"We have a house with a roof; I think we'll be fine," Russell said. "Are you going to tell me what's going on?"

Cindy felt the empty pocket of her jeans. "I lost my new phone."

"Do you want me to call it to help you find it?" Russell offered as Davey and Julia went back onto the large swing.

Cindy leaned against Russell and watched the approaching storm. "No. I'm pretty sure it's gone."

THE NEW PLANET

By Jane Yolen

So, we discovered it,
Named it,
Farmed it,
Tamed it,
Rolled in its earth,
Climbed its limited trees,
Swam in its silken seas.
So, why were we surprised
that we woke up the sleeping residents,
who had their own ideas
about what or who was edible,
after a long year's nap?

HOSTILE UNIVERSE

By K. Eason

The word came up from Science in a condensed squirt over the comps: *Atmosphere ninety-two percent carbon dioxide, surface temperate ranges between minus one hundred and minus fifteen C.* And added, only half sarcastic: *Wear your suit out there.*

"Helpful," Mercx muttered. "Someone topside's got a sense of humour. Check it."

Jenner materialized over her shoulder, ghost-image in the comp-screen's black and green. He flashed her a grin. "Nah. See. Thought I'd go down naked. What you think of that, Mercx?"

"I think you should've volunteered that thirty solar days ago," she murmured. "Save BioHaz some work. Scare the indigenes to death."

Jenner leaned on the back of her chair. The springs sighed protest. "Way I heard, the indigenes got no *eyes*."

Mercx had her own ideas about the indigenes. Sounded to her like bored BioHaz personnel entertaining themselves. But the indigene rumour kept Jenner interested. Gave her team something to think about besides a lot of nothing on the other side of the ship and a distinct shortage of action inside it.

"We'll find out, won't we? Dirtside in our future." She shifted counterbalance against Jenner's weight, kept her hands near the keypad. Slanted a look at him through the screen's reflection. "Maybe they'll want us to bring back a sample."

"Live or dead?"

"They're sending *us*, aren't they?"

"So, dead."

"'S my guess. Wait for the brief." Which would be incoming—now, looked like. Mercx watched the flat green bar on the bottom of the screen. Percentage download, it told her, fifteen percent. Forty. *Big* report. Meant a lot of reading. Meant pulling weapons out of lockers, and priming the suits, and doing something, God and finally. The only conflict Carlen Mercx, Sergeant, Special Environments Commando Tactical Reconnaissance, had met so far this run was the third-shift tech-chief. Big man, hair like copper wire, who made a habit of looming in garrison corridors and scowling disapproval at anyone in a uniform.

Fuggin' janissaires are nothin' but a waste of resources.

As if the ship had a shortage. As if somehow, her team's presence might mean some other crewman slept in an airlock and ate nutripaste for all his meals. Mercx wondered what the tech-chief would do in *her* place if he had to go dirtside with a polyceramic rig between him and a hostile universe. What he'd do with non-standard G, and a horizon that curved the wrong way and klicks of nothing except air and gravity between self and cold space, or with weather cutting around the suit's slopes and angles, precip spatter and rattle on the faceplate.

Bets he'd need decontamination in his suit, that was what.

"What's it say? Car?"

"Hm?" She blinked Jenner's face back to focus. Harder to see his reflection in the screen now, with the orange lines of text marching past. Her gaze snagged on geological data, seismic reports, mineralogy—

Hell. Oh *hell*. She stabbed the keypad, backed up in a series of violent clicks. An equipment manifest. A passenger list, for *IC-274 Drakkar*.

"Got your answer, Jen. Why we're here. This isn't a survey run. This is—" *search and rescue*, she almost said, and then she saw the crash date. Her pride prickled. "—salvage and secure."

"What?"

She leaned sideways to let him read the screen. "That's why we've been sitting in orbit. They've been scanning for wreckage."

And had found it, apparently. There were drop coordinates in the report and high-orbit images. Scans showed no domes on the surface. No EM output that didn't come from rocks and the star's radiation. That wasn't a surprise. But the deepscans had coughed up those anomalous readings that BioHaz claimed could be—

"Indigenes," she muttered and wished she hadn't.

"Indigenes," Jenner said in the same breath and swore after. "Or maybe it's survivors?"

"You think anyone walked away from a crash like that? *Drakkar* wasn't built for landing. Chunks of metal made it down. Scrap. Look at the images."

"Maybe part of the inner ring made it."

"Sure. You've seen atmospherics, Jen. *Nothing's* breathing down there."

"Something is," he repeated darkly. "BioHaz says so."

"BioHaz, hell. We've been circling this rock for three tendays, haven't we? Everyone's bored. Even BioHaz." She twisted and laid a hand on Jenner's arm, where it weighted the back of her chair. "The reactor's probably leaking. That'd set BioHaz off."

"Maybe it's the Nanny."

"Hell. Nannies run ships. That costs power. There's nothing down there to feed a nanny." But there were those readings from BioHaz, so, "It's probably microbes. Bacteria. That shit's tough. And it'd get BioHaz's attention."

"Except—"

"No except. This rock's useless dirt if it's got organic contamination. We're here to see that it doesn't. So we go down, haul out the scrap, scrub the place down, and InterCorp can get back to the business of building a colony."

Jenner's jaw squared off stubborn. "So why are they sending *us* on an s-and-s?"

A good question, sure, and one that OpSec hadn't put in the report. But it wouldn't've mattered if they had. Jenner wouldn't believe it. He had an answer in mind already, had *indigene* fever-bright in his eyes. And he'd take that down to the team, and when they dropped, she'd have janissaires distracted, looking for aliens and chattering *what if* instead of minding *what was.*

So Mercx snapped out, sergeant-voiced: "Assemble everyone in the mess for a briefing, 1500. *Don't* start with the indigene stuff. This is a salvage-and-secure op. That's all you say. That's an order, Corporal. Savvy?"

"Yes, *sir.*"

Jenner cut her a salute, stiff-shouldered, spun on his heel. Didn't quite stomp, no, but she pitied the deckplate. So he was angry. Hurt, which he had a right to be, hell. She'd apologize later. Make it up, after the drop, when they could joke about indigenes and BioHaz pranks and maybe, then, he'd laugh with her.

But after Jenner was gone—bawling names loud enough for

OpSec to hear him on the bridge—Mercx pulled up the images again. Gouges in the landscape, churned sand, a shallow trench, dark on the edges, that wasn't from any catastrophic flood. That was the crash site. Reports placed most of *Drakkar* inside that, with a scattering of debris on the red sand.

Hell. The trench wasn't that far, really, from the subterranean channels. Someone in a rig might make it that far. And a mining colony would've brought sealed ground transport.

Mercx ran the numbers, a dozen most-likely scenarios—if *Drakkar* had spun just so, if she *hadn't* broken up in atmosphere, if she *had,* and in how many pieces—and couldn't get the comp to predict a single survivor. Improbable, nudging up on impossible, that anyone had lived through impact even *if* equipment survived.

But she stared at the BioHaz readings, and she wondered.

"THIS PLACE HAVE A NAME?"

Private Kibrya aimed a kick at a rock, sent it arcing three metres over the red sands. The dropship had set them on the broad plain half a klick from the trench. *Can't get closer,* the pilot had said. *Wind shearing's bad.*

Damn right it was. Mercx's rig sang a constant click-and-whir adjustment against gusts and spurts and blasts that pinked her atmo-readings on the HUD. Lot of sand blowing. Hell on the filters.

"Sure," Teel said. She stretched the word into three syllables. "It's called Bad Investment."

"Hell it is." Kibrya hesitated. "Is it?"

Teel made an airless sound. Mercx intervened before Kibrya recognized himself as the butt of a joke.

"It's got a survey tag. ICS-1399G4-point-7." And added, because this was Kibrya's first drop, "InterCorp doesn't waste real names on dead dirt."

The HUD flickered. Com-channel blue, which meant command channel, which meant Jenner and for her ears only. His voice smoked like a burned wire. "Maybe we ask the indigenes what they call the place when we find 'em, huh, Car?"

She imagined Jenner's eyebrows, the insolent line of his lips. "Sure, Jen. You can ask 'em. But I don't think bacteria's got much imagination."

Oblivious, cheerful, Kibrya kicked another rock. It skipped and stuttered a metre to the edge of the trench. Teetered a moment before the sands slid and dragged it over. "How about we call it Hell's Asshole?"

"Ha," said Teel, "or maybe—"

Jenner cut in like seal doors in a hull breach. "Keep it clean, Kibrya. OpSec keeps a transcript."

Sand hissed on Mercx's face shield in the sudden silence. Then Kibrya coughed.

"Sorry, Corporal."

On the other side of the rigs, Mercx would wave Kibrya off, roll eyes, and hitch a smile. All she had now was a bright green strip on her HUD with his name under it. Her face went through the motions anyway.

"Don't worry about it," she said, as Jenner snapped, "Keep your mind on the mission, Private."

"Sir," Kibrya said, addressing both commanders with one syllable. And then came more silence, rig-com pure. Mercx listened to her own breath compete with the wind and wished for static. Watched Kibrya's readings hitch closer to yellow: elevated heart rate, blood pressure. He'd be shuffling his feet now if they were ship-side, ears red and eyes fixed on the deck.

She keyed blue-com. "You know OpSec won't care about profanity. They don't listen to our transcripts unless shit goes sideways."

"He needs to stay focused."

She turned her head out of reflex, fired a scowl through HUD and helmet that Jenner did not see. She hadn't argued when Jenner insisted on bringing the big RB-22s or the concussion rounds. Had thought—and been wrong, evidently—that he'd relax once they hit dirt and saw what she did: nothing but sand and rocks and wreckage.

The moment passed for a retort, and Mercx said nothing else. She walked against the wind drag and sand-slip, with the horizon curved and cut with distant mountains and a watery unfiltered sun carving shadows in her wake. The terrain changed only slightly. The countdown on her navpoint ticked down to *proximity* and then *stop*.

Mercx paused at the top of the trench. Stared down at a shattered ship's tangled bones. Hours down, hours back, God knew how long navving the wreckage. It would be full planet-night when they got back, and the winds always got worse after sunset. They might spend a full dirtside revolution down here, waiting for a pick-up, and the danger had nothing to do with anything Jenner could shoot at. Lose a coil, a filter, and a body would die down here. Hostile universe. And

Hell's Asshole

ICS-1399G4-point-7 already had a taste for human flesh.

BLACK TANGLED ALLOY crunched under Mercx's boots, sent the faintest shiver up through polyceramic and synthrubber soles. The highbeam on her helmet bleached circles of solid reality into the wreckage. Rocks. Sand. Metal and melted plastic.

There was no place down here for the indigenes. No room even for sunlight. Just black overhead. Black all around. Space-black and impenetrable, except space was safely empty. More treacherous down here in the vault and tangle of *Drakkar's* bones. Teel had already collided with a fallen deckplate that lurked sharp and edge-on in the shadows. She'd walked knee-first into it and damn near split a joint seal. Teel had gone down, swearing. Alarms had gone off in Mercx's helmet, *impact* and red-flashing *Teel* on her HUD. But the rig had held, and Mercx consoled herself by blistering the inside of her helmet with a litany of Teel's failings, from birth-tank to basic to present, while Kibrya helped her up.

Jenner had said nothing, then and since. Except for the steady green presence on her HUD and the footprints gouged into the sand, he might not have been there at all. She sent him to the bones of the bridge, sent herself to engineering. Protocol said they should be two-person teams, but she didn't want an extra minute in the wreck she didn't need. *Pray* Kibrya and Teel could keep from impaling themselves on anything, pray that they found nothing at all.

Not much of a prayer. Nothing down here. BioHaz and their damned readings had been a mistake.

Mercx keyed her com. "Kibrya. Teel. Anything in medlab?"

"If by 'anything' you mean 'lots of broken stuff,' then yes, Sergeant. But the hardware's totally fragged."

"Looks like they lost pressure in here," Teel said, in the same tone she might've used to say *it's soy-fish for dinner tonight*. "The tanks imploded. There's organic contamination. But," she added, "nothing alive."

Of course, there wasn't. Mercx bit back an entirely petty urge to say *tell that to BioHaz*. "How's your knee?"

"Fine, Sergeant."

Not quite the report on her readout. Those numbers said elevated endorphins, which meant pain, and an uneven gait that the servos corrected with only a minor drain on the batteries. Nothing to worry about, long as

nothing goes wrong

the battery held through the climb back to the surface. It had been an ugly descent. Up would be worse, with everyone tired. The chrono said eight-point-two hours elapsed. Bet at least that much more until the dropship returned. Mercx thought about the climb again, and the spreading ache in her back, and the pinpoint pain in the needle slot at the base of her neck that would only get worse, the longer she stayed in the suit.

Hell with salvage and clean-up. Nothing down here worth one of her people. *Dead* planet, whatever BioHaz said.

"Bring it in," Mercx said. "Return to the rendezvous. Jenner?"

Insolent two beats, then: "Nothing yet."

"Yet. What's left?"

"I'm looking at the bridge seal now. There's a three-level hole in the decking. Took me a while to get up here."

"Hold position. I'm coming up."

"Negative. This won't take long. Nothing in there except the Nanny pod, and it's long dead, right? I'm going in."

She could argue with him, open-channel. She could take it to blue-com, too, with only the rig's recorders as witness. *Hell* if she'd grant him that satisfaction. She'd see him court-martialed for this, charge him with insubordination and confine him to quarters.

No. Better. Reassign him to maintenance, have him dis-and-re-assemble every one of the rigs, seal and bolt and circuit. Let him work with that third-shift tech-chief for a tenday, and Jenner would ask for—

His vitals surged toward a sudden yellow. Elevated heart rate, blood pressure, respiration, and breathless: "Car, it's here, the—"

The com crackled. Then Mercx's whole rig dimmed and dropped her into sudden and absolute black. She strangled a moment of panic. Stopped moving, held breath, and waited for the secondary systems. The life support came online first, mechanical sigh and groan, before her HUD flickered. Before the com did, in a hiss of static and Teel's fooling-nobody calm:

"—geant? Do you copy?" That was Teel, sounding panicked.

"Affirm." The primaries flickered on, light by light. That power drain shouldn't've happened. Shouldn't be able to happen, with all the rig's redundancies and shielding. Mercx let her breath out slowly. "Did you feel that, too? Some kind of settling in the debris?"

Expecting a yes, and surprised when Teel hesitated. "No, Sergeant. I mean—we didn't feel it. And it wasn't shifting debris. We registered an EM disturbance down there. *Real* localized. Like a weapon discharge, sir."

"Origin?" Mercx asked, already knowing.

"Looks like the bridge."

Mercx's gut dropped into freefall. *Now* she noticed the orange RIG OFFLINE on her HUD and the flat grey line of Jenner's vitals. There should have been an alarm when it happened. Might've been, and she hadn't heard it, being offline herself.

Teel said, "We're on our way, Sergeant."

It wasn't protocol, and OpSec might skin her for it, but she didn't need to risk two more lives. "Negative, Teel. You and Kibrya hold position."

"But, Sergeant—"

A plague of insubordination, clearly. "I said *hold position*. You lose contact with me, you go topside and can, and you wait for the dropship. Savvy that? You don't come after us."

"Yes, sergeant," said Teel, unhappily. And after a moment, a grim little "Yessir" from Kibrya.

Mercx squinted out the skeleton lines of the ship's guts. Her rig's lights seemed too dim, now, wholly insufficient against the dark. She followed the twist and tangle of the ruined corridor, overlaid with the specs on her HUD. Stopped when she found Jenner's three-level hole to the bridge and swore. Easy to see why he'd taken so long to climb up there. Jagged metal, that's all it was, no resemblance to decking or bulkheads or ductwork. She wedged her gloves and boots where she found room for them and climbed and hoped she didn't slip and impale herself on something harder than the suit's polyceramic.

Jenner's vitals stayed flat. His com did, each time she tried it. Which she did—

"Jenner, you copy? Jen, dammit, *respond*."

—until the HUD map told her she'd found the bridge corridor and the first of the breached seals. She ducked through the first hatch and damn near stepped on Jenner's rifle. Damn near stepped on Jenner, sprawled face down and halfway into the corridor. Mercx panned across his back. Saw no trace of impact, no cracks in the rig or his tanks. A tiny red e-light glowed steady and desperate near the power pack.

Empty, that meant. Both batteries drained, down to reserves and a handful of minutes. The EM pulse had done that. She could recharge him. Sacrifice one of her batteries to his rig and hope their pick-up happened on schedule.

Hope wasn't something command encouraged. They liked hard numbers and secure zones. Didn't like risks to personnel or equipment. One man down, bad enough, but a half-drained rig in a red zone might lead to two dead and more at risk on retrieval.

So let them court-martial her corpse if she got it wrong. She knelt beside Jenner and snaked an umbilical to his suit.

"Teel," she said, past her suit's advisory beep. "Teel, Kibrya, you copy?"

Nothing. Her suit beeped again. Did she really want to initiate power transfer, y/n? Yes. Numbers spilled onto the HUD, front and centre.

She noticed, then, that her com-lights were grey. She wasted five seconds swearing while her own vitals spiked until she strangled the panic. Worst that would happen, Kibrya and Teel would disobey and come down, and she might need them to haul Jenner topside. No goddamn idea what'd got him. The source of the BioHaz readings, he'd said, which apparently packed a *hell* of an EM charge behind it.

Her rig hadn't reported anything, but sometimes the sensors missed things. She looked up, then, and into the bridge. The

too dim

headlamp rubbed out the shadows. Sweat prickled her scalp, chilled on the back of her neck. She'd been wrong. God, she had.

There *were* survivors.

The whole bridge crew, it must be, the ones who might've survived the impact, here in the centre of the ship. A half-dozen e-suits—the soft ones meant for in-ship emergencies—dangled and flapped from a tangle of cables and wires snaking through them, anchoring them to overhead and bulkhead. There were strange bulges in some of the suits, organic softness that seemed to change shape when Mercx looked too closely. And there, in the centre: the Nanny pod. The AI should be long dead and dark and wasn't, oh God. Little green lights on the console, that meant *live*.

The silvered suit visors turned toward her with inhuman precision. A half-dozen tiny screens flickered into awareness, white noise to blank black. Text began on the far left and crept from visor to visor.

IC-274 Drakkar *to any ships. Mayday. Help us. Have lost primary drives, life support critical, high casualties, mayday.*

Flash, and another chrono-stop: *life support critical.*

Flash again and then names, God, one for each suit, with the InterCorp command sigil and alphanumeric strings that must be command overrides.

Bile burned at the base of her throat. Mercx tried hard not to think about the faces behind those visors, what they might look like now, this many years dirtside, this many years mated up to the Nanny. They wouldn't be human anymore. Not quite.

Indigene.

A Nanny managed a ship's biosystems. And when the biosystems were down to six crew, running short on air and out of water—hell. Oh hell. It was one thing to modify a Nanny to manage an e-suit. But it was something else to refit it for human life support. A Nanny needed a power source, and the ship's drives were long dead. So guess, just *guess*, what it was using for batteries.

The crew must've known that InterCorp would investigate a loss big as *Drakkar*. Take that as faith. But not for years, in the time-stretch of deep space. Delay the inevitable, that's all they'd done, one last snatch at living. Merge with the Nanny. Wait for rescue. There wasn't any sunlight down here for the batteries, though, and the Nanny—hell, the *crew*—needed to metabolize something.

Mercx looked, really looked, at the bridge. Her headlamp wandered across exposed wires and cables and metal peeled into strange shapes. Might be crash damage, sure. Might be adaptation, too. The crew's last attempt to survive. Or, *or* . . . maybe the Nanny just hadn't wanted its supper crawling away.

God. Don't think of that. Don't think of what was *in* there, moving around in those suits. Something alive, for some value of living, that'd triggered the BioHaz sensors and got rumours flying and crossed OpSec's desk. But not something recognizably human or recognizably Nanny. Something else.

Indigene. Organic contamination. The reason OpSec would send janissaires on a salvage-and-secure mission. OpSec knew about it, or suspected, and OpSec didn't want this thing alive.

Well. The indigene seemed to have other plans.

The rig advised her it had completed the power transfer. Jenner's rig reappeared in her HUD. Jenner's vitals spiked from grey to orange. Mercx had time to realize that *extremely* local transmission between the rigs still worked, to be pleased about that, before the coms flickered live, static hiss and cough and gasp.

"—shot me, motherf—"

Her own heart stuttered. Relief and horror because the silvered visors were still staring at them. "Easy, Jen. Just breathe." She didn't like his vitals.

Jenner never listened. "The Nanny, Car. The damned Nanny *killed* those people."

The damned Nanny was *moving* now, a drift of saggy suits. Mercx fought her voice steady. "I think the crew is still in there. The Nanny, the crew—that's the indigene. Savvy? I got no coms beyond you and me," she said conversationally. "I think it's jamming. I told Teel and Kibrya to wait topside and leave if we didn't show. Think they will? Or you think they'll come here looking because we're both offline?"

He swore, raw-voiced. Take that as a yes.

"Me, either. Got a discipline problem in this unit. Got to work on it when we get back." The indigene had stopped moving. Seemed to be waiting. Watching her. Watching Jenner. She swallowed dust and glass and said, rough-voiced: "Might need the help to get you out. My rig's at half. I can't haul us both."

"No. Don't—*listen*." Wet sound, like spilled soup. "It didn't hit me. Until I tried to leave. You savvy?"

"I savvy." Of course, the EM pulse hadn't been an accident. An attack, she'd thought first, to keep the indigene's secret. A pulse would cost power, and the indigene had a limited supply. An EM pulse would be an insupportable waste unless the indigene had the means to recover that cost. From a rig's power pack. From a rig's occupant.

It *knew* Jenner hadn't been alone in the wreck. It *knew* someone would come looking.

The indigene's composite eye watched her, blank screen faces reflecting six versions of herself and Jenner. She had no way to communicate with it. There wasn't enough atmosphere down here for external audio, and *hell* if she'd try an uplink. She had Jenner to worry about, linked to her rig, and it had—itself. Themselves. And if she could talk to it, what could she even promise?

Let us go, and InterCorp will leave you alone. We'll send batteries.

And in exchange, what would the indigene offer?

Sure, janissaire, we'll let our first meal in five standard years just walk out the door.

Best that might happen is BioHaz would come down and collect it for study, and *damn* sure they'd kill it first.

Mercx moved experimental fingers onto her rifle stock. Some of the cables shifted near the suits, rippled and resettled in front of the Nanny. A thick once-blue cable writhed on the deckplate. A disk of charred metal winked from the end.

So *that's* what it did to Jenner.

Through her teeth: "My rifle's still got a charge, Jen. All you have to do is get out the door. I'll cover you."

"Car." That was his serious voice, which could mean apologies or thanks or *I'm dying.*

And he wasn't. Damn him, he wasn't. Couldn't.

But of course, that wasn't true. Any EM that got through rig shielding wouldn't leave flesh undamaged. Guess at the harm to organic material. Guess why his lungs wouldn't clear. Guess why his vitals were flashing now and verging on red. Jenner couldn't fight like that. Couldn't *move* like that.

He knew it. She did. How many combat drops had they done together? How many campaigns? Neither of them was young anymore. Not like Teel and Kibrya. Any *you'll be all right, soldier* speeches would waste air they both needed.

Jenner sounded like his own ghost. "I can give you a couple seconds. Keep it busy. Got enough juice for that."

And God, she wished for eye contact, to see his face instead of her own rig reflected in his faceplate. It would be easy to die down here, her and Jenner together. But do that, and Kibrya and Teel died too when they came looking, and so would everyone else sent into the wreckage. There was a whole garrison up there in the ship to feed it that would come through this door in pairs until OpSec figured it out and ordered an orbital strike.

Jenner knew that. Expected her to know it, too. And they didn't have the extra air for

goodbye

discussion.

Mercx swallowed her voice back to steady. "Copy. On three. Your count."

Another cough. She knew he'd be nodding his head in the helmet's confines. "Three."

Jenner's flashing vitals retreated to her HUD's margins. She moved her rifle's targeting link front and centre. Armed it.

"Two."

The indigene rippled, a sheaf of black e-suits flashing *Mayday, Mayday* across its screens.

Jenner released the umbilical between their rigs and rolled onto one knee. One last burst of power from the rig, machine to get him where meat wouldn't.

"One," he said and surged forward.

The silver-faced e-suits peeled aside like an honour guard. Now Mercx could see the Nanny pod where it rested behind them. Its casing and cables had never been meant for the conditions on this planet. Cracked joints bled frozen fluids that turned briefly liquid as Jenner turned his combat rig into a slow-moving missile and punched into the heart of it.

The suits fluttered, closing ranks behind him.

Silence in her helmet. Mercx held her eyes wide against blinking as Jenner's vitals flickered into desperate red. One more flash, and then—gone. RIG OFFLINE filled in the gap, impersonal and orange and, this time, permanent.

Mercx let herself blink. Shifted the rifle to her shoulder. Steadied it. Blinked again to clear the blur. And stopped, breathless, as the indigene shivered, an internal wind rippling through the e-suits. A green light bloomed in her HUD, where *RIG OFFLINE* had been. Stretched and grew and pulsed into a steady heartbeat that was not *entirely*

Jenner's.

The com crackled. Whispered her name.

Mercx fired. The e-suits shredded in the first explosion, peeled and flapped and melted where the incendiary round touched them. Jenner had gotten all the way to the Nanny, had punched a hole in its already cracked casing. And it, in turn, had already threaded filaments into his rig. Into *him*.

Her second shot caught Jenner's rig square in the back. It burst in a shower of quick-frozen air, blood and oxygen and polyceramic sparkling like crystal in her headlamp.

In silence, all of it. There wasn't enough air for sound.

Mercx emptied her rifle, round after methodical round, until it clicked empty. Only her own breath for company, coming hard enough she left fog on the faceplate. Through it, she could see the bulk of the indigene—polymer and biological compounds—fused into a slick, shapeless mass. Tiny white fires dotted its surface, where there was still something living to burn. They died, one by one, as she watched.

SEND THEM FLOWERS

By Walter Jon Williams

W e skipped through the borderlands of Probability, edging farther and farther away from the safe universes that had become so much less safe for us, and into the fringe areas where stars were cloudy smears of phosphorescent gas and the Periodic Table wasn't a guide, but a series of ever-more-hopeful suggestions.

Our ship was fuelled for another seven years, but our flight ended at Socorro for the most prosaic reason possible: we had run out of food. Exchange rates and docking fees ate most of what little money we had, and that left us on Socorro with enough cash for two weeks' food or one good party.

Guess which we chose?

For five months, we'd been running from Shawn, or at any rate, the cloaked, dagger-bearing assassins we imagined him sending after us. I'd had nothing but Tonio's company and freeze-dried food to eat, and the only wine we'd drunk had been stuff that Tonio brewed in plastic bags out of kitchen waste. We hadn't realized how foul the air on the *Olympe* had grown until we stepped out of the docking tube and smelled the pure recycled air of Socorro Topside, the station floating in geosynchronous orbit at the end of its tether.

The delights of Topside glittered ahead of us, all lights and music, the sizzle of grilled meats and the clink of glasses. How could we resist?

Besides, freaky Probability was fizzing in our veins. Our metabolisms were pumped by a shift in the electromagnetic fine-structure constant. Oxygen was captured and transported and burned and united with carbon and exhaled with greater efficiency. We didn't have to breathe as often as in our home Probability, and still, our bodies ran a continuous fever from the boost in our metabolic rate.

Another few more steps into Probability and the multiverse would start fucking with the strong and weak nuclear forces, causing our bodies to fly apart or the calcium in our bones to turn radioactive. But here, we remained more or less ourselves even as certain chemical reactions become much easier.

Which was why Socorro and its Topside had been built on this strange outpost of the multiverse, to create alloys that weren't possible in our home probabilities and to refine pure chemicals in industrial-sized quantities at a fraction of the energy it would have taken elsewhere.

Probability specialists in the employ of the Pryor corporate gene line had laboured hard to locate this particular Probability, with its unique physical properties—some theorists would argue, in fact, that they'd *created* it, like magicians bringing an entire universe into being with their spell. Once the Pryors had found the place, they'd explored it for years while putting together the right industrial base to properly exploit it. When they finally came, they came in strength, a whole industrial colony jigsawing itself into the Socorro system practically overnight.

Once they started shipping product out, they had to declare to the authorities where it came from, and this particular Probability was no longer secret. Others could come and exploit it, but the Pryors already had their facilities in place, and the profits pouring out.

Nobody lived in Socorro permanently. There was something about this reality that was conducive to forming tumours. You came in on a three-year contract and then shipped out, with cancer-preventing chemicals saturating your tissues.

"Oh yisss," Tonio said as we walked down Topside's main avenue. "Scrutinize the fine ladies yonder, my compeer. I desire nothing so much as to bond with them chemically, oh yisss."

The local fashion for women was weirdly modest and demure, covering the whole body and with a hood for the head, and the outfit looked *inflated*—as if they were wearing full-body life preservers, designed to keep them floating even if Topside fell out of orbit and dropped into the ocean.

But even these outfits couldn't entirely disguise the female form or the female walk. My blood seemed to fizz at the sight, and perhaps, in this quirky Probability, it did.

Music floated out of a place called the Flesh Pit, all suggestive dark windows and colourful electric ads for cheap drinks. "Let us sample the pleasures of this charming bistro," Tonio suggested.

"How about some food, first?" I said, but Tonio was already halfway through the door.

The Flesh Pit had alcohol and other conventional stimulants, and also others that were designed for our current reality, taking advantage of the local biochemistry to deliver a packaged high aimed at our pumped metabolisms. The charge was delivered from a pressure cylinder into a cheap plastic face mask. The masks weren't hygienic, but after a few huffs, we didn't much care.

While getting refills at the bar, we met a short, brown-skinned man named Frank. He was drinking alcohol and joined us at our table. After two drinks, he was groping my thigh, but he didn't take it amiss when I moved his hand away.

The Flesh Pit was a disappointment. The music was bottom-grade puti-puti, and the women weren't very attractive even after they took off their balloon-suits. After we bought Frank another drink, he agreed to be our guide to Topside's delights, such as they were.

He took us up a flight of stairs to a place that didn't seem to actually have a name. The very second I stepped into the front room, a woman attached herself to me, spreading herself across my front like a cephalopod embracing its prey. My eyes were still adjusting to the dim light, and I hadn't seen her until she'd engulfed me.

My eyes adapted, and I looked around. We were in what appeared to be a small dance hall: there was a bar at one end and a live band at the other, and benches along the sides where women smoked and waited for partners. There were a few couples shuffling around on the dance floor, each man in the octopus clutch of his consort.

"Buy me a drink, space man?" my partner said. Her name was Étoile, and she wore a gardenia above one ear. I looked longingly at the prettier girls sitting on the benches and then sighed and headed for the bar. On my way, I noticed that Tonio had snagged the most beautiful woman in the place, a tall, tawny-haired lioness with a wicked smile.

I bought Étoile an overpriced cocktail and myself a whiff of some exotic gas. We took a turn on the dance floor, then went to the bedroom. Then back to the bar, then to the bedroom. Frank was sent out for food and came back with items on skewers. Then the bar, then the bedroom. I had to pay for clean sheets each time. Étoile was very efficient about collecting. Occasionally, I would run into Tonio and his girl in the corridor.

By morning, the bar was closed and locked, the dance floor was empty, I was hungry and broke and melancholy, and Tonio's girl had gone insane. She was crying and clutching Tonio's leg and begging him to stay.

"If you leave, I'll never see you again!" she said. "If you leave, I'll kill myself!" Then she took a bottle from the bar and smashed it on a table, and tried to cut her wrist with a piece of glass.

I grabbed her and knocked the broken glass out of her hand, and then I pinned her against the wall while she screamed and sobbed, with tears running down her beautiful face, and Étoile tried to find the management or the bartender or someone to get Tonio's girl a dose of something to calm her down.

I gave Tonio an annoyed look.

He had driven his woman crazy in only one night.

"That's a new record," I told him.

ÉTOILE RETURNED with an irritated and sleepy-eyed manager, who unlocked the bar and got an inhaler. He plastered the mask over the weeping woman's face and cracked the valve, and held the mask over her mouth and nose till she relaxed and drifted off to sleep. Then Tonio and I carried her to her room and laid her on the bed.

"She ever done this before?" I asked the manager.

He slapped at the wisp of hair atop his bald head as if it had bitten him. "No," he said.

"You'll have to watch her," I said.

He shrugged his little moustache. "I'm going back to bed," he said.

I looked at Étoile. "Not me," she said. "Unless you pay."

"It is necessary at this juncture," said Tonio, "for me to confess the infortunate condition of our finances."

Infortunate. Tonio was always making up words that he thought were real.

"Then get your asses out of here," said the manager. Étoile glared at me as if it weren't her fault I had no money left.

We dragged ourselves back to the *Olympe.* The ship smelled a lot better with air being cycled in from the station. I wondered if I'd ever be able to pay for the air I was breathing.

"I hope Fanny will recover, yiss," Tonio said as he headed for his rack.

"What did you *do* to her?" I said.

"We did things, yiss. It was Fanny did all the talking."

I looked again at Tonio and tried to figure out yet again why so many women loved him. He wasn't any better-looking than I was, and he was too skinny, and he had dirt under his nails. His hands were too big for the rest of him. He had blue eyes, which probably didn't hurt.

Maybe the attraction was the broken nose, the big knot in the middle of his face that made it all a little off-centre. Maybe that's all it took.

"Listen, Gaucho," he said. He had his sincere face on. "I am aware that this contingency is entirely my fault."

"It's too late to worry about that," I said.

"Yiss, well." He reached down and took the ring off his finger, the one with the big emerald that Adora had given him, and he held it out to me. "This is the only valuable thing I own," he said. "I desire that you take it."

"I don't want your ring," I said.

He took my hand and pressed the ring into it. "If necessity bides, you can sell it," he said. "I don't cognizate how much it's worth, but it's a lot, yiss. It will pay for docking fees and enough food to peregrinate to some other Probability where you might be able to make a success."

I looked at him. "Are you saying goodbye, Tonio?"

He shrugged. "Compeer, I have no plans. But who knows what the future may necessitate?"

He ambled away to his rack. I looked at the ring on my palm— all the intricate little designs on it, the dolphins of the Feeneys and the storks of the Storch line all woven together in little knots.

I went into my stateroom, where I closed the door. I put the ring on my desk and looked at it for a while, and then I went to bed.

When I woke in the morning, the ring was still there, shining like all the unpaid debts in all the multiverse.

I MET Tonio when I was working with my wife, Karen, on a mining concession owned by her family, an asteroid known only by an identification number. We were supervising the robots that did the actual mining, following the vein of gold and sending it streaming out into the void to be caught by the processor that hovered overhead. Gold was a common metal, and prices were low. The robots were old and kept breaking down.

Tonio turned up in a draft of new workers, and we became

friends. He had his charm and his strange Andevin accent, and the vocabulary he'd got in prison, where he had nothing to read for months but a dictionary. He said the prison term was the result of a misunderstanding about whether or not he could borrow someone else's blazemobile.

Tonio and I became friends. After Karen and Tonio became friends, I equipped myself with a heavy pry bar and went looking for him. When he opened the door to his little room and saw me standing there, he just looked at me and then shrugged.

"Do whatsoever thou must, compeer," he said, backing away from the door. "For I deserve it in all truth."

I stepped in and hefted the pry bar, and realized that I couldn't hit him. I lowered the bar, and then Tonio and I talked for about six hours, after which I realized that my marriage hadn't been working in a long time, and that I wanted out and that Tonio could have Karen for all I cared.

After the divorce, when everything had played itself out, and there was no point in staying on the claim of a family to which I was no longer tied, I left the scene along with Tonio.

Of the various options, it was the course that promised the most fun.

THE OLYMPE ISN'T A FREIGHTER; it's a small private vessel—a yacht, in fact, though I'm far from any kind of yachtsman. The boat can carry cargo, but only a modest amount. In practice, if I wanted to carry cargo, there were three alternatives: Passengers. Compact but valuable cargo, which often means contraband. And information: dispatches so private that the sender doesn't want to broadcast them, even in cipher. Usually, the dispatches are carried by a courier.

Once we docked on Socorro, I advertised *Olympe*—I even offered references—but didn't get any takers, not right away. Fortunately, docking on Socorro was cheap—this wasn't a tourist spot but an industrial colony with too much docking capacity— and the air was nearly free. So Tonio got a job Upside, selling roasted chestnuts from a little wheeled grill—and with his blue eyes and broken nose working for him, he soon sold more chestnuts than anyone in the history of the whole pushcart business.

I took my aurora onto the station and went looking for work as a musician. I did some busking till I got a job with a band whose aurorista was on vacation in another Probability, and my little salary and Tonio's got us through the first month even though the puti-puti music bored me stiff. Then I auditioned for a band that had a series of regular gigs in upscale bars, and they took me on. I got a full split and a share of tips instead of a tiny salary, and things eased a bit. Even the music was better. We played popular songs while the tables were full of the dinner crowd, but afterward, we played what we liked, and when I got a good grind going, I could make the room sizzle the way my blood sizzled in this little corner of the multiverse.

During our flight, I'd had nothing to do but practice, and I'd got pretty good.

A couple of months went by. I didn't see Tonio much—he'd got a girlfriend named Mackey and was spending his free time with her. But he sent a piece of his pay into my account every month to help pay for *Olympe*.

I didn't have to sell the ring. I put it in the captain's safe and tried not to think about it.

The docking fees got paid, and our air and water bill. I had

Olympe cleaned and the crudded-up old air filters replaced. I polished the wood and the ornate metalwork in my stateroom till it glistened and put up some of Aram's old things in case I wanted to impress a potential passenger with the luxury we could offer. I started stocking the larder against the day it was time to leave.

I began to relax. Perhaps Shawn's vengeance was not quite so hot on our tail. I even spent some dinars on my own pleasures.

Not knowing whether or not it was a good idea, I went back to the place where Frank had taken us that first night. I wanted to find out if Tonio's tawny-haired woman was all right. But I didn't see her, and I had barely started chatting with a couple of the employees when the manager recognized me and threw me out.

Which was an answer, I guess.

There were other places to have fun, though, that didn't come with bad memories. My band played in a lot of them. I met any number of women in them, and we had a good time with the sizzling in the blood, and nobody went crazy.

So it went until a friend of Frank's made an offer to hire *Olympe*. Eldridge was a short man with fast, darting hands and genes left over from some long-ago fashion for albinism. His pale hair was shaggy, and his eyes looked at you with irises the colour of blood.

Eldridge offered a very generous sum to ship a small cargo out to one of the system's outer moons, a place called Vantage, where a lot of mining and processing habitats were perched on vast seams of ore. The trip would take five days out and five back, and I was free to take any other cargo on the return trip. Half our fee would be paid in advance, half on delivery. The one condition Eldridge made was that the seals on the packages should not be broken.

I'd been scraping a living aboard *Olympe* long enough to know what that stipulation meant, and I knew what I meant to do about it, too.

The band hired a temporary aurora player, and Tonio quit his chestnut-selling job even though his boss offered him a bonus. We had no sooner cleared Upside than the two of us went into the cargo space and broke every seal on every container, digging like maniacs through cushions of spray foam to find exactly what was supposed to be there, bottles of rare brandy or expensive lubricating oil for robots or canister filters for miners' vac suits. We searched until the air was filled with a blizzard of foam, and I began to wonder if we'd misjudged Eldridge entirely.

But in what was literally the final container, we found what we were looking for, about forty kilos of blue salt, exactly the stimulant to keep miners working those extra hours to earn that end-of-the-year bonus, to keep them all awake and alert and safe until the salt turned them into sweating, shivering skeletons, every synapse turned to pork cracklings while heavy metals collected in their livers and their zombie bodies ran on chemical fumes.

Well, well, I thought. I looked at Tonio. He looked at me.

Vantage would have been a couple of months away except that *Olympe* could shift to a Probability where we could make better time, a place where the stars hung in the sky like hard little pearls on a background of green baize. We made a couple of course changes outside our regular flight plan, then docked at Vantage and waited for the police to come and tear our ship apart.

Which they did. It was all part of Eldridge's plan. The griffs would find the blue salt in our cargo hold, and we'd be arrested. The salt would find its way from police lockers to Eldridge's dealers on Vantage, who would sell it and give the griffs a piece. In the meantime, the griffs would collect our fee from Eldridge in fines, and the money would be returned to Eldridge. I'd be coerced into signing over *Olympe* in exchange for a reduced sentence, and *Olympe* would be sold, with the profits split between Eldridge and the griffs.

It's the sort of trap that tourists in the Probabilities walk into all the time. But Tonio and I aren't tourists.

The griffs came in with chemical sniffers and found nothing, which meant they had to break into the cargo containers, and of course, found that they'd been broken into already. "A freelance captain's got to protect himself," I told the griff lieutenant. "If I find contraband, it gets spaced."

I wouldn't admit to actually having found the salt. I didn't know the local laws well enough to know whether that admission would implicate me or not, so I refused to admit anything.

The lieutenant in charge of the search just kept getting more and more angry. I was worried that she or one of her cronies would plant some contraband on the ship, so I made a point of telling her that I'd turned on all the ship's cameras, one in every room and cargo space, and was livecasting the whole search back to a lawyer's office on Upside. If she tried to plant anything, it would be caught on camera.

That sent her in a towering rage, and she tossed all the state-rooms for spite, ripping the mattresses and blankets off the beds and emptying the closets onto the deck before she stomped off.

I planned to unload the cargo and leave the second we could get clearance, but thanks to the griff lieutenant's temper tantrum, we had to do some cleanup first. That's why we had time for a passenger to find us. That's how we met Katarina.

Katarina was one of the Pryors, the incorporated gene line that pretty much owned the system, all of Upside and most of Down-side, as well as every facility on Vantage. She'd been on some kind of inspection tour of the Pryor facilities on the various moons, but she'd been unexpectedly called back to Socorro and needed a ride.

When the message first came that someone wanted passage to Socorro, I'd been worried that Katarina was a plant from the police or from Eldridge, but as soon as I looked at her, I knew that she was going to be a lot more trouble than that.

I don't understand the way the gene lines operate internally, with all the cloning and use of cartridge memories and marriages by cousins to keep all the money and power in the same pedigree, but it was clear from the second she came aboard *Olympe* that she ranked high in the structure. She had that eerie perfection that came with her status. Geneticists had sweated over her body years before she'd ever been born. Flawless complexion, perfect black hair, perfect white teeth. Full expressive lips, intense black eyes that looked at me for a full half-second before they had added up my entire life and riches, found them unworthy of further consideration and looked away. She wore an outfit that was the opposite of the balloon-suits women wore in Socorro, a dark fabric that outlined perfectly every curve of that genetically ideal body. I got dizzy just looking at her.

She looked at my stateroom—I'd moved my stuff out of it—and spared an extra glance for the painting I'd put over a cabinet door that had been ripped off its hinges by the griffs. The painting is of a woman nude on a sofa, with a black ribbon around her neck and a bangle on her wrist. She has a cat and a servant bringing her flowers from the admirer that's obviously just walked into the room. She looks out of the painting at her visitor with eyes hard and objective and cutting as obsidian.

Aram had that painting in the stateroom when he'd died. I'd kept it for a while but put it away later. It is true that travellers, stuck in their ships for months at a time, like to look at pictures of naked ladies, but not the same lady all the time, and not one who looks back at you the way this one does.

I looked for a startled moment at Katarina and the woman in the painting, and I realized they had the same look in their eyes, that same hard, indifferent calculation. She turned those eyes to me.

"I'll take it," she said. "There's a room for my secretary?"

"Of course." With a torn mattress and a smashed chair, but I didn't mention that.

She left the stateroom to call for her secretary and her baggage. In the corridor, she encountered Tonio.

He grinned at her, blue eyes set on either side of that broken nose. Those hard black eyes gazed back, then softened.

"Who is *this*?" she asked.

Trouble, I thought.

"I'm the cook," Tonio said.

Of course, she was married. They almost always are.

Tonio and I had first come aboard *Olympe* as crew. Aram was the owner and captain—he was a Maheu and had inherited money and power and responsibility, but after eight hundred years, he'd given up everything but the money and travelled aimlessly in *Olympe*, looking for something that he hadn't seen somewhere before.

He also used massive amounts of drugs, which were sent to him by Maheu's special courier service. To show the drugs were legitimate, he had doctors' prescriptions for everything—he collected them the way he had once collected art.

Physically, he had the perfection of the high-bred gene lines, with broad shoulders, mahogany skin, and an arched nose. It was only if you looked closely that you saw that the eyes were pouchy and vague, that his muscles were wasting away, and that his skin was as slack as his first-rate genetics would permit. He was giving away his body the same way he'd given away his collection.

He was lonely, too, because he would talk to Tonio and me about history, and art, and poetry. He could recite whole volumes of poetry from memory, and it was beautiful even though most of it was in old languages, like Persian, that I'd never heard before and didn't understand.

I asked him about his gene line, his connections, what he did before he'd started his wandering.

"It was prostitution," he said with a look at the painting on his stateroom wall. "I don't want to talk about it, now I'm trying to regain my virtue."

These conversations happened in the morning, after breakfast. Then he'd put the first patch of the day on his arm and nod off, his head in Maud's lap.

Maud Rain was his girlfriend. She looked maybe seventeen, and maybe she was. She appeared as if her genetics had been intending to create a lily, or cornflower, or some other fragile blossom, and then been surprised to discover they'd produced a human being. She was blonde and green-eyed and blushed easily, and she loved Aram completely. I was a little in love with her myself.

Life aboard *Olympe* was pleasant, if somewhat pointless. We wandered around the multiverse without a schedule. We'd stop for a while, and Aram would leave the ship to visit old friends or see something new that he thought might interest him, and we wouldn't hear from him for anywhere between three days and three months, then abruptly, we'd be on our way again. Aram paid us well and gave us a good deal of time off, and once, he bailed Tonio out of a scrape involving the wife of a Creel station superintendent.

I don't pretend to understand the chemistry between users and their consorts, and I don't know whether Aram talked Maud into using or whether it was her own idea. I do know that, like all users, Aram wanted to make everyone around him use, too. He offered the stuff often enough to me and Tonio, though I never heard him make the same offer to Maud.

Whoever made up Maud's mind for her, she then went on to make a stupid, elementary mistake. She gave herself the same dose that Aram gave himself, without his magic genes and all the immunity he'd built up over the decades, and she screamed and thrashed and went into convulsions. Tonio got his fingers savagely bitten trying to keep the vomit clear of her mouth while I madly shifted the ship through about eight Probabilities to get her to a hospital. By the time we got her there, she didn't have much of a brain left. She still blushed easily and looked at you with dreamy green eyes. She had the sweet-natured smile, but there was nothing behind it but the void.

We left her in a place they'd look after her, a stately white building on a pleasant green lawn, and *Olympe* resumed its wanderings. Aram deteriorated quickly. He no longer talked in the mornings. We'd find him alone and crying, the tears pouring down his face in silence, and then he'd put a new patch on his arm and drift away. One afternoon, we found him dead with six patches on his arm.

In his will, he left all his money to a trust for Maud, and he left *Olympe* and its contents to me. He left Tonio some money. I gave Tonio everything in the pharmacy, and he sold it to someone on Burnes Upside, and we gave Aram a long, crazy wake with the profits. The rest of Tonio's money went to lawyers to fix a misunderstanding that occurred during the course of the wake.

When we sobered up, I realized I had a yacht but no money to support it.

Tonio was the only crew I ever had because he didn't expect to be paid. He did the job of a crew, and when he had money, he paid me as if he were a passenger. When I had money, I shared it with him.

We kept moving, the same kind of random shifts we'd made with Aram.

It was almost enough to keep us out of trouble.

TONIO SPENT that first night in the stateroom with Katarina Pryor. I tried to console myself with the fact that this was all happening in a whole other Probability from the one Katarina normally lived in. I also tried to concentrate on how I was going to handle Eldridge when I saw him again.

I checked some data sources and inquired about Katarina Pryor. She was about fifty years old, though she looked half that and would for the next millennium if she so desired. She was one of the Council of Seven that ran Socorro on behalf of the Pryor gene line.

Her husband, Denys, was one of the other Seven.

I let that settle in my brain for a while. Then I sent a message to Eldridge telling him that I wanted to meet him as soon as *Olympe* docked Topside. He replied that it would be his pleasure to do so.

We'd see how much fun he'd have.

I told Tonio of this development as we were walking to the

lounge. As he stepped into the room, he gave me the news. "Katarina has invited me to accompany her to Downside on completion of our returnment. I have accepted, yiss, pending, of course, my captain's sanction."

Katarina's secretary, a young Pryor named Andrew, happened to be sitting in the lounge as we entered, and he looked as if someone had hit him in the head with a brick.

"It's not as if people are going out of their way to hire us," I said, "so the ship can spare you. But . . ." I hesitated, aware of the presence of Andrew. "Doesn't this *remind* you of anything, Tonio?"

He gave me a look of offended dignity. "The situation of which you speak was on an entirely different plane," he said. "This, on the contrary, is *real*."

The conversation was taking place in a Probability where stars looked like spinning billiard balls on a felt-green sky, and he and Katarina were travelling to another place where oxygen burned in their blood like naphtha. Who knew how real *anything* could be under such circumstances?

I asked Tonio if he could delay his departure with Katrina until Eldridge came aboard.

"Oh yiss. Most assuredly."

He seemed perfectly confident.

I wish I could have echoed his assurance.

ELDRIDGE WAS present when *Olympe* arrived at Upside, and he had brought a couple of thick-necked thugs with him. They were hanging back from the personnel lock because there was plainclothes Pryor security present, waiting to escort Katarina and her new beau on the first stage of their planetary honeymoon.

I called Eldridge from the control room. "Come on in," I said. "Leave your friends behind."

When he came on board, he looked as if he was fully capable of dismembering me all by himself, his small size notwithstanding. I escorted him through the lounge, where Katarina and Andrew waited for Tonio to finish his packing job, a job that would not be completed until I gave him the high sign.

His eyes went wide as he saw Katarina. She wore a compromise between the local balloon-suits and the form-fitting outfit she'd worn when she came aboard, which amounted to a slinky suit with a puffy jacket on top. But I don't think it was her looks that riveted his attention.

He recognized her.

"This is Miss Katarina Pryor," I told him, redundantly, I hoped, "and Mr. Andrew Pryor."

"Pryor," Eldridge repeated as if he wanted to confirm this striking fact for himself.

Andrew gave him a barely civil nod. Katarina just gave him her stone-eyed stare, letting him know he had been measured and found wanting.

I went to the bar and poured myself a cup of coffee. You have to drink coffee quickly there because in that Probability, it cools very fast.

"Eldridge," I remarked. "I haven't received my on-delivery fee."

He gave me a scarlet stare out of his white face. "The cargo did not arrive intact."

"One crate went missing," I said. "It was probably the fault of the loaders, but since I signed for it, you should feel free to deduct its value from the delivery fee." I made a show of looking at the manifest on my pocket adjutant. "What was in that crate—? Ah, jugs of spray foam mix. Value three hundred—would you say that's a correct value, Miss Pryor?"

Katarina drummed her fingers on the arm of the sofa. "Sounds about right, Captain Crossbie," she said in a voice that also said *Don't bother me with this crap.*

I called up my bank account. "Might as well do the transfer now," I said.

Eldridge's eyes cut to Katarina, then cut back. His lips went even whiter than usual.

If the Pryors decided to step on him, he wouldn't leave so much as a grease spot on their shoes. He knew that, as did I.

He got out his own adjutant and tapped in codes with his one long thumbnail. I saw my bank account jump by the anticipated amount, and I put away my adjutant and sipped my coffee. It was already lukewarm.

"Want some coffee, by the way?" I asked.

Eldridge gazed at me out of those flaming eyes. "No," he said.

"We have some other business, but there's no reason to bother Miss Pryor with it," I said.

He followed me into the control room, where I closed the door and gestured him toward a chair.

"Consider that a penalty," I said, "for thinking I was new to the multiverse."

"The Pryors aren't really protecting you," he said. "They can't be."

"They're old family friends," I said. I sat in the padded captain's chair—genuine Tibetan goat hide, Aram had told me—and swivelled it toward him. He just stared at me, his busy fingers plucking at his knees.

"I'm willing to sell you coordinates," I said.

He licked his lips, pink tongue on paper-white. "Coordinates to what?" he asked.

"What do you think?"

He didn't answer.

We had put the blue salt in orbit around an ice moon, one that circled the same gas giant as Vantage.

"The coordinates go for the same price as the cargo." I smiled. "Plus three hundred."

He just kept staring. Probably that agate gaze had frightened a lot of people, but I wasn't scared at all.

Five days around Katarina Pryor had given me immunity to lesser terrors.

"If you don't want the coordinates," I said, "your competition will."

He sneered. "There *is* no competition."

"There will be if Katarina takes you and your tame police out of the equation," I said.

So, in the end, he paid. Once the money was in the account, I gave Eldridge the seven orbital elements that described the salt's amble about its moon. Someone from Vantage could easily hop over and pick up the salt for him, and the strung-out miners would go on getting their daily nerve-searing dose of fate.

I showed Eldridge out, and as he bustled away, he cast a look over his shoulder that promised payback.

I sent a message to Tonio telling him to solve his packing crisis, and as I returned to the lounge, he came loping out of his quarters, his belongings carried in a rucksack on one shoulder. Andrew raised an eyebrow at the tiny amount of baggage that had taken so long to pack.

Katarina rose to embrace Tonio. I watched as she moulded her body to his.

"I am primed, lover mine," Tonio said.

"So am I."

I showed them to the door. "Thank you, Captain," Andrew said and, with an expression like someone passing gas at a funeral, handed me a tip in an envelope.

I looked at the envelope. *This* had never happened before.

"See you later, compeer." Tonio grinned.

"You bet."

I watched them walk toward their waiting transport, arms around each other's waists. People stared. Wary guards circled them. Eldridge and his people were long gone.

I decided it was time to buy and stow a lot of rations. A year's worth, at least.

For two fools, running.

BUT FIRST, I wanted to celebrate the fact that I now possessed more money than I'd ever had in my life, even if you didn't count my tip—which was two thousand, by the way, an inept attempt to buy my silence. I couldn't make up my mind whether Eldridge was going to be a problem or not—if I were him, Katarina would have scared the spleen right out of me, but I didn't know Eldridge well enough to know how stubborn or stupid he was.

While I considered this, it occurred to me to wonder how many years it had been since I'd had a planet under my feet.

Too many, I thought.

I opened my safe and put Tonio's emerald ring in my pocket— no sense in leaving it behind for people like Eldridge to find—and then I followed in the footsteps of Tonio and Katrina and took the next ride down the grapevine to Downside. I looked for tourist resorts and exotic sights, and though I discovered there were none of the former, there were plenty of the latter. There were mountains, gorges, and colossal wildlife—the chemical bonding of the local Probability led to plants, even those with Earth genetics, running amok. I saw rose blossoms bigger than my head and with a smell like vinegar—chemistry not quite right, you see. Little pine trees grew to the size of Douglas firs. Socorro's internal workings had thrust huge reefs of nearly-pure minerals right out of the ground, many of which the miners had not yet begun to disassemble and carry away. For a brief time, wearing a protective raincoat, breathing apparatus, and crinkly plastic overshoes, I walked on the Whitewashed Desert that surrounded Mount Cyanide. I bathed in the Red Sea. Then the Green Sea, the Yellow Sea, and the Winedark Sea. The Yellow Sea stained my skin for days. It looked as if I were dying of cirrhosis.

I kept the ring in a special trouser pocket that would open only to a code from my personal adjutant. After a while, I got used to the feel of it, and days went by before I remembered it was there.

I'd brought my aurora. Along the way, there were music, bars, and happy moments. I met women named Meimei, Sally June, and Soda. We had good times together. None of them died, went crazy, or slit their wrists.

Carried away by the sheer carefree joy of it all, I began to think of going back to the *Olympe* and sailing away on the sea of Probability. Tonio was probably still happy with Katarina, and I could leave with his blessing.

I would be safe. Shawn wasn't after *me*. And Tonio, provided he stayed put, would be as safe as he ever was, probably safer.

I contemplated this possibility for a few too many days because one morning, I woke from a dense, velvety dream to the birdlike tones of my adjutant. I told it to answer.

"Compeer," said Tonio. "Wherewhich art thou?"

"Shadows and fog," I said because the voice seemed to be coming from my dream.

"There's a party on the morrow. Come and share it with me. Katarina would be delighted to see you."

I'll bet, I thought.

―――――――――

THE HOTEL LOOKED like a hovership that had stranded itself on land, a series of swoops and terraces surrounded by cypress trees the size of skyscrapers, with gardenias as long as my leg tumbling brightly down from the balconies. Katarina had installed Tonio and his rucksack in a five-room suite and given him an expense account that, so far, he'd been unable to dent.

Tonio greeted me as I stepped into the suite. His blue eyes sparkled with joy. He looked well-scrubbed and well-tended, and his hair was sleek.

"Did you bring your aurora, Gaucho?" he said. "Let us repair to a suitable location, with drinks and the like, and partake of heavenly music."

"I thought we were going to a party."

"That is later. Right now, we've got to have you measured for clothes."

A tailor with a double chin and a ponytail stepped out of a side room, had me take off my jacket, and got my measurements with a laser scriber. He vanished. Tonio led me out of the apartment and down a confusing series of stairs and lifts to a sub-basement garage. Empty space echoed around us, supported by fluted pillars with lotus-leaf capitals. Tonio whispered a code into his adjutant, and turbines began their soft whine somewhere in the darkness. Spotlights flared. A blaze-mobile came whispering toward us on its cushion of air. I felt its breath on my face and hands. The colours were grey and silver, blending into each other as if they were somehow forged together. The lines were clean and sharp. It looked purposeful as a sword.

"Nice," I said. "Is this Katarina's?" I had a hard time not calling her *Miss Pryor.*

"It's mine," Tonio said. "Katarina purchased it for me after, ah, the incident."

I looked at him.

"There was a misunderstanding about another vehicle," Tonio said. "I thought I had the owner's permission to take it."

Ah, I thought. *One of* those *misunderstandings.*

"Are you driving?" I asked.

"Why don't you drive? You're better than I am."

I settled into the machine gingerly. It folded around me like a piece of origami. Tonio settled into the passenger seat. I drove the car with care till I got out of town, then let the turbines off their leash, and we were soon zooming down a highway under the system's fluorescing, shivering smear of a sun, huge jungle growth on either side of the road turning the highway into a tunnel beneath vines and wild, drooping blossoms.

"There's another car behind us," I said, looking at the displays. I was surprised it could keep up.

"That would be Katarina's security," Tonio said. "It is a mark of her love. They follow me everywhere to render me safe."

And to prevent, I thought, *any of those misunderstandings about who owns what.*

A blissful smile crossed Tonio's face. "Katharine and I are so in love," he said. "I sing her to sleep every night."

The thought of Tonio crooning made me smile. "That sounds great," I said.

"We wish to have many babies, but there are complicatories."

"Like her husband?"

"He is obstacular, yiss, but the principal problem is legal."

It turned out that Katarina did not legally own her own womb, as well as other parts, which were part of the Pryor family trust. She could not become pregnant without the permission of certain high-ranking members of her line, who alone knew the codes that would unlock her fertility.

"That's . . . not the usual problem," I said, stunned. I don't know much about how the big corporate gene lines work, but this seemed extreme, even for them.

"Can you hire a surrogate?" I asked. "Use an artificial womb?"

"It's not the same." He cast a glance over his shoulder. "Those individuals behind us—mayhap you can outspeed them?"

"I'll try."

I set the jets alight. My vision narrowed with acceleration, but oxygen still blazed in my blood. Alarms began to chirp. The vehicle trailing us fell back, but before long, we came to a town and had to slow.

It was a sad little mining town, covered with the dust of the huge magnesite reef that loomed over the town. Vast movers were in the process of disassembling the entire formation while being careful not to ignite it and incinerate the entire county.

Tonio pointed to a bar called the Reefside. "Pull in here, compeer. Mayhap we may discover refreshment."

The bar sat on its tracks, ready to move to another location when the last chunk of magnesite was finally carried away. I put the blazemobile in a side street so as not to attract attention to ourselves. We climbed up into the bar and blinked in its dark, musty-scented interior. We had arrived during an off-peak period, and only a few faces stared back at us.

We huffed some gas and shared a bag of crisps. After ten minutes, the security detail barged in, two broad-shouldered, clean-cut, thick-necked young men in city suits. After they saw us, one went back outside, and the other ordered fruit juice.

The regulars stared at him.

I asked the bartender if it was all right to play my aurora.

"You can if you want," he said, "but if the music's shit, I'll tell you to stop."

"That's fair," I said. I opened the case and adjusted the sonics for the room and put the aurora against my shoulder, and touched the strings. A chord hung in the air, with just a touch of sourness. The bartender frowned. I tuned and began to play.

The bartender turned away with a grudging smile. I made the aurora sound like chimes, like drums, like brass. Our fellow drinkers began to bob their heads and call for the bartender to refill their glasses. One gent bought us rounds of beer.

The shifts changed at the diggings, and miners spilled in, their clothes dusty, their respirators hanging loose around their necks. Some were highly specialized gene types, with sleek skin and implants for remote control of heavy equipment. Others were generalized humans, like us. One woman had lost an arm in an accident, and they were growing it back—it was a formless pink bud on the end of her shoulder.

I played my aurora. I played fierce, then slow. The miners nodded and grinned and tapped their booted feet on the grainy plastic floor. The security man clung unhappily to his glass of fruit juice. I played angry, I played tender, I played the sound of birds in the air and bees in their hive. Tonio borrowed a cap from one of the diggers and passed it around. It came back full of money, which he stuffed in my pockets.

My fingers and mind were numb, and I paused for a moment. There was a round of applause, and the diggers called for more refreshment. A few others asked who we were, and I told them we were off a ship and just travelling around the country.

Tonio had a blazing white grin on his face. "It is *spectacular!*" he said. "This is the true joy!"

"More than with Katarina?"

He shrugged. "With Katarina, it is sensational, but she is terribly occupied, and I don't know anyone else in this coincidence of spacetime. People fear to be in my vicinity, and when I corner one, they only speak to me because they are afraid of Katarina. I have nothing in my day but to wait for Katarina to come home."

"Can't she give you a job? Make you her secretary, maybe?"

"She has Andrew."

"Her social secretary, then." I couldn't help but laugh at the idea.

He gave a big grin. "*She* knows the social rules, yiss. I am signally lacking in that area of expertise."

"You could be a prospector. Travel around looking for minerals or whatever."

"For this task, they have satellites and artificial intelligences." He gazed for a long moment off into nowhere. "I am filled with gladness that you came to see me, Gaucho."

"I'm glad I came." Though I'm not certain I was telling the truth.

Tonio was getting bored with his life with Katarina. A bored Tonio was a dangerous Tonio.

We talked and drank with the miners till Tonio said it was time to leave. Our guard was relieved to follow us out of the bar. His partner had been guarding our blazemobile all this time.

We were both too drunk to drive, so we got in the car and told the autopilot to take us home. Once we arrived, I had a fitting from the tailor, who had run up my suit while we were off enjoying ourselves. I had this deep-blue outfit, all spider silk, with lots of gold braid on my cuffs.

"What's this?" I asked Tonio.

"You are my captain," he said, "and now you are dressed like one."

"I feel ridiculous," I said.

"Wait till you see what *I* am compelled to wear."

The tailor adjusted the suit, then gave me the codes so that I could alter the fit of the suit if I wanted to or add a pocket here or there. In the meantime, Tonio changed. His suit was the latest mode, with ruffles and fringes that seemed to triple the volume of his thin body. He looked unusual, but he carried himself with his usual jaunty style as if he wanted it made clear to everyone that he was only *pretending* to be the person in the suit.

Katarina arrived and wrapped herself around Tonio without caring if I was there or not. I was reminded of my little limpet-girl Étoile.

Katarina began tearing at Tonio's ruffles and fringes. They went off to the bedroom for a lust break. I went out onto the balcony and watched the sun set over the jade forest. The sweet smell of flowers rose on the twilight air.

Tonio and Katarina returned. She wore a dark, lacy sheath that was as simple as Tonio's suit was elaborate. Gemstones glittered sunset-red about her neck, and a languid post-coital glow seemed to float around her like a halo. I could feel sweat prickling my forehead at her very presence.

"You're looking very well, Captain Crossbie," she said.

"You're looking well yourself," I said. There was a bit more regard in her glance than I usually got. I wondered if Tonio had been telling her stories that made me seem, well, interesting.

We went to the party, which was in the same building. It celebrated the fact that some production quota or other had been exceeded, and the room was full of Pryors and their minions. Katarina took Tonio's arm and pressed herself to him all night, making it clear they were a couple.

The place was filled with people who were perfectly perfect, perfect everywhere, from their dress to their genetics. All the talk I heard was of business, and complex business, at that. If I'd been a spy sent by the competition, I would have heard a lot, but it would have been opaque to me.

Don't let anyone tell you that people like the Pryors don't work for their riches and power. They do nothing else.

I was introduced as Captain Crossbie, and people took me for a yachtsman, which technically, I suppose I was. People asked me about regattas and famous captains, and I admitted that I only used my yacht for travel. I was then asked where I'd been, and I managed to tell a few stories.

I was talking about yachts to an engineer named Bond—his dream was to buy a ship when he retired, and travel—when a blond man came up to talk to him. I thought the newcomer looked familiar but didn't place him right away.

He talked to Bond about some kind of bottleneck on the Downside grapevine station that was threatening to interfere with shipments to Upside, and Bond assured him that the problem would be engineered out of existence in a couple of weeks. He asked after Bond's family. Bond told him that his son had won some kind of prize from the Pryor School of Economics. It was then that the blond man turned to me.

He had the chiselled perfection that came with his flawless genes, and violet eyes, and around his mouth was a tight-lipped tension that nature—or his designers—had not quite intended for him.

"This is Mister Denys Pryor," Bond said. "Denys, this is Captain Crossbie."

He realized who I was about the same instant that I finally recognized him as Katarina's husband. The violet eyes narrowed.

"Ah," he said. "The accomplice."

"I don't have any response to that," I said, "that I'd expect you to believe."

He gave me a contemptuous look and stalked away. Bond looked after him in surprise, then looked at me. Then the light dawned. Panic flashed across his face.

"If you'll excuse me," he said and was gone before I could even reply.

That was the last conversation I had at the party. Word about my connection to Tonio flashed through the room faster than lightning, and soon, I was alone. I got tired of standing around by myself, so I went out onto the terrace, where a group of women in immaculate white balloon-suits were grilling meats. I was considering chatting up one of them when Tonio came up, carrying a pair of drinks. He handed me one.

"My apologies, compeer," he said. "They are stuck-up here, yiss."

"I've been treated worse."

He looked up at the strangely infirm stars. "I have Katarina by way of compensation," he said. "You have nothing."

"I have *Olympe*," I said. "I've been thinking maybe it's time she and I flew away to the next Probability."

He looked at me sombrely. "I will miss your companionhood," he said.

"You'll have Katarina." I looked at the sky, where Upside glittered on its invisible tether. "I hope Eldridge isn't still looking for me," I said.

"You don't have to worry about Eldridge," Tonio said. "I told Katarina all about him."

Hot terror flashed through my nerves.

"What did you tell her?" I asked.

"I told her that Eldridge tried to use us to smuggle his salt and that we found the stuff and spaced it."

I relaxed a little. The scene that Eldridge and I had played in front of Katarina might not seem that suspicious if, of course, she believed her lover.

"You didn't hear the news?" Tonio said. "About that police officer that was found in the vacuum, over on Vantage?"

My mouth was dry. "That griff lieutenant?" I asked.

"Her captain. The lieutenant is learning a new job, floating in zero gravity and sucking up industrial wastes with a big vacuum cleaner." He rubbed his chin. "The Pryors don't like people fucking up their workers with drugs."

"They don't seem to mind all those enhanced production quotas, though," I said. "Do you think those come from workers who aren't spiked up?" There was a moment of silence. The scent of sizzling meat gusted past. "What happened to Eldridge?" I asked.

"Don't know. Didn't bother to ask."

If anything was going to harden my determination to leave Socorro as quickly as I could, it was this.

I turned to Tonio. "I'll miss you," I said. I raised a glass. "To happy endings."

Before Tonio could respond, there was a sudden brilliant radiance in the sky, and we looked up. An enormous structure had appeared in the sky above Socorro, a vast black octahedron covered with thousands of brilliant lights, windows enabling the 1.4 million people aboard to gaze out at the passing Probabilities. To gaze down at *us.*

"It's the Chrysalis," I said aloud.

Surrounding the structure were half a dozen birds, each larger than the habitat, long necks outstretched. The storks that were the emblem of the Storch gene line, each with ghostly white wings flapping in utter silence, holograms projected into space by enormous lasers.

Suddenly, I remembered Tonio's emerald ring, in its special pocket on the old trousers I'd left back at Tonio's flat.

Too late, I thought. Shawn had come for us.

———————

"WE CAN'T KEEP THEM OUT," Katarina said. "This Probability isn't a secret any longer, and anyone can exploit it now that it's registered."

I doubted the Pryors could keep the Chrysalis out even if they wanted to. The Pryors maintained a police force here, not an army, and I knew the Chrysalis had weapons for self-defence. They had those huge lasers they'd used to project their flying stork blazons, for one thing, and those could be tuned to military use at any time.

We sat on Tonio's terrace the morning following the Storchs' arrival, soaking in the scent of blossoms. The Chrysalis was still visible in daylight, its edges rimmed with silver.

Breakfast was curdling on our plates. Nobody was very hungry.

"The Chrysalis is a state-of-the-art industrial colony," I said. "They can park it here and start exporting materials in just weeks."

Katarina gave me a tell-me-something-I-don't-know look.

"They have also made an official request," she said. "They want the two of you arrested on charges of theft and turned over to them."

I felt myself turn pale, a chill touching my lips and cheeks. "What are we supposed to have stolen?" I asked.

Katarina permitted herself a thin smile. "They haven't said. We have requested clarification." She turned her black eyes to me. "They have also asked that your ship be impounded until it can be determined whether you obtained it by forging Aram Maheu's will."

"That was all settled in the chancery court on Burnes Upside," I said. "Besides, if I was going to forge a will to give myself a yacht, I'd give myself the money to keep it going."

"The request is a delaying tactic," Katarina said. "It's to tie up your vessel for an indeterminate period and prevent you from escaping.,"

"Is it going to work?" I asked.

Katarina didn't bother to answer.

The previous night's party had ended with the appearance of the Chrysalis, as the Council of Seven went into executive session and their employees scattered to duty stations to do research on the Chrysalis and the implication of its arrival.

Apparently, at some point in the night, Tonio had told Katarina about Adora and Shawn, and Katarina must have believed him because neither of us was being tied to a chair and tortured by Pryor security armed with shock wands.

Katarina rose and gave Tonio a kiss. "I've got a lot of meetings," she said.

"See you tonight, lover mine," Tonio said.

We sat in silence for a while as Socorro's strange sun climbed above the horizon. I turned to Tonio.

"Are you certain," I asked, "that Adora gave you that ring?"

He gave me a wounded look. "Surely I am not hearing what I am hearing, my compeer.'

"It wasn't one of those misunderstandings?" I pressed. "Where you're certain she gave it to you, but she doesn't remember doing it?"

"I am certain she told Shawn it was stolen," Tonio said with dignity, "but this is what happened in sooth. He presented her with the ring at their wedding, a sentimental token, I imagine. But later, she was angry at Shawn for a scene he'd made, where he was complaining about how she had behaved with me at a certain social function, and out of anger, she bestowed the ring upon me."

"And when you left, and she went back to Shawn," I said, "she couldn't admit it, so she told him it was stolen."

"That is my postulation."

Or that was the postulation that Tonio wanted me to believe.

Tonio had been to prison, and in prison, you learn to manipulate people. You learn to tell them what they want to hear. Is it lying if there is no harm intended? If it's just saying the thing that's most convenient for everyone?

I didn't steal anything. How often in prison do you hear *that*?

I think Tonio was sincere in everything he said and did. But what he was sincere *about* could change from one minute to the next.

In any case, this had to be more than just about the ring. The ring was valuable, but it didn't justify moving over a million Storch employees to this Probability and opening mining operations.

"Why did Shawn and Adora marry in the first place?" I asked.

"Their families told them to. They hadn't met until a few days before the ceremony."

"But *why*? Usually, line members marry each other, like Katarina and Denys. It keeps the money in the family. When they merge or take another outfit over, they do it by adoption. But Shawn and Adora were different—each was ordered to marry *out*. The Storches do heavy industry. The Feeneys specialize in biotech and research. What did they have in common?"

Tonio waved a hand in dismissal. "There was a special project. I did not ask for details, no. Why would I? It was connected to Shawn, and when I was with Adora, I had no wish to talk about Shawn. Why spoil a bliss that was so perfect with such a subject?"

"If it was so perfect, why did you leave Adora?" I asked. "When I last saw you together, you seemed so . . . connected."

"She grew too onerous," Tonio said. "Once we began to live together, she began giving orders. *Go here. Do this. Put on these clothes. What do you want to name the children?* Under the oppression, my spirit began to chafe, yiss. She loved me, but only as a pet."

"Still," I said, "you had good times."

"Oh yiss." There was a soft light in his eyes. "They were magical, so many of our times. When we were sneaking away together, to make love in an isolated corner of the Chrysalis . . . that was bliss, my compeer."

I looked up at the Chrysalis, hovering over our heads like the Big Heavy Shiny Object of Damocles.

"Do you think she's up there?" I asked. "It was Adora who was the member of the Storch line. Shawn was the Feeney half of the alliance. He could only command the Chrysalis with the permission of his in-laws."

Tonio looked at the sky in wonder. His face screwed up as he tried to think.

I rose and left him to his thoughts. I needed to do a lot of thinking myself.

FOR THE NEXT SEVERAL DAYS, we bounced around the apartment with increasing energy and frustration. The news was grim. Shuttles from the Chrysalis were exploring uninhabited parts of Socorro. There had been one near-miss between a Storch shuttle and a Pryor transport. Fail-safes normally kept ships from getting remotely close to one another, so the miss had been a deliberate provocation.

Guards stood on our door and even on the next terrace, sensors deployed, looking for any assassins lurking on the horizon. Tonio's blazemobile privileges had been revoked, and he wasn't allowed out of the building.

"I love my little Katarina, yiss," he said one day as he stalked about the main room. "But this is growing onerous."

A bored Tonio was a dangerous Tonio. If he walked out on Katarina, we were both just so much dog food.

"She's just trying to protect you," I said. "It'll only last until the business with the Storches is resolved."

He flung out his arms. "But how long will that be?"

I looked at him. "What if Adora's up there, Tonio?"

He gave me an exasperated look. "What if she is?"

"Do you think you can talk to her? Find out what she wants?"

Tonio stopped his pacing. His startled face began to look thoughtful.

"Do you think I can?" he asked.

"If you try it from here, Katarina will be listening in before you can spit."

"But she won't let me *leave* here!"

"Let me work on that."

His adjutant bleeped, and he answered. His face broke into a look of pure joy as he said, "Hello, lover."

Go on pleasing them, Tonio, I thought.

I went to one of the security guards on our door and told him that I needed to speak to Denys Pryor.

"I DON'T KNOW why I'm even talking to you," said Denys. I had been called into his office, the design of which told me that he liked clean sight lines, no clutter, curved geometries, and a terrace with a water view. He remained at his desk as I entered and was turned slightly away so that I saw his perfect chiselled features in three-quarter profile. He wore fewer ruffles in his office than at the party.

There was no chair for me to sit in. Not anywhere in the room. I had a choice of responses—Denys would probably have preferred an awkward shuffle—so instead, I leaned on his immaculate white wall.

"I'm here to solve your problems," I said.

He raised an eyebrow.

No wonder Katarina is dissatisfied with him, I thought. She could have conveyed the same suspicion and contempt without twitching a single hair.

"Your Chrysalis problem," I clarified, "and your Tonio problem."

"Tonio Hope," he said, "is welcome to my wife. They deserve each other, and I hope you'll tell them that. But the problem represented by the Chrysalis is rather more urgent." He turned in his chair to face me. "Tell me your scheme, please. Then I can have a good hearty laugh and have you thrown out of here."

Cuckolded husbands, I have observed, are rarely models of courtesy.

"Tell me one thing first," I said. "Is Adora Storch on the Chrysalis?"

"Your friend's former lover? Yes." His tone was bored. "Apparently, he stole something from her, but she's too embarrassed to admit what it was."

"Her heart," I said. He looked away suddenly, toward the distant lake.

"What I would like," I said, "is a secure means of communication between Tonio and Adora." And then, at the sudden sharp violet-eyed look, I added, "Secure, I mean, from Katarina."

"START WITH FLOWERS," I suggested. Tonio contacted a florist on the Chrysalis and sent an extravagant bouquet with a humble little message. There was no reply. "Just call her," I said finally.

Her secretary kept him waiting for half an hour while he paced about gripping the adjutant I'd got from Denys. I played quiet, tinkly music on the aurora to keep him calmed down while I watched the muscles leaping on his face. Finally, I heard Adora's voice.

"Tonio! You have the nerve to call me after the way you walked out on me?"

Adora had taken half an hour to work up sufficient anger to decide to confront Tonio instead of just leaving him hanging. Things had worked out more or less as I'd hoped.

Tonio looked at the adjutant's screen. Over his shoulder, I saw Adora's brilliant red hair, her flashing green eyes, her pale-rose complexion. He didn't reply.

"What's the matter with you?" she demanded. "Have the lies stuck in your throat for the first time in your life?"

"I—I am but stunned, seeing you again," Tonio said. "I know you're angry and suchlike, but—at least the anger shows you still care."

Adora began screaming at that point, and I left the room.

Just do what you do best, I told Tonio silently.

I heard Tonio murmur and more fury from Adora, and then a lot of silence, which meant Adora was doing the talking and Tonio was listening. It went on for nearly two hours.

While it went on, I strummed the aurora, volume at a low setting. I really didn't want to know how Tonio did these things: I didn't think I could be trusted with the knowledge.

After the murmuring stopped, I walked back out into the main room. Tonio sat on the sofa, his hands dangling over his knees. He shook his head.

"I'd forgotten what Adora was like," he said. "How beautiful she is. How passionate."

"You've got to tell Katarina," I said. He looked up in shock.

"Tell her that I—"

"Tell her that you're in touch with Adora. Tell her it was my idea, and I made you do it."

"Why?"

"Because if you don't, Denys will. He'll use it to turn Katarina against you."

He rubbed his face with one of his big hands. "This is complicated."

"Tell Katarina the next time you see her," I said.

Which he did that night. By morning, he had Katarina thinking this was a good idea, and the three of us plotted strategy over breakfast.

When, later that day, Denys told her of Tonio's supposed treachery, she laughed in his face.

WHILE DENYS WAS FUMING, and Tonio and Adora were cooing at each other with Katarina's approval, I decided it was time to find out as much as I could about the ring. I got free of security by telling them I was going to report to Denys and took the ring to a jeweller. If I got no answer there, I'd take it to a laboratory.

I could feel my blood sizzle as I walked into the shop. There was a little extra oxygen in the air there, I thought, to make the customers happy and more willing to buy.

The jeweller was a dark-haired woman with a low, scratchy voice and long, elegant hands. She stood amid cases of brilliant splendour but refused to be distracted by them. Her attention was devoted entirely to the customer.

"Splendid work," she said, gazing at a hologram of the ring as big as her head. "The emerald is a natural emerald, which makes it slightly more valuable than an artificial one."

"How do you know?" I asked. She'd made the judgment a split second after she'd put the ring into the laser scanner.

"Natural gems have flaws," the jeweller said. "Artificial gems are perfect."

Imperfection is worth more. Perhaps that says something about our world. Perhaps that says something about how women relate to Tonio.

"The setting is common gold and platinum," the jeweller continued, "but it's more valuable than the gem because it's clearly hand-made and by a master. Let me see if it's signed anywhere."

She called up a program that would scan the ring thoroughly for numbers or letters. "No," she said and then cocked her head. She rotated the image, then magnified it.

"This is curious. There are letters laser-inscribed in the gem, and that's not unusual—most gems are coded that way. But *this* is a type of code I've never seen.." She frowned, and her long fingers reached for her keyboard. "Let me check—"

"No," I said quickly. "That's not necessary."

I only recognized the number sequence because I was a pilot. The numbers had nothing to do with the gem. They weren't a code, they were a set of *coordinates*.

For a Probability. And given how badly Shawn wanted it back, it was almost certainly a *brand-new* Probability.

Feeney researchers must have developed it, very possibly a Probability with one of the Holy Grails of Probability research, like a Probability where electromagnetism never broke into a separate force from gravity, or where atoms heavier than uranium have a greater stability than in the Home Universe, thus allowing atomic power with reduced radioactivity. The Feeneys had discovered this new universe, but they needed an industrial combine with the power of the Storches to exploit it properly. Hence a marriage to seal the bargain. Hence a gem given by one line to the other with the coordinates secretly graven onto it.

I wasn't foolish enough to think the ring held the only copy of the coordinates—the Feeneys wouldn't have been that stupid. But it was the *only copy outside the gene lines' control*. If we gave the coordinates to the Pryors, the Storches would have competition in their new realm before they ever made their investment back.

No wonder something as huge and powerful as the Chrysalis had been sent after us.

I asked the jeweller an estimate of the ring's worth—"so I know how much insurance to buy"—and then I took the ring and walked out of the shop with billions on my finger. The store's oxygenated atmosphere boiled in my blood.

The ring was the best insurance in the world, I thought. Shawn didn't dare kill us until he got his wedding present back.

That night, Tonio and Katarina had their first fight. She complained about the time he was spending talking to Adora. He pointed out that he was stuck here in the apartment and had nothing else to do. It degenerated from there.

I went to my room and played the aurora, loudly this time, and tried to decide what needed to happen next. It might be a good idea to get Tonio closer to Adora, just in case he needed a fast transfer from one girlfriend to another.

I went to Denys and suggested that we all go up the grapevine to Upside in case any face-to-face meetings became necessary. He understood my point at once.

And so, we all moved off the planet, spending a day and a half in the first-class compartment of a car roaring up the grapevine. Katarina spent the time adhered to Tonio, who looked uncomfortable. Denys kept to a cubicle where he worked, except for his occasional parades through the lounge, where he was all ostentatious about paying no attention to his wife.

The atmosphere on the car was sullen and ominous and filled with electricity, like the air before a thunderstorm. Even the other passengers felt it.

To dispel the lowering atmosphere, I played my aurora, until some pompous rich bastard told me to stop that damned noise, or he'd call an attendant. "I'm with Miss Katarina Pryor," I told him. "Take it up with her."

He turned pale. I played on for a while, but the mood, such as it was, had been completely spoiled. I went to my cabin and lay on my bed, and tried to sleep.

I needed to get away from Tonio and Katarina and Denys. I needed to get away from this freakish Probability where my blood sizzled all the time and my skin burned with fever. I needed to get *away*.

"I'd like to move onto *Olympe*," I told Katarina. She was curled around the spot on a lounge sofa where Tonio had just been sitting. He had gone to the bar for a cup of coffee, but you could still see his impression on the cushions.

Her cold eyes drifted over me. "Why?"

"I'll be out of your way. And it's where I *live*." When she didn't answer, I added, "Look, I can't leave the dock without your permission. I'm not *going* anywhere."

She turned away, dismissing me. "I'll tell the guards to let you pass," she said.

"There are *guards*?"

The only answer was an exasperated set to her lips as if she didn't consider the question worthy of answer.

So it was that I showed the guards my ID and moved back onto *Olympe*. The air was stale, the corridors silent. I stepped into the stateroom and told the lights to go on, and the first thing I saw was the painting of the naked woman, staring at me. She reminded me too much of some people I'd grown to know, so I put the painting in storage.

I went to the pilot's station, where I'd talked to Eldridge, and checked the ship's systems, which were normal. I wondered what would happen if I powered up the engines and decided not to find out.

For a few days, I indulged myself in the fantasy that I was going to escape. I filled the larder with food and drink, enough for eight months of flight to whatever Probability struck my fancy. I tuned every system on the ship except the drive. I made plans about where I'd like to travel next.

I thought about putting the ring back in the safe, but I figured the safe was no real obstacle to people like Denys or Shawn, so I kept the ring in the special pocket in my trousers. Maybe Denys or Shawn were less likely to rip off my pants than rip off the door to the safe.

I went to some of the places I'd enjoyed when I was living Topside the first time. All the bars and restaurants that had seemed so bright and inviting when I was just off a five-month voyage now seemed garish and third-rate. Guards followed me and tried to be inconspicuous. Without a friend, I didn't seem to be having any fun.

It really was time to leave.

I brought a bottle home to the *Olympe* and drank while I worked out a plan. I'd sell the ring's coordinates to Denys in exchange for our safety and a lot of money. Then I'd sell the ring itself back to Shawn for the same thing. I'd split the money with Tonio, and then I'd run for it while the running was good.

I looked at the plan again the next morning, when I was sober, and it still seemed good. I was trying to work out my best approach to Denys when Tonio came aboard. He was a reminder of everything I was trying to escape, and his presence annoyed me, but he was exasperated and didn't notice.

"Katarina is more onerous than ever before," he said. He flapped his big hands. "I am watched every moment, yiss. She says she is protecting me, but I know it's all because she doesn't want me to speak to Adora. Yet out of every port, I see the Chrysalis floating in the sky, with Adora so near."

"You've got to keep Katarina's trust," I said.

"*Olympe* is the only place where I'm free," Tonio said. "Katarina doesn't mind if I come here. And that's why you've got to help me get Adora on board."

"Adora?" I said. "Here?"

"There's no place else."

"But the ship's being watched. So is the Chrysalis. If Adora comes here, they'll see her."

Tonio smiled. "The Pryors and the Storches do not confront each other all the time. Even if they're playing chicken with each other's cargo ships, both the Chrysalis and Socorro possess resources the other finds useful. There are ships coming from the Chrysalis to purchase certain commodities and sell others and perform transactions of that nature. Adora will come in one of these ships, and when the business is being transacted by her minions, she will fly here to me in a vacuum suit and enter through our very airlock, bypassing those inconvenient guards upon the door."

I was appalled. Tonio smiled. "Adora assures me that it will be perfectly safe."

For whom? I wondered.

"I don't want to be on board when this happens," I said.

WHEN TONIO ENTERTAINED Adora on my ship, I spent the time shopping for stuff I never bought, and when I got bored with that, I found a bar and huffed some gas. I didn't return to *Olympe* until Tonio sent me a prearranged little beep on my adjutant.

Olympe's lounge still smelled faintly of Adora's flowery perfume. Tonio splayed on the couch. Energy filled his skinny body. His blue eyes were aglow.

"Such a passion it was!" he said. "Such zealocity! Such a twining of bodies and souls!"

"Glad to know she doesn't want to kill you anymore," I said.

He waved a hand. "All in the past." He heaved a sigh and looked around the lounge at the old furniture and Aram's brass-and-mahogany trim. "I am glad to bring happiness here," he said, "to counter those memories of sorrow and tragedy."

I looked at him. "What memories are those?"

"The afternoon I spent here with beautiful little Maud. The day before she gave herself that overdose."

I stared at Tonio. Drugs whirled in my head as insects crawled along my nerves.

"You're telling me that—"

He looked away and brushed a cushion with the back of his knuckles. "She was so sweet, yiss. So giving."

I had been off the ship that day, I remembered, making final preparations for departure. Aram was saying goodbye to some of his friends and picking up a new shipment of drugs from the Maheu office. That must have been the time when Maud Rain had finally succumbed to the magic that was Tonio.

And then, in remorse, she'd decided to grow closer to Aram. By becoming a user like him.

And now she lived in a little white room in the country, her mind as white and blank as the walls that surrounded her.

I stood over Tonio. I felt sick. "Remember, you're spending tonight with Katarina," I said.

The glow in his eyes faded. "I know," he said. "It is not that I am not fond of her, but the circumstances—"

"I don't want to hear about the circumstances," I said. "Right now, I need to be alone, so I can think."

Tonio was on his feet at once. "I know I have made an imposition upon you," he said. "I hope you understand my gratitude."

"I understand," I said. "But I need to be by myself."

"Whatsoever thou desirest, my captain." Tonio rose and loped away.

I went to the captain's station and sat on the goatskin chair, and decided that I had better get my escape plan underway. I called Denys's office and asked for an appointment. His secretary told me to come early the next day.

Tonio had been in prison, I thought. In prison, you learn how to handle people. You learn how to tell them what they want and how to please them.

I wondered if Tonio had been playing me all along. Telling me what I wanted in exchange for a place to stay and a tour of the multiverse and its attractions.

I had many hours before my appointment, but alcohol helped.

THIS REALITY's blazing oxygen had burned the hangover out of my blood by the time I stepped into Denys's office. The geometries of the room were even more curved than his place Downside, and there were even more windows. Outside the office, the structures of Upside glittered, and beyond them was the ominous octahe-dron of the Chrysalis, glowing on the horizon of Socorro.

There were two chairs in the room this time, but neither of them was for me. Both were on the far side of Denys's desk. One held Denys and the other the black-skinned, broad-shouldered form of Shawn Feeney.

Denys raised his brows. "Surprised, Captain Crossbie? Surely you don't imagine that you and Tonio are the only people who employ backchannel communications?"

He was enjoying himself far too much. Cuckolds, as I've stated elsewhere, are rarely models of deportment.

"I'd asked for a private meeting," I said, without hope.

"Shawn and I have decided," Denys said, "that it's time for you and your friend to leave this reality. We know that your ship is provisioned for a long journey, and we intend that you take it."

"How do I know," I said, "that there isn't a bomb hidden some-where in my ship's pantry?"

The two looked at each other and smirked. Denys answered.

"Because if you and Tonio disappear or die mysteriously, that makes *us* the villains," he said. "Whereas, if you simply abandon this Probability, leaving the two ladies behind . . ." He couldn't resist a grin.

"Then *you* are the bad guys," Shawn finished in his deep voice.

I considered this. "I suppose that makes sense," I said.

"And in exchange for the free passage," Denys said, "I'll take the ring."

"*You?*" I said and then looked at Shawn.

"Oh, I'll get it back eventually," Shawn said. "And I'll get the credit for it, too."

"The Storch line," Denys said, "will have at least a couple of years to exploit the new Probability before we Pryors arrive in force. But even so, we'll get there years ahead of the rest of the competition..... and *I'll* get the credit for that."

Shawn smiled at me. "And *you'll* get the blame for selling our secret to our rivals. But by then, I'm sure you'll have lots of practice at running."

"I could tell the truth," I said.

"I'm sure you can," Shawn said. He leaned closer to me. "And the very best of luck with that plan, by the way."

"The ring?" Denys reminded.

I thought about it for a moment and could see no alternative.

"To get the ring," I said, "I have to take my pants off."

Shawn's smile broadened. "We'll watch," he said, "and enjoy your embarrassment."

Tonio was in *Olympe* by the time I returned. Delight danced in his blue eyes.

"I have received a missive from Adora!" he said. "We are to flee together, she and I—and you, of course, my compeer. She has bribed someone in Socorro Traffic Control, yiss, to let us leave the station without alerting the Pryors. We then fly to the coordinates she has provided, where she will join us. From this point on, we exist in our own Probability of bliss and complete happiness!"

I let Tonio dance around the ship while I went to the captain's station and began the start-up sequence. Socorro Traffic Control let us go without a murmur. I manoeuvred clear of the station and engaged the drive.

As we raced to the coordinates the message had provided, there was no pursuit. No ships came out of some alternate Probability to collide with us. No lasers lanced out of the Chrysalis to incinerate the ship. No bomb blew us into fragments.

As we neared the rendezvous point, Tonio grew anxious. "Where is my darling?" he demanded. "Where is Adora?" His hands turned to fists. "I hope that something has not gone amiss with the plan."

"The plan is working fine," I said, "and Adora isn't coming."

I told him about my meeting with Denys and Shawn and what I had been ordered to do. Tonio raged and shouted. He demanded I turn *Olympe* around and take him back to his beloved Adora at once.

I refused. I fed coordinates into the Probability drive, and an instant later, the stars turned to hard little pebbles and we were racing away from Socorro, leaving its quirky electromagnetic structure in our wake.

Tonio and I were on the run. Again. Trapped with one another in Reality, whether we liked it or not.

I had let Tonio play me, just as he had played Adora and Katarina and Maud and the others. Now we were in a place where we had no choice but to play each other.

Tonio was in despair. "Adora and Katarina will think I deserted them!" he said. "Their rage will know no bounds! They may send assassins—fleets—armies! What can I do?"

"Start," I said, "by sending them flowers."

ABOUT THE AUTHORS

GRIFFIN BARBER spent his youth in four different countries, learning three languages and burning all his bridges. Finally settled in Northern California and retired from a day job as a police officer in a major metropolitan department, he lives the good life with his lovely wife, crazy-smart daughter, tiny Bengal, and needy dog. *1636: Mission to the Mughals*, co-authored *with Eric Flint, was his first novel.* 1637: The Peacock Throne is now available. He's also collaborated with Kacey Ezell on a novel set in their Last Stop Station Universe, titled *Second Chance Angel*. He's also collaborated with Chuck Gannon, penning *Man-Eater* and *Infiltration*, novellas set in the Murphy's Lawless annex of the Caine Riordan Universe. He has a number of short stories set in different universes coming out in 2022.

GERALD BRANDT is an International Bestselling Author of Science Fiction and Fantasy. He is a member of the Science Fiction and Fantasy Writers of America. His current novel is *Threader God*, Book Three of the Quantum Empirica, published by DAW Books. His first novel, *The Courier*, in the San Angeles series was listed by the Canadian Broadcasting Corporation as one of the ten Canadian science fiction books you need to read and was a finalist for the prestigious Aurora Award. Both *The Courier* and its sequel, *The Operative*, appeared on the *Locus* Bestsellers List. You can find Gerald online at www.geraldbrandt.com, on Facebook as Gerald Brandt—Author, and on Twitter @geraldbrandt.

CHRISTIAN/MILES CAMERON is s full-time writer of speculative and historical fiction living in Toronto, Canada with his partner, Sarah, daughter, Beatrice, and a surprising number of cats. He is an avid swordperson and loves travel and wilderness camping and, above all, writing.

SEBASTIEN DE CASTELL had just finished a degree in Archaeology when he started work on his first dig. Four hours later he realized how much he actually hated archaeology and left to pursue a very focused career as a musician, ombudsman, interaction designer, fight choreographer, teacher, project manager, actor, and product strategist. Sebastien's acclaimed swashbuckling fantasy series, The Greatcoats, was shortlisted for the 2014 Goodreads Choice Award for Best Fantasy, the Gemmell Morningstar Award for Best Debut, the Prix Imaginales for Best Foreign Work, and the John W. Campbell Award for Best New Writer. His YA fantasy series, Spellslinger, was nominated for the Carnegie Medal and is published in more than a dozen languages. Sebastien lives in Vancouver, Canada with his lovely wife and two belligerent cats.

KRISTI CHARISH is the author of *Kincaid Strange*, an urban fantasy about a voodoo practitioner living in Seattle with the ghost of a grunge rocker, and *The Adventures of Owl*, an "Indiana Jane"-style adventure about ex-archaeology grad student turned international antiquities thief who reluctantly navigates the hidden supernatural world. Kristi writes what she loves: adventure-heavy stories featuring strong, savvy female protagonists, pop culture, and the occasional RPG fantasy game thrown in the mix. Kristi is also a scientist. She has a BSc and MSc from Simon Fraser University in Molecular Biology and Biochemistry and a PhD in Zoology from the University of British Columbia. She specializes in genetics, cell biology, and molecular biology, and gratuitously uses her expertise throughout her fiction. You can find Kristi on her laptop writing videogames and making science comprehensible.

CORY DOCTOROW (craphound.com) is a science fiction author, activist and journalist. He is the author of many books, most recently *Radicalized* and *Walkaway*, science fiction for adults; *How to Destroy Surveillance Capitalism*, nonfiction about monopoly and conspiracy; *In Real Life*, a graphic novel; and the picture book *Poesy the Monster Slayer*. His latest book is *Attack Surface*, a standalone adult sequel to *Little Brother*; his next nonfiction book is *Chokepoint Capitalism*, with Rebecca Giblin, about monopoly, monopsony, and fairness in the creative-arts labour market (Beacon Press, 2022). In 2020, he was inducted into the Canadian Science Fiction and Fantasy Hall of Fame.

K. EASON lives with her husband and a trio of disreputable cats in Southern California, where she teaches first-year college students about zombies and food (not at the same time!). Her short fiction has appeared in *Cabinet-des-Fées*, *Postcards from Hell: The First Thirteen*, *Jabberwocky 4*, *Crossed Genres*, *Kaleidotrope*, and *Ink: Queer Sci Fi Anthology*. She has written the On the Bones of Gods trilogy, The Thorne Chronicles, and The Weep series, the second book of which, *Nightwatch Over Windscar*, is forthcoming from DAW Books in November 2022. When she's not writing or commenting on essays, she's probably playing D&D.

DAVID EBENBACH is the author of nine books of fiction, non-fiction, and poetry, including his recent novel, *How to Mars*, a book that's been called, "A poignant examination of what it means to be human" (*Kirkus Reviews*). His books have won such awards as the Juniper Prize and the Drue Heinz Literature Prize, among others. Ebenbach lives with his family in Washington, DC, where he teaches and supports other teachers' development at Georgetown University. You can find out more at www.davidebenbach.com.

MARK EVERGLADE has spent his life studying social conflict as a sociologist. He runs the website www.markeverglade.com where he reviews cyberpunk media and interviews the legends. He also helps run Cyberpunk Day each year to bring hopeful, yet dystopian, fiction to a new generation. His newest book, *Song of Kitaba*, revolves around themes of human freedom in an age of increased cyber surveillance.

FRANK J. FLEMING is a novelist and a script creator for *The Daily Wire*. He has also written satire books, wrote approximately 666 articles for *The Babylon Bee*, and wrote columns for *The New York Post*, *USA Today*, and *The Washington Times*. Frank is a Carnegie Mellon University graduate and used to be a really good electrical and software engineer back when he was inclined to have a more useful occupation than writing. He lives in Austin with his wife and four kids and is a really cool dude.

JOSEPH HURTGEN holds a doctorate in English Literature from Ball State University, where he specialized in American Literature and Science Fiction. Hurtgen's most recent novel is *tae kwon Go*. He teaches writing and literature at Western Kentucky University and lives in Campbellsville, KY, with his wife, Rebecca, and children, Frances and Ira.

VIOLETTE MALAN is the author of the Dhulyn and Parno sword-and-sorcery series and The Mirror Lands series of primary world fantasies. As VM Escalada, she's the author of the Faraman Prophecy, including *Halls of Law* and *Gift of Griffins*. She's on Facebook and she's on Twitter (@Violette Malan). Violette lives in Spain with her husband, Paul, and Luna the Cat, and she strongly urges you to remember that no one expects the Spanish Inquisition.

ANNA MOCIKAT is the award-winning, internationally published author of *Behind Blue Eyes*, the Tales of the Shadow City series, and the MUC series. Before becoming a novelist, she graduated from film school and worked as a screenwriter and game writer for over a decade. She lives in Greenville, South Carolina.

Born in 1947, JAMES MORROW has been writing fiction ever since. As a seven-year-old living in the Philadelphia suburbs, he dictated "The Story of the Dog Family" to his mother, who dutifully typed it up and bound the pages with yarn. Upon reaching adulthood, Jim channelled his storytelling urge toward the production of theologically inflected satiric fiction, including the critically acclaimed Godhead Trilogy. He has twice won the World Fantasy Award (for *Only Begotten Daughter* and *Towing Jehovah*), and twice the Nebula Award (for "The Deluge" and *City of Truth*). In recent years Jim has composed historical fiction informed by a *fantastika* sensibility, including *The Last Witchfinder* and *Galápagos*

Regained, the French translation of which received the *Grand Prix de l'Imaginaire*.

JESS E. OWEN is a professional author and artist. With her BFA in technical theatre, she worked for nearly a decade as a stage manager before leaving the industry to focus on writing. She has served as president of her local writing organization, and speaks frequently in classes and workshops. Jess published her own young adult fantasy series featuring gryfon characters, the Summer King Chronicles, and also writes contemporary YA under the name Jessica Kara. All her books, whether modern or high fantasy, are "noblebright" at their core, written with a spirit of hope, belief in the power of kindness, and the faith that good will overcome. "Together As One" is set in the world of the Summer King Chronicles, in an earlier Age. Find her online at www.jessowen.com.

ROBERT G. PENNER is the author of *Strange Labour*, one of *Publishers Weekly*'s Best Science Fiction Books of 2020. He's also the editor of the online science fiction zine *Big Echo*, and has published more than thirty short stories in a wide range of speculative and literary journals under the pseudonym of William Squirrell. After seven years in western Pennsylvania, he has recently returned to Winnipeg.

CAT RAMBO's 250+ fiction publications include stories in *Asimov's*, *Clarkesworld Magazine*, and *The Magazine of Fantasy and Science Fiction*. In 2020 they won the Nebula Award for fantasy novelette *Carpe Glitter*. They are a former two-term President of the Science Fiction and Fantasy Writers of America (SFWA). Their most recent works are the space opera *You Sexy Thing* (Tor

Macmillan) and an anthology, *The Reinvented Heart* (Arc Manor, March, 2022), co-edited with Jennifer Brozek. For more about Cat, as well as links to fiction and their popular online school, The Rambo Academy for Wayward Writers, see their website.

K.M. RICE (Kellie) is a national award-winning screenwriter and author. Her first novel, *Darkling*, is a young adult dark fantasy that now has a companion novel titled *The Watcher*. Over the years, her love of storytelling has led to producing and geeking out in various web shows and short films. When not writing or filming, she can be found hiking in the woods, baking, gardening, and enjoying the company of the many animals on her family ranch in the Santa Cruz Mountains of California. Her latest publications are the novels in her historical fantasy series Afterworld, which launched with Book 1, *Ophelia*.

EDWARD WILLETT is the Aurora Award-winning author of more than sixty books of science fiction, fantasy, and non-fiction for readers of all ages, including twelve novels for DAW Books, the latest of which is *The Tangled Stars*, a humorous far-future space-opera heist novel featuring a talking genetically modified AI-uplifted cat who becomes a starship captain. Ed owns and operates Shadowpaw Press, which publishes new work by established and emerging authors and new editions of notable, previously published work. A past president of SF Canada, he is currently vice-president of SaskBooks, the professional association of publishers in Saskatchewan. He has a university-age daughter, Alice, and lives in Regina, Saskatchewan, with his wife, Margaret Anne Hodges, P.Eng., and their black Siberian cat, Shadowpaw.

WALTER JON WILLIAMS is an award-winning author who has been listed on the best-seller lists of the *New York Times* and the *Times of London*. He is the author of forty volumes of fiction. His first novel to attract serious public attention was *Hardwired* (1986), described by Roger Zelazny as "a tough, sleek juggernaut of a story, punctuated by strobe-light movements, coursing to the wail of jets and the twang of steel guitars." In 2001 he won a Nebula Award for his novelette, "Daddy's World," and won again in 2005 for "The Green Leopard Plague." His latest work is *Lord Quillifer*, the latest installment in his popular Quillifer fantasy series. Walter has also written for comics, the screen, and for television, and has worked in the gaming field. He was a writer for the alternate reality game *Last Call Poker*, and has scripted the mega-hit *Spore*.

F. PAUL WILSON is the award-winning, *New York Times*-bestselling author of eighty books and numerous short stories spanning medical thrillers, SF, horror, adventure, and virtually everything between. More than nine million copies of his books are in print in the US and his work has been translated into 24 languages. He also has written for the stage, screen, comics, and interactive media. Best known for *The Keep* and his notorious urban mercenary, Repairman Jack, he currently resides at the Jersey Shore. Find him online at www.repairmanjack.com.

JANE YOLEN is a Grand Master for SFWA, World Fantasy, and the Science Fiction Poetry Association, plus the winner of two Nebulas and several World Fantasy Awards; has six honourary doctorates; and was the first woman to give the St. Andrews University Andrew Lang lecture. She is the author of well over 400 books and has published much more than a thousand poems so far. She has been called the "Hans Christian Andersen of America," but more appropriate would be the "Hans Jewish Andersen of America." She has also been called the "Aesop of the 20th century," but careful readers will note we are on the cusp of the 22nd-23rd centuries. And as she is a folklorist, she needs to point out that calling her legendary is actually a back-handed insult as she is (for now) alive, still writing, and very real.

ACKNOWLEDGMENTS

This anthology would not have been possible without the generous support of the many people who pledged to back it on Kickstarter. You not only made this terrific collection of science fiction and fantasy stories possible, you've set the stage for more *Shapers of Worlds* anthologies in the future.

This anthology only includes guests from the third year of *The Worldshapers* podcast. With luck and supporters like you, there'll be a Volume IV next year featuring guests from the podcast's fourth year—an equally stellar collection of authors. Huge thanks to everyone listed below, and to those who chose to remain anonymous, for helping to bring this book to life.

KICKSTARTER BACKERS

Sarah Ogden, Faizaan Alam, Judith Silverthorne, Tosca Lee, Karen Lytle Sumpter, Nancy BueSpider Tice, James S. O'Brien, Jordan Theyel, Steve Mashburn, John Crouch, Michael Fedrowitz, Lisa Kruse, Michael Feir, Rick Straker, Melanie Marttila, Konstanze Tants, dennis chambers, Jennifer Berk, Brendan Lonehawk, Tony E. Calidonna, C. Kierstead, David Myers, Chris Gerrib, Simo Muinonen, Robert Tienken, Kim Stoker, Pat, Mary Jo Rabe, Pat Hayes, maileguy, Jacques Toupin, GMarkC, Evan Ladouceur, Joe and Gay Haldeman, RJ Hopkinson, Anna Fultz, Stu Glennie,

Adam Rajski, Robert Claney, Dan Neely, Krystal Bohannan, Richard Norton, Julian White, Luis Manuel Sánchez García, Moe Lane, Eric, Elizabeth Raum, Leo Valiquette, Sheryl R. Hayes, Richard D. Grant, Caroline Westra, John Mead, Nick Hlavacek, James Lucas, James Kennedy, Carol J. Guess, Kate Mallooy, Mike Rimar, Joseph Geary, Natasha Liff, Jennifer Flora Black, Tony Pi, Kal Powell, Renee Rathjen, Adam Corey, Ward R. Pederson, Debbie Matsuura, Jared Nelson, Jakub Narębski, Brian Smyth, Connor Bliss, Sean Chappell, Lucas K. Law, Ross Emery, Jim Willett, Gary Phillips, Ernesto Pavan, Greg Hansford, Patrick Fowler, Jeroen Teitsma, Dustin Bilyk, Matt Knepper, Isaac 'Will It Work' Dansicker, Gareth Jones, Sharon Waller, Brian Schrader, Taka Mounspell, Matthew R Gaglio, Seamus Sands, TC McG, A.J. Bohne, Christine Price, Kelly Snyder, Richard O'Shea, Christine A. Cooney, Dina S Willner, Jacen Leonard, Avid Supporter, Herbert Eder, Aramanth Dawe, Julian Tysoe, Jessica Meade, Piet Wenings, Patrick E Johnson, Craig "Stevo" Stephenson, W D Stancil, Katy Manck - BooksYALove, Brynn, Andrew Whitwham, Jeffrey Allan Boman, Don Meyer, Glenn Allen, Jason Boissiere, Rob Wittmer, Rob Morrison, Cameron greatorex, Astra Crompton, Pete Gedzyk, Brett Mitchell, Reuben Talbott, Janet Louise Wilson, Brad Anderson, Mark Carter, Mike Hein, Scott Phyrebird, Sueann Snow, Anna R. Dunster, Eric Allsop, S Klotz, Virginia Wilkinson, Chris Thomas, Mark Meyer, TracyN, Dominik Plejić, Raúl Castro, Eron Wyngarde, Rachel Burdorf, Chantelle Wilson, Emily Lynn, Ruth Ann Orlansky, Mervi Hamalainen, Fernando Autran, R. Goodman Gaghan, Gavran, Mike Manzer, V. Jakubovic, Marcelle Dubé, ben 'blarg' wong, Giuseppe Lo Turco, Steve Arensberg, Jace Chretin, Xavier Walker, Yankton Robins, Margaret Hodges, Sharon and Mike Sheffield, Dr. Charles E. Norton III, Catherine Seeligson, Barbara Tomporowski, Dan-o, Ian Hecht, David Schumacher,

Charley Kneifel, Joanne B Buurows, Dome from Sci Fi Saturday Night, Margaret A. Menzies, Jessa Willson, Axisor and Firestar, Cathy Green, Martin Beijer, Margaret Bumby, Stephanie Lucas, Adam Eaton, Curtis and Maryrita Steinhour, R.J.H., Kari Blocker, E.L. Winberry, Tania, Joshua Palmatier, Peter Halasz, Mark Newman, Stephen Ballentine, Fenric Cayne, Camielle Adams, Heather Armstrong, DK Perlmutter, Larry Strome, Lisa Johnson, Jesse N. Klein, Thomas Bull, Ira Nayman, Dr. Mary C. Crowell, Brad Weckman, Kerry aka Trouble, Patrick Osbaldeston, Andrew MacLeod, Andrew Hatchell, Adria, Sharon Eisbrenner, Robert Cram, Carol Bachelu, James McCoy, Margaret St. John, Joe Mahoney, David Rowe, Simon Matthews, Andromeda Taylor-Wallace, Jess Turner, Parker & Malcolm Curtis, Rhonda Harms, Henrik Sörensen, Tyler Hulsey, Andrew, Colleen Feeney, Jim Putz, Stephen Dowling, Derek Kumar, PJ, Aurora Nelson, Brian Bygland, David Hopkinson, Michèle Laframboise, SindrElf, Tara Zrymiak, Rhel ná DecVandé, Jan Pedro Tumusok, Joseph J Connell, E.M. Middel, Nathan Ari Breitenbach, ET, James & Shannon, Hennie vd Merwe, Brent Guild, Nancy, Frankie Mundens, Sharon Plumb, Yusa, Kai Hutchence, Margaret Bessai, Karen M, Ian Chung, Ryan Hughes, Darren Fry, Dwight Willett, Terrance R. Jacobs III, Ethan Partington, Brooks Moses, Joseph Cox, Meo, Amira, Kali Alston, and Gina Jordan.